Honoré de Balzac

A Distinguished Provincial at Paris and Z. Marcas

Honoré de Balzac

A Distinguished Provincial at Paris and Z. Marcas

ISBN/EAN: 9783337428556

Printed in Europe, USA, Canada, Australia, Japan

Cover: Foto ©Andreas Hilbeck / pixelio.de

More available books at **www.hansebooks.com**

H. DE BALZAC

A DISTINGUISHED PROVINCIAL AT PARIS

(UN GRAND HOMME DE PROVINCE À PARIS)

AND Z. MARCAS

TRANSLATED BY

ELLEN MARRIAGE

WITH A PREFACE BY

GEORGE SAINTSBURY

PHILADELPHIA

THE GEBBIE PUBLISHING CO., Ltd.

1898

CONTENTS

LIST OF ILLUSTRATIONS

Drawn by W. Boucher.

PREFACE.

THE central part of "Illusiones Perdues," which in reason stands by itself, and may do so ostensibly with considerably less than the introduction explanatory which Balzac often gives to his own books, is one of the most carefully worked out and diversely important of his novels. It should, of course, be read before "Splendeurs et Misères des Courtesanes," which is avowedly its second part, a small piece of "Eve et David" serving as the link between them. But it is almost sufficient by and to itself. "Lucien de Rubempré ou le Journalisme" would be the most straightforward and descriptive title for it, and one which Balzac, in some of his moods, would have been content enough to use.

The story of it is too continuous and interesting to need elaborate argument, for nobody is likely to miss any important link in it. But Balzac has nowhere excelled in *finesse* and success of analysis the double disillusion which introduces itself at once between Madame de Bargeton and Lucien, and which makes any *redinte-gratio amoris* of a valid kind impossible, because each cannot but be aware that the other has anticipated the rupture. It will not, perhaps, be matter of such general agreement whether he has or has not exceeded the fair license of the novelist in attributing to Lucien those charms of body and gifts of mind which make him, till his moral weakness and worthlessness are exposed, irresistible, and enable him for a time to repair his faults by a sort of fairy good-luck. The sonnets of "Les Marguerites," which were given to the author by poetical friends—Gautier, it is said, supplied the "Tulip"—are undoubtedly good and sufficient. But Lucien's first article, which is (according to a practice the rashness of which cannot be too much deprecated) given like-

wise, is certainly not very wonderful; and the Paris press
must have been rather at a low ebb if it made any sensation.
As we are not favored with any actual portrait of Lucien, de-
tection is less possible here, but the novelist has perhaps a
very little abused the privilege of making a hero, " Like Paris
handsome, and like Hector brave," or, rather, " Like Paris
handsome, and like Phœbus clever." There is no doubt,
however, that the interest of the book lies partly in the vivid
and severe picture of journalism given in it, and partly in the
way in which the character of Lucien is adjusted to show up
that of the abstract journalist still farther.

How far is this picture true? It must be said, in fairness
to Balzac, that a good many persons of some competence in
France have pronounced for its truth there; and if that be so,
all one can say is, " So much the worse for French journalists."
It is also certain that a lesser, but still not inconsiderable
number of persons in England—generally persons who, not
perhaps with Balzac's genius, have like Balzac published
books, and are not satisfied with their reception by the press—
agree more or less as to England. For myself, I can only say
that I do not believe things have ever been quite so bad in
England, and that I am quite sure there never has been any
need for them to be. There are, no doubt, spiteful, unprin-
cipled, incompetent practitioners of journalism as of everything
else ; and it is of course obvious that while advertisements, the
favor of the chiefs of parties, and so forth, are temptations to
newspaper managers not to hold up a very high standard of
honor, anonymity affords to newspaper writers a dangerously
easy shield to cover malice or dishonesty. But I can only say
that during long practice in every kind of political and literary
journalism, I never was seriously asked to write anything I
did not think, and never had the slightest difficulty in con-
fining myself to what I did think.

In fact Balzac, like a good many other men of letters who
abuse journalism, put himself very much out of court by con-

tinually practicing it, not merely during his struggling period, but long after he had made his name, indeed almost to the very last. And it is very hard to resist the conclusion that when he charged journalism generally not merely with envy, hatred, malice, and all uncharitableness, but with hopeless and pervading dishonesty, he had little more ground for it than an inability to conceive how any one, except from vile reasons of this kind, could fail to praise Honoré de Balzac.

At any rate, either his art by itself, or his art assisted and strengthened by that personal feeling which, as we have seen, counted for much with him, has here produced a wonderfully vivid piece of fiction—one, I think, inferior in success to hardly anything he has done. Whether, as at a late period a very well-informed, well-affected, and well-equipped critic hinted, his picture of the Luciens and the Lousteaus did not a little to propagate both is another matter. The seriousness with which Balzac took the accusation perhaps shows a little sense of galling. But, putting this aside, "Un Grand Homme de Province à Paris" must be ranked, both for comedy and tragedy, both for scheme and execution, in the first rank of his work.

(For bibliography, see Preface to "The Two Poets.")

"Z. Marcas."—Numerous and often good as are the stories by all manner of hands, eminent and other, of the strange neighbors and acquaintance which the French habit of living in apartments brings about, this may vie with almost the best of them for individuality and force. Of course, it may be said that its brevity demanded no very great effort; and also, a more noteworthy criticism, that Balzac has not made it so very clear, after all, why the political ingratitude of those for whom Marcas labored made it impossible for him to gain a living more amply and comfortably than by copying. The former carp needs no answer; the sonnet *is* the equal of the long poem if it is a perfect sonnet. The latter, more respectable, is also more damaging.   But it is a fair, if not quite full, defense to say that Balzac is here once more exemplifying his favorite notion of the *maniaque* in the French sense—of the man with one idea, who is incapable not only of making a dishonorable surrender of that idea, but of entering into even the most honorable armistice in his fight for it.   Not only will such a man not bow in the House of Rimmon, but the fullest liberty to stay outside will not content him—he must force himself in and be at the idol.   The external as well as the internal portraiture of " Z. Marcas " is also as good as it can be : and it cannot but add legitimate interest to the sketch to remember, first, that Balzac attributes to Marcas his own favorite habits and times of work ; and, secondly, that, like some other men of letters, he himself was an untiring, and would fain have been an influential, politician.

 " Z. Marcas," written in 1840, appeared in the " Revue Parisienne " for July of that year, made its first book appearance in a miscellany by different hands called " Le Fruit Défendu " (1841), and five years later took rank in the " Comédie."

G. S.

A DISTINGUISHED PROVINCIAL
AT PARIS.

PART I.

MME. DE BARGETON and Lucien de Rubempré had left
Angoulême behind, and were traveling together upon the
road to Paris. Not one of the party who made that journey
alluded to it afterward ; but it may be believed that an infatuated youth who had looked forward to the delights of an
elopement must have found the continual presence of Gentil,
the manservant, and Albertine, the maid, not a little irksome
on the way. Lucien, traveling post for the first time in his
life, was horrified to see pretty nearly the whole sum on which
he meant to live in Paris for a twelvemonth dropped along
the road. Like other men who combine great intellectual
powers with the charming simplicity of childhood, he openly
expressed his surprise at the new and wonderful things which
he saw, and thereby made a mistake. A man should study a
woman very carefully before he allows her to see his thoughts
and emotions as they arise in him. A woman, whose nature
is large as her heart is tender, can smile upon childishness
and make allowances ; but let her have ever so small a spice
of vanity herself, and she cannot forgive childishness, or
littleness, or vanity in her lover. Many a woman is so extravagant a worshiper that she must always see the god in her
idol ; but there are yet others who love a man for his sake
and not for their own, and adore his failings with his greater
qualities.

Lucien had not guessed as yet that Mme. de Bargeton's
love was grafted on pride. He made another mistake when
he failed to discern the meaning of certain smiles which

(1)

flitted over Louise's lips from time to time; and instead of
keeping himself to himself, he indulged in the playfulness of
the young rat emerging from his hole for the first time.

The travelers were set down before daybreak at the sign of
the Gaillard-Bois in the Rue de l'Échelle, both so tired out
with the journey that Louise went straight to bed and slept,
first bidding Lucien to engage the room immediately over-
head. Lucien slept on until four o'clock in the afternoon,
when he was awakened by Mme. de Bargeton's servant, and,
learning the hour, made a hasty toilet and hurried downstairs.

Louise was sitting in the shabby inn sitting-room. Hotel
accommodation is a blot on the civilization of Paris; for with
all its pretensions to elegance, the city as yet does not boast a
single inn where a well-to-do traveler can find the surroundings to which he is accustomed at home. To Lucien's just-
awakened, sleep-dimmed eyes, Louise was hardly recognizable
in this cheerless, sunless room, with the shabby window-cur-
tains, the comfortless polished floor, the hideous furniture
bought second-hand, or much the worse for wear.

Some people no longer look the same when detached from
the background of faces, objects, and surroundings which
serve as a setting, without which, indeed, they seem to lose
something of their intrinsic worth. Personality demands its
appropriate atmosphere to bring out its values, just as the
figures in Flemish interiors need the arrangement of light and
shade in which they are placed by the painter's genius if they
are to live for us. This is especially true of provincials.
Mme. de Bargeton, moreover, looked more thoughtful and
dignified than was necessary now, when no barriers stood
between her and happiness.

Gentil and Albertine waited upon them, and while they
were present Lucien could not complain. The dinner, sent
in from a neighboring restaurant, fell far below the provincial
average, both in quantity and quality; the essential goodness
of country fare was wanting, and in point of quantity the

portions were cut with so strict an eye to business that they savored of short commons. In such small matters Paris does not show its best side to travelers of moderate fortune. Lucien waited till the meal was over. Some change had come over Louise, he thought, but he could not explain it.

And a change had, in fact, taken place. Events had occurred while he slept; for reflection is an event in our inner history, and Mme. de Bargeton had been reflecting.

About two o'clock that afternoon, Sixte du Châtelet made his appearance in the Rue de l'Échelle and asked for Albertine. The sleeping damsel was aroused, and to her he expressed his wish to speak with her mistress. Mme. de Bargeton had scarcely time to dress before he came back again. The unaccountable apparition of M. du Châtelet roused the lady's curiosity, for she had kept her journey a profound secret, as she thought. At three o'clock the visitor was admitted.

"I have risked a reprimand from headquarters to follow you," he said, as he greeted her; "I foresaw coming events. But if I lose my post for it, *you*, at any rate, shall not be lost."

"What do you mean?" exclaimed Mme. de Bargeton.

"I can see plainly that you love Lucien," he continued, with an air of tender resignation. "You must love indeed if *you* can act thus recklessly and disregard the conventions which you know so well. Dear adored Naïs, can you really imagine that Madame d'Espard's salon, or any other salon in Paris, will not be closed to you as soon as it is known that you have fled from Angoulême, as it were, with a young man, especially after the duel between de Bargeton and de Chandour? The fact that your husband has gone to the Escarbas looks like a separation. Under such circumstances a gentleman fights first and afterward leaves his wife at liberty. Give Monsieur de Rubempré your love and your countenance; do just as you please; but you must not live in the same house. If anybody here in Paris knew that you had traveled together, the whole world that you have a mind to see would point the finger at you.

"And, Naïs, do not make these sacrifices for a young man whom you have as yet compared with no one else; he, on his side, has been put to no proof; he may forsake you for some Parisienne, better able, as he may fancy, to further his ambitions. I mean no harm to the man you love, but you will permit me to put your own interests before his, and to beg you to study him, to be fully aware of the serious nature of this step that you are taking. And, then, if you find all doors closed against you, and that none of the women call upon you, make sure at least that you will feel no regret for all that you have renounced for him. Be very certain first that he for whom you will have given up so much will always be worthy of your sacrifices and appreciate them.

"Just now," continued Châtelet, "Madame d'Espard is the more prudish and particular because she herself is separated from her husband, nobody knows why. The Navarreins, the Lenoncourts, the Blamont-Chauvrys, and the rest of the relations have all rallied round her; the most strait-laced women are seen at her house, and receive her with respect, and the Marquis d'Espard has been put in the wrong. The first call that you pay will make it clear to you that I am right; indeed, knowing Paris as I do, I can tell you beforehand that you will no sooner enter the Marquise's salon than you will be in despair lest she should find out that you are staying at the Gaillard-Bois with an apothecary's son, though he may wish to be called Monsieur de Rubempré.

"You will have rivals here, women far more astute and shrewd than Amélie; they will not fail to discover whom you are, where you are, where you come from, and all that you are doing. You have counted upon your incognito, I see, but you are one of those women for whom an incognito is out of the question. You will meet Angoulême at every turn.

There are the deputies from the Charente coming up for the opening of the session; there is the commandant in Paris on leave. Why, the first man or woman from Angoulême who happens to see you would cut your career short in a strange fashion. You would simply be Lucien's mistress.

"If you need me at any time, I am staying with the re-' ceiver-general in the Rue du Faubourg Saint-Honoré, two steps away from Madame d'Espard's. I am sufficiently ac- quainted with the Maréchale de Carigliano, Madame de Sérizy, and the president of the council to introduce you to them; but you will meet so many people at Madame d'Espard's that you are not likely to require me. So far from wishing to gain admittance to this set or that, every one will be longing to make your acquaintance."

Châtelet talked on; Mme. de Bargeton made no inter- ruption. She was struck with his perspicacity. The queen of Angoulême had, in fact, counted upon preserving her in- cognito.

"You are right, my dear friend," she said at length; "but what am I to do?"

"Allow me to find suitable furnished lodgings for you," suggested Châtelet; "that way of living is less expensive than an inn. You will have a home of your own; and, if you will take my advice, you will sleep in your new rooms this very night."

"But how did you know my address?" queried she.

"Your traveling carriage is easily recognized; and, beside, I was following you. At Sèvres your postillion told mine that he had brought you here. Will you permit me to act as your harbinger? I will write as soon as I have found lodg- ings."

"Very well, do so," said she. And in those seemingly insignificant words, all was said. The Baron du Châtelet had spoken the language of worldly wisdom to a woman of the world. He had made his appearance before her in faultless dress, a neat cab was waiting for him at the door; and Mme. de Bargeton, standing by the window thinking over the position, chanced to see the elderly dandy drive away.

A few moments later Lucien appeared, half-awake and hastily dressed. He was handsome, it is true; but his clothes, his last year's nankeen trousers, and his shabby tight jacket were ridiculous. Put Antinous or the Apollo Belvedere himself into a water-carrier's blouse, and how shall you recognize the godlike creature of the Greek or Roman chisel? The eyes note and compare before the heart has time to revise the swift involuntary judgment; and the contrast between Lucien and Châtelet was so abrupt that it could not fail to strike Louise.

Toward six o'clock that evening, when dinner was over, Mme. de Bargeton beckoned Lucien to sit beside her on the shabby sofa, covered with a flowered chintz—a yellow pattern on a red ground.

"Lucien mine," she said, "don't you think that if we have both of us done a foolish thing, suicidal for both our interests, that it would only be commonsense to set matters right? We ought not to live together in Paris, dear boy, and we must not allow any one to suspect that we traveled together. Your career depends so much upon my position that I ought to do nothing to spoil it. So, to-night, I am going to remove into lodgings near by. But you will stay on here, we can see each other every day, and nobody can say a word against us."

And Louise explained conventions to Lucien, who opened wide eyes. He had still to learn that when a woman thinks better of her folly, she thinks better of her love; but one thing he understood—he saw that he was no longer the Lucien of Angoulême. Louise talked of herself, of *her* interests, *her* reputation, and of the world; and, to veil her egoism, she tried to make him believe that this was all on his account. He had no claim upon Louise thus suddenly transformed into Mme. de Bargeton, and, more serious still, he had no power over her. He could not keep back the tears that filled his eyes.

"If I am your glory," cried the poet, "you are yet more to me—you are my one hope, my whole future rests with you. I thought that if you meant to make my successes yours, you would surely make my adversity yours also, and here we are going to part already."

"You are judging my conduct," said she; "you do not love me."

Lucien looked at her with such a dolorous expression that, in spite of herself, she said—

"Darling, I will stay if you like. We shall both be ruined; we shall have no one to come to our aid. But when we are both equally wretched, and every one shuts their door upon us both; when failure (for we must look all possibilities in the face), when failure drives us back to the Escarbas, then remember, love, that I foresaw the end, and that at the first I proposed that we should make your way by conforming to established rules."

"Louise," he cried, with his arms round her, "you are wise; you frighten me! Remember that I am a child, that I have given myself up entirely to your dear will. I myself should have preferred to overcome obstacles and win my way among men by the power that is in me; but if I can reach the goal sooner through your aid, I shall be very glad to owe all my success to you. Forgive me! You mean so much to me that I cannot help fearing all kinds of things; and, for me, parting means that desertion is at hand, and desertion is death."

"But, my dear boy, the world's demands are soon satisfied," she returned. "You must sleep here; that is all. All day long you will be with me, and no one can say a word."

A few kisses set Lucien's mind completely at rest. An hour later Gentil brought in a note from Châtelet. He told Mme. de Bargeton that he had found lodgings for her in the

Rue Neuve-de-Luxembourg. Mme. de Bargeton informed herself of the exact place, and found that it was not very far from the Rue de l'Échelle. "We shall be neighbors," she told Lucien.

Two hours afterward Louise stepped into the hired carriage sent by Châtelet for the removal to the new rooms. The apartments were of the class that upholsterers furnish and let to wealthy deputies and persons of consideration on a short visit to Paris — showy and uncomfortable. It was eleven o'clock when Lucien returned to his inn, having seen nothing as yet of Paris except the part of the Rue Saint-Honoré which lies between the Rue Neuve-de-Luxembourg and the Rue de l'Échelle. He lay down in his miserable little room, and could not help comparing it in his own mind with Louise's sumptuous apartments.

Just as he came away the Baron du Châtelet came in, gorgeously arrayed in evening dress, fresh from the minister for foreign affairs, to inquire whether Mme. de Bargeton was satisfied with all that he had done on her behalf. Naïs was uneasy. The splendor was alarming to her mind. Provincial life had reacted upon her; she was painfully conscientious over her accounts and economical to a degree that is looked upon as miserly in Paris. She had brought with her twenty thousand francs in the shape of a draft on the receiver-general, considering that the sum would more than cover the expenses of four years in Paris; she was afraid already lest she should not have enough and should run into debt; and now Châtelet told her that her rooms would only cost six hundred francs per month.

"A mere trifle," added he, seeing that Naïs was startled. "For five hundred francs a month you can have a carriage from a livery stable; fifty louis in all. You need only think of your dress. A woman moving in good society could not well do less; and if you mean to obtain a receiver-general's appointment for de Bargeton, or a post in the household, you ought not to look poverty-stricken. Here, in Paris, they only give to the rich. It is most fortunate that you brought Gentil to go out with you, and Albertine for your own woman, for servants are enough to ruin you here. But with your introductions you will seldom be at home to a meal."

Mme. de Bargeton and the Baron du Châtelet chatted about Paris. Châtelet gave her all the news of the day, the myriad nothings that you are bound to know, under penalty of being a nobody. Before very long the Baron also gave advice as to shopping, recommending Herbault for toques and Juliette for hats and bonnets; he added the address of a fashionable dressmaker to supersede Victorine. In short, he made the lady see the necessity of rubbing off Angoulême. Then he took his leave after a final flash of happy inspiration.

"I expect I shall have a box at one of the theatres to-morrow," he remarked carelessly; "I will call for you and Monsieur de Rubempré, for you must allow me to do the honors of Paris."

"There is more generosity in his character than I thought," said Mme. de Bargeton to herself when Lucien was included in the invitation.

In the month of June ministers are often puzzled to know what to do with boxes at the theatre; ministerialist deputies and their constituents are busy in their vineyards or harvest-fields, and their more exacting acquaintances are in the country or traveling about; so it comes to pass that the best seats are filled at this season with heterogeneous theatre-goers, never seen at any other time of year, and the house is apt to look as if it were tapestried with very shabby material. Châtelet had thought already that this was his opportunity of giving Naïs the amusements which provincials crave most eagerly, and that with very little expense.

The next morning, the very first morning in Paris, Lucien went to the Rue Neuve-de-Luxembourg and found that Louise had gone out. She had gone to make some indispensable purchases, to take counsel of the mighty and illustrious authorities in the matter of the feminine toilet, pointed out to her by Châtelet, for she had written to tell the Marquise d'Espard of her arrival. Mme. de Bargeton possessed the self-confidence born of a long habit of rule, but she was exceedingly afraid of appearing to be provincial. She had tact enough to know how greatly the relations of women among themselves depend upon first impressions; and though she felt that she was equal to taking her place at once in such a distinguished set as Mme. d'Espard's, she felt also that she stood in need of good-will at her first entrance into society, and was resolved, in the first place, that she would leave nothing undone to secure success. So she felt boundlessly thankful to Châtelet for pointing out these ways of putting herself in harmony with the fashionable world.

A singular chance so ordered it that the Marquise was delighted to find an opportunity of being useful to a connection of her husband's family. The Marquis d'Espard had just withdrawn himself without apparent reason from society, and ceased to take any active interest in affairs, political or domestic. His wife, thus left mistress of her actions, felt the need of the support of public opinion, and was glad to take the Marquis' place and give her countenance to one of her husband's relations. She meant to be ostentatiously gracious, so as to put her husband more evidently in the wrong; and that very day she wrote " Mme. de Bargeton *née* Nègrepelisse " a charming billet, one of the prettily worded compositions of which time alone can discover the emptiness.

" She was delighted that circumstances had brought a relative, of whom she had heard, whose acquaintance she had desired to make, into closer connection with her family. Friendships in Paris were not so solid but that she longed to find one more to love on earth ; and if this might not be, there would only be one more illusion to bury with the rest. She put herself entirely at her cousin's disposal. She would have called upon her if indisposition had not kept her to the house, and she felt that she lay already under obligations to the cousin who had thought of her."

Lucien, meanwhile, taking his first ramble along the Rue de la Paix and through the boulevards, like all new-comers, was much more interested in the things that he saw than in the people he met. The general effect of Paris is wholly engrossing at first. The wealth in the shop windows, the high houses, the streams of traffic, the contrast everywhere between the last extremes of luxury and want struck him more than anything else. In his astonishment at the crowds of strange faces, the man of imaginative temper felt as if he himself had shrunk, as it were, immensely. A man of any consequence in his native place, where he cannot go out but he meets with some recognition of his importance at every step, does not readily accustom himself to the sudden and total extinction of his consequence. You are somebody in your own country—in Paris you are nobody. The transition between the first state and the last should be made gradually, for the too abrupt fall is something like annihilation. Paris could not fail to be an appalling wilderness for a young poet, who looked for an echo for all his sentiments, a confident for all his thoughts, a soul to share his least sensations.

Lucien had not gone in search of his luggage and his best blue coat; and painfully conscious of the shabbiness, to say no worse of his clothes, he went to Mme. de Bargeton, feeling sure that she must have returned. He found the Baron du Châtelet, who carried them both off to dinner at the Rocher de Cancale. Lucien's head was dizzy with the whirl of Paris, the Baron was in the carriage, he could say nothing to Louise, but he squeezed her hand, and she gave a warm response to the mute confidence.

After dinner Châtelet took his guests to the Vaudeville.

Lucien, in his heart, was not over well pleased to see Châtelet again, and cursed the chance that had brought the Baron to Paris. The Baron said that ambition had brought him to town; he had hopes of an appointment as secretary-general to a government department, and meant to take a seat in the council of state as master of requests. He had come to Paris to ask for fulfillment of the promises that had been given him, for a man of his stamp could not be expected to remain a comptroller all his life; he would rather be nothing at all, and offer himself for election as deputy, or re-enter diplomacy. Châtelet grew visibly taller; Lucien dimly began to recognize in this elderly beau the superiority of the man of the world who knows Paris; and, most of all, he felt ashamed to owe his evening's amusement to his rival. And while the poet looked ill at ease and awkward, her royal highness' ex-secretary was quite in his element. He smiled at his rival's hesitations, at his astonishment, at the questions he put, at the little mistakes which the latter ignorantly made, much as an old salt laughs at an apprentice who has not found his sea legs; but Lucien's pleasure at seeing a play for the first time in Paris outweighed the annoyance of these small humiliations.

That evening marked an epoch in Lucien's career; he put away a good many of his ideas as to provincial life in the course of it. His horizon widened; society assumed different proportions. There were fair Parisiennes in fresh and elegant toilets all about him; Mme. de Bargeton's costume, tolerably ambitious though it was, looked dowdy by comparison; the material, like the fashion and the color, was out of date. That way of arranging her hair, so bewitching in Angoulême, looked frightfully ugly here among the daintily devised coiffures which he saw in every direction.

"Will she always look like that?" he said to himself, ignorant that the morning had been spent in preparing a transformation.

In the provinces comparison and choice are out of the question; when a face has grown familiar it comes to possess a certain beauty that is taken for granted. But transport the pretty woman of the provinces to Paris and no one takes the slightest notice of Her; her prettiness is of the comparative degree illustrated by the saying that among the blind the one-eyed are kings. Lucien's eyes were now busy comparing Mme. de Bargeton with other women, just as she herself had contrasted him with Châtelet on the previous day. And Mme. de Bargeton, on her part, permitted herself some strange reflections upon her lover. The poet cut a poor figure notwithstanding his singular beauty. The sleeves of his jacket were too short; with his ill-cut country gloves and a waistcoat too scanty for him, he looked prodigiously ridiculous, compared with the young men in the balcony—"positively pitiable," thought Mme. de Bargeton. Châtelet, interested in her without presumption, taking care of her in a manner that revealed a profound passion; Châtelet, elegant, and as much at home as an actor treading the familiar boards of his theatre, in two days had recovered all the ground lost in the past six months.

Ordinary people will not admit that our sentiments toward each other can totally change in a moment, and yet certain it is that two lovers not seldom fly apart even more quickly than they drew together. In Mme. de Bargeton and in Lucien a process of disenchantment was at work; Paris was the cause. Life had widened out before the poet's eyes, as society came to wear a new aspect for Louise. Nothing but an accident now was needed to sever finally the bond that united them; nor was that blow, so terrible for Lucien, very long delayed.

Mme. de Bargeton set Lucien down at his inn, and drove home with Châtelet, to the intense vexation of the luckless lover.

"What will they say about me?" he wondered, as he climbed the stairs to his dismal room.

"That poor fellow is uncommonly dull," said Châtelet, with a smile, when the door was closed.

"That is the way with those who have a world of thoughts in their heart and brain. Men who have so much in them to give out in great works long dreamed of profess a certain contempt for conversation, a commerce in which the intellect spends itself in small change," returned the haughty Nègre-pelisse. She still had courage to defend Lucien, but less for Lucien's sake than for her own.

"I grant it you willingly," replied the Baron, "but we live with human beings and not with books. There, dear Naïs, I see how it is, there is nothing between you yet, and I am delighted that it is so. If you decide to bring an interest of a kind hitherto lacking into your life, let it not be this so-called genius, I implore you. How if you have made a mistake? Suppose that in a few days' time, when you have compared him with men whom you will meet, men of real ability, men who have distinguished themselves in good earnest; suppose that you should discover, dear and fair siren, that it is no lyre-bearer that you have borne into port on your dazzling shoulders, but a little ape, with no manners and no capacity; a presumptuous fool who may be a wit in L'Houmeau, but turns out a very ordinary specimen of a young man in Paris? And, after all, volumes of verse come out every week here, the worst of them better than all this Chardon's poetry put together. For pity's sake, wait and compare! To-morrow, Friday, is opera night," he continued, as the carriage turned into the Rue Neuve-de-Luxembourg; "Mme. d'Espard has the box of the first gentlemen of the chamber, and will take you, no doubt. I shall go to Mme. de Sérizy's box to behold you in your glory. They are giving 'Les Danaïdes.'"

"Good-by," said she.

Next morning Mme. de Bargeton tried to arrange a suitable toilet in which to call on her cousin, Mme. d'Espard. The weather was rather chilly. Looking through the dowdy wardrobe from Angoulême, she found nothing better than a certain green velvet gown, trimmed fantastically enough. Lucien, for his part, felt that he must go at once for his celebrated blue best coat; he felt aghast at the thought of his tight jacket, and determined to be well dressed, lest he should meet the Marquise d'Espard or receive a sudden summons to her house. He must have his luggage at once, so he took a cab, and in two hours' time spent three or four francs, matter for much subsequent reflection on the scale of the cost of living in Paris. Having dressed himself in his best, such as it was, he went to the Rue Neuve-de-Luxembourg, and on the door-step encountered Gentil in company with a gorgeously be-feathered chasseur.

"I was just going round to you, sir; madame gave me a line for you," said Gentil, ignorant of Parisian forms of re-spect, and accustomed to homely provincial ways. The chas-seur took the poet for a servant.

Lucien tore open the note, and learned that Mme. de Bargeton had gone to spend the day with the Marquise d'Espard. She was going to the opera in the evening, but she told Lucien to be there to meet her. Her cousin per-mitted her to give him a seat in her box. The Marquise d'Espard was delighted to procure the young poet that pleasure.

"Then she loves me! my fears were all nonsense!" said Lucien to himself. "She is going to present me to her cousin this very evening."

He jumped for joy. He would spend the day that separ-ated him from the happy evening as joyously as might be. He dashed out in the direction of the Tuileries, dreaming of walking there until it was time to dine at Véry's. And now, behold Lucien frisking and skipping, light of foot because light of heart, on his way to the Terrasse des Feuillants to take a look at the people of quality on promenade there. Pretty women walk arm in arm with men of fashion, their adorers; couples greet each other with a glance as they pass; how

different it is from the terrace at Beaulieu! How far finer
the birds on this perch than the Angoulême species! It is as
if you beheld all the colors that glow in the plumage of the
feathered tribes of India and America, instead of the sober
European families.

Those were two wretched hours that Lucien spent in the
garden of the Tuileries. A violent revulsion swept through
him, and he sat in judgment upon himself.

In the first place, not a single one of these gilded youths
wore a swallow-tailed coat. The few exceptions, one or
two poor wretches, a clerk here and there, an annuitant
from the Marais, could be ruled out on the score of age;
and hard upon the discovery of a distinction between
morning and evening dress, the poet's quick sensibility and
keen eyes saw likewise that his shabby old clothes were
not fit to be seen; the defects in his coat branded that
garment as ridiculous; the cut was old-fashioned, the color
was the wrong shade of blue, the collar outrageously un-
gainly, the coat-tails, by dint of long wear, overlapped each
other, the buttons were reddened, and there were fatal white
lines along the seams. Then his waistcoat was too short,
and so grotesquely provincial, that he hastily buttoned his
coat over it; and, finally, no man of any pretension to
fashion wore nankeen trousers. Well-dressed men wore
charming fancy materials or immaculate white, and every one
had straps to his trousers, while the shrunken hems of Lucien's
nether garments manifested a violent antipathy for the heels
of shoes which they wedded with obvious reluctance. Lucien
wore a white cravat with embroidered ends; his sister had
seen that M. du Hautoy and M. de Chandour wore such
things, and hastened to make similar ones for her brother.
Here, no one appeared to wear white cravats of a morning
except a few grave seniors, elderly capitalists, and austere
public functionaries, until, in the street on the other side of the
railings, Lucien noticed a grocer's boy walking along the Rue

de Rivoli with a basket on his head; him the man of Angoulême detected in the act of sporting a cravat, with both ends
adorned by the handiwork of some adored shop-girl. The
sight was a stab to Lucien's breast; penetrating straight to
that organ as yet undefined, the seat of our sensibility, the
region whither, since sentiment has had any existence, the
sons of men carry their hands in any excess of joy or
anguish. Do not accuse this chronicle of puerility. The
rich, to be sure, never having experienced sufferings of this
kind, may think them incredibly petty and small; but the
agonies of less fortunate mortals are as well worth our attention as crises and vicissitudes in the lives of the mighty and
privileged ones of earth. Is not the pain equally great for
either? Suffering exalts all things. And, after all, suppose
that we change the terms, and for a suit of clothes, more or
less fine, put instead a ribbon, or a star, or a title; have not
brilliant careers been tormented by reason of such apparent
trifles as these? Add, moreover, that for those people who
must seem to have that which they have not, the question of
clothes is of enormous importance, and not unfrequently the
appearance of possession is the shortest road to possession at
a later day.

A cold sweat broke out over Lucien as he bethought himself
that to-night he must make his first appearance before the
Marquise in this dress—the Marquise d'Espard, relative of a
first gentleman of the bedchamber, a woman whose house was
frequented by the most illustrious among illustrious men in
every field.

"I look like an apothecary's son, a regular shop-drudge,"
he raged inwardly, watching the youth of the Faubourg de
Saint-Germain pass under his eyes; graceful, spruce, fashion-
ably dressed, with a certain uniformity of air, a sameness due
to a fineness of contour, and a certain dignity of carriage and
expression; though, at the same time, each one differed from
the rest in the setting by which he had chosen to bring his

2

personal characteristics into prominence.   Each one made
the most of his personal advantages.   Young men in Paris
understand the art of presenting themselves quite as well as
women.   Lucien had inherited from his mother the invaluable physical distinction of race, but the metal was still in the
ore, and not set free by the craftsman's hand.

His hair was badly cut.   Instead of holding himself upright
with an elastic corset, he felt that he was cooped up inside a
hideous shirt-collar; he hung his dejected head without resistance on the part of a limp cravat.   What woman could guess
that a handsome foot was hidden by the clumsy boots which
he had brought from Angoulême?   What young man could
envy him his graceful figure, disguised by the shapeless blue
sack which hitherto he had mistakenly believed to be a coat?
What bewitching studs he saw on those dazzling white shirt
fronts, his own looked dingy by comparison; and how marvelously all these elegant persons were gloved, his own gloves
were only fit for a policeman!   Yonder was a youth toying
with a cane exquisitely mounted; there, another with dainty
gold studs in his wristbands.   Yet another was twisting a
charming riding-whip while he talked with a woman; there
were specks of mud on the ample folds of his white trousers,
he wore clanking spurs and a tight-fitting jacket, evidently
he was about to mount one of the two horses held by a hop-
o'-my-thumb of a tiger.   A young man who went past drew
a watch no thicker than a five-franc piece from his pocket,
and looked at it with the air of a person who is either too
early or too late for an appointment.

Lucien, seeing these pretty trifles, hitherto unimagined, became aware of a whole world of indispensable superfluities,
and shuddered to think of the enormous capital needed by a
professional pretty fellow!   The more he admired these gay
and careless beings, the more conscious he grew of his own
outlandishness; he knew that he looked like a man who has
no idea of the direction of the streets, who stands close to

the Palais Royal and cannot find it, and asks his way to the
Louvre of a passer-by, who tells him, " Here you are." Lucien saw a great gulf fixed between him and this new world,
and asked himself how he might cross over, for he meant to
be one of these delicate, slim youths of Paris, these young
patricians who bowed before women divinely dressed and
divinely fair. For one kiss from one of these, Lucien was
ready to be cut in pieces, like Count Philip of Konigsmark.
Louise's face rose up somewhere in the shadowy background
of memory—compared with these queens, she looked like an
old woman. He saw women whose names will appear in the
history of the nineteenth century, women no less famous than
the queens of past times for their wit, their beauty, or their
lovers ; one who passed was the heroine Mlle. des Touches,
so well known as Camille Maupin, the great woman of letters,
great by her intellect, great no less by her beauty. He overheard the name pronounced by those who went by.

"Ah ! " he thought to himself, " she is Poetry."

What was Mme. de Bargeton in comparison with this angel
in all the glory of youth, and hope, and promise of the future,
with that sweet smile of hers, and the great dark eyes with all
heaven in them, and the glowing light of the sun ? She was
laughing and chatting with Mme. Firmiani, one of the most
charming women in Paris. A voice indeed cried, " Intellect
is the lever by which to move the world," but another voice
cried no less loudly that money was the fulcrum.

He would not stay any longer on the scene of his collapse
and defeat, and went toward the Palais Royal. He did not
know the topography of his quarter yet, and was obliged to
ask his way. Then he went to Véry's and ordered dinner by
way of an initiation into the pleasures of Paris and a solace
for his discouragement. A bottle of Bordeaux, oysters from
Ostend, a dish of fish, a partridge, a dish of macaroni and
dessert—this was the *ne plus ultra* of his desire. He enjoyed
this little debauch, studying the while how to give the Mar-

quise d'Espard proof of his wit, and redeem the shabbiness
of his grotesque accoutrements by the display of intellectual
riches. The total of the bill drew him down from these
dreams, and left him the poorer by fifty of the francs which
were to have gone such a long way in Paris. He could have
lived in Angoulême for a month on the price of that dinner.
Wherefore he closed the door of the palace with awe, thinking as he did so that he should never set foot in it again.

"Eve was right," he said to himself, as he went back
under the stone arcading for some more money. "There is
a difference between Paris prices and prices in L'Houmeau."

He gazed in at the tailors' windows on the way, and
thought of the costumes in the garden of the Tuileries.

"No," he exclaimed, "I will *not* appear before Mme.
d'Espard dressed out as I am."

He fled to his inn, fleet as a stag, rushed up to his room,
took out a hundred crowns, and went down again to the
Palais Royal, where his future elegance lay scattered over
half a score of shops. The first tailor whose door he entered
tried as many coats upon him as he would consent to put on,
and persuaded his customer that all were in the very latest
fashion. Lucien came out the owner of a green coat, a pair
of white trousers, and a "fancy waistcoat," for which outfit
he gave two hundred francs. Ere long he found a very elegant pair of ready-made shoes that fitted his foot; and finally,
when he had made all necessary purchases, he ordered the
tradespeople to send them to his address, and inquired for a
hairdresser. At seven o'clock that evening he called a cab
and drove away to the opera, curled like a Saint John of a
procession day, elegantly waistcoated and gloved, but feeling
a little awkward in this kind of sheath in which he found himself for the first time.

In obedience to Mme. de Bargeton's instructions, he asked
for the box reserved for the first gentlemen of the bedchamber.
The man at the box office looked at him, and beholding

"M. DE RUBEMPRÉ," SAID THE MARQUISE——"TAKE THIS SEAT."

Lucien in all the grandeur assumed for the occasion, in which he looked like a best man at a wedding, asked Lucien for his order.

" I have no order."

" Then you cannot go in," said the man at the box office · drily.

" But I belong to Madame d'Espard's party."

" It is not our business to know that," said the man, who could not help exchanging a barely perceptible smile with his colleague.

A carriage stopped under the peristyle as he spoke. A chasseur, in a livery which Lucien did not recognize, let down the step, and two women in evening dress came out of the brougham. Lucien had no mind to lay himself open to an insolent order to get out of the way from the official. He stepped aside to let the two ladies pass.

" Why, that lady is the Marquise d'Espard, whom you say you know, sir," the man said ironically.

Lucien was so much the more confounded because Mme. de Bargeton did not seem to recognize him in his new plumage; but when he stepped up to her, she smiled at him and said—

" This has fallen out wonderfully—come ! "

The functionaries at the box office grew serious again as Lucien followed Mme. de Bargeton. On their way up the great staircase the lady introduced M. de Rubempré to her cousin. The box belonging to the first gentlemen of the bedchamber is situated in one of the angles at the back of the house, so that its occupants see and are seen all over the theatre. Lucien took his seat on a chair behind Mme. de Bargeton, thankful to be in the shadow.

" Monsieur de Rubempré," said the Marquise with flattering graciousness, "this is your first visit to the opera, is it not ? You must have a view of the house ; take this seat, sit in front of the box ; we give you permission."

Lucien obeyed as the first act came to an end.

"You have made good use of your time," Louise said in his ear, in her first surprise at the change in his appearance.

Louise was still the same. The near presence of the Marquise d'Espard, a Parisian Mme. de Bargeton, was so damaging to her; the brilliancy of the Parisienne brought out all the defects in her country cousin so clearly by contrast, that Lucien, looking out over the fashionable audience in the superb building, and then at the great lady, was twice enlightened, and saw poor Anaïs de Nègrepelisse as she really was, as Parisians saw her—a tall, lean, withered woman, with a pimpled face and faded complexion; angular, stiff; affected in her manner; pompous and provincial in her speech; and, above all these things, dowdily dressed. As a matter of fact, the creases in an old dress from Paris still bear witness to good taste, you can tell what the gown was meant for; but an old dress made in the country is inexplicable, it is a thing to provoke laughter. There was neither charm nor freshness about the dress or its wearer; the velvet, like the complexion, had seen wear. Lucien felt ashamed to have fallen in love with this cuttle-fish bone, and vowed that he would profit by Louise's next fit of virtue to leave her for good. Having an excellent view of the house, he could see the opera glasses pointed at the aristocratic box *par excellence*. The best-dressed women must certainly be scrutinizing Mme. de Bargeton, for they smiled at each other as they talked among themselves.

If Mme. d'Espard knew the object of their sarcasms from those feminine smiles and gestures, she was perfectly insensible to them. In the first place, anybody must see that her companion was a poor relation from the country, an affliction with which any Parisian family may be visited. And, in the second, when her cousin had spoken to her of her dress with manifest misgivings, she had reassured Anaïs, seeing that, when once properly dressed, her relative would very easily acquire the tone of Parisian society. If Mme. de Bargeton needed polish, on the other hand, she possessed the native haughtiness of good birth, and that indescribable something which may be called "pedigree." So, on Monday her turn would come. And, moreover, the Marquise knew that as soon as people learned that the stranger was her cousin, they would suspend their banter and look twice before they condemned her.

Lucien did foresee the change in Louise's appearance shortly to be worked by a scarf about her throat, a pretty dress, an elegant coiffure, and Mme. d'Espard's advice. As they came up the staircase even now, the Marquise told her cousin not to hold her handkerchief unfolded in her hand. Good or bad taste turns upon hundreds of such almost imperceptible shades, which a quick-witted woman discerns at once, while others will never grasp them. Mme. de Bargeton, plentifully apt, was more than clever enough to discover her shortcomings. Mme. d'Espard, sure that her pupil would do her credit, did not decline to form her. In short, the compact between the two women had been confirmed by self-interest on either side.

Mme. de Bargeton, enthralled, dazzled, and fascinated by her cousin's manner, wit, and acquaintances, had suddenly declared herself a votary of the idol of the day. She had discerned the signs of the occult power exerted by the ambitious great lady, and told herself that she could gain her end as the satellite of this star, so she had been outspoken in her admiration. The Marquise was not insensible to the artlessly admitted conquest. She took an interest in her cousin, seeing that she was weak and poor; she was, beside, not indisposed to take a pupil with whom to found a school, and asked nothing better than to have a sort of lady-in-waiting in Mme. de Bargeton, a dependent who would sing her praises, a treasure even more scarce among Parisian women than a stanch and loyal critic among the literary tribe. The flutter of curiosity in the house was too marked to be ignored, however, and

Mme. d'Espard politely endeavored to turn her cousin's mind from the truth.

"If any one comes to our box," she said, "perhaps we may discover the cause to which we owe the honor of the interest that these ladies are taking——"

"I have a strong suspicion that it is my old velvet gown and Angoumoisin air which Parisian ladies find amusing," Mme. de Bargeton answered, laughing.

"No, it is not you ; it is something that I cannot explain," she added, turning to the poet, and, as she looked at him for the first time, it seemed to strike her that he was singularly dressed.

"There is Monsieur du Châtelet," exclaimed Lucien at that very moment, and he pointed a finger toward Mme. de Sérizy's box, which the renovated beau had just entered.

Mme. de Bargeton bit her lips with chagrin as she saw that gesture, and saw beside the Marquise's ill-suppressed smile of contemptuous astonishment. "Where does the young man come from?" her look said, and Louise felt humbled through her love, one of the sharpest of all pangs for a Frenchwoman, a mortification for which she cannot forgive her lover.

In these circles where trifles are of such importance, a gesture or a word at the outset is enough to ruin a new-comer. It is the principal merit of fine manners and the highest breeding that they produce the effect of a harmonious whole, in which every element is so blended that nothing is startling or obtrusive. Even those who break the laws of this science, either through ignorance or carried away by some impulse, must comprehend that it is with social intercourse as with music, a single discordant note is a complete negation of the art itself, for the harmony exists only when all its conditions are observed down to the least particular.

"Who is the gentleman?" asked Mme. d'Espard, looking toward Châtelet. "And have you made Madame de Sérizy's acquaintance already?"

"Oh! is that the famous Madame de Sérizy who has had so many adventures and yet goes everywhere?"

"An unheard-of thing, my dear, explicable but unexplained. The most formidable men are her friends, and why? Nobody dares to fathom the mystery. Then is this person the lion of Angoulême?"

"Well, Monsieur le Baron du Châtelet has been a good deal talked about," answered Mme. de Bargeton, moved by vanity to give her adorer the title which she herself had called in question. "He was Monsieur de Montriveau's traveling companion."

"Ah!" said the Marquise d'Espard, "I never hear that name without thinking of the Duchesse de Langeais, poor thing. She vanished like a falling star. That is Monsieur de Rastignac with Madame de Nucingen," she continued, indicating another box; "she is the wife of a contractor, a banker, a city man, a broker on a large scale; he forced his way into society with his money, and they say that he is not very scrupulous as to the methods of making it. He is at endless pains to establish his credit as a stanch upholder of the Bourbons, and has tried already to gain admittance into my set. When his wife took Madame de Langeais' box, she thought that she could take her charm, her wit, and her success as well. It is the old fable of the jay in the peacock's feathers!"

"How do Monsieur and Madame de Rastignac manage to keep their son in Paris, when, as we know, their income is under a thousand crowns?" asked Lucien, in his astonishment at Rastignac's elegant and expensive dress.

"It is easy to see that you come from Angoulême," said Mme. d'Espard, ironically enough, as she continued to gaze through her opera-glass.

Her remark was lost upon Lucien; the all-absorbing spectacle of the boxes prevented him from thinking of anything else. He guessed the comments made upon Mme. de Bargeton, and saw that he himself was an object of no small curiosity. Louise, on the other hand, was exceedingly mortified by the evident slight esteem in which the Marquise held Lucien's beauty.

" He cannot be so handsome as I thought him," she said to herself; and between " not so handsome " and " not so clever as I thought him " there was but one step.

The curtain fell. Châtelet was paying a visit to the Duchesse de Carigliano in an adjoining box; Mme. de Bargeton acknowledged his bow by a slight inclination of the head. Nothing escapes a woman of the world; Châtelet's air of distinction was not lost upon Mme. d'Espard. Just at that moment four personages, four Parisian celebrities, came into the box, one after another.

The most striking feature of the first comer, M. de Marsay, famous for the passions which he had inspired, was his girlish beauty; but its softness and effeminacy were counteracted by the expression of his eyes, unflinching, steady, untamed, and hard as a tiger's. He was loved and he was feared. Lucien was no less handsome; but Lucien's expression was so gentle, his blue eyes so limpid, that he scarcely seemed to possess the strength and power which attract women so strongly. Nothing, moreover, so far had brought out the poet's merits; while de Marsay, with his flow of spirits, his confidence in his power to please, and appropriate style of dress, eclipsed every rival by his presence. Judge, therefore, the kind of figure that Lucien, stiff, starched, unbending in clothes as new and unfamiliar as his surroundings, was likely to cut in de Marsay's vicinity. De Marsay with his wit and charm of manner was privileged to be insolent. From Mme. d'Espard's reception of this personage his importance was at once evident to Mme. de Bargeton.

The second comer was a Vandenesse, the cause of the scandal in which Lady Dudley was concerned. Félix de Vandenesse, amiable, intellectual, and modest, had none of the characteristics on which de Marsay prided himself and owed his success to diametrically opposed qualities. He had been warmly recommended to Mme. d'Espard by her cousin Mme. de Mortsauf.

The third was General de Montriveau, the author of the Duchesse de Langeais' ruin.

The fourth, M. de Canalis, one of the famous poets of the day, and as yet a newly risen celebrity, was prouder of his birth than of his genius, and dangled in Mme. d'Espard's train by way of concealing his love for the Duchesse de Chaulieu. In spite of his graces and the affectation that spoiled them, it was easy to discern the vast, lurking ambitions that plunged him at a later day into the storms of political life. A face that might be called insignificantly pretty and caressing manners thinly disguised the man's deeply rooted egoism and habit of continually calculating the chances of a career which at the time looked problematical enough ; though his choice of Mme. de Chaulieu (a woman past forty) made interest for him at court, and brought him the applause of the Faubourg Saint-Germain and the gibes of the liberal party, who dubbed him " the poet of the sacristy."

Mme. de Bargeton, with these remarkable figures before her, no longer wondered at the slight esteem in which the Marquise held Lucien's good looks. And when conversation began, when intellects so keen, so subtle, were revealed in two-edged words with more meaning and depth in them than Anaïs de Bargeton heard in a month of talk at Angoulême ; and, most of all, when Canalis uttered a sonorous phrase, summing up a materialistic epoch, and gilding it with poetry —then Anaïs felt all the truth of Châtelet's dictum of the previous evening. Lucien was nothing to her now. Every one cruelly ignored the unlucky stranger ; he was so much like a foreigner listening to an unknown language that the Marquise d'Espard took pity on him. She turned to Canalis.

" Permit me to introduce Monsieur de Rubempré," she

said. "You rank too high in the world of letters not to welcome a *débutant.* Monsieur de Rubempré is from Angoulême,
and will need your influence, no doubt, with the powers that
bring genius to light. So far, he has no enemies to help him
to success by their attacks upon him. Is there enough originality in the idea of obtaining for him by friendship all that
hatred has done for you to tempt you to make the experiment?"

The four new-comers all looked at Lucien while the Marquise was speaking. De Marsay, only a couple of paces
away, put up an eyeglass and looked from Lucien to Mme. de
Bargeton, and then again at Lucien, coupling them with some
mocking thought, cruelly mortifying to both. He scrutinized them as if they had been a pair of strange animals, and
then he smiled. The smile was like a stab to the distinguished
provincial. Félix de Vandenesse assumed a charitable air.
Montriveau, with insolent contempt, looked Lucien through·
and through.

"Madame," M. de Canalis answered with a bow, "I will
obey you, in spite of the selfish instinct which prompts us to
show a rival no favor; but you have accustomed us to
miracles."

"Very well, do me the pleasure of dining with me on
Monday with Monsieur de Rubempré, and you can talk of
matters literary at your ease. I will try to enlist some of the
tyrants of the world of letters and the great people who protect them, the author of 'Ourika,' and one or two young
poets with sound views."

"Madame la Marquise," said de Marsay, "if you give·
your support to this gentleman for his intellect, I will support
him for his good looks. I will give him advice which will
put him in a fair way to be the luckiest dandy in Paris. After
that, he may be a poet—if he has a mind."

Mme. de Bargeton thanked her cousin by a grateful glance.

"I did not know that you were jealous of intellect," Montriveau said, turning to de Marsay; "good fortune is the death of a poet."

"Is that why your lordship is thinking of marriage?" inquired the dandy, addressing Canalis, and watching Mme. d'Espard to see if the words went home.

Canalis shrugged his shoulders, and Mme. d'Espard, Mme. de Chaulieu's niece, began to laugh. Lucien in his new clothes felt as if he were an Egyptian statue in its narrow sheath; he was ashamed that he had nothing to say for himself all this while. At length he turned gracefully to the Marquise.

"After your kindness, madame, I am pledged to make no failures," he said in those soft tones of his.

Châtelet came in as he spoke; he had seen Montriveau, and by hook or crook snatched at the chance of a good introduction to the Marquise d'Espard through one of the kings of Paris. He bowed to Mme. de Bargeton, and begged Mme. d'Espard to pardon him for the liberty he took in invading her box; he had been separated so long from his traveling companion! Montriveau and Châtelet met for the first time since they parted in the desert.

"To part in the desert, and meet again in the opera house!" said Lucien.

"Quite a theatrical meeting!" said Canalis.

Montriveau introduced the Baron du Châtelet to the Marquise, and the Marquise received her royal highness' ex-secretary the more graciously because she had seen that he had been very well received in three boxes already. Mme. de Sérizy knew none but unexceptionable people, and, moreover, he was Montriveau's traveling companion. So potent was this last credential that Mme. de Bargeton saw from the manner of the group that they accepted Châtelet as one of themselves without demur. Châtelet sultan's airs in Angoulême were suddenly explained.

At length the Baron saw Lucien, and favored him with a

cool, disparaging little nod, indicative to men of the world of the recipient's inferior station. A sardonic expression accompanied the greeting, "How does *he* come here?" he seemed to say. This was not lost on those who saw it; for de Marsay leaned toward Montriveau, and said in tones audible to Châtelet—

"Do ask him who the queer-looking young fellow is that looks like a dummy at a tailor's store-door."

Châtelet spoke a few words in his traveling companion's ear, and, while apparently renewing his acquaintance, no doubt cut his rival to pieces.

If Lucien was surprised at the apt wit and the subtlety with which these gentlemen formulated their replies, he felt bewildered with epigram and repartee, and, most of all, by their off-hand way of talking and their ease of manner. The material luxury of Paris had alarmed him that morning; at night he saw the same lavish expenditure of intellect. By what mysterious means, he asked himself, did these people make such piquant reflections on the spur of the moment, those repartees which he could only have made after much pondering. And not only were they at ease in their speech, they were at ease in their dress, nothing looked new, nothing looked old, nothing about them was conspicuous, everything attracted the eyes. The fine gentleman of to-day was the same yesterday and would be the same to-morrow. Lucien guessed that he himself looked as if he were dressed for the first time in his life.

"My dear fellow," said de Marsay, addressing Félix de Vandenesse, "that young Rastignac is soaring away like a paper-kite. Look at him in the Marquise de Listomère's box; he is making progress, he is putting up his eyeglass at us! He knows this gentleman, no doubt," added the dandy, speaking to Lucien, but looking elsewhere.

"He can scarcely fail to have heard the name of a great man of whom we are proud," said Mme. de Bargeton.

"Quite lately his sister was present when Monsieur de Rubempré read us some very fine poetry."

Félix de Vandenesse and de Marsay then took leave of the Marquise d'Espard, and went off to Mme. de Listomère, Vandenesse's sister. The second act began, and the three were left to themselves again. The curious women learned how Mme. de Bargeton came to be there from some of the party, while the others announced the arrival of a poet and made fun of his costume. Canalis went back to the Duchesse de Chaulieu and no more was seen of him.

Lucien was glad when the rising of the curtain produced a diversion. All Mme. de Bargeton's misgivings with regard to Lucien were increased by the marked attention which the Marquise d'Espard had shown to Châtelet; her manner toward the Baron was very different from the patronizing affability with which she treated Lucien. Mme. de Listomère's box was full during the second act, and, to all appearance, the talk turned upon Mme. de Bargeton and Lucien. Young Rastignac was evidently entertaining the party; he had raised laughter that needs fresh fuel every day in Paris, the laughter that seizes upon a topic and exhausts it, and leaves it stale and threadbare in a moment. Mme. d'Espard grew uneasy. She knew that an ill-natured speech is not long in coming to the ears of those whom it will wound, and waited till the end of the act.

After a revulsion of feeling such as had taken place in Mme. de Bargeton and Lucien, strange things come to pass in a brief space of time, and any revolution within us is controlled by laws that work with great swiftness. Châtelet's sage and politic words as to Lucien, spoken on the way home from the Vaudeville, were fresh in Louise's memory. Every phrase was a prophecy; it seemed as if Lucien had set himself to fulfill the predictions one by one. When Lucien and Mme. de Bargeton had parted with their illusions concerning each other, the luckless youth, with a destiny not unlike Rousseau's,

went so far in his predecessor's footsteps that he was capti-
vated by the great lady and smitten with Mme. d'Espard at
first sight.   Young men and men who remember their young
emotions can see that this was only what might have been
looked for. Mme. d'Espard with her dainty ways, her delicate
enunciation, and the refined tones of her voice; the fragile
woman so envied, of such high place and high degree, appeared before the poet as Mme. de Bargeton had appeared to
him in Angoulême.   His fickle nature prompted him to desire
influence in that lofty sphere at once, and the surest way to
secure such influence was to possess the woman who exerted
it, and then everything would be his.   He had succeeded at
Angoulême, why should he not succeed in Paris?

Involuntarily, and despite the novel counter-fascination of
the stage, his eyes turned to this Célimène in her splendor;
he glanced furtively at her every moment; the longer he
looked, the more he desired to look at her.   Mme. de
Bargeton caught the gleam in Lucien's eyes, and saw that he
found the Marquise more interesting than the opera.   If
Lucien had forsaken her for the fifty daughters of Danaus, she
could have borne his desertion with equanimity; but another
glance—bolder, more ardent, and unmistakable than any before—revealed the state of Lucien's feelings.   She grew jealous,
but not so much for the future as for the past.

"He never gave me such a look?" she thought.   "Dear
me!   Châtelet was right!"

Then she saw that she had made a mistake; and when a
woman once begins to repent of her weaknesses she sponges
out the whole past.   Every one of Lucien's glances roused her
indignation, but to all outward appearance she was calm.   De
Marsay came back in the interval, bringing M. de Listomère
with him; and that serious person and the young coxcomb
soon informed the Marquise that the wedding-guest in his
holiday suit, whom she had the bad luck to have in her box,
had as much right to the appellation of Rubempré as a Jew to

a baptismal name. Lücien's father was an apothecary named
Chardon. M. de Rastignac, who knew all about Angoulême,
had set several boxes laughing already at the mummy whom
the Marquise styled her cousin, and at the Marquise's forethought in having an apothecary at hand to sustain an artificial
life with drugs. In short, de Marsay brought a selection
from the thousand-and-one jokes made by Parisians on the
spur of the moment, and no sooner uttered than forgotten.
Châtelet was at the back of it all and the real author of this
Punic faith.

Mme. d'Espard turned to Mme. de Bargeton, put up her
fan, and said, "My dear, tell me if your protégé's name is
really Monsieur de Rubempré?"

"He has assumed his mother's name," said Anaïs, uneasily.

"But who was his father?"

"His father's name was Chardon."

"And what was this Chardon?"

"A druggist."

"My dear friend, I felt quite sure that all Paris could not
be laughing at any one whom I took up. I do not care to
stay here when wags come in in high glee because there is an
apothecary's son in my box. If you will follow my advice, we
will leave it, and at once."

Mme. d'Espard's expression was insolent enough; Lucien
was at a loss to account for her change of countenance. He
thought that his waistcoat was in bad taste, which was true;
and that his coat looked like a caricature of the fashion, which
was likewise true. He discerned, in bitterness of soul, that
he must put himself in the hands of an expert tailor, and
vowed that he would go the very next morning to the most
celebrated artist in Paris. On Monday he would hold his own
with the men at the Marquise's house.

Yet, lost in thought though he was, he saw the third act to
an end, and, with his eyes fixed on the gorgeous scene upon

3

the stage, dreamed out his dream of Mme. d'Espard. He was
in despair over her sudden coldness; it gave a strange check
to the ardent reasoning through which he advanced upon this
new love, undismayed by the immense difficulties in the way,
difficulties which he saw and resolved to conquer. He roused
himself from these deep musings to look once more at his new
idol, turned his head, and saw that he was alone; he had heard
a faint rustling sound, the door closed—Mme. d'Espard had
taken her cousin with her. Lucien was surprised to the last
degree by the sudden desertion; he did not think long about
it, however, simply because it was inexplicable.

When the carriage was rolling along the Rue de Richelieu
on the way to the Faubourg Saint-Honoré, the Marquise
spoke to her cousin in a tone of suppressed irritation.

" My dear child, what are you thinking about ? Pray wait
till an apothecary's son has made a name for himself before
you trouble yourself about him. The Duchesse de Chaulieu
does not acknowledge Canalis even now, and he is famous
and a man of good family. This young fellow is neither your
son nor your lover, I suppose?" added the haughty dame,
with a keen, inquisitive glance at her cousin.

" How fortunate for me that I kept the little scapegrace at
a distance !" thought Mme. de Bargeton.

" Very well," continued the Marquise, taking the expression in her cousin's eyes for an answer, " drop him, I beg of
you. Taking an illustrious name in that way ! Why, it is a
piece of impudence that will meet with its desserts in society.
It is his mother's name, I dare say ; but just remember, dear,
that the King alone can confer, by a special ordinance, the
title of de Rubempré on the son of a daughter of the house.
If she made a *mésalliance*, the favor would be enormous, only
to be granted to vast wealth, or conspicuous services, or very
powerful influence. The young man looks like a shopman in
his Sunday suit ; evidently he is neither wealthy nor noble ;
he has a fine head, but he seems to me to be very silly ; he

has no idea what to do, and has nothing to say for himself; in fact, he has no breeding. How came you to take him up?"

Mme. de Bargeton renounced Lucien as Lucien himself had renounced her; a ghastly fear lest her cousin should learn the manner of her journey shot through her mind.

"Dear cousin, I am in despair that I have compromised you."

"People do not compromise me," Mme. d'Espard said, smiling; "I am only thinking of you."

"But you have asked him to dine with you on Monday."

"I shall be ill," the Marquise said quickly; "you can tell him so, and I shall leave orders that he is not to be admitted under either name."

During the interval Lucien noticed that every one was walking up and down in the lobby. He would do the same. In the first place, not one of Mme. d'Espard's visitors recognized him nor paid any attention to him, their conduct seemed nothing less than extraordinary to the provincial poet; and, secondly, Châtelet, on whom he tried to hang, watched him out of the corner of his eye and fought shy of him. Lucien walked to and fro watching the eddying crowd of men, till he felt convinced that his costume was absurd, and he went back to his box, ensconced himself in a corner, and stayed there until the end. At times he thought of nothing but the magnificent spectacle of the ballet in the great Inferno scene in the fifth act; sometimes the sight of the house absorbed him, sometimes his own thoughts; he had seen society in Paris, and the sight had stirred him to the depths.

"So this is my kingdom," he said to himself; "this is the world that I must conquer."

As he walked home through the streets he thought over all that had been said by Mme. d'Espard's courtiers; memory reproducing with strange faithfulness their demeanor, their gestures, their manner of coming and going.

Next day, toward noon, Lucien betook himself to Staub,

the great tailor of that day. Partly by dint of entreaties, and partly by virtue of cash, Lucien succeeded in obtaining a promise that his clothes should be ready in time for the great day. Staub went so far as to give his word that a perfectly elegant coat, a waistcoat, and a pair of trousers should be forthcoming. Lucien then ordered linen and pocket-hand-kerchiefs, a little outfit, in short, of a linen draper, and a celebrated bootmaker measured him for shoes and boots. He bought a neat walking-cane at Verdier's; he went to Mme. Irlande for gloves and shirt studs; in short, he did his best to reach the climax of dandyism. When he had satisfied all his fancies, he went to the Rue Neuve-de-Luxembourg and found that Louise had gone out.

"She was dining with Madame la Marquise d'Espard," her maid said, "and would not be back until late."

Lucien dined for two francs at a restaurant in the Palais Royal, and went to bed early. The next day was Sunday. He went to Louise's lodging at eleven o'clock. Louise had not yet risen. At two o'clock he returned once more.

"Madame cannot see anybody yet," reported Albertine, "but she gave me a line for you."

"Cannot see anybody yet?" repeated Lucien. "But I am not anybody——"

"I do not know," Albertine answered very impertinently; and Lucien, less surprised by Albertine's answer than by a note from Mme. de Bargeton, took the billet and read the following discouraging lines:

"Mme. d'Espard is not well; she will not be able to see you on Monday. I am not feeling very well myself, but I am about to dress and go to keep her company. I am in despair over this little disappointment; but your talents reassure me, you will make your way without charlatanism."

"And no signature!" Lucien said to himself. He found

himself in the Tuileries before he knew whither he was walking. With the gift of second-sight, which accompanies genius, he began to suspect that the chilly note was but a warning of the catastrophe to come. Lost in thought, he walked on and on, gazing at the monuments in the Place Louis Quinze.

It was a sunny day; a stream of fine carriages went past him on the way to the Champs Élysées. Following the direction of the crowd of strollers, he saw the three or four thousand carriages that turn the Champs Élysées into an improvised Longchamp on Sunday afternoons in summer. The splendid horses, the toilets and liveries bewildered him; he went further and further, until he reached the Arc de Triomphe, then unfinished. What were his feelings when, as he returned, he saw Mme. de Bargeton and Mme. d'Espard coming toward him in a wonderfully appointed calèche, with a chasseur behind it in waving plumes and that gold-embroidered green uniform which he knew only too well. There was a block somewhere in the row, and the carriages waited. Lucien beheld Louise transformed beyond recognition. All the colors of her toilet had been carefully subordinated to her complexion; her dress was delicious, her hair gracefully and becomingly arranged, her hat, in exquisite taste, was remarkable even beside Mme. d'Espard, that leader of fashion.

There is something in the art of wearing a hat that escapes definition. Tilted too far to the back of the head, it imparts a bold expression to the face; bring it too far forward, it gives you a sinister look; tipped to one side, it has a jaunty air; a well-dressed woman wears her hat exactly as she means to wear it, and exactly at the right angle. Mme. de Bargeton had solved this curious problem at sight. A dainty girdle outlined her slender waist. She had adopted her cousin's gestures and tricks of manner; and now, as she sat by Mme. d'Espard's side, she played with a tiny scent-bottle that dangled by a slender gold chain from one of her fingers, displaying a little, well-gloved hand without seeming to do so. She had modeled herself on Mme. d'Espard without mimicking her; the Marquise had found a cousin worthy of her, and seemed to be proud of her pupil. ·

The men and women on the footways all gazed at the splendid carriage, with the bearings of the d'Espards and Blamont-Chauvrys upon the panels. Lucien was amazed at the number of greetings received by the cousins; he did not know that the "all Paris," which consists in some score of salons, was well aware already of the relationship between the ladies. A little group of young men on horseback accompanied the carriage in the Bois; Lucien could recognize de Marsay and Rastignac among them, and could see from their gestures that the pair of coxcombs were complimenting Mme. de Bargeton upon her transformation. Mme. d'Espard was radiant with health and grace. So her indisposition was simply a pretext for ridding herself of him, for there had been no mention of another day!

The wrathful poet went toward the calèche; he walked slowly, waited till he came in full sight of the two ladies and made them a bow. Mme. de Bargeton would not see him; but the Marquise put up her eyeglass, and deliberately cut him. He had been disowned by the sovereign lords of Angoulême, but to be disowned by society in Paris was another thing; the booby-squires by doing their utmost to mortify Lucien admitted his power and acknowledged him as a man; for Mme. d'Espard he had positively no existence. This was no sentence, it was a refusal of justice. Poor poet! a deadly cold seized on him when he saw de Marsay eyeing him through his glass; and when the Parisian lion let that optical instrument fall, it dropped in so singular a fashion that Lucien thought of the knife-blade of the guillotine.

The calèche went by. Rage and a craving for vengeance took possession of his slighted soul. If Mme. de Bargeton had been in his power, he could have cut her throat at that moment; he was a Fouquier-Tinville gloating over the pleasure of sending Mme. d'Espard to the scaffold. If only he could have put de Marsay to the torture with refinements of savage cruelty! Canalis went by on horseback, bowing to the prettiest women, his dress elegant, as became the most dainty of poets.

"Great heavens!" exclaimed Lucien. "Money, money at all costs! money is the one power before which the world bends the knee." ("No!" cried conscience, "not money, but glory; and glory means work! Work! that was what David said.") "Great heavens! what am I doing here? But I will triumph. I will drive along this avenue in a calèche with a chasseur behind me! I will possess a Marquise d'Espard." And flinging out the wrathful words, he went to Hurbain's to dine for two francs.

Next morning, at nine o'clock, he went to the Rue Neuve-de-Luxembourg to upbraid Louise for her barbarity. But Mme. de Bargeton was not at home to him, and not only so, but the porter would not allow him to go up to her rooms; so he stayed outside in the street, watching the house till noon. At twelve o'clock Châtelet came out, looked at Lucien out of the corner of his eye and avoided him.

Stung to the quick, Lucien hurried after his rival; and Châtelet, finding himself closely pursued, turned and bowed, evidently intending to shake him off by this courtesy.

"Spare me one moment for pity's sake, sir," said Lucien; "I want just a word or two with you. You have shown me friendship, I now ask the most trifling service of that friendship. You have just come from Madame de Bargeton; how have I fallen into disgrace with her and Madame d'Espard? —please explain."

"Monsieur Chardon, do you know why the ladies left you at the opera that evening?" asked Châtelet, with treacherous good-nature.

"No," said the poor poet.

"Well, it was Monsieur de Rastignac who spoke against

you from the beginning. They asked him about you, and the young dandy simply said that your name was Chardon, and not de Rubempré; that your mother was a monthly nurse; that your father, when he was alive, was an apothecary in L'Houmeau, a suburb of Angoulême; and that your sister, a charming girl, gets up shirts to admiration, and is just about to be married to a local printer named Séchard. Such is the world! You no sooner show yourself than it pulls you to pieces.

"Monsieur de Marsay came to Madame d'Espard to laugh at you with her; so the two ladies, thinking that your presence put them in a false position, went out at once. Do not attempt to go to either house. If Madame de Bargeton continued to receive your visits, her cousin would have nothing to do with her. You have genius; try to avenge yourself. The world looks down upon you; look down in your turn upon the world. Take refuge in some garret, write your masterpieces, seize on power of any kind, and you will see the world at your feet. Then you can give back the bruises which you have received, and in the very place where they were given. Madame de Bargeton will be the more distant now because she has been friendly. That is the way with women. But the question now for you is not how to win back Anaïs' friendship, but how to avoid making an enemy of her. I will tell you of a way. She has written letters to you; send all her letters back to her, she will be sensible that you are acting like a gentleman; and at a later time, if you should need her, she will not be hostile. For my own part, I have so high an opinion of your future that I have taken your part everywhere; and if I can do anything here for you, you will always find me ready to be of use."

The elderly beau seemed to have grown young again in the atmosphere of Paris. He bowed with frigid politeness; but Lucien, woe-begone, haggard, and undone, forgot to return the salutation. He went back to his inn, and there found the great Staub himself, come in person, not so much to try his customer's clothes as to make inquiries of the landlady with regard to that customer's financial status. The report had been satisfactory. Lucien had traveled post; Madame de Bargeton brought him back from the Vaudeville last Thursday in her carriage. Staub addressed Lucien as "Monsieur le Comte," and called his customer's attention to the artistic skill with which he had brought a charming figure into relief.

"A young man in such a costume has only to walk in the Tuileries," he said, "and he will marry an English heiress within a fortnight."

Lucien brightened a little under the influence of the German tailor's joke, the perfect fit of his new clothes, the fine cloth, and the sight of a graceful figure which met his eyes in the looking-glass. Vaguely he told himself that Paris was the capital of chance, and for the moment he believed in chance. Had he not a volume of poems and a magnificent romance entitled "The Archer of Charles IX." in manuscript? He had hope for the future. Staub promised the overcoat and the rest of the clothes the next day. Following him came the other tradesmen.

The next day the bootmaker, linen-draper, and tailor all returned armed each with his bill, which Lucien, still under the charm of provincial habits, paid forthwith, not knowing how otherwise to rid himself of them. After he had paid, there remained but three hundred and sixty francs out of the two thousand which he had brought with him from Angoulême, and he had been but one week in Paris! Nevertheless, he dressed and went out to take a stroll on the Terrasse des Feuillants. He had his day of triumph. He looked so handsome and so graceful, he was so well dressed, that women looked at him; two or three were so much struck with his beauty that they turned their heads to look again. Lucien studied the gait and carriage of the young men on the Terrasse, and took a lesson in fine manners while he meditated on his three hundred and sixty francs.

That evening, alone in his chamber, an idea occurred to him which threw a light on the problem of his existence at the Gaillard-Bois, where he lived on the plainest fare, thinking to economize in this way. He asked for his account, as if he meant to leave, and discovered that he was indebted to his landlord to the extent of a hundred francs. The next morning was spent in running about the Latin Quarter, recommended for its cheapness by David. For a long while he looked about till, finally, in the Rue de Cluny, close to the Sorbonne, he discovered a place where he could have a furnished room for such a price as he could afford to pay. He settled with his hostess of the Gaillard-Bois and took up his quarters in the Rue de Cluny that same day. His removal only cost him the cab-fare.

When he had taken possession of his poor room, he made a packet of Mme. de Bargeton's letters, laid them on the table, and sat down to write to her; but before he wrote he fell to thinking over that fatal week. He did not tell himself that he had been the first to be faithless; that for a sudden fancy he had been ready to leave his Louise without knowing what would become of her in Paris. He saw none of his own short-comings, but he saw his present position and blamed Mme. de Bargeton for it. She was to have lighted his way; instead she had ruined him. He grew indignant, he grew proud, he worked himself into a paroxysm of rage, and set himself to compose the following epistle:

" What would you think, madame, of a woman who should take a fancy to some poor and timid child full of the noble superstitions which the grown man calls ' illusions,' and using all the charm of woman's coquetry, all her most delicate ingenuity, should feign a mother's love to lead that child astray? Her fondest promises, the card-castles which raised his wonder, cost her nothing; she leads him on, tightens her hold upon him, sometimes coaxing, sometimes scolding him for his want of confidence, till the child leaves his home and follows her blindly to the shores of a vast sea. Smiling, she lures him into a frail skiff, and sends him forth alone and helpless to face the storm. Standing safe on the rock, she laughs and wishes him luck. You are that woman; I am that child.

" The child has a keepsake in his hands, something which might betray the wrongs done by your beneficence, your kindness in deserting him. You might have to blush if you saw him struggling for life, and chanced to recollect that once you clasped him to your breast. When you read these words the keepsake will be in your own safe-keeping; you are free to forget everything.

"Once you pointed out fair hopes to me in the skies, I awake to find reality in the squalid poverty of Paris. While you pass, and others bow before you, on your brilliant path in the great world, I, whom you deserted on the threshold, shall be shivering in the wretched garret to which you consigned me. Yet some pang may perhaps trouble your mind amid festivals and pleasures; you may think sometimes of the child whom you thrust into the depths. If so, madame, think of him without remorse. Out of the depths of his misery the child offers you the one thing left to him—his forgiveness in a last look. Yes, madame, thanks to you, I have nothing left. Nothing! Was not the world created from nothing? Genius should follow the Divine example; I begin with Godlike forgiveness, but as yet I know not whether I possess the God-like power. You need only tremble lest I should go astray; for you would be answerable for my sins. Alas! I pity you, for you will have no part in the future toward which I go, with work as my guide."

After penning this rhetorical effusion, full of the sombre dignity which an artist of one-and-twenty is rather apt to overdo, Lucien's thoughts went back to them at home. He saw the pretty rooms which David had furnished for him, at the cost of part of his little store, and a vision rose before him of quiet, simple pleasures in the past. Shadowy figures came about him ; he saw his mother and Eve and David, and heard their sobs over his leave-taking, and at that he began to cry himself, for he felt very lonely in Paris, and friendless and forlorn.

Two or three days later he wrote to his sister :

" My dear Eve :—When a sister shares the life of a brother who devotes himself to art, it is her sad privilege to take more sorrow than joy into her life ; and I am beginning to fear that I shall be a great trouble to you. Have I not abused your goodness already ? have not all of you sacrificed yourselves to me ? It is the memory of the past, so full of family happiness, that helps me to bear up in my present loneliness. Now that I have tasted the first beginnings of poverty and the treachery of the world of Paris, how my thoughts have flown to you, swift as an eagle back to his eyrie, so that I might be with true affection again. Did you see sparks in the candle? Did a coal pop out of the fire ? Did you hear singing in your ears ? And did mother say, ' Lucien is thinking of us,' and David answer, ' He is fighting his way in the world ? '

" My Eve, I am writing this letter for your eyes only. I cannot tell any one else all that has happened to me, good and bad, blushing for both, as I write, for good here is as rare as evil ought to be. You shall have a great piece of news in a very few words. Mme. de Bargeton was ashamed of me, disowned me, would not see me, and gave me up nine days after we came to Paris. She saw me in the street and looked another way ; when, simply to follow her into the society to which she meant to introduce me, I had spent seventeen hundred and sixty francs out of the two thousand I brought from Angoulême, the money so hardly scraped together. 'How did you spend it?' you will ask. Paris is a strange bottomless gulf, my poor sister; you can dine here for less than a franc, yet the simplest dinner at a fashionable restaurant costs fifty francs; there are waistcoats and trousers to be had for four francs and two francs each; but a fashionable tailor never charges less than a hundred francs. You pay for everything; you pay a halfpenny to cross the kennel in the street when it rains; you cannot go the least little way in a cab for less than thirty-two sous.

"I have been staying in one of the best parts of Paris, but now I am living at the Hôtel de Cluny, in the Rue de Cluny, one of the poorest and darkest slums, shut in between three churches and the old buildings of the Sorbonne. I have a furnished room on the fourth floor; it is very bare and very dirty, but, all the same, I pay fifteen francs a month for it. For breakfast I spend a penny on a roll and a halfpenny for milk, but I dine very decently for twenty-two sous at a restaurant kept by a man named Flicoteaux in the Place de la Sorbonne itself. My expenses every month will not exceed sixty francs, everything included, until the winter begins— at least I hope not. So my two hundred and forty francs ought to last me for the first four months. Between now and then I shall have sold 'The Archer of Charles IX.' and the 'Marguerites,' no doubt. Do not be in the least uneasy on my account. If the present is cold and bare and poverty-stricken, the blue distant future is rich and splendid; most great men have known the vicissitudes which depress but cannot overwhelm me.

"Plautus, the great comic Latin poet, was once a miller's lad. Machiavelli wrote 'The Prince' at night, and by day was a common workingman like any one else; and more than all, the great Cervantes, who lost an arm at the battle of Lepanto, and helped to win that famous day, was called a 'base-born, hand-less dotard' by the scribblers of his day;

there was an interval of ten years between the appearance of
the first part and the second of his sublime 'Don Quixote'
for lack of a publisher. Things are not so bad as that nowadays. Mortifications and want only fall to the lot of unknown writers; as soon as a man's name is known, he grows
rich, and I will be rich. And, beside, I live within myself,
I spend half the day at the Bibliothèque (Library) Sainte-
Geneviève, learning all that I want to learn ; I should not go
far unless I knew more than I do. So at this moment I am
almost happy. In a few days I have fallen in with my life
very gladly. I begin the work that I love with daylight, my
subsistence is secure, I think a great deal, and I study. I do
not see that I am open to attack at any point, now that I have
renounced a world where my vanity might suffer at any
moment. The great men of every age are obliged to lead
lives apart. What are they but birds in the forest ? They
sing, nature falls under the spell of their song, and no one
should see them. That shall be my lot, always supposing that
I can carry out my ambitious plans.

"Mme. de Bargeton I do not regret. A woman who
could behave as she behaved does not deserve a thought. Nor
am I sorry that I left Angoulême. She did wisely when she
flung me into the sea of Paris to sink or swim. This is the
place for men of letters and thinkers and poets ; here you
cultivate glory, and I know how fair the harvest is that we
reap in these days. Nowhere else can a writer find the living
works of the great dead, the works of art which quicken the
imagination in the galleries and museums here ; nowhere else
will you find great reference libraries always open in which
the intellect may find pasture. And, lastly, here in Paris
there is a spirit which you breathe in the air ; it infuses the
least details, every literary creation bears traces of its influence. You learn more by talk in a café, or at a theatre, in
one half-hour, than you would learn in ten years in the
provinces. Here, in truth, wherever you go, there is always

something to see, something to learn, some comparison to
make. Extreme cheapness and excessive dearness—there is
Paris for you; there is honeycomb here for every bee, every
nature finds its own nourishment. So, though life is hard
for me just now, I repent of. nothing. On the contrary, a
fair future spreads out before me, and my heart rejoices though
it is saddened for the moment. Good-by, my dear sister.
Do not expect letters from me regularly; it is one of the
peculiarities of Paris that one really does not know how the
time goes. Life is so alarmingly rapid. I kiss the mother •
and you and David more tenderly than ever.''

The name of Flicoteaux is engraved on many memories.
Few indeed were the students who lived in the Latin Quarter
during the last twelve years of the restoration and did not frequent that temple sacred to hunger and impecuniosity. There
a dinner of three courses, with a quarter-bottle of wine or a
bottle of beer, could be had for eighteen sous; or for twenty-
two sous the quarter-bottle became a bottle. Flicoteaux, that
friend of youth, would beyond a doubt have amassed a
colossal fortune but for a line on his bill of fare, a line which
rival establishments are wont to print in capital letters, thus—
BREAD AT DISCRETION, which, being interpreted, should read
'' indiscretion.''

Flicoteaux has been nursing-father to many an illustrious
name. Verily, the heart of more than one great man ought
to wax warm with innumerable recollections of inexpressible
enjoyment at the sight of the small, square window-panes
that look upon the Place de la Sorbonne and the Rue Neuve-
de-Richelieu. Flicoteaux II. and Flicoteaux III. respected the
old exterior, maintaining the dingy hue and general air of a
respectable, old-established house, showing thereby the depth
of their contempt for the charlatanism of the store-front, the
kind of advertisement which feasts the eyes at the expense of
the stomach, to which your modern restaurant almost always

has recourse. Here you beheld no piles of straw-stuffed game never destined to make the acquaintance of the spit, no fantastical fish to justify the mountebank's remark, " I saw a fine carp to-day ; I expect to buy it this day week." Instead of the prime vegetables, more fittingly described by the word primeval, artfully displayed in the window for the delectation of the military man and his fellow-countrywoman the nursemaid, honest Flicoteaux exhibited full salad-bowls adorned with many a rivet, or pyramids of stewed prunes to rejoice the sight of the customer, and assure him that the word "dessert," with which other handbills made too free, was in this case no charter to hoodwink the public. Loaves of six pounds' weight, cut in four quarters, made good the promise of "bread at discretion." Such was the plenty of the establishment that Molière would have celebrated it if it had been in existence in his day, so comically appropriate is the name.

Flicoteaux still subsists ; so long as students are minded to live, Flicoteaux will make a living. You feed there, neither more nor less; and you feed as you work, with morose or cheerful industry, according to the circumstances and the temperament.

At that time his well-known establishment consisted of two dining-halls, at right angles to each other ; long, narrow low-ceiled rooms, looking respectively on the Rue Neuve-de-Richelieu and the Place de la Sorbonne. The furniture must have come originally from the refectory of some abbey, for there was a monastic look about the lengthy tables, where the serviettes of regular customers, each thrust through a numbered ring of crystallized tin plate, were laid by their places. Flicoteaux I. only changed the serviettes of a Sunday ; but Flicoteaux II. changed them twice a week, it is said, under pressure of competition which threatened his dynasty.

Flicoteaux's restaurant is no banqueting-hall, with its refinements and luxuries; it is a workshop where suitable tools are provided, and everybody gets up and goes as soon as he has

finished. The coming and going within is swift. There is
no dawdling among the waiters; they are all busy; every one
of them is wanted.

The fare is not very varied. The potato is a permanent
institution; there might not be a single tuber left in Ireland,
and prevailing dearth elsewhere, but you would still find pota-
toes at Flicoteaux's. Not once in thirty years shall you miss
its pale gold (the color beloved of Titian), sprinkled with
chopped verdure; the potato enjoys a privilege that women
might envy; such as you see it in 1814, so shall you find it
in 1840. Mutton cutlets and fillet of beef at Flicoteaux's
represent black game and fillet of sturgeon at Véry's; they
are not on the regular bill of fare, that is, and must be ordered
beforehand. Beef of the feminine gender there prevails; the
young of the bovine species appears in all kinds of ingenious
disguises. When the whiting and mackerel abound on our
shores, they are likewise seen in large numbers at Flicoteaux's;
his whole establishment, indeed, is directly affected by the
caprices of the season and the vicissitudes of French agricul-
ture. By eating your dinners at Flicoteaux's you learn a host
of things of which the wealthy, the idle, and folk indifferent
to the phases of nature have no suspicion, and the student
penned up in the Latin Quarter is kept accurately informed
of the state of the weather and good or bad seasons. He
knows when it is a good year for peas or French beans, and
the kind of salad stuff that is plentiful; when the Great Market is glutted with cabbages, he is at once aware of the fact,
and the failure of the beet-root crop is brought home to his
mind. A slander, old in circulation in Lucien's time, connected the appearance of beefsteaks with a mortality among
horseflesh.

Few Parisian restaurants are so well worth seeing. Every
one at Flicoteaux's is young; you see nothing but youth;
and although earnest faces and grave, gloomy, anxious faces
are not lacking, you see hope and confidence and poverty

4

gaily endured. Dress, as a rule, is careless, and regular comers in decent clothes are marked exceptions. Everybody knows at once that something extraordinary is afoot; a mistress to visit, a theatre party, or some excursion into higher spheres. Here, it is said, friendships have been made among students who became famous men in after-days, as will be seen in the course of this narrative; but with the exception of a few knots of young fellows from the same part of France who make a group about the end of a table, the gravity of the diners is hardly relaxed. Perhaps this gravity is due to the catholicity of the wine, which checks good fellowship of any kind.

Flicoteaux's frequenters may recollect certain sombre and mysterious figures enveloped in the gloom of the chilliest penury; these beings would dine there daily for a couple of years and then vanish, and the most inquisitive regular comer could throw no light on the disappearance of such goblins of Paris. Friendships struck up over Flicoteaux's dinners were sealed in neighboring cafés in the flames of heady punch, or by the generous warmth of a small cup of black coffee glorified by a dash of something hotter and stronger.

Lucien, like all neophytes, was modest and regular in his habits in those early days at the Hôtel de Cluny. After the first unlucky venture in fashionable life which absorbed his capital, he threw himself into his work with the first earnest enthusiasm, which is fritted away so soon over the difficulties or in the by-paths of every life in Paris. The most luxurious and the very poorest lives are equally beset with temptations which nothing but the fierce energy of genius or the morose persistence of ambition can overcome.

Lucien used to drop in at Flicoteaux's about half-past four, having remarked the advantages of an early arrival; the bill-of-fare was more varied, and there was still some chance of obtaining the dish of your choice. Like all imaginative persons, he had taken a fancy to a particular seat, and showed discrimination in his selection. On the very first day he had noticed a table near the counter, and from the faces of those who sat about it, and chance snatches of their talk, he recognized brothers of the craft. A sort of instinct, moreover, pointed out the table near the counter as a spot whence he could parley with the owners of the restaurant. In time an acquaintance would grow up, he thought, and then in the day of distress he could no doubt obtain the necessary credit. So he took his place at a small square table close to the desk, intended probably for casual comers, for the two clean serviettes were unadorned with rings. Lucien's opposite neighbor was a thin, pallid youth, to all appearance as poor as he himself; his handsome face was somewhat worn: already it told of hopes that had vanished, leaving lines upon his forehead and barren furrows in his soul, where seeds had been sown that had come to nothing. Lucien felt drawn to the stranger by these tokens; his sympathies went out to him with irresistible fervor.

After a week's exchange of small courtesies and remarks, the poet from Angoulême found the first person with whom he could chat. The stranger's name was Étienne Lousteau. Two years ago he had left his native place, a town in Berri, just as Lucien had come from Angoulême. His lively gestures, bright eyes, and occasionally curt speech revealed a bitter apprenticeship to literature. Étienne had come from Sancerre with his tragedy in his pocket, drawn to Paris by the same motives that impelled Lucien—hope of fame and power and money.

Sometimes Étienne Lousteau came for several days together; but in a little while his visits became few and far between and he would stay away for five or six days in succession. Then he would come back, and Lucien would hope to see his poet next day, only to find a stranger in his place. When two young men meet daily, their talk harks back to their last conversation; but these continual interruptions obliged Lu-

cien to break the ice afresh each time, and further checked
an intimacy which made little progress during the first few
weeks. On inquiry of the damsel at the counter, Lucien was
told that his future friend was on the staff of a small newspaper, and wrote reviews of books and dramatic criticism of
pieces played at the Ambigu-Comique, the Gaité, and the
Panorama-Dramatique. The young man became a personage
all at once in Lucien's eyes. Now, he thought, he would
lead the conversation on rather more personal topics, and
make some effort to gain a friend so likely to be useful to a
beginner. The journalist stayed away for a fortnight. Lucien
did not know that Étienne only dined at Flicoteaux's when
he was hard up, and hence his gloomy air of disenchantment
and the chilly manner, which Lucien met with gracious smiles
and amiable remarks. But, after all, the project of a friendship called for mature deliberation. This obscure journalist
appeared to lead an expensive life in which *petits verres* (little
glasses), cups of coffee, punch-bowls, sight-seeing, and suppers
played a part. In the early days of Lucien's life in the Latin
Quarter, he behaved like a poor child bewildered by his first
experience of Paris life ; so that when he had made a study
of prices and weighed his purse, he lacked courage to make
advances to Étienne; he was afraid of beginning a fresh
series of the blunders of which he was still repenting. And
he was still under the yoke of provincial creeds; his two
guardian angels, Eve and David, rose up before him at the
least approach of an evil thought, putting him in mind of all
the hopes that were centred on him, of the happiness that he
owed to the old mother, of all the promises of his genius.

He spent his mornings in studying history at the Bibliothèque Sainte-Geneviève. His very first researches made
him aware of frightful errors in the memoirs of "The Archer
of Charles IX." When the library closed, he went back to
his damp, chilly room to correct his work, cutting out whole
chapters and piecing it together anew. And after dining at

Flicoteaux's, he went down to the Passage du Commerce to see the newspapers at Blosse's reading-room, as well as new books and magazines and poetry, so as to keep himself informed of the movements of the day. And when, toward midnight, he returned to his wretched lodgings, he had used neither fuel nor candle-light. His reading in those days made such an enormous change in his ideas that he revised his volume of flower-sonnets, his beloved "Marguerites," working them over to such purpose that scarce a hundred lines of the original verses were allowed to stand.

So in the beginning Lucien led the honest, innocent life of the country lad who never leaves the Latin Quarter; devoting himself wholly to his work, with thoughts of the future always before him; who finds Flicoteaux's ordinary luxurious after the simple home-fare; and strolls for recreation along the alleys of the Luxembourg, the blood surging back to his heart as he gives timid side-glances to the pretty women. But this could not last. Lucien, with his poetic temperament and boundless longings, could not withstand the temptations held out by the play-bills.

The Théâtre-Français, the Vaudeville, the Variétés, the Opéra-Comique relieved him of some sixty francs, although he always went to the pit. What student could deny himself the pleasure of seeing Talma in one of his famous rôles? Lucien was fascinated by the theatre, that first love of all poetic temperaments; the actors and actresses were awe-inspiring creatures; he did not so much as dream of the possibility of crossing the footlights and meeting them on familiar terms. The men and women who gave him so much pleasure were surely marvelous beings, whom the newspapers treated with as much gravity as matters of national interest. To be a dramatic author, to have a play produced on the stage! What a dream was this to cherish! A dream which a few bold spirits like Casimir Delavigne had actually realized! Thick swarming thoughts like these, and moments of belief in himself, followed by despair, gave Lucien no rest, and kept him in the narrow way of toil and frugality, in spite of the smothered grumblings of more than one frenzied desire.

Carrying prudence to an extreme, he made it a rule never to enter the precincts of the Palais Royal, that place of perdition where he had spent fifty francs at Véry's in a single day, and nearly five hundred francs on his clothes ; and when he yielded to temptation, and saw Fleury, Talma, the two Baptistes, or Michot, he went no further than the murky passage where theatre-goers used to stand in a string from half-past five in the afternoon till the hour when the door opened, and belated comers were compelled to pay ten sous for a place near the ticket-office. And, after waiting for two hours, the cry of "All tickets are sold !" rang not infrequently in the ears of disappointed students. When the play was over, Lucien went home with downcast eyes, through streets lined with living attractions, and, perhaps, fell in with one of those commonplace adventures which loom so large in a young and timorous imagination.

One day Lucien counted over his remaining stock of money, and took alarm at the melting of his funds; a cold perspiration broke out upon him when he thought that the time had come when he must find a publisher, and try also to find work for which a publisher would pay him. The young journalist, with whom he had made a one-sided friendship, never came now to Flicoteaux's. Lucien was waiting for a chance— which failed to present itself. In Paris there are no chances except for men with a very wide circle of acquaintance ; chances of success of every kind increase with the number of your connections; and, therefore, in this sense also the chances are in favor of the big battalions. Lucien had sufficient provincial foresight still left, and had no mind to wait until only a last few coins remained to him. He resolved to face the publishers.

So one tolerably chilly September morning Lucien went

down the Rue de là Harpe, with his two manuscripts under
his arm. As he made his way to the Quai des Augustins,
and went along, looking into the booksellers' windows on one
side and into the Seine on the other, his good genius might
have counseled him to pitch himself into the water sooner
than plunge into literature. After heart-searching hesitations,
after a profound scrutiny of the various countenances, more or
less encouraging, soft-hearted, churlish, cheerful, or melancholy, to be seen through the window-panes or in the door-
ways of the booksellers' establishments, he espied a house
where the shopmen were busy packing books at a great rate.
Goods were being dispatched. The walls were plastered with
bills:

JUST OUT.

LE SOLITAIRE, by M. le Vicomte d'Arlincourt.
Third edition.

LÉONIDE, by Victor Ducange; five volumes,
12mo, printed on fine paper. 12 francs.

INDUCTIONS MORALES, by Kératry.

" They are lucky, that they are ! " exclaimed Lucien.
The placard, a new and original idea of the celebrated
Ladvocat, was just beginning to blossom out upon the walls.
In no long space Paris was to wear motley, thanks to the
exertions of his imitators, and the Treasury was to discover a
new source of revenue.

Anxiety sent the blood surging to Lucien's heart, as he
who had been so great at Angoulême, so insignificant of late
in Paris, slipped past the other houses, summoned up all his
courage, and at last entered the shop thronged with assistants,
customers, and booksellers—" And authors too, perhaps ! "
thought Lucien.

" I want to speak with Monsieur Vidal or Monsieur Porchon," he said, addressing a shopman. He had read the

names on the signboard—VIDAL & PORCHON (it ran), *French and foreign booksellers' agents.*

" Both gentlemen are engaged," said the man.

" I will wait."

Left to himself, the poet scrutinized the packages, and amused himself for a couple of hours by scanning the titles of books, looking into them, and reading a page or two here and there. At last, as he stood leaning against a window, he heard voices, and suspecting that the green curtains hid either Vidal or Porchon, he listened to the conversation.

" Will you take five hundred copies of me? If you will, I will let you have them at five francs, and give fourteen to the dozen."

" What does that bring them in at ? "

" Sixteen sous less."

" Four francs four sous ? " said Vidal or Porchon, whichever it was.

" Yes," said the vendor.

" Credit your account? " inquired the purchaser.

" Old humbug ! you would settle with me in eighteen months' time, with bills at a twelvemonth."

" No. Settled at once," returned Vidal or Porchon.

" Bills at nine months ? " asked the publisher or author, who evidently was selling his book.

" No, my dear fellow, twelve months," returned one of the firm of booksellers' agents.

There was a pause.

" You are simply cutting my throat ! " said the visitor.

" But in a year's time shall we have placed a hundred copies of ' Léonide? ' " said the other voice. " If books went off as fast as the publishers would like, we should be millionaires, my good sir; but they don't, they go as the public pleases. There is some one now bringing out an edition of Scott's novels at eighteen sous per volume, three livres twelve sous per copy, and you want me to give you more for your stale remainders? No. If you mean me to push this novel of yours, you must.make it worth my while. Vidal!"

A stout man, with a pen behind his ear, came down from his desk.

"How many copies of Ducange did you place last journey?" asked Porchon of his partner.

"Two hundred of 'Le Petit Vieillard de Calais;' but to sell them I was obliged to cry down two books which pay in less commission, and uncommonly fine 'nightingales' they are now."

(A "nightingale," as Lucien afterward learned, is a bookseller's name for books that linger on hand, perched out of sight in the loneliest nooks in the store.)

"And, beside," added Vidal, "Picard is bringing out some novels, as you know. We have been promised twenty per cent. on the published price to make the thing a success."

"Very well, at twelve months," the publisher answered in a piteous voice, thunderstruck by Vidal's confidential remark.

"Is it an offer?" Porchon inquired curtly.

"Yes." The stranger went out. After he had gone, Lucien heard Porchon say to Vidal—

"We have three hundred copies on order now. We will keep him waiting for his settlement, sell the 'Léonides' for five francs net, settlement in six months, and——"

"And that will be fifteen hundred francs into our pockets," said Vidal.

"Oh, I saw quite well that he was in a fix. He is giving Ducange four thousand francs for two thousand copies."

Lucien cut Vidal short by appearing in the entrance of the den.

"I have the honor of wishing you a good-day, gentlemen," he said, addressing both partners. The booksellers nodded slightly.

"I have a French historical romance after the style of

Scott.   It is called 'The Archer of Charles IX.;' I propose
to offer it to you——''

Porchon glanced at Lucien with lustreless eyes, and laid
his pen down on the desk.   Vidal stared rudely at the author.

"We are not publishing booksellers, sir ; we are booksellers' agents," he said.   "When we bring out a book ourselves, we only deal in well-known names ; and, beside, we
only take serious literature—history and epitomes."

"But my book is very serious.   It is an attempt to set the
struggle between Catholics and Calvinists in its true light ;
the Catholics were supporters of absolute monarchy and the
Protestants for a republic."

"Monsieur Vidal !" shouted an assistant.   Vidal fled.

"I don't say, sir, that your book is not a masterpiece,"
replied Porchon, with scanty civility, "but we only deal in
books that are ready printed.   Go and see somebody that
buys manuscripts.   There is old Doguereau in the Rue du
Coq, near the Louvre, he is in the romance line.   If you had
only spoken sooner, you might have seen Pollet, a competitor
of Doguereau and of the publishers in the Wooden Galleries."

"I have a volume of poetry——"

"Monsieur Porchon !" somebody shouted.

"*Poetry!*" Porchon exclaimed angrily.   "For what do
you take me ?" he added, laughing in Lucien's face.   And
he dived into the regions of the back shop.

Lucien went back across the Pont Neuf absorbed in reflection.   From all that he understood of this mercantile dialect,
it appeared that books, like cotton nightcaps, were to be regarded as articles of merchandise to be sold dear and bought
cheap.

"I have made a mistake," said Lucien to himself ; but, all
the same, this rough-and-ready practical aspect of literature
made an impression upon him.

In the Rue du Coq he stopped in front of a modest-looking
store, which he had passed before.   He saw the inscription,

Doguereau, Bookseller, painted above it in yellow letters on a green ground, and remembered that he had seen the name at the foot of the title-page of several novels at Blosse's reading-room. In he went, not without the inward trepidation which a man of any imagination feels at the prospect of a battle. Inside the shop he discovered an odd-looking old man, one of the queer characters of the trade in the days of the empire.

Doguereau wore a black coat with vast square skirts, when fashion required swallow-tail coats. His waistcoat was of some cheap material, a checked pattern of many colors; a steel chain, with a copper key attached to it, hung from his fob and dangled down over a roomy pair of black nether garments. The bookseller's watch must have been the size of an onion. Iron-gray ribbed stockings and shoes with silver buckles completed his costume. The old man's head was bare, and ornamented with a fringe of grizzled locks, quite poetically scanty. "Old Doguereau," as Porchon styled him, was dressed half like a professor of belles-lettres as to his trousers and shoes, half like a tradesman with respect to the variegated waistcoat, the stockings, and the watch; and the same odd mixture appeared in the man himself. He united the magisterial, dogmatic air and the hollow countenance of the professor of rhetoric with the sharp eyes, suspicious mouth, and vague uneasiness of the bookseller.

"Monsieur Doguereau?" asked Lucien.

"That is my name, sir."

"I am the author of a romance," began Lucien.

"You are very young," remarked the bookseller.

"My age, sir, has nothing to do with the matter."

"True," and the old bookseller took up the manuscript. "Ah, begad! 'The Archer of Charles IX.,' a good title. Let us see now, young man, just tell me your subject in a word or two."

"It is a historical work, sir, in the style of Scott. The

character of the struggle between the Protestants and Catholics is depicted as a struggle between two opposed systems of government, in which the throne is seriously endangered. I have taken the Catholic side."

"Eh! but you have ideas, young man. Very well, I will read your book, I promise you. I would rather have had something more in Mrs. Radcliffe's style; but if you are industrious, if you have some notion of style, conceptions, ideas, and the art of telling a story, I don't ask better than to be of use to you. What do we want but good manuscripts?"

"When may I come back?"

"I am going into the country this evening; I shall be back again the day after to-morrow. I shall have read your manuscript by that time; and if it suits me, we might come to terms that very day."

Seeing his acquaintance so easy, Lucien was inspired with the unlucky idea of bringing the "Marguerites" upon the scene.

"I have a volume of poetry as well, sir——" he began.

"Oh! you are a poet! Then I don't want your romance," and the old man handed back the manuscript. "The rhyming fellows come to grief when they try their hands at prose. In prose you can't use words that mean nothing; you absolutely must say something."

"But Sir Walter Scott, sir, wrote poetry as well as——"

"That is true," said Doguereau, relenting. He guessed that the young fellow before him was poor, and kept the manuscript. "Where do you live? I will come and see you."

Lucien, all unsuspicious of the ideas at the back of the old man's head, gave his address; he did not see that he had to do with a bookseller of the old school, a survival of the eighteenth century, when booksellers tried to keep Voltaires and Montesquieus starving in garrets under lock and key.

"The Latin Quarter. I am coming back that very way," said Doguereau, when he had read the address.

"Good man!" thought Lucien, as he took his leave. "So I have met a friend to young authors, a man of taste, who knows something. That is the kind of man for me! It is just as I said to David—talent soon makes its way in Paris."

Lucien went home again, happy and light of heart; he dreamed of glory. He gave not another thought to the ominous words which fell on his ear as he stood by the counter in Vidal and Porchon's store; he beheld himself the richer by twelve hundred francs at least. Twelve hundred francs! It meant a year in Paris, a whole year of preparation for the work that he meant to do. What plans he built on that hope! What sweet dreams, what visions of a life established on a basis of work! Mentally he found new quarters and settled himself in them; it would not have taken much to set him making a purchase or two. He could only stave off impatience by constant reading at Blosse's.

Two days later old Doguereau came to the lodgings of his budding Sir Walter Scott. He was struck with the pains which Lucien had taken with the style of this his first work, delighted with the strong contrasts of character sanctioned by the epoch, and surprised at the spirited imaginations which a young writer always displays in the scheming of a first plot. —he had not been spoiled, had not old Daddy Doguereau. He had made up his mind to give a thousand francs for "The Archer of Charles IX.;" he would buy the copyright out and out, and bind Lucien by an engagement for several books. But when he came to look at the house, the old fox thought better of it.

"A young fellow that lives here has none but simple tastes," said he to himself; "he is fond of study, fond of work; I need not give more than eight hundred francs."

"Fourth floor," answered the landlady, when he asked for M. Lucien de Rubempré. The old bookseller, peering up, saw nothing but the sky above the fourth floor.

"This young fellow," thought he, "is a good-looking lad;

one might go so far as to say that he is very handsome. If
he were to make too much money, he would only fall into
dissipated ways and then he would not work. In the interests
of us both, I shall only offer six hundred francs, in coin
though, not paper."

He climbed the stairs and gave three taps at the door.
Lucien came to open it. The room was forlorn in its bare-
ness. A bowl of milk and a penny roll stood on the table.
The destitution of genius made an impression on Daddy
Doguereau.

"Let him preserve these simple habits of life, this frugality,
these modest requirements," thought he. Aloud he said:
"It is a pleasure to me to see you. Thus, sir, lived Jean-
Jacques, whom you resemble in more ways than one. Amid
such surroundings the fire of genius shines brightly; good
work is done in such rooms as these. This is how men of
letters should work, instead of living riotously in cafés and
restaurants, wasting their time and talent and our money."

He sat down.

"Your romance is not bad, young man. I was a professor
of rhetoric once; I know French history, there are some
capital things in it. You have a future before you, in fact."

"Oh! sir."

"No; I tell you so. We may do business together. I
will buy your romance."

Lucien's heart swelled and throbbed with gladness. He
was about to enter the world of literature; he should see himself in print at last.

"I will give you four hundred francs," continued Doguereau in honeyed accents, and he looked at Lucien with an
air which seemed to betoken an effort of generosity.

"The volume?" queried Lucien.

"For the romance," said Doguereau, heedless of Lucien's
surprise. "In ready money," he added; "and you shall
undertake to write two books for me every year for six years.

If the first book is out of print in six months, I will give you six hundred francs for the others. So, if you write two books each year, you will be making a hundred francs a month; you will have a sure income; you will be well off. There are some authors whom I only pay three hundred francs for a romance; I give two hundred for translations of English books. Such prices would have been exorbitant in the old days."

"Sir, we cannot possibly come to an understanding. Give me back my manuscript, I beg," said Lucien, in a cold chill.

"Here it is," said the old bookseller. "You know nothing of business, sir. Before an author's first book can appear, a publisher is bound to sink sixteen hundred francs on the paper and the printing of it. It is easier to write a romance than to find all that money. I have a hundred romances in manuscript, and I have not a hundred and sixty thousand francs in my cash box, alas! I have not made so much in all these twenty years that I have been a bookseller. So you don't make a fortune by printing romances, you see. Vidal and Porchon only take them of us on conditions that grow harder and harder day by day. You have only your time to lose, while I am obliged to disburse two thousand francs. If we fail, *habent sua fata libelli*, I lose two thousand francs; while, as for you, you simply hurl an ode at the thick-headed public. When you have thought over this that I have the honor of telling you, you will come back to me. *You will come back to me!*" he asserted authoritatively, by way of reply to a scornful gesture made involuntarily by Lucien. "So far from finding a publisher obliging enough to risk two thousand francs for an unknown writer, you will not find a publisher's clerk that will trouble himself to look through your screed. Now that I have read it, I can point out a good many slips in grammar. You have put *observer* for *faire observer* and *malgré que*. *Malgré* is a preposition, and requires an object."

Lucien appeared to be humiliated.   He was dumfounded.

"When I see you again, you will have lost a hundred francs," he added.   "I shall only give a hundred crowns."

With that he arose and took his leave.   On the threshold he said, "If you had not something in you, and a future before you; if I did not take an interest in studious youth, I should not have made you such a handsome offer.   A hundred francs per month!   Think of it!   After all, a romance in a drawer is not eating its head off like a horse in a stable, nor will it find you in victuals either, and that's a fact."

Lucien snatched up his manuscript and dashed it on the floor.

"I would rather burn it, sir!" he exclaimed.

"You have a poet's head," returned his senior.

Lucien devoured his bread and supped his bowl of milk, then he went downstairs.   His room was not large enough for him; he was turning round and round in it like a lion in a cage at the Jardin des Plantes.

At the Bibliothèque Sainte-Geneviève, whither Lucien was going, he had come to know a stranger by sight; a young man of five and twenty or thereabouts, working with the sustained industry which nothing can disturb nor distract, the sign by which your genuine literary worker is known.   Evidently the young man had been reading there for some time, for the librarian and the attendants all knew him and paid him special attention; the librarian would even allow him to take away books, with which Lucien saw him return in the morning.   In the stranger student he recognized a brother in penury and hope.

Pale-faced and slight and thin, with a fine forehead hidden by masses of black, tolerably unkempt hair, there was something about him that attracted indifferent eyes : it was a vague resemblance which he bore to portraits of the young Bonaparte, engraved from Robert Lefebvre's picture.   That engraving is a poem of melancholy intensity, of suppressed ambition, of power working below the surface. Study the face carefully, and you will discover genius in it and discretion and all the subtlety and greatness of the man. The portrait has speaking eyes like a woman's; they look out, greedy of space, craving difficulties to vanquish. Even if the name of Bonaparte were not written beneath it, you would gaze long at that face.

Lucien's young student, the incarnation of this picture, usually wore footed trousers, shoes with thick soles to them, an overcoat of coarse cloth, a black cravat, a waistcoat of some gray-and-white material buttoned to the chin, and a cheap hat. Contempt for superfluity in dress was visible in his whole person. Lucien also discovered that the mysterious stranger with that unmistakable stamp which genius sets upon the forehead of its slaves was one of Flicoteaux's most regular customers; he ate to live, careless of the fare which appeared to be familiar to him, and drank water. Wherever Lucien saw him, at the library or at Flicoteaux's, there was a dignity in his manner, springing doubtless from the consciousness of a purpose that filled his life, a dignity which made him unapproachable. He had the expression of a thinker, meditation dwelt on the fine, nobly carved brow. You could tell from the dark bright eyes, so clear-sighted and quick to observe, that their owner was wont to probe to the bottom of things. He gesticulated very little, his demeanor was grave. Lucien felt an involuntary respect for him.

Many times already the pair had looked at each other at the Bibliothèque or at Flicoteaux's; many times they had been on the point of speaking, but neither of them had ventured so far as yet. The silent young man went off to the further end of the library, on the side at right angles to the Place de la Sorbonne, and Lucien had no opportunity of making his acquaintance, although he felt drawn to a worker whom he knew by indescribable tokens for a character of no common order. Both, as they came to know afterward,

5

were unsophisticated and shy, given to fears which cause a
pleasurable emotion to solitary creatures.   Perhaps they never
would have been brought into communication if they had not
come across each other that day of Lucien's disaster; for, as
Lucien turned into the Rue des Grès, he saw the student coming away from the Bibliothèque Sainte-Geneviève.

"The library is closed; I don't know why, monsieur,"
said he.

Tears were standing in Lucien's eyes; he expressed his
thanks by one of those gestures that speak more eloquently
than words and unlock hearts at once when two men meet in
youth.   They went together along the Rue des Grès toward
the Rue de la Harpe.

"As that is so, I shall go to the Luxembourg for a walk,"
said Lucien.   "When you have come out, it is not easy to
settle down to work again."

"No; one's ideas will not flow in the proper current," remarked the stranger.   "Something seems to have annoyed
you, monsieur?"

"I have just had a queer adventure," said Lucien, and he
told the history of his visit to the quai, and gave an account
of his subsequent dealings with the old bookseller.   He gave
his name and said a word or two of his position.   In one
month or thereabouts he had spent sixty francs on his board,
thirty for lodging, twenty more francs in going to the theatre,
and ten at Blosse's reading-room—one hundred and twenty
francs in all, and now he had just a hundred and twenty
francs in hand.

"Your story is mine, monsieur, and the story of ten or
twelve hundred young fellows beside who come from the
country to Paris every year.   There are others even worse off
than we are.   Do you see that theatre?" he continued, indicating the turrets of the Odéon.   "There came one day to
lodge in one of the houses in the square a man of talent who had
fallen into the lowest depths of poverty.   He was married, in

addition to the misfortunes which we share with him, to a wife whom he loved; and the poorer or the richer, as you will, by two children. He was burdened with debt, but he put his faith in his pen. He took a comedy in five acts to the Odéon; the comedy was accepted, the management arranged to bring it out, the actors learned their parts, the stage manager urged on the rehearsals. Five several bits of luck; five dramas to be performed in real life, and far harder tasks than the writing of a five-act play. The poor author lodged in a garret; you can see the place from here. He drained his last resources to live until the first representation; his wife pawned her clothes, they all lived on dry bread. On the day of the final rehearsal the household owed fifty francs in the Quarter to the baker, the milkwoman, and the porter. The author had only the strictly necessary clothes—a coat, a shirt, trousers, a waistcoat, and a pair of boots. He felt sure of success; he kissed his wife. The end of their troubles was at hand. 'At last! There is nothing against us now,' cried he. 'Yes, there is fire,' said his wife; 'look, the Odéon is on fire!' The Odéon was on fire, monsieur. So do not you complain. You have clothes, you have neither wife nor child, you have a hundred and twenty francs for emergencies in your pocket, and you owe no one a penny. Well, the piece went through a hundred and fifty representations at the Théâtre Louvois. The King allowed the author a pension. 'Genius is patience,' as Buffon said. And patience after all is man's nearest approach to nature's processes of creation. What is art, monsieur, but nature concentrated?" He paused as if to impress these thoughts upon Lucien.

By this time the young men were striding along the walks of the Luxembourg, and in no long time Lucien learned the name of the stranger who was doing his best to administer comfort. That name has since grown famous. Daniel d'Arthez is one of the most illustrious of living men of letters; one of the rare few who show us an example of "a noble gift with a noble nature combined," to quote a poet's fine thought.

"There is no cheap route to greatness," Daniel went on in his kind voice. "The works of genius are watered with tears. The gift that is in you, like an existence in the physical world, passes through childhood and its maladies. Nature sweeps away sickly or deformed creatures, and society rejects an imperfectly developed talent. Any man who means to rise above the rest must make ready for a struggle and be undaunted by difficulties. A great writer is a martyr who does not die; that is all. There is the stamp of genius on your forehead," d'Arthez continued, enveloping Lucien by a glance; "but unless you have within you the will of genius, unless you are gifted with angelic patience, unless, no matter how far the freaks of fate have set you from your destined goal, you can find the way to your infinite as the turtles in the Indies find their way to the ocean, you had better give up at once."

"Then do you yourself expect these ordeals?" asked Lucien.

"Trials of every kind, slander and treachery, and effrontery and cunning, the rivals who act unfairly, and the keen competition of the literary market," his companion said resignedly. "What is a first loss, if only your work was really good?"

"Will you look at mine and give me your opinion?" asked Lucien.

"So be it," said d'Arthez. "I am living in the Rue des Quatre-Vents. Desplein, one of the most illustrious men of genius in our time, the greatest surgeon the world has known, once endured the martyrdom of early struggles with the first difficulties of a glorious career in the same house. I think of that every night, and the thought gives me the stock of courage that I need every morning. I am living in the very room where, like Rousseau, he often ate bread and cherries, but, unlike Rousseau, he had no Theresa. Come in about an hour's time. I shall be in, and waiting anxiously for your return.''

The poets grasped each other's hands with a rush of melancholy and tender feeling inexpressible in words, and went their separate ways ; Lucien to fetch his manuscript, Daniel d'Arthez to pawn his watch and buy a couple of faggots. The weather was cold, and his new-found friend should find a fire in his room.

Lucien was punctual. He noticed at once that the house was of an even poorer class than the Hôtel de Cluny. A staircase gradually became visible at the further end of a dark passage ; he mounted to the fifth floor, and found d'Arthez's room.

A bookcase of dark-stained wood, with rows of labeled cardboard cases on the shelves, stood between the two crazy windows. A gaunt, painted wooden bedstead, of the kind seen in school dormitories, a night-table, picked up cheaply somewhere, and a couple of horsehair armchairs, filled the further end of the room. The wall-paper, a Highland plaid pattern, was glazed over with the grime of years. Between the window and the grate stood a long table littered with papers, and opposite the fireplace there was a cheap mahogany chest of drawers. A second-hand carpet covered the floor—a necessary luxury, for it saved firing. A common office armchair, cushioned with leather, crimson once, but now hoary with wear, was drawn up to the table. Add half-a-dozen rickety chairs, and you have a complete list of the furniture. Lucien noticed an old-fashioned candle sconce for a card-table, with an adjustable screen attached, and wondered to see four wax-candles in the sockets. D'Arthez explained that he could not endure the smell of tallow, a little trait denoting great delicacy of sense-perception and the exquisite sensibility which accompanies it.

The reading lasted for seven hours. Daniel listened con-

scientiously, forbearing to interrupt by word or comment—
one of the rarest proofs of good taste in a listener.

"Well?" queried Lucien, laying the manuscript on the
chimney-shelf.

"You have made a good start on the right way," d'Arthez
answered judicially, " but you must go over your work again.
You must strike out a different style for yourself if you do not
mean to ape Sir Walter Scott, for you have taken him for
your model. You begin, for instance, as he begins, with
long conversations to introduce your characters, and only
when they have said their say does description and action
follow.

" This opposition, necessary in all work of a dramatic kind,
comes last. Just put the terms of the problem the other way
round. Give descriptions, to which our language lends itself
so admirably, instead of diffuse dialogue, magnificent in Scott's
work, but colorless in your own. Lead naturally up to your
dialogue. Plunge straight· into the action. Treat your subject from different points of view, sometimes in a side-light,
sometimes retrospectively; vary your methods, in fact, to
diversify your work. You may be original while adapting
the Scotch novelist's form of dramatic dialogue to French
history. There is no passion in Scott's novels; he ignores
passion, or perhaps it was interdicted by the hypocritical
manners of his country. Woman for him is duty incarnate.
His heroines, with possibly one or two exceptions, are all
exactly alike; he has drawn them all from the same model, as
painters say. They are, every one of them, descended from
Clarissa Harlowe. And returning continually, as he did, to
the same idea of woman, how could he do otherwise than
produce a single type, varied only by degrees of vividness in
the coloring? Woman brings confusion into society through
passion. Passion gives infinite possibilities. Therefore depict
passion; you have one great resource open to you, foregone by
the great genius for the sake of providing family reading for

prudish England. In France you have the charming sinner, the brightly colored life of Catholicism, contrasted with sombre Calvinistic figures on a background of the times when passions ran higher than at any other period of our history.

" Every epoch which has left authentic records since the time of Charles the Great calls for at least one romance. Some require four or five ; the periods of Louis XIV., of Henry IV., of Francis I., for instance. You would give us in this way a picturesque history of France, with the costumes and furniture, the houses and their interiors, and domestic life; giving us the spirit of the time instead of a laborious narration of ascertained facts. Then there is further scope for originality. You can remove some of the popular delusions which disfigure the memories of most of our kings. Be bold enough in this first work of yours to rehabilitate the great magnificent figure of Catherine, whom you have sacrificed to the prejudices which still cloud her name. And, finally, paint Charles IX. for us as he really was, and not as Protestant writers have made him. Ten years of persistent work, and fame and fortune will be yours.''

By this time it was nine o'clock; Lucien followed the example set in secret by his future friend by asking him to dine at Édon's, and spent twelve francs at that restaurant. During the dinner Daniel admitted Lucien into the secret of his hopes and studies. Daniel d'Arthez would not allow that any writer could attain to a pre-eminent rank without a profound knowledge of metaphysics. He was engaged in ransacking the spoils of ancient and modern philosophy, and in the assimilation of it all ; he would be like Molière, a profound philosopher first, and a writer of comedies afterward. He was studying the world of books and the living world about him—thought and fact. His friends were learned naturalists, young doctors of medicine, political writers and artists, a number of earnest students full of promise.

D'Arthez earned a living by a conscientious and ill-paid

work; he wrote articles for encyclopædias, dictionaries of biography and natural science, doing just enough to enable him to live while he followed his own bent, and neither more nor less. He had a piece of imaginative work on hand, undertaken solely for the sake of studying the resources of language, an important psychological study in the form of a novel, unfinished as yet, for d'Arthez took it up or laid it down as the humor struck him, and kept it for days of great distress. D'Arthez's revelations of himself were made very simply, but to Lucien he seemed like an intellectual giant; and by eleven o'clock, when they left the restaurant, he began to feel a sudden, warm friendship for this nature, unconscious of its loftiness, this unostentatious worth.

Lucien took d'Arthez's advice unquestioningly, and followed it out to the letter. The most magnificent palaces of fancy had been suddenly flung open to him by a nobly gifted mind, matured already by thought and critical examinations undertaken for their own sake, not for publication, but for the solitary thinker's own satisfaction. The burning coal had been laid on the lips of the poet of Angoulême, a word uttered by a hard student in Paris had fallen upon ground prepared to receive it in the provincial. Lucien set about recasting his work.

In his gladness at finding in this wilderness of Paris a nature abounding in generous and sympathetic feeling, the distinguished provincial did, as all young creatures hungering for affection are wont to do; he fastened, like a chronic disease, upon this one friend that he had found. He called for d'Arthez on his way to the Bibliothèque, walked with him on fine days in the Luxembourg Gardens, and went with his friend every evening as far as the door of his lodging-house after sitting next him at Flicoteaux's. He pressed close to his friend's side as a soldier might keep by a comrade on the frozen Russian plains.

During those early days of his acquaintance, he noticed,

not without chagrin, that his presence imposed a certain restraint on the circle of Daniel's intimates. The talk of those superior beings of whom d'Arthez spoke to him with such concentrated enthusiasm kept within the bounds of a reserve but little in keeping with the evident warmth of their friendships. At these times Lucien discreetly took his leave, a feeling of curiosity mingling with the sense of something like pain at the ostracism to which he was subjected by these strangers, who all addressed each other by their Christian names. Each one of them, like d'Arthez, bore the stamp of genius upon his forehead.

After some private opposition, overcome by d'Arthez without Lucien's knowledge, the new-comer was at length judged worthy to make one of the *cénacle* of lofty thinkers. Henceforward he was to be one of a little group of young men who met almost every evening in d'Arthez's room, united by the keenest sympathies and by the earnestness of their intellectual life. They all foresaw a great writer in d'Arthez ; they looked upon him as their chief since the loss of one of their number, a mystical genius, one of the most extraordinary intellects of the age. This former leader had gone back to his province for reasons on which it serves no purpose to enter, but Lucien often heard them speak of this absent friend as "Louis." Several of the group were destined to fall by the way; but others, like d'Arthez, have since won all the fame that was their due. A few details as to the circle will readily explain Lucien's strong feeling of interest and curiosity.

One among those who still survive was Horace Bianchon, then a house-student at the Hôtel-Dieu ; later, a shining light at the École de Paris, and now so well known that it is needless to give any description of his appearance, genius, or character.

Next came Léon Giraud, that profound philosopher and bold theorist, turning all systems inside out, criticising, expressing, and formulating, dragging them all to the feet of

his idol—Humanity; great even in his errors, for his honesty ennobled his mistakes.   An intrepid toiler, a conscientious scholar, he became the acknowledged head of a school
of moralists and politicians.   Time alone can pronounce upon
the merits of his theories; but if his convictions have drawn
him into paths in which none of his old comrades tread, none
the less he is still their faithful friend.

Art was represented by Joseph Bridau, one of the best
painters among the younger men.   But for a too impression-
able nature, which made havoc of Joseph's heart, he might
have continued the tradition of the great Italian masters,
though, for that matter, the last word has not yet been said
concerning him.   He combines Roman outline with Venetian
color; but love is fatal to his work, love not merely transfixes
his heart, but sends his arrow through the brain, deranges the
course of his life, and sets the victim describing the strangest
zigzags.   If the mistress of the moment is too kind or too
cruel, Joseph will send into the exhibition sketches where the
drawing is clogged with color, or pictures finished under the
stress of some imaginary woe, in which he gave his whole
attention to the drawing, and left the color to take care of
itself.   He is a constant disappointment to his friends and
the public; yet Hoffmann would have worshiped him for his
daring experiments in the realms of art, for his caprices, for a
certain fantastic streak in his work.   When Bridau is wholly
himself he is admirable, and, as praise is sweet to him, his
disgust is great when no one praises the failures in which he
alone discovers all that is lacking in the eyes of the public.
He is whimsical to the last degree.   His friends have seen
him destroy a finished picture because, in his eyes, it looked
too smooth.   "It is overdone," he would say; "it is nig-
gling work."

With his eccentric, yet lofty nature, with a nervous organization and all that it entails of torment and delight, the craving for perfection becomes morbid.   Intellectually he is akin

to Sterne, though he is not a literary worker. There is an indescribable piquancy about his epigrams and sallies of thought. He is eloquent, he knows how to love, but the uncertainty that appears in his execution is a part of the very nature of the man. The brotherhood loved him for the very qualities which the Philistine would style defects.

Last among the living comes Fulgence Ridal. No writer of our time possesses more of the exuberant spirit of pure comedy than this poet, careless of fame, who will fling his more commonplace productions to theatrical managers and keep the most charming scenes in the seraglio of his brain for himself and his friends. Of the public he asks just sufficient to secure his independence, and then declines to do anything more. Indolent and prolific as Rossini, compelled, like great poet-comedians, as Molière and Rabelais, to see both sides of everything, and all that is to be said both for and against, he is a skeptic, ready to laugh at all things. Fulgence Ridal is a great practical philosopher. His worldly wisdom, his genius for observation, his contempt for fame (" fuss," as he calls it) have not seared a kind heart. He is as energetic on behalf of another as he is careless where his own interests are concerned; and if he bestirs himself, it is for a friend. Living up to his Rabelaisian mask, he is no enemy to good-cheer, though he never goes out of his way to find it; he is melancholy and gay. His friends dubbed him the "Dog of the Regiment." You could have no better portrait of the man than his nickname.

Three more of the band, at least as remarkable as the friends who have just been sketched in outline, were destined to fall by the way. Of these, Meyraux was the first. Meyraux died after stirring up the famous controversy between Cuvier and Goeffroy Saint-Hilaire, a great question which divided the whole scientific world into two opposite camps, with these two men of equal genius as leaders. This befell some months before the death of the champion of rigorous analytical science as opposed to the pantheism of one who is still living to bear an honored name in Germany. Meyraux was the friend of that "Louis" of whom death was so soon to rob the intellectual world.

With these two, both marked by death, and unknown to-day in spite of their wide knowledge and their genius, stands a third, Michel Chrestien, the great republican thinker, who dreamed of European federation, and had no small share in bringing about the Saint-Simonian movement of 1830. A politician of the calibre of Saint-Just and Danton, but simple, meek as a maid, and brimful of illusions and loving-kindness; the owner of a singing voice which would have sent Mozart, or Weber, or Rossini into ecstasies, for his singing of certain songs of Béranger's could intoxicate the heart in you with poetry, or hope, or love—Michel Chrestien, poor as Lucien, poor as Daniel d'Arthez, as all the rest of his friends, gained a living with the hap-hazard indifference of a Diogenes. He indexed lengthy works, he drew up prospectuses for book-sellers, and kept his doctrines to himself as the grave keeps the secrets of the dead. Yet the gay Bohemian of intellectual life, the great statesman who might have changed the face of the world, fell as a private soldier in the cloister of Saint-Merri; some storekeeper's bullet struck down one of the noblest creatures that ever trod French soil, and Michel Chrestien died for other doctrines than his own. His federation scheme was more dangerous to the aristocracy of Europe than the republican propaganda; it was more feasible and less extravagant than the hideous doctrines of indefinite liberty proclaimed by the young madcaps who assume the character of heirs of the convention. All who knew the noble plebeian wept for him; there is not one of them but remembers, and often remembers, a great obscure politician.

Esteem and friendship kept the peace between the extremes of hostile opinion and conviction represented in the brotherhood. Daniel d'Arthez came of a good family in Picardy.

His belief in the monarchy was quite as strong as Michel
Chrestien's faith in European federation. Fulgence Ridal
scoffed at Léon Giraud's philosophical doctrines, while Giraud
himself prophesied for d'Arthez's benefit the approaching end
of Christianity and the extinction of the institution of the
family. Michel Chrestien, a believer in the religion of
Christ, the divine lawgiver, who taught the equality of men,
would defend the immortality of the soul from Bianchon's
scalpel, for Horace Bianchon was before all things an analyst.

There was plenty of discussion, but no bickering. Vanity
was not engaged, for the speakers were also the audience.
They would talk over their work among themselves and take
counsel of each other with the delighful openness of youth.
If the matter in hand was serious, the opponent would ·leave
his own position to enter into his friend's point of view ; and,
being an impartial judge in a matter outside his own sphere,
would prove the better helper ; envy, the hideous treasure of
disappointment, abortive talent, failure, and mortified vanity,
was quite unknown among them. All of them, moreover,
were going their separate ways. For these reasons, Lucien
and others admitted to their society felt at their ease in it.
Wherever you find real talent, you will find frank good-fellowship and sincerity and no sort of pretension ; the wit that
caresses the intellect and is never aimed at self-love.

When the first nervousness, caused by respect, wore off, it
was unspeakably pleasant to make one of this elect company
of youth. Familiarity did not exclude in each a consciousness of his own value, nor a profound esteem for his neighbor ; and, finally, as every member of the circle felt that he
could afford to receive or give, no one made a difficulty of
accepting. Talk was unflagging, full of charm, and ranging
over the most varied topics ; words light as arrows sped to the
mark. There was a strange contrast between the dire material
poverty in which the young men livèd and the splendor of
their intellectual wealth. They looked upon the practical

problems of existence simply as matter for friendly jokes.
The cold weather happened to set in early that year.   Five
of d'Arthez's friends appeared one day, each concealing firewood under his cloak ; the same idea had occurred to the five,
as it sometimes happens that all the guests at a picnic are inspired with the notion of bringing a pie as their contribution.

All of them were gifted with the moral beauty which reacts
upon the physical form, and, no less than work and vigils,
overlays a youthful face with a shade of divine gold; purity
of life and the fire of thought had brought refinement and
regularity into features somewhat pinched and rugged.   The
poet's amplitude of brow was a striking characteristic common to them all; the bright, sparkling eyes told of cleanli-
ness of life.   The hardships of penury, when they were felt at
all, were so gaily borne and embraced with such enthusiasm that
they had left no trace to mar the serenity peculiar to the faces
of the young who have no grave errors laid to their charge as
yet, who have not stooped to any of the base compromises
wrung from impatience of poverty by the strong desire to
succeed.   The temptation to use any means to this end is the
greater since that men of letters are lenient with bad faith
and extend an easy indulgence to treachery.

There is an element in friendship which doubles its
charm and renders it indissoluble—a sense of certainty
which is lacking in love.   These young men were sure of
themselves and of each other; the enemy of one was the
enemy of all; the most urgent personal considerations would
have been shattered if they had clashed with the sacred
solidarity of their fellowship.   All alike incapable of disloy-
alty, they could oppose a formidable NO to any accusation
brought against the absent and defend them with perfect
confidence.   With a like nobility of nature and strength of
feeling, it was possible to think and speak freely on all matters of intellectual or scientific interest ; hence the honesty
of their friendships, the gaiety of their talk, and with this

intellectual freedom of the community there was no fear of being misunderstood; they stood upon no ceremony with each other; they shared their troubles and joys, and gave thought and sympathy from full hearts. The charming delicacy of feeling which makes the tale of "Deux Amis" (Two Friends) a treasury for great souls was the rule of their daily life. It may be imagined, therefore, that their standard of requirements was not an easy one; they were too conscious of their worth, too well aware of their happiness, to care to trouble their life with the admixture of a new and unknown element.

This federation of interests and affection lasted for twenty years without a collision or disappointment. Death alone could thin the numbers of the noble Pleiades, taking first Louis Lambert, later Meyraux and Michel Chrestien.

When Michel Chrestien fell in 1832 his friends went, in spite of the perils of the step, to find his body at Saint-Merri; and Horace Bianchon, Daniel d'Arthez, Léon Giraud, Joseph Bridau, and Fulgence Ridal performed the last duties to the dead, between two political fires. By night they buried their beloved in the cemetery of Père-Lachaise; Horace Bianchon, undaunted by the difficulties, cleared them away one after another—it was he indeed who besought the authorities for permission to bury the fallen insurgent and confessed to his old friendship with the dead Federalist. The little group of friends present at the funeral with those five great men will never forget that touching scene.

As you walk in the trim cemetery you will see a grave purchased in perpetuity, a grass-covered mound with a dark wooden cross above it, and the name in large red letters—MICHEL CHRESTIEN. There is no other monument like it. The friends thought to pay a tribute to the sternly simple nature of the man by the simplicity of the record of his death.

So, in that chilly garret, the fairest dreams of friendship

were realized. These men were brothers leading lives of intellectual effort, loyally helping each other, making no reservations, not even of their worst thoughts; men of vast acquirements, natures tried in the crucible of poverty. Once admitted as an equal among such elect souls, Lucien represented beauty and poetry. They admired the sonnets which he read to them; they would ask him for a sonnet as he would ask Michel Chrestien for a song. And in the desert of Paris Lucien found an oasis of restful peace in the Rue des Quatre-Vents.

At the beginning of October, Lucien had spent the last of his money on a little firewood; he was half-way through the task of recasting his work, the most strenuous of all toil, and he was penniless. As for Daniel d'Arthez, burning blocks of spent tan and facing poverty like a hero, not a word of complaint came from him; he was as sober as any elderly spinster and methodical as a miser. This courage called out Lucien's courage; he had only newly come into the circle, and shrank with invincible repugnance from speaking of his straits. One morning he went out, manuscript in hand, and reached the Rue du Coq; he would sell "The Archer of Charles IX." to Doguereau; but Doguereau was out. Lucien little knew how indulgent great natures can be to the weaknesses of others. Every one of the friends had thought of the peculiar troubles besetting the poetic temperament, of the prostration which follows upon the struggle, when the soul has been overwrought by the contemplation of that nature which it is the task of art to reproduce. And strong as they were to endure their own ills, they felt keenly for Lucien's distress; they guessed that his stock of money was failing; and after all the pleasant evenings spent in friendly talk and deep meditations, after the poetry, the confidences, the bold flights over the fields of thought or into the far future of the nations, yet another trait was to prove how little Lucien had understood these new friends of his.

"Lucien, dear fellow," said Daniel, "you did not dine at Flicoteaux's yesterday, and we know why."

Lucien could not keep back the overflowing tears.

"You showed a want of confidence in us," said Michel Chrestien; "we shall chalk that up over the chimney, and when we have scored ten we will——"

"We have all of us found a bit of extra work," said Bianchon; "for my own part, I have been looking after a rich patient for Desplein; d'Arthez has written an article for the 'Revue Encyclopédique;' Chrestien thought of going out to sing in the Champs-Élysées of an evening with a pocket-handkerchief and four candles, but he found a pamphlet to write instead for a man who has a mind to go into politics, and gave his employer six hundred francs' worth of Machiavelli; Léon Giraud borrowed fifty francs of his publisher; Joseph sold one or two sketches; and Fulgence's piece was given on Sunday, and there was a full house."

"Here are two hundred francs," said Daniel, "and let us say no more about it."

"Why, if he is not going to hug us all as if we had done something extraordinary!" cried Chrestien.

Lucien, meanwhile, had written to the home circle. His letter was a masterpiece of sensibility and good-will, as well as a sharp cry wrung from him by distress. The answers which he received the next day will give some idea of the delight that Lucien took in this living encyclopedia of angelic spirits, each one of whom bore the stamp of the art or science which he followed:

David Séchard to Lucien.

"MY DEAR LUCIEN :—Enclosed herewith is a bill at ninety days, payable to your order, for two hundred francs. You can draw on M. Métivier, paper merchant, our Paris correspondent in the Rue Serpente. My good Lucien, we have

6

absolutely nothing. Eve has undertaken the charge of the printing-house, and works at her task with such devotion, patience, and industry that I bless heaven for giving me such an angel for a wife. She herself says that it is impossible to send you the least help. But I think, my friend, now that you are started in so promising a way, with such great and noble hearts for your companions, that you can hardly fail to reach the greatness to which you were born, aided as you are by intelligence almost divine in Daniel d'Arthez and Michel Chrestien and Léon Giraud, and counseled by Mey-raux and Bianchon and Ridal, whom we have come to know through your dear letter. So I have drawn this bill without Eve's knowledge, and I will contrive somehow to meet it when the time comes. Keep on your way, Lucien; it is rough, but it will be glorious. I can bear anything but the thought of you sinking into the sloughs of Paris, of which I saw so much. Have sufficient strength of mind to do as you are doing, and keep out of scrapes and bad company, wild young fellows and men of letters of a certain stamp, whom I learned to take at their just valuation when I lived in Paris. Be a worthy compeer of the divine spirits whom we have learned to love through you. Your life will soon meet with its reward. Farewell, dearest brother; you have sent trans-ports of joy to my heart. I did not expect such courage of you.

" DAVID."

Eve Séchard to Lucien.

" DEAR :—Your letter made all of us cry. As for the noble hearts to whom your good angel surely led you, tell them that a mother and a poor young wife will pray for them night and morning; and if the most fervent prayers can reach the Throne of God, surely they will bring blessings upon you all. Their names are engraved upon my heart. Ah ! some day I shall see your friends ; I will go to Paris, if I have to walk the whole way, to thank them for their friendship for you, for to me the thought has been like balm to smarting wounds. We are working like day laborers here, dear. This husband of mine, the unknown great man whom I love more and more every day, as I discover moment by moment the wealth of his nature, leaves the printing-house almost entirely to me. Why, I guess. Our poverty—yours, and ours, and our mother's—is heart-breaking to him. Our adored David is a Prometheus gnawed by a vulture, a haggard, sharp-beaked regret. As for himself, dear, noble fellow, he scarcely thinks of himself; he is hoping to make a fortune for *us*. He spends his whole time in experiments in paper-making; he begged me to take his place and look after the business, and gives me as much help as his pre-occupation allows. Alas! I shall be a mother soon. That should have been a crowning joy; but as things are, it saddens me. Poor mother! she has grown young again; she has found strength to go back to her tiring nursing. We should be happy if it were not for these money cares. Old Father Séchard will not give his son a farthing. David went over to see if he could borrow a little for you, for we were in despair over your letter. 'I know Lucien,' David said; 'he will lose his head and do something rash.' I gave him a good scolding. 'My brother disappoint us in any way!' I told him, 'Lucien knows that I should die of sorrows.' Mother and I have pawned a few things; David does not know about it, mother will redeem them as soon as she has made a little money. In this way we have managed to put together a hundred francs, which I am sending you by the coach. If I did not answer your last letter, do not remember it against me, dear; we were working all night just then. I have been working like a man. Oh, I had no idea that I was so strong!

"Mme. de Bargeton is a heartless woman; she has no soul; even if she cared for you no longer, she owed it to herself to use her influence for you and to help you when she had torn you from us to plunge you into that dreadful sea of Paris.

Only by the special blessing of heaven could you have met with true friends there among those crowds of men and innumerable interests. She is not worth a regret. I used to wish that there might be some devoted woman always with you, a second myself; but now I know that your friends will take my place, and I am happy. Spread your wings, my dear great genius, you will be our pride as well as our beloved.

" Eve."

"My darling," the mother wrote, "I can only add my blessing to all that your sister says, and assure you that you are more in my thoughts and in my prayers (alas!) than those whom I see daily; for some hearts the absent are always in the right, and so it is with the heart of your mother."

So two days after the loan was offered so graciously, Lucien repaid it. Perhaps life had never seemed so bright to him as that moment; but the touch of self-love in his joy did not escape the delicate sensibility and searching eyes of his friends.

"Any one might think that you were afraid to owe us anything," exclaimed Fulgence.

"Oh! the pleasure that he takes in returning the money is a very serious symptom to my mind," said Michel Chrestien. "It confirms some observations of my own. There is a spice of vanity in Lucien."

"He is a poet," said d'Arthez.

"But do you grudge me such a very natural feeling?" asked Lucien.

"We should bear in mind that he did not hide it," said Léon Giraud; "he is still open with us; but I am afraid that he may come to feel shy of us."

"And why?" Lucien asked.

"We can read your thoughts," answered Joseph Bridau.

"There is a diabolical spirit in you that will seek to justify courses which are utterly contrary to our principles. Instead of being a sophist in theory, you will be a sophist in practice."

"Ah! I am afraid of that," said d'Arthez. "You will carry on admirable debates in your own mind, Lucien, and take up a lofty position in theory, and end by blameworthy actions. You will never be at one with yourself."

"What ground have you for these charges?"

"Thy vanity, dear poet, is so great that it intrudes itself even into thy friendships!" cried Fulgence. "All vanity of that sort is a symptom of shocking egoism, and egoism poisons friendship."

"Oh! dear," said Lucien, "you cannot know how much I love you all."

"If you loved us as we love you, would you have been in such a hurry to return the money which we had such pleasure in lending? or have made so much of it?"

"We don't lend here; we give," said Joseph Bridau roughly.

"Don't think us unkind, dear boy," said Michel Chrestien; "we are looking forward. We are afraid lest some day you may prefer a petty revenge to the joys of pure friendship. Read Goethe's 'Tasso,' the great master's greatest work, and you will see how the poet-hero loved gorgeous stuffs and banquets and triumph and applause. Very well, be Tasso without his folly. Perhaps the world and its pleasures tempt you? Stay with us. Carry all the cravings of vanity into the world of imagination. Transpose folly. Keep virtue for daily wear, and let imagination run riot, instead of doing, as d'Arthez says, thinking high thoughts and living beneath them."

Lucien hung his head. His friends were right.

"I confess that you are stronger than I," he said, with a charming glance at them. "My back and shoulders are not made to bear the burden of Paris life; I cannot struggle bravely. We are born with different temperaments and facul-

ties, and you know better than I that faults and virtues have
their reverse side.   I am tired already, I confess.''

"We will stand by you,'' said d'Arthez; "it is just in
these ways that a faithful friendship is of use.''

" The help that I have just received is precarious, and
every one of us is just as poor as another; want will soon
overtake me again.   Chrestien, at the service of the first that
hires him, can do nothing with the publishers; Bianchon is
quite out of it; d'Arthez's booksellers only deal in scientific
and technical books—they have no connection with publishers of new literature; and as for Horace and Fulgence
Ridal and Bridau, their work lies miles away from the booksellers.   There is no help for it; I must make up my mind
one way or another.''

" Stick by us, and make up your mind. to it,'' said Bian- ·
chon.   " Bear up bravely, and trust in hard work.''

" But what is hardship for you is death for me,'' Lucien
put in quickly.

"Before the cock crows thrice,'' smiled Léon Giraud,
" this man will betray the cause of work for an idle life and
the vices of Paris.''

"Where has work brought you?'' asked Lucien, laughing.

" When you start out from Paris for Italy, you don't find
Rome half-way,'' said Joseph Bridau.   " You want your peas
to grow ready buttered for you.''

" They only grow like that for young dukes,'' said Michel
Chrestien.   " But the rest of us sow them and water them,
and like the flavor of them all the better.''

The conversation ended in a joke, and they changed the
subject.   Lucien's friends, with their perspicacity and delicacy of heart, tried to efface the memory of the little quarrel;
but Lucien knew thenceforward that it was no easy matter to
deceive them.   He soon fell into despair, which he was careful to hide from such stern mentors as he imagined them to
be; and the Southern temper that runs so easily through the

whole gamut of mental dispositions set him making the most contradictory resolutions.

Again and again he talked of making the plunge into journalism; and time after time did his friends reply with a " Mind you do nothing of the sort ! "

" It would be the tomb of the beautiful, gracious Lucien whom we love and know," said d'Arthez.

" You would not hold for long between the two extremes of toil and pleasure which make up a journalist's life, and resistance is the very foundation of virtue. You would be so delighted to exercise your power of life and death over the offspring of the brain that you would be an out-and-out journalist in two months' time. To be a journalist—that is to turn Herod in the republic of letters. The man who will say anything will end by sticking at nothing. That was Napoleon's maxim, and it explains itself."

" But you would be with me, would you not ? " asked Lucien.

" Not by that time," said Fulgence. " If you were a journalist, you would no more think of us than the opera girl in all her glory, with her adorers and her silk-lined carriage, thinks of the village at home and her cows and her sabots. You could never resist the temptation to pen a witticism, though it should bring tears to a friend's eyes. I come across journalists in theatre lobbies ; it makes me shudder to see them. Journalism is an inferno, a bottomless pit of iniquity and treachery and lies ; no one can traverse it undefiled, unless, like Dante, he is protected by Virgil's sacred laurel."

But the more the set of friends opposed the idea of journalism, the more Lucien's desire to know its perils grew and tempted him. He began to debate within his own mind ; was it not ridiculous to allow want to find him a second time defenseless? He bethought him of the failure of his attempts to dispose of his first novel, and felt but little tempted to

begin a second.   How, beside, was he to live while he was
writing another romance?   One month of privation had exhausted his stock of patience.   Why should he not do nobly
that which journalists did ignobly and without principle?
His friends insulted him with their doubts; he would convince them of his strength of mind.   Some day, perhaps, he
would be of use to them; he would be the herald of their
fame !

" And what sort of a friendship is it which recoils from
complicity?" demanded he one evening of Michel Chrestien;
Lucien and Léon Giraud were walking home with their friend.

" We shrink from nothing," Michel Christien made reply.
" If you were so unlucky as to kill your mistress, I would help
you to hide your crime and could still respect you; but if
you were to turn spy, I should shun you with abhorrence, for
a spy is systematically shameless and base.   There you have
journalism summed up in a sentence.   Friendship can pardon
error and the hasty impulse of passion; it is bound to be
inexorable when a man deliberately traffics in his own soul,
and intellect, and opinions."

" Why can I not turn journalist to sell my volume of poetry
and the novel, and then give up at once?"

" Machiavelli might do so, but not Lucien de Rubempré,"
said Léon Giraud.

" Very well," exclaimed Lucien; "I will show you that I
can do as much as Machiavelli."

" Oh !" cried Michel, grasping Léon's hand, " you have
done it, Léon.   Lucien," he continued, " you have three
hundred francs in hand; you can live comfortably for three
months; very well, then, work hard and write another romance.   D'Arthez and Fulgence will help you with the plot;
you will improve, you will be a novelist.   And I, meanwhile,
will enter one of these *lupanars* of thought; for three months
I will be a journalist.   I will sell your books to some bookseller or other by attacking his publications; I will write the

articles myself; I will get others for you. We will organize a success; you shall be a great man, and still remain our Lucien."

"You must despise me very much, if you think that I should perish while you escape," said the poet.

"O Lord, forgive him; it is a child!" cried Michel Chrestien.

When Lucien's intellect had been stimulated by the evenings spent in d'Arthez's garret, he had made some study of the jokes and articles in the smaller newspapers. He was at least the equal, he felt, of the wittiest contributors; in private he tried some mental gymnastics of the kind, and went out one morning with the triumphant idea of finding some colonel of such light skirmishers of the press and enlisting in their ranks. He dressed in his best and crossed the bridges, thinking as he went that authors, journalists, and men of letters, his future comrades, in short, would show him rather more kindness and disinterestedness than the two species of booksellers who had so dashed his hopes. He should meet with fellow-feeling and something of the kindly and grateful affection which he found in the *cénacle* of the Rue des Quatre-Vents. Tormented by emotion, consequent upon the presentiments to which men of imagination cling so fondly, half-believing, half-battling with their belief in them, he arrived in the Rue Saint-Fiacre off the Boulevard Montmartre. Before a house, occupied by the offices of a small newspaper, he stopped, and at the sight of it his heart began to throb as heavily as the pulses of a youth upon the threshold of some evil haunt.

Nevertheless, upstairs he went, and found the offices in the low *entresol* between the ground floor and the first story. The first room was divided down the middle by a partition, the lower half of solid wood, the upper lattice work to the ceiling. In this apartment Lucien discovered a one-armed pensioner supporting several reams of paper on his head with his remaining hand, while between his teeth he held the passbook which the Internal Revenue Department requires every newspaper to produce with each issue.   This ill-favored individual, owner of a yellow countenance covered with red excrescences, to which he owed his nickname of " Coloquinte," indicated a personage behind the lattice as the Cerberus of the paper. This latter was an elderly officer with a medal on his chest and a black silk skull-cap on his head ; his nose was almost hidden by a pair of grizzled mustaches, and his person was hidden as completely in an ample blue overcoat as the body of the turtle in its carapace.

" From what date do you wish your subscription to com- mence, sir ? " inquired the Emperor's officer.

" I did not come about a subscription," returned Lucien. Looking about him, he saw a placard fastened on a door, corresponding to the one by which he had entered, and read the words—EDITOR'S OFFICE, and below, in smaller letters, *No admittance except on business.*

" A complaint, I expect ? " replied the veteran.   " Ah ! yes ; we have been hard on Mariette.   What would you have ? I don't know the why and wherefore of it yet.   But if you want satisfaction, I am ready for you," he added, glancing at a collection of small arms and foils stacked in a corner, the armory of the modern warrior.

" That was still further from my intention, sir.   I have come to speak to the editor."

" Nobody is ever here before four o'clock."

" Look you here, Giroudeau, old chap," remarked a voice, " I make it eleven columns ; eleven columns at five francs apiece is fifty-five francs, and I have only been paid forty ; so you owe me another fifteen francs, as I have been telling you."

These words proceeded from a little weasel-face, pallid and semi-transparent as the half-boiled white of an egg ; two slits of eyes looked out of it, mild blue in tint, but appallingly malignant in expression ; and the owner, an insignificant young man, was completely hidden by the veteran's opaque person. It was a blood-curdling voice, a sound between the mewing of a cat and the wheezy chokings of a hyena.

"Yes, yes, my little militiaman," retorted he of the medal, "but you are counting the headings and white lines. I have Finot's instructions to add up the totals of the lines, and to divide them by the proper number for each column; and after I performed that concentrating operation on your copy, there were three columns less."

"He doesn't pay for the blanks, the Jew! He reckons them in though when he sends up the total of his work to his partner, and he gets paid for them too. I will go and see Étienne Lousteau, Vernou——"

"I cannot go beyond my orders, my boy," said the veteran. "What! do you cry out against your foster-mother for a matter of fifteen francs? you that turn out an article as easily as I smoke a cigar. Fifteen francs! why, you will give a bowl of punch the less to your friends or win an extra game of billiards, and there's an end of it!"

"Finot's savings will cost him very dear," said the contributor as he took his departure.

"Now, would not anybody think that he was Rousseau and Voltaire rolled in one?" the cashier remarked to himself as he glanced at Lucien.

"I will come in again at four, sir," said Lucien.

While the argument proceeded, Lucien had been looking about him. He saw upon the walls the portraits of Benjamin Constant, General Foy, and the seventeen illustrious orators of the Left, interspersed with caricatures at the expense of the government; but he looked more particularly at the door of the sanctuary where, no doubt, the paper was elaborated, the witty paper that amused him daily, and enjoyed the privilege of ridiculing kings and the most portentous events, of calling anything and everything in question with a jest. Then he sauntered along the boulevards. It was an entirely novel

amusement ; and so agreeable did he find it, that, looking at
the turret clocks, he saw the hour hands were pointing to four,
and only then remembered that he had not breakfasted.

He went at once in the direction of the Rue Saint-Fiacre,
climbed the stair, and opened the door.

The veteran officer was absent ; but the old pensioner, sitting on a pile of stamped papers, was munching a crust and
acting as sentinel resignedly.   Coloquinte was as much accustomed to his work in the office as to the fatigue duty of
former days, understanding as much or as little about it as
of the why and wherefore of forced marches made by the
Emperor's orders.   Lucien was inspired with the bold idea
of deceiving that formidable functionary.   He settled his hat
on his head, and walked into the editor's office as if he were
quite at home.

Looking eagerly about him, he beheld a round table covered
with green cloth, and half-a-dozen cherry-wood chairs, newly
reseated with straw.   The colored brick floor had not been
waxed, but it was clean ; so clean that the public, evidently,
seldom entered the room.   There was a mirror above the
chimney-piece, and on the ledge below, amid a sprinkling of
visiting-cards, stood a storekeeper's clock, smothered with
dust, and a couple of candlesticks with tallow dips thrust into
their sockets.   A few antique newspapers lay on the table
beside an inkstand containing some black lacquer-like substance, and a collection of quill pens twisted into stars.
Sundry dirty scraps of paper, covered with almost undeci-
pherable hieroglyphs, proved to be manuscript articles torn
across the top by the compositor to check off the sheets as
they were set up.   He admired a few rather clever caricatures,
sketched on bits of brown paper by somebody who evidently
had tried to kill time by killing something else to keep his
hand in.

Other works of art were pinned to the cheap sea-green wall-
paper.   These consisted of nine pen-and-ink illustrations for

"La Solitaire." The work had attained to such an unheard-of European popularity that journalists evidently were tired of it. "The Solitary makes its first appearance in the provinces; sensation among the women. The Solitary perused at a château. Effect of the Solitary on domestic animals. The Solitary explained to savage tribes, with the most brilliant results. The Solitary translated into Chinese and presented by the author to the Emperor at Pekin. The Mont Sauvage, Rape of Élodie." (Lucien thought this caricature very shocking, but he could not help laughing at it.) "The Solitary under a canopy conducted in triumphal procession by the newspapers. The Solitary breaks the press to splinters and wounds the printers. Read backward, the superior beauties of the Solitary produce a sensation at the Académie." On a newspaper-wrapper Lucien noticed a sketch of a contributor holding out his hat, and beneath it the words, "Finot! my hundred francs," and a name, since grown more notorious than famous.

Between the window and the chimney-piece stood a writing-table, a mahogany armchair, and a waste-paper basket on a strip of hearth-rug; the dust lay thick on all these objects. There were short curtains in the windows. About a score of new books lay on the writing-table, deposited there apparently during the day, together with prints, music, snuff-boxes of the "Charter" pattern, a copy of the ninth edition of "Le Solitaire" (the great joke of the moment), and some ten unopened letters.

Lucien had taken stock of this strange furniture and made reflections of the most exhaustive kind upon it, when, the clock striking five, he returned to question the pensioner. Coloquinte had finished his crust and was waiting with the patience of a commissionaire for the man of medals, who, perhaps, was taking an airing on the boulevard.'

At this conjuncture the rustle of a dress sounded on the stair, and the light, unmistakable footstep of a woman on the threshold. The new-comer was passably pretty. She addressed herself to Lucien.

"Sir," she said, "I know why you cry up Mademoiselle Virginie's hats so much; and I have come to put down my name for a year's subscription, in the first place; but tell me your conditions——"

"I am not connected with the paper, madame."

"Oh!"

"A subscription dating from October?" inquired the pensioner.

"What does the lady want to know?" asked the veteran, reappearing on the scene.

The fair milliner and the retired military man were soon deep in converse; and when Lucien, beginning to lose patience, came back to the first room, he heard the conclusion of the matter.

"Why, I shall be delighted, quite delighted, sir. Mademoiselle Florentine can come to my shop and choose anything she likes. Ribbons are in my department. So it is all quite settled. You will say no more about Virginie, a botcher that cannot design a new shape, while I have ideas of my own, I have."

Lucien heard a sound as of coins dropping into a cashbox, and the veteran began to make up his books for the day.

"I have been waiting here for an hour, sir," Lucien began, looking not a little annoyed.

"And 'they' have not come yet!" exclaimed Napoleon's veteran, civilly feigning concern. "I am not surprised at that. It is some time since I have seen 'them' here. It is the middle of the month, you see. Those fine fellows only turn up on pay-days—the 29th or the 30th."

"And Monsieur Finot?" asked Lucien, having caught the editor's name.

"He is in the Rue Feydeau, that's where he lives. Coloquinte, old chap, just take him everything that has come in to-day when you go with the paper to the printers."

"Where is the newspaper put together?" Lucien said half to himself.

"The newspaper?" repeated the officer, as he received the rest of the stamp money from Coloquinte, "the news-paper?—broum! broum! (Mind you are round at the prin-ters by six o'clock to-morrow, old chap, to send off the porters.) The newspaper, sir, is written in the street, at the writers' houses, in the printing-office between eleven and twelve o'clock at night. In the Emperor's time, sir, these shops for spoiled paper were not known. Oh! he would have cleared them out with four men and a corporal; they would not have come over *him* with their talk. But that is enough of prattling. If my nephew finds it worth his while, and so long as they write for the son of the Other (broum! broum!)—— after all, there is no harm in that. Ah! by the way, subscribers don't seem to me to be advancing in serried columns; I shall leave my post."

"You seem to know all about the newspaper, sir," Lucien began.

"From a business point of view, broum! broum!" coughed the soldier, clearing his throat. "From three to five francs per column, according to ability. Fifty lines to a column, forty letters to a line; no blanks; there you are! As for the staff, they are queer fish, little youngsters whom I wouldn't take on for the commissariat; and, because they make fly-tracks on sheets of white paper, they look down, forsooth, on an old captain of dragoons of the Guard, that retired with a major's rank after entering every European capital with Napoleon."

The soldier of Napoleon brushed his coat and made as if he would go out, but Lucien, swept to the door, had courage enough to make a stand.

"I came to be a contributor of the paper," he said. "I

am full of respect, I vow and declare, for a captain of the Imperial Guard, those men of bronze——''

'' Well said, my little civilian, there are several kinds of contributors ; which kind do you wish to be ? '' replied the trooper, bearing down on Lucien, and descending the stairs. At the foot of the flight he stopped, but it was only to light a cigar at the porter's box.

'' If any subscribers come, you see them and take note of them, Mother Chollet.   Simply subscribers, never know any-thing but subscribers,'' he added, seeing that Lucien followed him.   '' Finot is my nephew ; he is the only one of my fam-ily that has done anything to relieve me in my position.   So when anybody comes to pick a quarrel with Finot, he finds old Giroudeau, captain of the dragoons of the Guard, that set out as a private in a cavalry regiment in the army of the Sambre-et-Meuse, and was fencing-master for five years to the First Hussars, Army of Italy !   One, two, and the man that had any complaints to make would be turned off into the dark,'' he added, making a lunge.   '' Now writers, my boy, are in different corps ; there is the writer who writes and draws his pay ; there is the writer who writes and gets nothing (a volunteer we call him) ; and, lastly, there is the writer who writes nothing, and he is by no means the stupidest, for he makes no mistakes ; he gives himself out for a literary man, he is on the paper, he treats us to dinners, he loafs about the theatres, he keeps an actress, he is very well off.   What do you mean to be ? ''

'' The man that does good work and gets good pay.''

'' You are like the recruits ; they all want to be marshals of France.   Take old Giroudeau's word for it, and turn right about, in double-quick time, and go and pick up nails in the gutter like that good fellow yonder ; you can tell by the look of him that he has been in the army.   Isn't it a shame that an old soldier who has walked into the jaws of death hun-dreds of times should be picking up old iron in the streets of

Paris? Ah! God A'mighty! 'twas a shabby trick to desert the Emperor. Well, my boy, the individual you saw this morning has made his forty francs a month. Are you going to do better? And, according to Finot, he the cleverest man on the staff."

" When you enlisted in the Sambre-et-Meuse, did they talk about danger?"

" Rather."

" Very well?"

" Very well. Go and see my nephew Finot, a good fellow, as good a fellow as you will find, if you can find him that is, for he is like a fish, always on the move. In his way of business, there is no writing, you see, it is setting others to write. That sort like gallivanting about with actresses better than scribbling on sheets of paper, it seems. Oh! they are queer customers, they are. Hope I may have the honor of seeing you again."

With that the cashier raised his formidable loaded cane, one of the defenders of Germanicus, and walked off, leaving Lucien in the street, as much bewildered by this picture of the newspaper world as he had formerly been by the practical aspects of literature at Messrs. Vidal and Porchon's establishment.

Ten several times did Lucien repair to the Rue Feydeau in search of Andoche Finot, and ten times he failed to find that gentleman. He went the first thing in the morning, Finot had not come in. At noon, Finot had gone out; he was breakfasting at such and such a café. At the café, in answer to inquiries of the waitress, made after surmounting unspeakable repugnance, Lucien heard that Finot had just left the place. Lucien, at length tired out, began to regard Finot as a mythical and fabulous character; it appeared simpler to waylay Étienne Lousteau at Flicoteaux's. That youthful journalist would, doubtless, explain the mysteries that enveloped the paper for which he wrote.   .

7

Since the day, a hundred times blessed, when Lucien made the acquaintance of Daniel d'Arthez, he had taken another seat at Flicoteaux's. The two friends dined side by side, talking in lowered voices of the higher literature, of suggested subjects, and ways of presenting, opening up, and developing them. At the present time Daniel d'Arthez was correcting the manuscript of "The Archer of Charles IX." He reconstructed whole chapters, and wrote the fine passages found therein, as well as the magnificent preface, which is, perhaps, the best thing in the book, and throws so much light on the work of the young school of literature. One day it so happened that Daniel had been waiting for Lucien, who now sat with his friend's hand in his own, when he saw Étienne Lousteau turn the door-handle. Lucien instantly dropped Daniel's hand, and told the waiter that he would dine at his old place by the counter. D'Arthez gave Lucien a glance of divine kindness, in which reproach was wrapped in forgiveness. The glance cut the poet to the quick; he took Daniel's hand and grasped it anew.

"It is an important question of business for me; I will tell you about it afterward," said he.

Lucien was in his old place by the time that Lousteau reached the table as the first comer, he greeted his acquaintance; they soon struck up a conversation, which grew so lively that Lucien went off in search of the manuscript of the "Marguerites," while Lousteau finished his dinner. He had obtained leave to lay his sonnets before the journalist, and mistook the civility of the latter for willingness to find him a publisher or a place on the paper. When Lucien came hurrying back again he saw d'Arthez resting an elbow on the table in a corner of the restaurant, and knew that his friend was watching him with melancholy eyes, but he would not see d'Arthez just then; he felt the sharp fangs of poverty, the goading of ambition, and followed Lousteau.

In the late afternoon the journalist and the neophyte went

to the Luxembourg, and sat down under the trees in that part
of the gardens which lies between the broad Avenue de l'Observatoire and the Rue de l'Ouest. The Rue de l'Ouest at
that time was a long morass, bounded by planks and market-
gardens; the houses were all at the end nearest the Rue de
Vaugirard; and the walk through the gardens was so little frequented that, at the hour when Paris dines, two lovers might
fall out and exchange the earnest of reconciliation without
fear of intruders. The only possible spoil-sport was the pensioner on duty at the little iron gate on the Rue de l'Ouest,
if that gray-headed veteran should take it into his head to
lengthen his monotonous beat. There, on a bench beneath
the lime trees, Étienne Lousteau sat and listened to sample
sonnets from the "Marguerites."

Étienne Lousteau, after two years' apprenticeship, was on
the staff of a newspaper; he had his foot in the stirrup; he
reckoned some of the celebrities of the day among his friends;
altogether, he was an imposing personage in Lucien's eyes.
Wherefore, while Lucien untied the string about the "Marguerites," he judged it necessary to make some sort of preface.

"The sonnet, monsieur," said he, "is one of the most difficult forms of poetry. It has fallen almost entirely into disuse.
No Frenchman can hope to rival Petrarch; for the language
in which the Italian wrote, being so infinitely more pliant
than French, lends itself to play of thought which our posi-
tivism (pardon the use of the expression) rejects. So it
seemed to me that a volume of sonnets would be something
quite new. Victor Hugo has appropriated the ode, Canalis
writes lighter verse, Béranger has monopolized songs, Casimir
Delavigne has taken tragedy, and Lamartine the poetry of
meditation."

"Are you a 'Classic' or a 'Romantic?'" asked Lousteau.

Lucien's astonishment betrayed such complete ignorance
of the state of affairs in the republic of letters that Lousteau
thought it necessary to enlighten him.

"You have come up in the middle of a pitched battle, my dear fellow; you must make your decision at once. Literature is divided, in the first place, into several zones, but our great men are ranged in two hostile camps. The royalists are 'Romantics,' the liberals are 'Classics.' The divergence of taste in matters literary and divergence of political opinion coincide; and the result is a war with weapons of every sort, double-edged witticisms, subtle calumnies and nicknames *à outrance* (to the extreme), between the rising and the waning glory, and ink is shed in torrents. The odd part of it is that the royalist-romantics are all for liberty in literature and for repealing laws and conventions; while the liberal-classics are for maintaining the unities, the Alexandrine, and the classical theme. So opinions in politics on either side are directly at variance with literary taste. If you are eclectic, you will have no one for you. Which side do you take?"

"Which is the winning side?"

"The liberal newspapers have far more subscribers than the royalist and ministerial journals; still, though Canalis is for Church and King, and patronized by the court and the clergy, he reaches other readers. Pshaw! sonnets date back to an epoch before Boileau's time," said Étienne, seeing Lucien's dismay at the prospect of choosing between two banners. "Be a romantic. The romantics are young men and the classics are pedants; the romantics will gain the day."

The word "pedant" was the latest epithet taken up by romantic journalism to heap confusion on the classical faction.

Lucien began to read, choosing first of all the title-sonnets:

EASTER DAISIES.

The daisies in the meadows, not in vain,
  In red and white and gold before our eyes,
  Have written an idyll for man's sympathies,
And set his heart's desire in language plain.

Gold stamens set in silver filigrane
  Reveal the treasures which we idolize;
  And all the cost of struggle for the prize
Is symboled by a secret blood-red stain.

Was it because your petals once uncurled
When Jesus rose upon a fairer world,
And from wings shaken for a heav'nward flight
  Shed grace, that still as autumn reappears
You bloom again to tell of dead delight,
  To bring us back the flower of twenty years?

Lucien felt piqued by Lousteau's complete indifference during the reading of the sonnet; he was unfamiliar as yet with the disconcerting impassibility of the professional critic, wearied by much reading of poetry, prose, and plays. Lucien was accustomed to applause. He choked down his disappointment and read another, a favorite with Mme. de Bargeton and with some of his friends in the Rue des Quatre-Vents. "This one, perhaps, will draw a word from him," he thought:

THE MARGUERITE.

I am the Marguerite, fair and tall I grew
  In velvet meadows, 'mid the flowers a star.
  They sought me for my beauty near and far;
My dawn, I thought, should be for ever new.

But now an all unwished-for gift I rue,
  A fatal ray of knowledge shed to mar
  My radiant star-crown grown oracular,
For I must speak and give an answer true.

An end of silence and of quiet days.
The Lover with two words my counsel prays;
And when my secret from my heart is reft,
  When all my silver petals scattered lie,
I am the only flower neglected left,
  Cast down and trodden under foot to die.

At the end the poet looked up at his Aristarchus.   Étienne
Lousteau was gazing at the trees in the Pépinière.

"Well?" asked Lucien.

"Well, my dear fellow, go on!   I am listening. to you,
am I not?   That fact in itself is as good as praise in Paris."

"Have you had enough?" Lucien inquired.

"Go on," the other answered, abruptly enough.

Lucien proceeded to read the following sonnet, but his
heart was dead within him; Lousteau's inscrutable composure
froze his utterance.   If he had come a little further upon the
road, he would have known that, between writer and writer,
silence or abrupt speech, under such circumstances, is a betrayal of jealousy, and outspoken admiration means a sense of
relief over the discovery that the work is not above the
average, after all.

THE CAMELLIA.

In Nature's book, if rightly understood,
   The rose means love, and red for beauty glows;
   A pure, sweet spirit in the violet blows,
And bright the lily gleams in lowlihood.

But this strange bloom, by sun and wind unwooed,
   Seems to expand and blossom 'mid the snows,
   A lily sceptreless, a scentless rose,
For dainty listlessness of maidenhood.

Yet at the opera-house the petals trace
   For modesty a fitting aureole;
An alabaster wreath to lay, methought,
In dusky hair o'er some fair woman's face
   Which kindles ev'n such love within the soul
As sculptured marble forms by Phidias wrought.

"What do you think of my poor sonnets?" Lucien asked,
coming straight to the point.

"Do you want the truth?"

" I am young enough to like the truth and so anxious to succeed that I can hear it without taking offense, but not without despair," replied Lucien. .

"Well, my dear fellow, the first sonnet, from its involved style, was evidently written at Angoulême; it gave you so much trouble, no doubt, that you cannot give it up. The second and third smack of Paris already; but read us one more sonnet," he added, with a gesture that seemed charming to the provincial.

Encouraged by the request, Lucien read with more confidence, choosing a sonnet which d'Arthez and Bridau liked best, perhaps on account of its color.

THE TULIP.

I am the Tulip from Batavia's shore;
  The thrifty Fleming for my beauty rare
  Pays a king's ransom, when that I am fair,
And tall, and straight, and pure my petal's core.

And, like some Yolande of the days of yore,
  My long and amply folded skirts I wear,
  O'er-painted with the blazon that I bear,
—Gules, a fess azure; purpure, fretty, or.

The fingers of the Gardener divine
Have woven for me my vesture fair and fine,
  Of threads of sunlight and of purple stain;
No flower so glorious in the garden bed,
But Nature, woe is me, no fragrance shed
  Within my cup of Orient porcelain.

"Well?" asked Lucien after a pause, immeasurably long, as it seemed to him.

" My dear fellow," Étienne said, gravely surveying the tips of Lucien's boots (he had brought the pair from Angoulême, and was wearing them out). " My dear fellow, I strongly recommend you to put your ink on your boots to save black-

ing, and to take your pens for toothpicks, so that when you
come away from Flicoteaux's you can swagger along this picturesque alley looking as if you had dined. Get a situation
of any sort or description. Run errands for a bailiff if you
have a heart, be a shopman if your back is strong enough,
enlist if you happen to have a taste for military music. You
have the stuff of three poets in you ; but before you can reach
your public, you will have time to die of starvation six times
over, if you intend to live on the proceeds of your poetry,
that is. And, from your too unsophisticated discourse, it
would seem to be your intention to coin money out of your
inkstand.

   " I say nothing as to your verses; they are a good deal
better than all the poetical wares that are cumbering the
ground in booksellers' backstores just now. Elegant ' nightingales ' of that sort cost a little more than the others, because they are printed on hand-made paper, but they nearly
all of them come down at last to the banks of the Seine. You
may study their range of notes there any day if you care to
make an instructive pilgrimage along the quais from old
Jérôme's stall by the Pont Notre Dame to the Pont Royal.
You will find them all there—all the ' Essays in Verse,' the
' Inspirations,' the lofty flights, the hymns, and songs, and
ballads, and odes ; all the nestfuls hatched during the last
seven years, in fact. There lie their muses, thick with dust,
bespattered by every passing cab, at the mercy of every pro-
. fane hand that turns them over to look at the vignette on the
title-page.

   " You know nobody ; you have access to no newspaper,
so your ' Marguerites ' will remain demurely folded as you
hold them now. They will never open out to the sun of publicity in fair fields, with broad margins enameled with the
florets which Dauriat the illustrious, the king of the Wooden
Galleries, scatters with a lavish hand for poets known to fame.
I came to Paris as you came, poor boy, with a plentiful stock

of illusions, impelled by irrepressible longings for glory—and I found the realities of the craft, the practical difficulties of the trade, the hard facts of poverty. In my enthusiasm (it is kept well under control now), my first ebullition of youthful spirits, I did not see the social machinery at work; so I had to learn to see it by bumping against the wheels and bruising myself against the shafts, covering myself with oil, hearing the clatter of fly-wheel and chains. Now you are about to learn, as I learned, that between you and all these fair dreamed-of things lies the strife of men, and passions, and necessities.

" Willy-nilly, you must take part in a terrible battle; book against book, man against man, party against party; make war you must, and that systematically, or you will be abandoned by your own party. And they are mean contests; struggles which leave you disenchanted, and wearied, and depraved, and all in pure waste; for it often happens that you put forth all your strength to win laurels for a man whom you despise, and maintain, in spite of yourself, that some second-rate writer is a genius.

" There is a world behind the scenes in the theatre of literature. The public in front sees unexpected or well-deserved success, and applauds; the public does *not* see the preparations, ugly as they always are, the painted supers, the *claqueurs* hired to applaud, the stage carpenters, and all that lies behind the scenes. You are still among the audience. Abdicate, there is still time, before you set your foot on the lowest step of the throne for which so many ambitious spirits are contending, and do not sell your honor, as I do, for a livelihood." Étienne's eyes filled with tears as he spoke.

" Do you know how I make a living?" he continued passionately. " The little stock of money they gave me at home was soon eaten up. A piece of mine was accepted at the Théâtre-Français just as I came to an end of it. At the Théâtre-Français the influence of a first gentleman of the

bedchamber, or of a prince of the blood, would not be
enough to secure a turn of favor; the actors only make concessions to those who threaten their self-love. If it is in your
power to spread a report that the *jeune premier* (leading juve-
nile) has the asthma, the leading lady a fistula where you
please, and the soubrette has foul breath, then your piece
would be played to-morrow. I do not know whether, in two
years' time, I who speak to you now shall be in a position to
exercise such power. You need so many to back you. And
where and how am I to gain my bread meanwhile?

"I tried lots of things; I wrote a novel, anonymously;
old Doguereau gave me two hundred francs for it, and he did
not make very much out of it himself. Then it grew plain
to me that journalism alone could give me a living. The
next thing was to find my way into those shops. I will not
tell you all the advances I made, nor how often I begged in
vain. I will say nothing of the six months I spent as extra
hand on a paper, and was told that I scared subscribers away,
when as a fact I attracted them. Pass over the insults I put
up with. At this moment I am doing the plays at the boulevard theatres, almost *gratis*, for a paper belonging to Finot,
that stout young fellow who breakfasts two or three times a
month, even now, at the Café Voltaire (but you don't go
there). I live by selling tickets that managers give me to
bribe a good word in the paper and reviewers' copies of books.
In short, Finot once satisfied, I am allowed to write for and
against various commercial articles, and I traffic in tribute
paid in kind by various tradesmen. A facetious notice of a
Carminative Toilet Lotion, 'Pâte des Sultanes,' Cephalic Oil,
or Brazilian Mixture brings me in twenty or thirty francs.

"I am obliged to dun the publishers when they don't send
in a sufficient number of reviewers' copies; Finot, as editor,
appropriates two and sells them, and I must have two to sell.
If a book of capital importance comes out, and the publisher
is stingy with copies, his life is made a burden to him. The

craft is vile, but I live by it, and so do scores of others. Do not imagine that things are any better in public life. There is corruption everywhere in both regions; every man is corrupt or corrupts others. If there is any publishing enterprise somewhat larger than usual afoot, the trade will pay me something to buy neutrality. The amount of my income varies, therefore, directly with the prospectuses. When prospectuses break out like a rash, money pours into my pockets; I stand treat all round. When trade is dull, I dine at Flicoteaux's.

" Actresses will pay you likewise for praise, but the wiser among them pay for criticism. To be passed over in silence is what they dread the most ; and the very best thing of all, from their point of view, is criticism which draws down a reply; it is far more effectual than bald praise, forgotten as soon as read, and it costs more in consequence. Celebrity, my dear fellow, is based upon controversy. I am a hired bravo; I ply my trade among ideas and reputations, commercial, literary, and dramatic; I make some fifty crowns a month; I can sell a novel for five hundred francs; and I am beginning to be looked upon as a man to be feared. Some day, instead of living with Florine at the expense of a druggist who gives himself the airs of a lord, I shall be in a house of my own; I shall be on the staff of a leading newspaper, I shall have a *feuilleton* (a fly-leaf or portion of a journal) ; and on that day, my dear fellow, Florine will become a great actress. As for me, I am not sure what I shall be when that time comes, a minister or an honest man—all things are still possible."

He raised his humiliated head, and looked out at the green leaves, with an expression of despairing self-condemnation dreadful to see.

"And I had a great tragedy accepted!" he went on. " And among my papers there is a poem, which will die. And I was a good fellow, and my heart was clean ! I used to dream lofty dreams of love for great ladies, queens in the great world; and—my mistress is an actress at the Panorama-Dramatique. And, lastly, if a bookseller declines to send a copy of a book to my paper, I shall run down work which is good, as I know."

Lucien was moved to tears, and he grasped Étienne's hand in his. The journalist rose to his feet, and the pair went up and down the broad Avenue de l'Observatoire, as if their lungs craved ampler breathing space.

"Outside the world of letters," Étienne Lousteau continued, "not a single creature suspects that every one who succeeds in that world—who has a certain vogue, that is to say, or comes into fashion, or gains reputation, or renown, or fame, or favor with the public (for by these names we know the rungs of the ladder by which we climb to the greater heights above and beyond them)—every one who comes even thus far is the hero of a dreadful Odyssey. Brilliant portents rise above the mental horizon through a combination of a thousand accidents; conditions change so swiftly that no two men have been known to reach success by the same road. Canalis and Nathan are two dissimilar cases; things never fall out in the same way twice. There is d'Arthez, who knocks himself to pieces with work—he will make a famous name by some other chance.

"This so much desired reputation is nearly always crowned prostitution. Yes; the poorest kind of literature is the hapless creature freezing at a street corner; second-rate literature is the kept-mistress picked out of the brothels of journalism, and I am her bully; lastly, there is lucky literature, the flaunting, insolent courtesan who has a house of her own and pays taxes, who receives great lords, treating or ill-treating them as she pleases, who has liveried servants and a carriage and can afford to keep greedy creditors waiting. Ah! and for yet others, for me not so very long ago, for you to-day—she is a white-robed angel with many-colored wings, bearing a green palm branch in the one hand, and in the other a

flaming sword. An angel, something akin to the mythological abstraction which lives at the bottom of a well, and to the
poor and honest girl who lives a life of exile in the outskirts
of the great city, earning every penny with a noble fortitude
and in the full light of virtue, returning to heaven inviolate
of body and soul; unless, indeed, she comes to lie at the last,
soiled, despoiled, polluted, and forgotten, on a pauper's bier.
As for the men whose brains are encompassed with bronze,
whose hearts are still warm under the snows of experience,
they are found but seldom in the country that lies at our feet,"
he added, pointing to the great city seething in the late afternoon light.

A vision of d'Arthez and his friends flashed upon Lucien's
sight and made appeal to him for a moment; but Lousteau's
appalling lamentation carried him away.

"They are very few and far between in that great ferment-
ing vat; rare as love in love-making, rare as fortunes honestly
made in business, rare as the journalist whose hands are clean.
The experience of the first man who told me all that I am
telling you was thrown away upon me, and mine no doubt
will be wasted upon you. It is always the same old story
year after year; the same eager rush to Paris from the provinces; the same, not to say a growing, number of beardless,
ambitious boys, who advance, head erect and the heart beating high in them, to storm the citadel of the fashion—that
Princess Tourandocte of the 'Mille et un Jours' (Thousand
and one Days)—each one of them fain to be her Prince Calaf.
But never a one of them reads the riddle. One by one they
drop, some into the trench where failures lie, some into the
mire of journalism, some again into the quagmires of the
booktrade.

"They pick up a living, these beggars, what with bio-
graphical notices, penny-a-lining, and scraps of news for the
papers. They become booksellers' hacks for the clear-headed
dealers in printed paper, who would sooner take the rubbish

that goes off in a fortnight than a masterpiece which requires
time to sell.   The life is crushed out of the grubs before they
reach the butterfly stage.   They live by shame and dishonor.
They are ready to write down a rising genius or to praise him
to the skies at a word from the pacha of the ' Constitutionnel,'
the ' Quotidienne,' or the ' Débats,' at a sign from a publisher, at the request of a jealous comrade, or (as not seldom
happens) simply for a dinner.   Some surmount the obstacles,
and these forget the misery of their early days.   I, who am
telling you this, have been putting the best that is in me into
newspaper articles for six months past for a blackguard who
gives them out as his own and has secured a *feuilleton* in
another paper on the strength of them.   He has not taken
me on as his collaborator, he has not given me so much as a
five-franc piece, but I hold out a hand to grasp his when we
meet ; I cannot help myself.''

" And why ? " Lucien asked indignantly.

" I may want to put a dozen lines into his *feuilleton* some
day," Lousteau answered coolly.   " In short, my dear fellow, in literature you will not make money by hard work,
that is not the secret of success ; the point is to exploit the
work of somebody else.   A newspaper proprietor is a contractor, we are the bricklayers.   The more mediocre the
man, the better his chance of getting on among mediocrities ;
he can play the toad-eater, put up with any treatment, and
flatter all the little base passions of the sultans of literature.
There is Hector Merlin, who came from Limoges a short time
ago ; he is writing political articles already for a Right Centre
daily, and he is at work on our little paper as well.   I have
seen an editor drop his hat and Merlin pick it up.   The fellow was careful never to give offense, and slipped into the
thick of the fight between rival ambitions.   I am sorry for
you.   It is as if I saw in you the self that I used to be, and
sure am I that in one or two years' time you will be what I
am now.   You will think that there is some lurking jealousy

or personal motive in this bitter counsel, but it is prompted by the despair of a damned soul that can never leave hell. No one ventures to utter such things as these. You hear the groans of anguish from a man wounded to the heart, crying like a second Job from the ashes, ' Behold my sores ! ' ''

'' But whether I fight upon this field or elsewhere, fight I must,'' said Lucien.

'' Then, be sure of this,'' returned Lousteau, '' if you have anything in you, the war will know no truce, the best chance of success lies in an empty head. The austerity of your conscience, clear as yet, will relax when you see that a man holds your future in his two hands, when a word from such a man means life to you, and he will not say that word. For, believe me, the most brutal bookseller in the trade is not so insolent, so hard-hearted to a new-comer as the celebrity of the day. The bookseller sees a possible loss of money, while the writer of books dreads a possible rival ; the first shows you the door, the second crushes the life out of you. To do really good work, my boy, means that you will draw out the energy, sap, and tenderness of your nature at every dip of the pen in the ink, to set it forth for the world in passion and sentiment and phrases. Yes ; instead of acting, you will write ; you will sing songs instead of fighting ; you will love and hate and live in your books ; and then, after all, when you shall have reserved your riches for your style, your gold and purple for your characters, and you yourself are walking the streets of Paris in rags, rejoicing in that, rivaling the state register, you have authorized the existence of a being styled Adolphe, Corinne or Clarissa, René or Manon ; when you shall have spoiled your life and your digestion to give life to that creation, then you shall see it slandered, betrayed, sold, swept away into the back waters of oblivion by journalists and buried out of sight by your best friends. How can you afford to wait until the day when your creation shall rise again, raised from the dead—how ? when ? and by whom ? Take a

magnificent book, the *pianto* of unbelief; 'Obermann' is a
solitary wanderer in the desert places of booksellers' warehouses, he has been a 'nightingale,' ironically so called, from
the very beginning: when will his Easter come? Who
knows? Try, to begin with, to find somebody bold enough
to print the 'Marguerites;' not to pay for them, but simply
to print them; and you will see some queer things."

The fierce tirade, delivered in every tone of the passionate
feeling which it expressed, fell upon Lucien's spirit like an
avalanche, and left a sense of glacial cold. For one moment
he stood silent; then, as he felt the terrible, stimulating charm
of difficulty beginning to work upon him, his courage blazed
up. He grasped Lousteau's hand.

"I will triumph!" he cried aloud.

"Good!" said the other, "one more Christian given over
to the wild beasts in the arena. There is a first-night performance at the Panorama-Dramatique, my dear fellow; it
doesn't begin till eight, so you can change your coat, come
properly dressed in fact, and call for me. I am living on the
fourth floor above the Café Servel, Rue de la Harpe. We
will go to Dauriat's first of all. You still mean to go on, do
you not? Very well, I will introduce you to one of the kings
of the trade to-night, and to one or two journalists. We will
sup with my mistress and several friends after the play, for
you cannot count that dinner as a meal. Finot will be there,
editor and proprietor of my paper. As Minette says in the
Vaudeville (do you remember?), 'Time is a great lean creature.' Well, for the like of us, Chance is a great lean creature, and must be tempted."

"I shall remember this day as long as I live," said
Lucien.

"Bring your manuscript with you, and be careful of
your dress, not on Florine's account, but for the booksellers'
benefit."

The comrade's good-nature, following upon the poet's passionate outcry, as he described the war of letters, moved Lucien quite as deeply as d'Arthez's grave and earnest words on a former occasion. The prospect of entering at once upon the strife with men warmed him. In his youth and inexperience he had no suspicion how real were the moral evils denounced by the journalist. Nor did he know that he was standing at the parting of two distinct ways, between two systems, represented by the brotherhood upon one hand and journalism ' upon the other. The first way was long, honorable, and sure; the second beset with hidden dangers, a perilous path, among muddy channels where conscience is inevitably bespattered. The bent of Lucien's character determined for the shorter way, and the apparently pleasanter way, and to snatch at the quickest and promptest means. At this moment he saw no difference between d'Arthez's noble friendship and Lousteau's easy camaraderie; his inconstant mind discerned a new weapon in journalism; he felt that he could wield it, so he wished to take it.

He was dazzled by the offers of this new friend, who had struck a hand in his in an easy way, which charmed Lucien. How should he know that while every man in the army of the press needs friends, every leader needs men. Lousteau, seeing that Lucien was resolute, enlisted him as a recruit and hoped to attach him to himself. The relative positions of the two were similar—one hoped to become a corporal, the other to enter the ranks.

Lucien went back gaily to his lodgings. He was as careful over his toilet as on that former unlucky occasion when he occupied the Marquise d'Espard's box; but he had learned by this time how to wear his clothes with a better grace. They looked as though they belonged to him. He wore his best tightly fitting, light-colored trousers, and a dress coat. His boots, a very elegant pair adorned with tassels, had cost him forty francs. His thick, fine, golden hair was scented and crimped into bright, rippling curls. Self-confidence and

8

belief in his future lighted up his forehead. He paid careful attention to his almost feminine hands, the filbert nails were a spotless rose-pink, and the white contours of his chin were dazzling by contrast with a black satin stock. Never did a more beautiful youth come down from the hills of the Latin Quarter.

Glorious as a Greek god, Lucien took a cab and reached the Café Servel at a quarter to seven. There the portress gave him some tolerably complicated directions for the ascent of four pair of stairs. Provided with these instructions, he discovered, not without difficulty, an open door at the end of a long, dark passage, and in another moment made the acquaintance of the traditional room of the Latin Quarter.

A young man's poverty follows him wherever he goes—into the Rue de la Harpe as into the Rue de Cluny, into d'Arthez's room, into Chrestien's lodging; yet everywhere no less the poverty has its own peculiar characteristics, due to the idiosyncrasies of the sufferer. Poverty in this case wore a sinister look.

A shabby, cheap carpet lay in wrinkles at the foot of a curtainless walnut-wood bedstead; dingy curtains, begrimed with cigar-smoke and fumes from a smoky chimney, hung in the windows; a Carcel lamp, Florine's gift, on the chimney-piece, had so far escaped the pawnbroker. Add a forlorn-looking chest of drawers, a table littered with papers and disheveled quill-pens, and the list of furniture is almost complete. All the books had evidently arrived in the course of the last twenty-four hours; and there was not a single object of any value in the room. In one corner you beheld a collection of crushed and flattened cigars, soiled pocket-handkerchiefs, shirts which had been turned to do double duty, and cravats that had reached a third edition; while a sordid array of old shoes stood gaping in another angle of the room among aged socks worn into lace.

The room, in short, was a journalist's bivouac, filled with

odds and ends of no value, and the most curiously bare apartment imaginable. A scarlet tinder-box glowed among a pile of books on the night-stand. A brace of pistols, a box of cigars, and a stray razor lay upon the mantel-shelf; a pair of foils, crossed under a wire mask, hung against a panel. Three chairs and a couple of armchairs, scacely fit for the shabbiest lodging-house in the street, completed the inventory.

The dirty, cheerless room told a tale of a restless life and a want of self-respect; some one came hither to sleep and work at high pressure, staying no longer than he could help, longing, while he remained, to be out and away. What a difference between this cynical disorder and d'Arthez's neat and self-respecting poverty! A warning came with the thought of d'Arthez; but Lucien would not heed it, for Étienne made a joking remark to cover the nakedness of a reckless bohemian life.

"This is my kennel; I appear in state in the Rue de Bondy, in the new apartments which our druggist has taken for Florine; we hold the house-warming this evening."

Étienne Lousteau wore black trousers and beautifully varnished shoes; his coat was buttoned up to the chin; he probably meant to change his linen at Florine's house, for his shirt collar was hidden by a velvet stock. He was trying to renovate his hat by an application of the brush.

"Let us go," said Lucien.

"Not yet. I am waiting for a bookseller to bring me some money; I have not a farthing; there will be play, perhaps, and in any case I must have gloves."

As he spoke the two new friends heard a man's step in the passage outside.

"There he is," said Lousteau. "Now you will see, my dear fellow, the shape that providence takes when he manifests himself to poets. You are going to behold Dauriat, the fashionable bookseller, in all his glory; but first you shall see the bookseller of the Quai des Augustins, the pawnbroker, the marine store-dealer of the trade, the Norman ex-green-grocer. Come along, old tartar!'' shouted Lousteau.

"Here am I,'' said a voice like a cracked bell.

"Brought the money with you?''

"Money? There is no money now in the trade,'' retorted the other, a young man who eyed Lucien curiously.

"*Imprimis:* you owe me fifty francs,'' Lousteau continued.

"There are two copies of 'Travels in Egypt' here, a marvel, so they say, swarming with woodcuts, sure to sell. Finot has been paid for two reviews that I am to write for him. *Item:* two works, just out by Victor Ducange, a novelist highly thought of in the Marais. *Item:* a couple of copies of a second work by Paul de Kock, a beginner in the same style. *Item:* two copies of 'Yseult of Dôle,' a charming provincial work. Total, one hundred francs net. Wherefore you owe me one hundred francs, my little Barbet.''

Barbet made a close survey of edges and binding.

"Oh! they are in perfect condition,'' cried Lousteau. "The 'Travels' are uncut, so is the Paul de Kock, so is the Ducange, so is that other thing on the chimney-piece, 'Considerations on Symbolism.' I will throw that in; myths weary me to that degree that I will let you have the thing to spare myself the sight of the swarms of mites coming out of it,'' he added.

"But,'' asked Lucien, "how are you going to write your reviews?''

Barbet, in profound astonishment, stared at Lucien; then he looked at Étienne and chuckled.

"One can see that the gentleman has not the misfortune to be a literary man,'' said he.

"No, Barbet—no. He is a poet, a great poet; he is going to cut out Canalis, and Béranger, and Delavigne. He will go a long way if he does not throw himself into the river, and even so he will get as far as the drag-nets in the Seine at Saint-Cloud.''

"If I had any advice to give the gentleman," remarked
Barbet, "it would be to give up poetry and take to prose.
Poetry is not wanted on the quais just now."

Barbet's shabby overcoat was fastened by a single button;
his collar was greasy; he kept his hat on his head as he spoke;
he wore low shoes; an open waistcoat gave glimpses of a
homely shirt of coarse linen. Good-nature was not wanting
in the round countenance, with its two slits of covetous eyes;
but there was likewise the vague uneasiness habitual to those
who have money to spend and hear constant applications for
it. Yet, to all appearance, he was plain-dealing and easy-
natured, his business shrewdness was so well wadded round
with fat. He had been an assistant until he took a wretched
little store on the Quai des Augustins two years since, and
issued thence on his rounds among journalists, authors, and
printers, buying up free copies cheaply, making in such ways
some ten or twenty francs daily. Now, he had money saved;
he knew instinctively where every man was pressed; he had a
keen eye for business. If an author was in difficulties, he
would discount a bill given by a publisher at fifteen or twenty
per cent.; then the next day he would go the publisher,
haggle over the price of some work in demand, and pay him
with his own bills instead of cash. Barbet was something of
a scholar; he had just enough education to make him careful
to steer clear of modern poetry and modern romances. He
had a liking for small speculations, for books of a popular
kind which might be bought outright for a thousand francs
and exploited at pleasure, such as the "Child's History of
France," "Bookkeeping in Twenty Lessons," and "Botany
for Young Ladies." Two or three times already he had
allowed a good book to slip through his fingers; the authors
had come and gone a score of times while he hesitated and
could not make up his mind to buy the manuscript. When
reproached for his pusillanimity, he was wont to produce the
account of a notorious trial taken from the newspapers; it

cost him nothing and had brought him in two or three thousand francs.

Barbet was the type of bookseller that goes in fear and trembling; he lives on bread and walnuts; rarely puts his name to a bill; filches little profits on invoices; makes deductions, and hawks his books about himself; heaven only knows where they go, but he sells them somehow, and gets paid for them. Barbet was the terror of printers, who could not tell what to make of him; he paid cash and took off the discount; he nibbled at their invoices whenever he thought they were pressed for money; and when he had fleeced a man once he never went back to him—he feared to be caught in his turn.

" Well," said Lousteau, " shall we go on with our business? "

" Eh ! my boy," returned Barbet in a familiar tone ; " I have six thousand volumes of stock on hand at my place, and ' paper is not gold,' as the old bookseller said. Trade is dull."

" If you went into his shop, my dear Lucien," said Étienne, turning to his friend, " you would see an oak counter from some bankrupt wine merchant's sale, and a tallow dip, never snuffed for fear it should burn too quickly, making darkness visible. By that anomalous light you descry rows of empty shelves with some difficulty. An urchin in a blue blouse mounts guard over the emptiness, and blows his fingers, and shuffles his feet, and slaps his chest, like a cabman on the box. Just look about you ! there are no more books there than I have here. Nobody could guess what kind of store he keeps."

" Here is a bill at three months for a hundred francs," said Barbet, and he could not help smiling as he drew it out of his pocket ; " I will take your old books off your hands. I can't pay cash any longer, you see ; sales are too slow. I thought that you would be wanting me ; I had not a penny, and I made out a bill simply to oblige you, for I am not fond of giving my signature."

" So you want my thanks and esteem into the bargain, do you ? "

" Bills are not met with sentiment," responded Barbet; " but I will accept your esteem, all the same."

" But I want gloves, and the perfumers will be base enough to decline your paper," said Lousteau. " Stop, there is a superb engraving in the top drawer in the chest there, worth eighty francs, proof before letters and after letter-press, for I have written a pretty droll article upon it. There was something to lay hold of in ' Hippocrates refusing the Presents of Artaxerxes.' A fine engraving, eh ? Just the thing to suit all the doctors, who are refusing the extravagant gifts of Parisian satraps. You will find two or three dozen novels underneath it. Come, now, take the lot and give me forty francs."

" *Forty francs !* " exclaimed the bookseller, emitting a cry like the squall of a frightened fowl. " Twenty at the very most ! And then I may never see the money again," he added.

" Where are your twenty francs ? " asked Lousteau.

" My word, I don't know that I have them," said Barbet, fumbling in his pockets. " Here they are. You are plundering me ; you have an ascendency over me——"

" Come, let us be off," said Lousteau, and, taking up Lucien's manuscript, he drew a line upon it in ink under the string.

" Have you anything else ? " asked Barbet.

" Nothing, you young Shylock. I am going to put you in the way of a bit of very good business," Étienne continued (" in which you shall lose a thousand crowns, to teach you to rob me in this fashion"), he added for Lucien's ear.

" But how about your reviews ? " said Lucien, as they rolled away to the Palais Royal.

" Pooh ! you do not know how reviews are knocked off. As for the ' Travels in Egypt,' I looked into the book here and there (without cutting the pages), and I found eleven

slips in grammar.   I shall say that the writer may have mastered the dicky-bird language on the flints that they call
'obelisks' out there in Egypt, but he cannot write 'in his
own, as I will prove to him in a column and a half.   I shall
say that instead of giving us natural history and archæology,
he ought to have interested himself in the future of Egypt,
in the progress of civilization, and the best method of strength-
ening the bond between Egypt and France.   France has won
and lost Egypt, but she may yet attach the country to her
interests by gaining a moral ascendency over it.   Then some
patriotic penny-a-lining, interlarded with diatribes on Mar-
seilles, the Levant, and our trade.''

"But suppose that he had taken that view, what would you
do?''

"Oh well, I should say that instead of boring us with
politics, he should have written about art, and described the
picturesque aspects of the country and the local color.   Then
the critic bewails himself.   Politics are intruded everywhere;
we are weary of politics—politics on all sides.   I should
regret those charming books of travel that dwelt upon the
difficulties of navigation, the fascination of steering between
two rocks, the delights of crossing the line, and all the things
that those who will never travel ought to know.   Mingle this
approval with scoffing at the travelers who hail the appearance
of a bird or a flying-fish as a great event, who dilate upon
fishing, and make transcripts from the log.   Where, you ask,
is that perfectly unintelligible scientific information, fascinating, like all that is profound, mysterious, and incompre-
hensible.   The reader laughs, that is all that he wants.   As for
novels, Florine is the greatest novel reader alive; she gives me
a synopsis and I take her opinion and put a review together.
When a novelist bores her with 'author's stuff,' as she calls it,
I treat the work respectfully, and ask the publisher for another
copy, which he sends forthwith, delighted to have a favorable
review.''

"Goodness! and what of criticism, the critic's sacred office?" cried Lucien, remembering the ideas instilled into him by the brotherhood.

"My dear fellow," said Lousteau, "criticism is a kind of brush which must not be used upon flimsy stuff, or it carries it all away with it. That is enough of the craft, now listen! Do you see that mark?" he continued, pointing to the manuscript of the "Marguerites." "I have put ink on the string and paper. If Dauriat reads your manuscript, he certainly could not tie the string and leave it just as it was before. So your book is sealed, so to speak. This is not useless to you for the experiment that you propose to make. And another thing: please to observe that you are not arriving quite alone and without a sponsor in the place, like the youngsters who make the round of half-a-score of publishers before they find one that will offer them a chair."

Lucien's experience confirmed the truth of this particular. Lousteau paid the cabman, giving him three francs—a piece of prodigality following upon such impecuniosity astonishing Lucien more than a little. Then the two friends entered the Wooden Galleries, where fashionable literature, as it is called, used to reign in state.

PART II.

The Wooden Galleries of the Palais Royal used to be one of the most famous sights of Paris. Some description of the squalid bazaar will not be out of place; for there are few men of forty who will not take an interest in recollections of a state of things which will seem incredible to a younger generation.

The great dreary, spacious Galerie d'Orléans, that flowerless hothouse, as yet was not; the space upon which it now stands was covered with booths; or, to be more precise, with small, wooden dens, pervious to the weather, and dimly illuminated on the side of the court and the garden by borrowed lights styled windows by courtesy, but more like the filthiest arrangements for obscuring daylight to be found in little wineshops in the suburbs.

The galleries, parallel passages about twelve feet in height, were formed by a triple row of stores. The centre row, giving back and front upon the galleries, was filled with the fetid atmosphere of the place, and derived a dubious daylight through the invariably dirty windows of the roof; but so thronged were these hives that rents were excessively high and as much as a thousand crowns was paid for a space scarce six feet by eight. The outer rows gave respectively upon the garden and the court, and were covered on that side by a slight trellis-work painted green, to protect the crazy plastered walls from continual friction with the passers-by. In a few square feet of earth at the back of the stores strange freaks of vegetable life unknown to science grew amid the products of various no less flourishing industries. You beheld a rosebush capped with printed paper in such a sort that the flowers of rhetoric were perfumed by the cankered blossoms of that ill-kept, ill-smelling garden. Handbills and ribbon streamers

(122)

of every hue flaunted gaily among the leaves; natural flowers competed unsuccessfully for an existence with odds and ends of millinery. You discovered a knot of ribbon adorning a green tuft; the dahlia admired afar proved on a nearer view to be a satin rosette.

The Palais seen from the court or from the garden was a fantastic sight, a grotesque combination of walls of plaster patchwork which had once been whitewashed, of blistered paint, heterogeneous placards, and all the most unaccountable freaks of Parisian squalor; the green trellises were prodigiously the dingier for constant contact with a Parisian public. So, upon either side, the fetid, disreputable approaches might have been there for the express purpose of warning away fastidious people; but fastidious folk no more recoiled before these horrors than the prince in the fairy stories turns tail at sight of the dragon or of the other obstacles put between him and the princess by the wicked fairy.

There was a passage through the centre of the galleries then as now; and, as at the present day, you entered them through the two peristyles begun before the revolution, and left unfinished for lack of funds; but, in place of the handsome modern arcade leading to the Théâtre-Français, you passed along a narrow, disproportionately lofty passage, so ill-roofed that the rain came through on wet days. All the roofs of the hovels indeed were in very bad repair, and covered here and again with a double thickness of tarpaulin. A famous silk mercer once brought an action against the Orleans family for damages done in the course of a night to his stock of shawls and stuffs, and gained the day and a considerable sum. It was in this last-named passage, called "The Glass Gallery" to distinguish it from the Wooden Galleries, that Chevet laid the foundations of his fortunes.

Here in the Palais you trod the natural soil of Paris, augmented by importations brought in upon the shoes of foot passengers; here, at all seasons, you stumbled among hills and hollows of dried mud swept daily by the store-clerk's besom, and only after some practice could you walk at your ease. The treacherous mud-heaps, the window-panes incrusted with deposits of dust and rain, the mean-looking hovels covered with ragged placards, the grimy unfinished walls, the general air of a compromise between a gypsy camp, the booths of a country fair, and the temporary structures which we in Paris build round about public monuments that remain unbuilt; the grotesque aspect of the mart as a whole was in keeping with the seething traffic of various kinds carried on within it; for here in this shameless, unblushing haunt, amid wild mirth and a babel of talk, an immense amount of business was transacted between the revolution of 1789 and the revolution of 1830.

For twenty years the Bourse stood just opposite, on the ground floor of the Palais. Public opinion was manufactured and reputations made and ruined here, just as political and financial jobs were arranged. People made appointments to meet in the galleries before or after 'Change; on showery days the Palais Royal was often crowded with weather-bound capitalists and men of business. The structure which had grown up, no one knew how, about this point was strangely resonant, laughter was multiplied; if two men quarreled, the whole place rang from one end to the other with the dispute. In the daytime milliners and booksellers enjoyed a monopoly of the place; toward nightfall it was filled with women of the town. Here dwelt poetry, politics, and prose, new books and classics, the glories of ancient and modern literature side by side with political intrigue and the tricks of the bookseller's trade. Here all the very latest and newest literature was sold to a public which resolutely declined to buy elsewhere. Sometimes several thousand copies of such and such a pamphlet by Paul-Louis Courier would be sold in a single evening; and people crowded thither to buy " Les aventures de la fille d'un Roi " (The Adventures of a King's Daughter), that first shot fired by the Orleanists at the charter promulgated by the émigré king, Louis XVIII.

When Lucien made his first appearance in the Wooden Galleries, some few of the shops boasted proper fronts and handsome windows, but these in every case looked upon the court or the garden. As for the centre row, until the day when the whole strange colony perished under the hammer of Fontaine the architect, every store was open back and front like a booth in a country fair, so that from within you could look out upon either side through gaps among the goods displayed or through the glass doors. As it was obviously impossible to kindle a fire, the tradesmen were fain to use charcoal chafing-dishes, and formed a sort of brigade for the prevention of fires among themselves; and, indeed, a little carelessness might have set the whole quarter blazing in fifteen minutes, for the plank-built republic, dried by the heat of the sun, and haunted by too inflammable human material, was bedizened with muslin and paper and gauze, and ventilated at times by a thorough draft.

The milliners' windows were full of impossible hats and bonnets, displayed apparently for advertisement rather than for sale, each on a separate iron spit with a knob at the top. The galleries were decked out in all the colors of the rainbow. On what heads would those dusty bonnets end their careers?—for a score of years the problem had puzzled frequenters of the Palais. Saleswomen, usually plain-featured but vivacious, waylaid the feminine foot passenger with cunning importunities, after the fashion of the market-women, and using much the same language; a store-girl, who made free use of her eyes and tongue, sat outside on a stool and harangued the public with "Buy a pretty bonnet, madame? Do let me sell you something!"—varying a rich and picturesque vocabulary with inflexions of the voice, with glances, and remarks upon the passers-by. Booksellers and milliners lived on terms of mutual good understanding.

But it was in the passage known by the pompous title of the "Glass Gallery" that the oddest trades were carried on. Here were ventriloquists and charlatans of every sort, and sights of every description, from the kind where there is really nothing to see to panoramas of the globe. One man, who has since made seven or eight hundred thousand francs by traveling from fair to fair, began here by hanging out a signboard, a revolving sun in a blackboard, and the inscription in red letters—"Here Man may see what God can never see. Admittance, two sous." The showman at the door never admitted one person alone, nor more than two at a time. Once inside, you confronted a great looking-glass; and a voice, which might have terrified Hoffmann of Berlin, suddenly spoke as if some spring had been touched, "You see here, gentlemen, something that God can never see through all eternity; that is to say, your like. God has not His like." And out you went, too shame-faced to confess to your stupidity.

Voices issued from every narrow doorway, crying up the merits of cosmoramas, views of Constantinople, marionettes, automatic chess players, and performing dogs who would pick you out the prettiest woman in the company. The ventriloquist, Fitz-James, flourished here in the Café Borel before he went to fight and fall at Montmartre with the young lads from the École Polytechnique. Here, too, there were fruit and flower shops, and a famous tailor whose gold-laced uniforms shone like the sun when the stores were lighted at night.

Of a morning the galleries were empty, dark, and deserted; the shopkeepers chatted among themselves. Toward two o'clock in the afternoon the Palais began to fill; at three, men came in from the Bourse, and Paris, generally speaking, crowded the place. Impecunious youth, hungering after literature, took the opportunity of turning over the pages of the books exposed for sale on the stalls outside the booksellers' stores; the men in charge charitably allowed a poor student

to pursue his course of free studies; and in this way a duodecimo volume of some two hundred pages, such as "Smarra"
or "Pierre Schlemihl," or "Jean Sbogar" or "Jocko,"
might be devoured in a couple of afternoons. There was
something very French in this alms given to the young, hun-
gry, starved intellect. Circulating libraries were not as yet;
if you wished to read a book, you were obliged to buy it; for
which reason novels of the early part of the century were
sold in numbers which now seem well-nigh fabulous to us.

But the poetry of this terrible mart appeared in all its
splendor at the close of the day. Women of the town, flock-
ing in and out from the neighboring streets, were allowed to
make a promenade of the Wooden Galleries. Thither came
prostitutes from every quarter of Paris to "do the Palais."
The Stone Galleries belonged to privileged houses, which
paid for the right of exposing women dressed like princesses
under such and such an arch, or in the corresponding
space of garden; but the Wooden Galleries were the common ground of women of the streets. This was *the* Palais,
a word which used to signify the temple of prostitution.
A woman might come and go, taking away her prey whither-
soever seemed good to her. So great was the crowd attracted thither at night by the women that it was impossible to move except at a slow pace, as in a procession
or at a masked ball. Nobody objected to the slowness;
it facilitated examination. The women dressed in a way
that is never seen nowadays. The bodices cut extremely
low both back and front; the fantastical head-dresses,
designed to attract notice; here a cap from the Pays de
Caux, and there a Spanish mantilla; the hair crimped
and curled like a poodle's or smoothed down in bandeaux
over the forehead; the close-fitting white stockings and
limbs, revealed it would not be easy to say how, but always
at the right moment—all this poetry of vice has fled. The
license of question and reply, the public cynicism in keeping

with the haunt, is now unknown even at masquerades or the
famous public balls.   It was an appalling, gay scene.   The
dazzling white flesh of the women's necks and shoulders stood
out in magnificent contrast against the men's almost invariably sombre costumes.   The murmur of voices, the hum of
the crowd, could be heard even in the middle of the garden
as a sort of droning bass, interspersed with shrieks of shrill
laughter or clamor of some rare dispute.   You saw gentlemen
and celebrities cheek by jowl with gallows-birds.   There was
something indescribably piquant about the anomalous assem-
blage ; the most insensible of men felt its charm, so much so,
that, until the very last moment, Paris came hither to walk up
and down on the wooden planks laid over the cellars where
men were at work on the new buildings ; and when the squalid
wooden erections were finally taken down great and unanimous regret was felt.

Ladvocat the bookseller had opened a store but a few days
since in the angle formed by the central passage which
crossed the galleries ; and immediately opposite another bookseller, now forgotten, Dauriat, a bold and youthful pioneer,
who opened up the paths in which his rival was to shine.
Dauriat's store stood in the row which gave upon the garden ;
Ladvocat's, on the opposite side, looked out upon the court.
Dauriat's establishment was divided into two parts ; his store
was simply a great trade warehouse, and the second room was
his private office.

Lucien, on this first visit to the Wooden Galleries, was bewildered by a sight which no novice can resist.   He soon lost
the guide who befriended him.

"If you were as good-looking as yonder young fellow I
would give you your money's worth," a woman said, pointing
out Lucien to an old man.

Lucien slunk through the crowd like a blind-man's dog,
following the stream in a state of stupefaction and excitement
difficult to describe.   Importuned by glances and white,

rounded contours, dazzled by the audacious display of bared throat and bosom, he gripped his roll of manuscript tightly lest somebody should steal it—innocent that he was!

" Well, what is it, sir!" he exclaimed, thinking, when some one caught him by the arm that his poetry had proved too great a temptation for some author's honesty, and, turning, he recognized Lousteau.

"I felt sure that you would find your way here at last," said his friend.

The poet was standing in the doorway of a shop crowded with persons waiting for an audience with the sultan of the publishing trade. Printers, paper-dealers, and designers were catechising Dauriat's assistants as to present or future business.

Lousteau drew Lucien into the shop. "There! that is Finot who edits my paper," he said; " he is talking with Félicien Vernou, who has abilities, but the little wretch is as dangerous as a hidden disease."

" Well, old boy, there is a first night for you," said Finot, coming up with Vernou. " I have disposed of the box."

" Sold it to Braulard ?"

"Well, and if I did, what then? You will get a seat. What do you want with Dauriat? Oh, it is agreed that we are to push Paul de Kock, Dauriat has taken two hundred copies, and Victor Ducange is refusing to give him his next. Dauriat wants to set up another man in the same line, he says. You must rate Paul de Kock above Ducange."

" But I have a piece on with Ducange at the Gaité," said Lousteau.

" Very well, tell him that I wrote the article. It can be supposed that I wrote a slashing review, and you toned it down ; and he will owe you thanks."

" Couldn't you get Dauriat's cashier to discount this bit of a bill for a hundred francs !" asked Étienne Lousteau. " We are celebrating Florine's house-warming with a supper to-night, you know."

9

"Ah! yes, you are treating us all," said Finot, with an apparent effort of memory. "Here, Gabusson," he added, handing Barbet's bill to the cashier, "let me have ninety francs for this individual. Fill in your illustrious name, old man."

Lousteau signed his name while the cashier counted out the money; and Lucien, all eyes and ears, lost not a syllable of the conversation.

"That is not all, my friend," Étienne continued; "I don't thank you, we have sworn an eternal friendship. I have taken it upon myself to introduce this gentleman to Dauriat and you must incline his ear to listen to us."

"What is on foot?" asked Finot.

"A volume of poetry," said Lucien.

"Oh!" said Finot, with a shrug of the shoulders.

"Your acquaintance cannot have had much to do with publishers, or he would have hidden his manuscript in the loneliest spot in his dwelling," remarked Vernou, looking at Lucien as he spoke.

Just at that moment a good-looking young man came into the shop, gave a hand to Finot and Lousteau, and nodded slightly to Vernou. The new-comer was Emile Blondet, who had made his first appearance in the "Journal des Débats," with articles revealing capacities of the very highest order.

"Come and have supper with us at midnight, at Florine's," said Lousteau.

"Very good," said the new-comer. "But who is going to be there?"

"Oh, Florine and Matifat the druggist," said Lousteau, "and du Bruel, the author who gave Florine the part in which she is to make her first appearance, a little old fogey named Cardot, and his son-in-law Camusot, and Finot, and Coralie, and——"

"Does your druggist do things properly?"

"He will not give us doctored wine," said Lucien.

"You are very witty, monsieur," Blondet returned gravely.
"Is he coming, Lousteau?"

"Yes."

"Then we shall have some fun."

Lucien had flushed red to the tips of his ears. Blondet
tapped on the window above Dauriat's desk.

"Is your business likely to keep you long, Dauriat?"

"I am at your service, my friend."

"That's right," says Lousteau, addressing his protégé.
"That young fellow is hardly any older than you are, and he
is on the 'Débats!' He is one of the princes of criticism.
They are afraid of him, Dauriat will fawn upon him, and then
we can put in a word about our business with the pasha of
vignettes and type. Otherwise we might have waited till
eleven o'clock and our turn would not have come. The
crowd of people waiting to speak with Dauriat is growing
bigger every moment."

Lucien and Lousteau followed Blondet, Finot, and Vernou
and stood in a knot at the back of the shop.

"What is he doing?" asked Blondet of the head clerk,
who rose to bid him good-evening.

"He is buying a weekly newspaper. He wants to put new
life into it, and set up a rival to the 'Minerve' and the
'Conservateur;' Eymery has rather too much of his own way
in the 'Minerve' and the 'Conservateur' is too romantic."

"Is he going to pay well?"

"Only too much—as usual," said the cashier.

Just as he spoke another young man entered; this was the
writer of a magnificent novel which had sold very rapidly
and met with the greatest possible success. Dauriat was
bringing out a second edition. The appearance of this odd
and extraordinary looking being, so unmistakably an artist,
made a deep impression on Lucien's mind.

"That is Nathan," Lousteau said in his ear.

Nathan, then in the prime of his youth, came up to the

group of journalists, hat in hand; and in spite of his look of fierce pride he was almost humble to Blondet, whom as yet he only knew by sight. Blondet did not remove his hat, neither did Finot.

"Monsieur, I am delighted to avail myself of an opportunity yielded by chance——"

("He is so nervous that he is committing a pleonasm," said Félicien in an aside to Lousteau.)

"To give expression to my gratitude for the splendid review which you were so good as to give me in the 'Journal des Débats.' Half the success of my book is owing to you."

"No, my dear fellow, no," said Blondet, with an air of patronage scarcely masked by good-nature. "You have talent, the deuce you have, and I'm delighted to know you."

"Now that your review has appeared, I shall not seem to be courting power; we can feel at ease. Will you do me the honor and the pleasure of dining with me to-morrow? Finot is coming. Lousteau, old man, you will not refuse me, will you?" added Nathan, shaking Étienne by the hand. "Ah, you are on the way to a great future, monsieur," he added, turning again to Blondet; "you will carry on the line of Dussaults, Fiévées, and Geoffrois! Hoffmann was talking about you to a friend of mine, Claud Vignon, his pupil; he said that he could die in peace, the 'Journal des Débats' would live for ever. They ought to pay you tremendously well."

"A hundred francs a column," said Blondet. "Poor pay when one is obliged to read the books, and read a hundred before you find one worth interesting yourself in, like yours. Your work gave me pleasure, upon my word."

"And brought him in fifteen hundred francs," said Lousteau for Lucien's benefit.

"But you write political articles, don't you?" asked Nathan.

"Yes; now and again."

Lucien felt like an embryo among these men; he had admired Nathan's book, he had reverenced the author as an
immortal; Nathan's abject attitude before this critic, whose
name and importance were both unknown to him, stupefied
Lucien.

"How if I should come to behave as he does?" he
thought. "Is a man obliged to part with his self-respect?
Pray put on your hat again, Nathan; you have written a
wonderfully great book and the critic has only written a review of it."

These thoughts set the blood tingling in his veins. Scarce
a minute passed but some young author, poverty-stricken and
shy, came in, asked to speak with Dauriat, looked round the
crowded shop despairingly, and went out saying, "I will
come back again." Two or three politicians were chatting
over the convocation of the Chambers and public business
with a group of well-known public men. The weekly newspaper for which Dauriat was in treaty was licensed to treat of
matters political, and the number of newspapers suffered to
exist was growing smaller and smaller, till a paper was a piece
of property as much in demand as a theatre. One of the
largest shareholders in the "Constitutionnel" was standing
in the midst of the knot of political celebrities. Lousteau
performed the part of cicerone to admiration; with every
sentence he uttered Dauriat rose higher in Lucien's opinion.
Politics and literature seemed to converge in Dauriat's shop.
He had seen a great poet prostituting his muse to journalism,
humiliating art, as woman was humiliated and prostituted in
those shameless galleries without, and the provincial took a
terrible lesson to heart. Money! That was the key to every
enigma. Lucien realized the fact that he was unknown and
alone, and that the fragile clue of an uncertain friendship was
his sole guide to success and fortune. He blamed the kind
and loyal little circle for painting the world for him in false
colors, for preventing him from plunging into the arena, pen

in hand. "I should be a Blondet at this moment!" he exclaimed within himself.

Only a little while ago they had sat looking out over Paris from the gardens of the Luxembourg, and Lousteau had uttered the cry of a wounded eagle; then Lousteau had been a great man in Lucien's eyes, and now he had shrunk to scarce visible proportions. The really important man for him at this moment was the fashionable bookseller, by whom all these men lived; and the poet, manuscript in hand, felt a nervous tremor that was almost like fear. He noticed a group of busts mounted on wooden pedestals, painted to resemble marble; Byron stood there, and Goethe and M. de Canalis. Dauriat was hoping to publish a volume by the last-named poet, who might see, on his entrance into the shop, the estimation in which he was held by the trade. Unconsciously Lucien's own self-esteem began to shrink, and his courage ebbed. He began to see how large a part this Dauriat would play in his destinies, and waited impatiently for him to appear.

"Well, children," said a voice, and a short, stout man appeared, with a puffy face that suggested a Roman proconsul's visage, mellowed by an air of good-nature which deceived superficial observers. "Well, children, here am I, the proprietor of the only weekly paper in the market, a paper with two thousand subscribers!"

"Old joker! The registered number is seven hundred, and that is over the mark," said Blondet.

"Twelve hundred, on my most sacred word of honor. I said two thousand for the benefit of the printers and paperdealers yonder," he added, lowering his voice, then raising it again. "I thought you had more tact, my boy," he added.

"Are you going to take any partners?" inquired Finot.

"That depends," said Dauriat. "Will you take a third at forty thousand francs?"

"It's a bargain, if you will take Emile Blondet here on the

staff, and Claud Vignon, Scribe, Theodore Leclercq, Félicien Vernou, Jay, Jouy, Lousteau, and——''

"And why not Lucien de Rubempré?" the provincial poet put in boldly.

" and Nathan," concluded Finot.

"Why not the people out there in the street?" asked Dauriat, scowling at the author of the "Marguerites." "To whom have I the honor of speaking?" he added, with an insolent glance.

"One moment, Dauriat," said Lousteau. "I have brought this gentleman to you. Listen to me, while Finot is thinking over your proposals."

Lucien watched this Dauriat, who addressed Finot with the familiar *tu*, which even Finot did not permit himself to use in reply; who called the redoubtable Blondet "my boy," and extended a hand royally to Nathan with a friendly nod. The provincial poet felt his shirt wet with perspiration when the formidable sultan looked indifferent and ill-pleased.

"Another piece of business, my boy!" exclaimed Dauriat. "Why, I have eleven hundred manuscripts on hand, as you know! Yes, gentlemen, I have eleven hundred manuscripts submitted to me at this moment; ask Gabusson. I shall soon be obliged to start a department to keep account of the stock of manuscripts, and a special office for reading them, and a committee to vote on their merits, with numbered counters for those who attend, and a permanent secretary to draw up the minutes for me. It will be a kind of local branch of the Académie, and the académiciens will be better paid in the Wooden Galleries than at the Institute."

"'Tis an idea," said Blondet.

"A bad idea," returned Dauriat. "It is not my business to take stock of the lucubrations of those among you who take to literature because they cannot be capitalists, and there is no opening for them as bootmakers, nor corporals, nor domestic servants, nor officials, nor bailiffs. Nobody comes here until he has made a name for himself! Make a name for yourself and you will find gold in torrents. I have made three great men in the last two years; and lo and behold three examples of ingratitude! Here is Nathan talking of six thousand francs for the second edition of his book, which cost me three thousand francs in reviews and has not brought in a thousand yet. I paid a thousand francs for Blondet's two articles, beside a dinner, which cost me at least five hundred——"

"But if all booksellers talked as you do, sir, how could a man publish his first book at all?" asked Lucien. Blondet had gone down tremendously in his opinion since he had heard the amount given by Dauriat for the articles in the "Débats."

"That is not my affair," said Dauriat, looking daggers at this handsome young fellow, who was smiling pleasantly at him. "I do not publish books for amusement, nor risk two thousand francs for the sake of seeing my money back again. I speculate in literature, and publish forty volumes of ten thousand copies each, just as Panckouke does and the Baudoins. With my influence and the articles which I secure, I can push a business of a hundred thousand crowns, instead of a single volume involving a couple of thousand francs. It is just as much trouble to bring out a new name and to induce the public to take up an author and his book, as to make a success with the 'Théâtres étrangers, Victoires et Conquêtes,' or 'Mémoires sur la Révolution,' books that bring in a fortune. I am not here as a stepping-stone to future fame, but to make money and to find it for men with distinguished names. The manuscripts for which I give a hundred thousand francs pay me better than work by an unknown author who asks six hundred. If I am not exactly a Mæcenas, I deserve the gratitude of literature; I have doubled the prices of manuscripts. I am giving you this explanation because you are a friend of Lousteau's, my boy," added Dauriat, clapping Lucien on the shoulder with odious familiarity. "If I were to talk to all the authors who have a mind that I should be their publisher, I should have to shut up shop ; I should.pass my time very agreeably no doubt, but the conversations would cost too much. I am not rich enough yet to listen to all the monologues of self-conceit. Nobody does, except in classical tragedies on the stage."

The terrible Dauriat's gorgeous raiment seemed in the provincial poet's eyes to add force to the man's remorseless logic.

"What is it about?" he continued, addressing Lucien's protector.

"It is a volume of magnificent poetry."

At that word, Dauriat turned to Gabusson with a gesture worthy of Talma.

"Gabusson, my friend," he said, "from this day forward, when anybody begins to talk of works in manuscript here. Do you hear that, all of you?" he broke in upon himself; and three assistants at once emerged from among the piles of books at the sound of their employer's wrathful voice. "If anybody comes here with manuscripts," he continued, looking at the finger-nails of a well-kept hand, "ask him whether it is poetry or prose ; and if he says poetry, show him the door at once. Verses mean *re*verses in the booktrade."

"Bravo ! well put, Dauriat," cried the chorus of journalists.

"It is true !" cried the bookseller, striding about his shop with Lucien's manuscript in his hand. "You have no idea, gentlemen, of the amount of harm that Byron, Lamartine, Victor Hugo, Casimir Delavigne, Canalis, and Béranger have done by their success. The fame of them has brought down an invasion of barbarians upon us. I know *this:* there are a thousand volumes of manuscript poetry going the round of the publishers at this moment, things that nobody can make head or tail of, stories in verse that begin in the middle, like

'The Corsair' and 'Lara.'   They set up to be original,
forsooth, and indulge in stanzas that nobody can understand,
and descriptive poetry after the pattern of the younger men
who discovered Delille, and imagine that they are doing
something new.   Poets have been swarming like cockroaches
for two years past.   I have lost twenty thousand francs
through poetry in the last twelvemonth.   You ask Gabusson!
There may be immortal poets somewhere in the world; I
know of some that are blooming and rosy and have no beards
on their chins as yet," he continued, looking at Lucien; "but
in the trade, young man, there are only four poets—Béranger,
Casimir Delavigne, Lamartine, and Victor Hugo; as for
Canalis—he is a poet made by sheer force of writing him up."

Lucien felt that he lacked the courage to hold up his head
and show his spirit before all these influential persons, who
were laughing with all their might.   He knew very well that
he should look hopelessly ridiculous, and yet he felt consumed by a fierce desire to catch the bookseller by the throat,
to ruffle the insolent composure of his cravat, to break the
gold chain that glittered on the man's chest, trample his watch
under his feet, and tear him in pieces.   Mortified vanity
opened the door to thoughts of vengeance, and inwardly he
swore eternal enmity to that bookseller.   But he smiled
amiably.

" Poetry is like the sun," said Blondet, " giving life alike to
primeval forests and to ants and gnats and mosquitoes.   There
is no virtue but has a vice to match, and literature breeds the
publisher."

"And the journalist," said Lousteau.

Dauriat burst out laughing.

" What is this, after all ?" he asked, holding up the manuscript.

"A volume of sonnets that will put Petrarch to the blush,"
said Lousteau.

" What do you mean ?"

"Just what I say," answered Lousteau, seeing the knowing smile that went round the group. Lucien could not take offense, but he chafed inwardly.

"Very well, I will read them," said Dauriat, with a regal gesture that marked the full extent of the concession. "If these sonnets of yours are up to the level of the nineteenth century, I will make a great poet of you, my boy."

"If he has brains to equal his good looks, you will run no great risks," remarked one of the greatest public speakers of the day, a deputy who was chatting with the editor of the "Minerve," and a writer for the "Constitutionnel."

"Fame means twelve thousand francs in reviews, and a thousand more for dinners, general," said Dauriat. "If Monsieur Benjamin de Constant means to write a paper on this young poet, it will not be long before I make a bargain with him."

At the title of general and the distinguished name of Benjamin Constant, the bookseller's shop took the proportions of Olympus for the provincial great man.

"Lousteau, I want a word with you," said Finot; "but I shall see you again later, at the theatre. Dauriat, I will take your offer, but on conditions. Let us step into your office."

"Come in, my boy," answered Dauriat, allowing Finot to pass before him. Then, intimating to some ten persons still waiting for him that he was engaged, he likewise was about to disappear when Lucien impatiently stopped him.

"You are keeping my manuscript. When shall I have an answer?"

"Oh, come back in three or four days, my little poet, and we will see."

Lousteau hurried Lucien away; he had not time to take leave of Vernou and Blondet and Raoul Nathan, nor to salute General Foy nor Benjamin Constant, whose book on the Hundred Days was just about to appear. Lucien scarcely caught a glimpse of fair hair, a refined oval-shaped face, keen eyes, and the pleasant-looking mouth belonging to the man who had played the part of a Potemkin to Mme. de Staël for twenty years, and now was at war with the Bourbons, as he had been at war with Napoleon. He was destined to win his cause and to die stricken to earth by his victory.

" What a store ! " exclaimed Lucien, as he took his place in the cab beside Lousteau.

" To the Panorama-Dramatique ; look sharp, and you shall have thirty sous," Étienne Lousteau called to the cabman. " Dauriat is a rascal who sells books to the amount of fifteen or sixteen hundred thousand francs every year. He is a kind of minister of literature," Lousteau continued. His self-conceit had been pleasantly tickled, and he was showing off before Lucien. " Dauriat is just as grasping as Barbet, but it is on a wholesale scale. Dauriat can be civil and he is generous, but he has a great opinion of himself; as for his wit, it consists in a faculty for picking up all that he hears, and his shop is a capital place to frequent. You meet all the best men at Dauriat's. A young fellow learns more there in an hour than by poring over books for half-a-score of years. People talk over articles and concoct subjects ; you make the acquaintance of great or influential people who may be useful to you. You must know people if you mean to get on nowadays. It is all luck, you see. And as for sitting by yourself in a corner alone with your intellect, it is the most dangerous thing of all."

" But what insolence ! " said Lucien.

" Pshaw ! we all of us laugh at Dauriat," said Étienne. " If you are in need of him, he tramples upon you ; if he has need of the 'Journal des Débats,' Emile Blondet sets him spinning like a top. Oh, if you take to literature, you will see a good many queer things. Well, what was I telling you, eh ? "

" Yes, you were right," said Lucien. " My experience in

that store was even more painful than I expected, after your programme."

"Why do you choose to suffer? You find your subject, you wear out your wits over it with toiling at night, you throw your very life into it; and after all your journeyings in the fields of thought, the monument reared with your life-blood is simply a good or a bad speculation for a publisher. Your work will sell or it will not sell; and therein, for them, lies the whole question. A book means so much capital to risk, and, the better the book, the less likely it is to sell. A man of talent rises above the level of ordinary heads; his success varies in direct ratio with the time required for his work to be appreciated. And no publisher wants to wait. To-day's book must be sold by to-morrow. Acting on this system, publishers and booksellers do not care to take real literature, books that call for the high praise that comes slowly."

"D'Arthez was right," exclaimed Lucien.

"Do you know d'Arthez?" asked Lousteau. "I know of no more dangerous company than solitary spirits like that fellow yonder, who fancy that they can draw the world after them. All of us begin by thinking that we are capable of great things; and when once a youthful imagination is heated by this superstition, the candidate for posthumous honors makes no attempt to move the world while such moving of the world is both possible and profitable; he lets the time go by. I am for Mahomet's system—if the mountain does not come to me, I am for going to the mountain."

The commonsense so trenchantly put in this sally left Lucien halting between the resignation preached by the brother-hood and Lousteau's militant doctrine. He said not a word until they reached the Boulevard du Temple.

The Panorama-Dramatique no longer exists. A dwelling-house stands on the sight of the once charming theatre in the Boulevard du Temple, where two successive managements

collapsed without making a single hit; and yet Vignol, who
has since fallen heir to some of Potier's popularity, made his
début there ; and Florine, five years later a celebrated actress,
made her first appearance in the theatre opposite the Rue
Charlot.   Play-houses, like men, have their vicissitudes.
The Panorama-Dramatique suffered from competition.   The
machinations of its rivals, the Ambigu, the Gaité, the Porte
Saint-Martin, and the Vaudeville, together with a plethora of
restrictions and a scarcity of good plays, combined to bring
about the downfall of the house.   No dramatic author cared
to quarrel with a prosperous theatre for the sake of the Panorama-Dramatique, whose existence was, to say the least,
problematical.   The management at this moment, however,
was counting on the success of a new melodramatic comedy
by M. du Bruel, a young author who, after working in collaboration with divers celebrities, had now produced a piece
professedly entirely his own.   It had been specially composed
for the leading lady, a young actress who began her stage
career as a supernumerary at the Gaité, and had been pro-
moted to small parts for the last twelvemonth.   But though
Mlle. Florine's acting had attracted some attention she obtained no engagement, and the Panorama accordingly had
carried her off.   Coralie, another actress, was to make her
début at the same time.

Lucien was amazed at the power wielded by the press.
" This gentleman is with me," said Étienne Lousteau, and
the box-office clerks bowed before him as one man.

" You will find it no easy matter to get seats," said the
head clerk.   " There is nothing left now but the stage-box."

A certain amount of time was wasted in controversies, with
the box-keepers in the lobbies, when Étienne said, " Let us
go behind the scenes ; we will speak to the manager, he will
take us into the stage-box ; and, beside, I will introduce you
to Florine, the heroine of the evening."

At a sign from Étienne Lousteau, the doorkeeper of the

orchestra took out a little key and unlocked a door in the thickness of the wall. Lucien, following his friend, went suddenly out of the lighted corridor into the black darkness of the passage between the house and the wings. A short flight of damp steps surmounted, one of the strangest of all spectacles opened out before the provincial poet's eyes. The height of the roof, the slenderness of the props, the ladders hung with argand lamps, the atrocious ugliness of scenery beheld at close quarters, the thick paint on the actors' faces, and their outlandish costumes, made of such coarse materials, the stage carpenters in greasy jackets, the firemen, the stage-manager strutting about with his hat on his head, the supernumeraries sitting among the hanging back-scenes, the ropes and pulleys, the heterogeneous collection of absurdities, shabby, dirty, hideous, and gaudy, was something so altogether different from the stage seen over the footlights that Lucien's astonishment knew no bounds. The curtain was just about to fall on a good old-fashioned melodrama entitled "Bertram," a play adapted from a tragedy by Maturin which Charles Nodier, together with Byron and Sir Walter Scott, held in the highest esteem, though the play was a conspicuous failure on the stage in Paris.

"Keep a tight hold of my arm, unless you have a mind to fall through a trap-door or bring down a forest on your head ; you will pull down a palace, or carry off a cottage, if you are not careful," said Étienne. "Is Florine in her dressing-room, my pet?" he added, addressing an actress who stood waiting for her cue.

"Yes, love. Thank you for the things you said about me. You are much nicer since Florine has come here."

"Come, don't spoil your entry, little one. Quick with you, look sharp, and say, 'Stop, wretched man !' nicely, for there are two thousand francs of takings."

Lucien was struck with amazement when the girl's whole face suddenly changed, and she shrieked, "Stop, wretched man ! '' a cry that froze the blood in your veins. She was no longer the same creature.

" So this is the stage," he said to Lousteau.

" It is like the bookseller's store in the Wooden Galleries, or a literary paper," said Étienne Lousteau; "it is a kitchen, neither more nor less."

Nathan appeared at this moment.

" What brings you here ? " inquired Lousteau.

"Why, I am doing the minor theatres for the ' Gazette ' until something better turns up."

" Oh ! come to supper with us this evening ; speak well of Florine, and I will do as much for you."

" Very much at your service," returned Nathan.

" You know ; she is living in the Rue du Bondy now," added Étienne.

" Lousteau, dear boy, who is the handsome young man that you have brought with you ? " asked the actress, now returned to the wings.

"A great poet, dear, that will have a famous name one of these days. Monsieur Nathan, I must introduce Monsieur Lucien de Rubempré to you, as your are to meet again at supper."

" You have a good name, monsieur," said Nathan.

" Lucien, Monsieur Raoul Nathan," continued Étienne.

" I read your book two days ago ; and, upon my word, I cannot understand how you, who have written such a book, and such poetry, can be so humble to a journalist."

" Wait until your first book comes out," said Nathan, and a shrewd smile flitted over his face.

" I say ! I say ! here are Ultras and Liberals actually shaking hands ! " cried Vernou, spying the trio.

"In the morning I hold the views of my paper," said Nathan ; " in the evening I think as I please ; all journalists see double at night."

Félicien Vernou turned to Lousteau.

"Finot is looking for you, Étienne ; he came with me, and —here he is."

"Ah, by-the-by, there is not a place in the house, is there ?" asked Finot.

"You will always find a place in our hearts," said the actress, with the sweetest smile imaginable.

"I say, my little Florville, are you cured already of your fancy? They told me that a Russian prince had carried you off."

"Who carries off women in these days?" said Florville (she who had cried, "Stop, wretched man ! ") "We stayed at Saint-Mandé for ten days, and my prince got off with paying the forfeit-money to the management. The manager will go down on his knees to pray for some more Russian princes," Florville continued, laughing; "the forfeit-money was so much clear gain."

"And as for you, child," said Finot, turning to a pretty girl in a peasant's costume, "where did you steal these diamond ear-drops? Have you hooked an Indian prince?"

"No, a blacking manufacturer, an Englishman, who has gone off already. It is not everybody who can find millionaire storekeepers, tired of domestic life, whenever they like, as Florine does and Coralie. Aren't they just lucky?"

"Florville, you will make a bad entry," said Lousteau; "the blacking has gone to your head ! "

"If you want a success," said Nathan, "instead of screaming, 'He is saved ! ' like a Fury, walk on quite quietly, go to the staircase, and say, 'He is saved,' in a chest voice, like Pasta's 'O patria' in 'Tancredi.' There, go along !" and he pushed her toward the stage.

"It is too late," said Vernou, "the effect has hung fire."

"What did she do? the house is applauding like mad," asked Lousteau.

"Went down on her knees and showed her bosom; that is her great resource," said the blacking-maker's widow.

10

"The manager is giving up the stage-box to us; you will find me there when you come," said Finot, as Lousteau walked off with Lucien.

At the back of the stage, through a labyrinth of scenery and corridors, the pair climbed several flights of stairs and reached a little room on a third floor, Nathan and Félicien Vernou following them.

"Good-day or good-night, gentlemen," said Florine. Then, turning to a short, stout man standing in a corner, "These gentlemen are the rulers of my destiny," she said, "my future is in their hands; but they will be under our table to-morrow morning, I hope, if Monsieur Lousteau has forgotten nothing——"

"Forgotten! You are going to have Blondet of the 'Débats,'" said Étienne, "the genuine Blondet, the very Blondet—Blondet himself, in short."

"Oh! Lousteau, you dear boy! stop, I must give you a kiss," and she flung her arms about the journalist's neck. Matifat, the stout person in the corner, looked serious at this.

Florine was thin; her beauty, like a bud, gave promise of the flower to come; the girl of sixteen could only delight the eyes of artists who prefer the sketch to the picture. All the quick subtlety of her character was visible in the features of the charming actress, who at that time might have sat for Goethe's Mignon. Matifat, a wealthy druggist of the Rue des Lombards, had imagined that a little boulevard actress would have no very expensive tastes, but in eleven months Florine had cost him sixty thousand francs. Nothing seemed more extraordinary to Lucien than the sight of an honest and worthy merchant standing like a statue of the god Terminus in the actress' narrow dressing-room, a tiny place some ten feet square, hung with a pretty wall-paper, and adorned with a full-length mirror, a sofa, and two chairs. There was a fire-place in the dressing-closet, a carpet on the floor, and cup-boards all round the room. A dresser was putting the finishing touches to a Spanish costume; for Florine was to take the part of a countess in an imbroglio.

"That girl will be the handsomest actress in Paris in five years' time," said Nathan, turning to Félicien Vernou.

"By-the-by, darlings, you will take care of me to-morrow, won't you?" said Florine, turning to the three journalists. "I have engaged cabs for to-night, for I am going to send you home as tipsy as Shrove Tuesday. Matifat has sent in wines—oh! wines worthy of Louis XVIII., and engaged the Prussian ambassador's cook."

"We expect something enormous from the look of the gentleman," remarked Nathan.

"And he is quite aware that he is treating the most dangerous men in Paris," added Florine.

Matifat was looking uneasily at Lucien; he felt jealous of the young man's good looks.

"But here is some one that I do not know," Florine continued, confronting Lucien. "Which of you has imported the Apollo Belvedere from Florence? He is as charming as one of Girodet's figures."

"He is a poet, mademoiselle, from the provinces. I forgot to present him to you; you are so beautiful to-night that you put the 'Complete Guide to Etiquette' out of a man's head——"

"Is he so rich that he can afford to write poetry?" asked Florine.

"Poor as Job," said Lucien.

"It is a great temptation for some of us," said the actress.

Just then the author of the play suddenly entered, and Lucien beheld Monsieur du Bruel, a short, attenuated young man in an overcoat, a composite human blend of the jack-in-office, the owner of house property, and the stockbroker.

"Florine, child," said this personage, "are you sure of your part, eh? No slips of memory, you know. And mind that scene in the second act, make the irony tell, bring out that subtle touch; say 'I do not love you' just as we agreed."

"Why do you take parts in which you have to say such things?" asked Matifat.

The druggist's remark was received with a general shout of laughter.

"What does it matter to you," said Florine, "so long as I don't say such things to you, great stupid? Oh! his stupidity is the pleasure of my life," she continued, glancing at the journalists. "Upon my word, I would pay him so much for every blunder, if it would not be the ruin of me."

"Yes, but you will look at me when you say it, as you do when you are rehearsing, and it gives me a turn," remonstrated the druggist.

"Very well, then, I will look at my friend Lousteau here."

A bell rang outside in the passage.

"Go out, all of you!" cried Florine; "let me read my part over again and try to understand it."

Lucien and Lousteau were the last to go. Lousteau set a kiss on Florine's shoulder, and Lucien heard her say, "Not to-night. Impossible. That stupid old animal told his wife that he was going out into the country."

"Isn't she very charming?" said Étienne, as they came away.

"But—but that Matifat, my dear fellow——"

"Oh! you know nothing of Parisian life, my boy. Some things cannot be helped. Suppose that you fell in love with a married woman, it comes to the same thing. It all depends on the way that you look at it."

Étienne and Lucien entered the stage-box and found the manager there with Finot. Matifat was in the first-floor box exactly opposite with a friend of his, a silk mercer named Camusot (Coralie's protector), and a worthy little old soul, his father-in-law. All three of these city men were polishing their opera-glasses, and anxiously scanning the house ; certain symptoms in the pit appeared to disturb them. The usual heterogeneous first-night elements filled the boxes—journalists and their mistresses, lorettes and their lovers, a sprinkling of the determined play-goers who never miss a first night if they can help it, and a very few people of fashion who care for this sort of sensation. The first box was occupied by the head of a department, to whom du Bruel, maker of vaude-villes, owed a snug little sinecure in the treasury.

Lucien had gone from surprise to surprise since the dinner at Flicoteaux's. For two months literature had meant a life of poverty and want ; in Lousteau's room he had seen it at its cynical worst ; in the Wooden Galleries he had met literature abject and literature insolent. The sharp contrasts of heights and depths; of compromise with conscience; of supreme power and want of principle ; of treachery and pleasure ; of mental elevation and bondage—all this made his head swim, he seemed to be watching some strange, unheard-of drama.

Finot was talking with the manager. "Do you think du Bruel's piece will pay?" he asked.

"Du Bruel has tried to do something in Beaumarchais' style. Boulevard audiences don't care for that kind of thing ; they like harrowing sensations; wit is not much appreciated here. Everything depends on Florine and Coralie to-night ; they are bewitchingly pretty and graceful, wear very short skirts, and dance a Spanish dance, and possibly they may carry off the piece with the public. The whole affair is a gambling speculation. A few clever notices in the papers and I may make a hundred thousand crowns, if the play takes."

"Oh ! come, it will only be a moderate success, I can see," said Finot.

"Three of the theatres have hatched a plot," continued the manager ; "they will even hiss the piece, but I have made arrangements to defeat their kind intentions. I have squared the men in their pay; they will make a muddle of it. A couple of city men yonder have taken a hundred tickets apiece to secure a triumph for Florine and Coralie and given them to acquaintances able and ready to act as chuckers out. The fellows, having been paid twice, will go quietly, and a scene of that sort always makes a good impression on the house.''

'' Two hundred tickets! What invaluable men!'' exclaimed Finot.

'' Yes. With two more actresses as handsomely kept as Florine and Coralie, I should make something out of the business.''

For the past two hours the word money had been sounding in Lucien's ears as the solution of every difficulty. In the theatre as in the publishing trade, and in the publishing trade as in the newspaper-office—it was everywhere the same; there was not a word of art or of glory. The steady beat of the great pendulum, Money, seemed to fall like hammer-strokes on his heart and brain. And yet while the orchestra played the overture, while the pit was full of noisy tumult of applause and hisses, unconsciously he drew a comparison between this scene and others that came up in his mind. Visions arose before him of David and the printing-office, of the poetry that he came to know in that atmosphere of pure peace, when together they beheld the wonders of art, the high successes of genius, and visions of glory borne on stainless wings. He thought of the evenings spent with d'Arthez and his friends and tears glittered in his eyes.

'' What is the matter with you?'' asked Étienne Lousteau.

'' I see poetry fallen into the mire.''

'' Ah! you have still some illusions left, my dear fellow.''

'' Is there nothing for it but to cringe and submit to thickheads like Matifat and Camusot, as actresses bow down to journalists and we ourselves to the booksellers?''

'' My boy, do you see that dull-brained fellow?'' asked

Étienne, lowering his voice, and glancing at Finot. "He has neither genius nor cleverness, but he is covetous; he means to make a fortune at all costs, and he is a keen man of business. Didn't you see how he made forty per cent. out of me at Dauriat's, and talked as if he were doing me a favor? Well, he gets letters from not a few unknown men of genius who go down on their knees to him for a hundred francs."

The words recalled the pen-and-ink sketch that lay on the table in the editor's office and the words, "Finot, my hundred francs!" Lucien's inmost soul shrank from the man in disgust.

"I would sooner die," he said.

"Sooner live," retorted Étienne.

The curtain rose, and the stage-manager went off to the wings to give orders. Finot turned to Étienne.

"My dear fellow, Dauriat has passed his word; I am proprietor of one-third of his weekly paper. I have agreed to give thirty thousand francs in cash, on condition that I am to be editor and director. 'Tis a splendid thing. Blondet told me that the government intends to take restrictive measures against the press; there will be no new papers allowed; in six months' time it will cost a million francs to start a new journal, so I struck the bargain though I have only ten thousand francs in hand. Listen to me. If you can sell one-half of my share, that is one-sixth of the paper, to Matifat for thirty thousand francs, you shall be editor of my little paper with a salary of two hundred and fifty francs per month. I want, in any case, to have the control of my old paper and to keep my hold upon it; but nobody need know that, and your name will appear as editor. You will be paid at the rate of five francs per column; you need not pay contributors more than three francs, and you keep the difference. That means another four hundred and fifty francs per month. But, at the same time, I reserve the right to use the paper to

attack or defend men or causes, as I please; and you may indulge your own likes and dislikes so long as you do not in-
terfere with my schemes.   Perhaps I may be a Ministerialist,
perhaps Ultra, I do not know yet; but I mean to keep up my
connection with the Liberal party (below the surface).   I can
speak out with you; you are a good fellow.   I might, perhaps,
give you the Chambers to do for another paper on which I
work; I am afraid I can scarcely keep on with it now.   So let
Florine do this bit of jockeying; tell her to put the screw on
her druggist.   If I can't find the money within forty-eight
hours I must cry off my bargain.   Dauriat sold another third
to his printer and paper-dealer for thirty thousand francs; so
he has his own third *gratis*, and ten thousand francs to the
good, for he only gave fifty thousand for the whole affair.
And in another year's time the magazine will be worth two
hundred thousand francs, if the court buys it up; if the
court has the good sense to suppress newspapers, as they say."

"You are lucky," said Lousteau.

"If you had gone through all that I have endured, you
would not say that of me.   I had my fill of misery in those
days, you see, and there was no help for it.   My father is a
hatter; he still keeps a shop in the Rue de Coq.   Nothing
but millions of money or a social cataclysm can open out the
way to my goal; and of the two alternatives, I don't know
now that the revolution is not the easier.   If I bore your
friend's name, I should have a chance to get on.   Hush, here
comes the manager.   Good-by," and Finot rose to his feet.
"I am going to the opera.   I shall very likely have a duel
on my hands to-morrow, for I have put my initials to a terrific
attack on a couple of dancers under the protection of two
generals.   I am giving it them hot and strong at the opera."

"Aha?" said the manager.

"Yes.   They are stingy with me," returned Finot, "now
cutting off a box and now declining to take fifty subscriptions.
I have sent in my ultimatum; I mean to have a hundred sub-

scriptions out of them and a box four times a month. If they take my terms, I shall have eight hundred readers and a thousand paying subscribers; and I know a way of getting another two hundred subscribers, so we shall have twelve hundred with the New Year."

"You will end by ruining us," said the manager.

"*You* are not much hurt with your ten subscriptions. I had two good notices put in the ' Constitutionnel.' "

" Oh! I am not complaining of you," cried the obsequious manager.

" Good-by till to-morrow evening, Lousteau," said Finot. " You can give me your answer at the Français; there is a new piece on there; and as I shall not be able to write the notice, you can take my box. I will give you the preference; you have worked yourself to death for me, and I am grateful. Félicien Vernou offered twenty thousand francs for a third share of my little paper, and to work without salary for a twelvemonth; but I want to be absolute master. Good-by."

" He is not named Finot" (*finaud*, slyboots) " for nothing," said Lucien.

" He is a gallows-bird that will get on in the world," said Étienne, careless whether the wily schemer overheard the remark or not, as he shut the door of the box.

" *He!* " said the manager. " He will be a millionaire; he will enjoy the respect of all who know him; he may, perhaps, have friends some day——"

" Good heavens! what a den!" said Lucien. " And are you going to drag that exquisite creature into such a business?" he continued, looking at Florine, who gave them side-glances from the stage.

" She will carry it through too. You do not know the devotion and the wiles of these beloved beings," said Lousteau.

" They redeem their failings and expiate all their sins by boundless love, when they love," said the manager. " A great

love is all the grander in an actress by reason of its violent
contrast with her surroundings.''

''And he who finds it, finds a diamond worthy of the
proudest crown lying in the mud,'' returned Lousteau.

'' But Coralie is not attending to her part,'' remarked the
manager. '' Coralie is smitten with our friend here, all unsuspicious of his conquest, and Coralie will make a *fiasco;*
she is missing her cues, this is the second time she has not
heard the prompter. Pray go into the corner, monsieur,'' he
continued. ''If Coralie is smitten with you, I will go and
tell her that you have left the house.''

'' No! no!'' cried Lousteau; ''tell Coralie that this gentleman is coming to supper and that she can do as she likes
with him, and she will play like Mademoiselle Mars.''

The manager went, and Lucien turned to Étienne. ''What!
do you mean to say that you will ask that druggist, through
Mademoiselle Florine, to pay thirty thousand francs for one-
half a share, when Finot gave no more for the whole of it?
and ask without the slightest scruple?——''

Lousteau interrupted Lucien before he had time to finish
his expostulation. '' My dear boy, what country can you
come from? The druggist is not a man; he is a strong box
delivered into our hands by his fancy for an actress.''

'' How about your conscience?''

'' Conscience, my dear fellow, is a stick which every one
takes up to beat his neighbor and not for application to his
own back. Come, now, who the devil are you angry
with? In one day chance has worked a miracle for you, a
miracle for which I have been waiting these two years, and
you must needs amuse yourself by finding fault with the
means? What! you appear to me to possess intelligence;
you seem to be in a fair way to reach that freedom from prej-
udice which is a first necessity to intellectual adventurers in
the world we live in; and are you wallowing in scruples
worthy of a nun who accuses herself of eating an egg with

concupiscence? If Florine succeeds, I shall be editor of a newspaper with a fixed salary of two hundred and fifty francs per month; I shall take the important plays and leave the vaudevilles to Vernou, and you can take my place and do the boulevard theatres, and so get a foot in the stirrup. You will make three francs per column and write a column a day— thirty columns a month means ninety francs; you will have some sixty francs' worth of books to sell to Barbet; and, lastly, you can demand ten tickets a month of each of your theatres—that is, forty tickets in all—and sell them for forty francs to a Barbet who deals in them (I will introduce you to the man), so you will have two hundred francs coming in every month. Then if you make yourself useful to Finot, you might get a hundred francs for an article in this new weekly review of his, in which case you should show uncommon talent, for all the articles are signed, and you cannot put in slipshod work as you can on a small paper. In that case you would be making a hundred crowns a month. Now, my dear boy, there are men of ability, like that poor d'Arthez, who dines at Flicoteaux's every day, who may wait for ten years before they will make a hundred crowns; and you will be making four thousand francs a year by your pen, to say nothing of the books you will write for the trade, if you do work of that kind.

" Now, a sub-prefect's salary only amounts to a thousand crowns, and there he stops in his arrondissement, wearing away time like the rung of a chair. I say nothing of the pleasure of going to the theatre without paying for your seat, for that is a delight which quickly palls; but you can go behind the scenes in four theatres. Be hard and sarcastic for a month or two, and you will be simply overwhelmed with invitations from actresses and their adorers will pay court to you; you will only dine at Flicoteaux's when you happen to have less than thirty sous in your pocket and no dinner engagement. At the Luxembourg, at five o'clock, you did not know which

way to turn ; now, you are on the eve of entering a privileged
class, you will be one of the hundred persons who tell France
what to think.　In three days' time, if all goes well, you can,
if you choose, make a man's life a curse to him by putting
thirty jokes at his expense in print at the rate of three a day ;
you can, if you choose, draw a revenue of pleasure from the
actresses at your theatres ; you can wreck a good play and
send all Paris running after a bad one.　If Dauriat declines to
pay you for your ' Marguerites,' you can make him come to
you, and meekly and humbly implore you to take two thousand francs for them.　If you have the ability and knock off
two or three articles that threaten to spoil some of Dauriat's
speculations, or to ruin a book on which he counts, you will
see him come climbing up your stairs like a clematis, and
always at the door of your dwelling.　As for your novel, the
booksellers who would show you more or less politely to the
door at this moment will be standing outside your attic in a
string, and the value of the manuscript, which old Doguereau
valued at four hundred francs, will rise to four thousand.
These are the advantages of the journalist's profession.　So
let us do our best to keep all new-comers out of it.　It needs
an immense amount of brains to make your way and a still
greater amount of luck.　And here are you quibbling over
your good fortune !　If we had not met to-day, you see, at
Flicoteaux's, you might have danced attendance on the booksellers for another three years, or starved like d'Arthez in a
garret.　By the time that d'Arthez is as learned as Bayle and
as great a writer of prose as Rousseau, we shall have made
our fortunes, you and I, and we shall hold his in our hands—
wealth and fame to give or to hold.　Finot will be a deputy
and proprietor of a great newspaper, and we shall be whatever we meant to be—peers of France, or prisoners for debt
in Sainte-Pélagie."

" So Finot will sell his paper to the highest bidder among
the ministers, just as he sells favorable notices to Madame

Bastienne and runs down Mademoiselle Virginie, saying that
Madame Bastienne's bonnets are superior to the millinery
which they praised at first ! " said Lucien, recollecting that,
to him, astonishing and laughable scene in the office when he
was awaiting Finot.

" My dear fellow, you are a simpleton," Lousteau remarked
drily. "Three years ago Finot was walking on the uppers
of his boots, dining for eighteen sous at Tabar's, and knocking
off a tradesman's prospectus (when he could get it) for ten
francs. His clothes hung together by some miracle as mysterious as the Immaculate Conception. *Now*, Finot has a
paper of his own, worth about a hundred thousand francs.
What with subscribers who pay and take no copies, genuine
subscriptions, and indirect taxes levied by his uncle, he is
making twenty thousand francs a year. He dines most sumptuously every day; he has set up a cabriolet within the last
month ; and now, at last, behold him the editor of a weekly
review with a sixth share, for which he will not pay one
penny, a salary of five hundred francs per month, and another
thousand francs for supplying matter which costs him nothing
and for which the firm pays. You yourself, to begin with, if
Finot consents to pay you fifty francs per sheet, will be only
too glad to let him have two or three articles for nothing.
When you are in his position, you can judge Finot ; a man
can only be tried by his peers. And for you, is there not an
immense future opening out before you if you will blindly
minister to his enmity, attack at Finot's bidding, and praise
when he gives the word ? Suppose that you yourself wish to
be revenged upon somebody, you can break a foe or friend
on the wheel. You have only to say to me, ' Lousteau, let us
put an end to So-and-so,' and we will kill him by a phrase
put in the paper morning by morning ; and afterward you
can slay the slain with a solemn article in Finot's weekly.
Indeed, if it is a matter of capital importance to you, Finot
would allow you to bludgeon your man in a big paper with

ten or twelve thousand subscribers, *if* you make yourself indispensable to Finot."

"Then are you sure that Florine can bring her druggist to make the bargain?" asked Lucien, dazzled by these prospects.

"Quite sure. Now comes the interval, I will go and tell her everything at once in a word or two; it will be settled to-night. If Florine once has her lesson by heart, she will have all my wit and her own beside."

"And there sits that honest tradesman, gaping with open-mouthed admiration at Florine, little suspecting that you are about to get thirty thousand francs out of him!——"

"More twaddle! Anybody might think that the man was going to be robbed!" cried Lousteau. "Why, my dear boy, if the Minister buys the newspaper, the druggist may make twenty thousand francs in six months on an investment of thirty thousand. Matifat is not looking at the newspaper, but at Florine's prospects. As soon as it is known that Matifat and Camusot—(for they will go shares)—that Matifat and Camusot are proprietors of a review, the newspapers will be full of friendly notices of Florine and Coralie. Florine's name will be made; she will perhaps obtain an engagement in another theatre with a salary of twelve thousand francs. In fact, Matifat will save a thousand francs every month in dinners and presents to journalists. You know nothing of men nor of the way things are managed."

"Poor man!" said Lucien, "he is looking forward to an evening's pleasure."

"And he will be sawn in two with arguments until Florine sees Finot's receipt for a sixth share of the paper. And to-morrow I shall be editor of Finot's paper, and making a thousand francs a month. The end of my troubles is in sight!" cried Florine's lover.

Lousteau went out and Lucien sat like one bewildered, lost

in the infinite of thought, soaring above this every-day world. In the Wooden Galleries he had seen the wires by which the trade in books is moved; he had seen something of the kitchen where great reputations are made; he had been behind the scenes; he had seen the seamy side of life, the consciences of men involved in the machinery of Paris, the mechanism of it all. As he watched Florine on the stage he almost envied Lousteau his good fortune; already, for a few moments, he had forgotten Matifat in the background. He was not left alone for long, perhaps for not more than five minutes, but those minutes seemed an eternity.

Thoughts rose within him that set his soul on fire, as the spectacle on the stage had heated his senses. He looked at the women with their wanton eyes, all the brighter for the red paint on their cheeks, at the gleaming bare necks, the luxuriant forms outlined by the lascivious folds of the basquina, the very short skirts, that displayed as much as possible of limbs encased in scarlet stockings with green clocks to them—a disquieting vision for the pit.

A double process of corruption was working within him in parallel lines, like two channels that will spread sooner or later in flood-time and make one. That corruption was eating into Lucien's soul, as he leaned back in his corner, staring vacantly at the curtain, one arm resting on the crimson velvet cushion and his hand drooping over the edge. He felt the fascination of the life that was offered to him, of the gleams of light among its clouds; and this so much the more keenly because it shone out like a blaze of fireworks against the blank darkness of his own obscure, monotonous days of toil.

Suddenly his listless eyes became aware of a burning glance that reached him through a rent in the curtain, and roused him from his lethargy. Those were Coralie's eyes that glowed upon him. He lowered his head and looked across at Camusot, who just then entered the opposite box.

That amateur was a worthy silk-mercer of the Rue des

Bourdonnais, stout and substantial, a judge in the commercial court, a father of four children, and the husband of a second wife. At the age of fifty-six, with a cap of gray hair on his head, he had the smug appearance of a man who has his eighty thousand francs of income; and having been forced to put up with a good deal that he did not like in the way of business, has fully made up his mind to enjoy the rest of life, and not to quit this earth until he has had his share of cakes and ale. A brow the color of fresh butter and florid cheeks like a monk's jowl seemed scarcely big enough to contain his exuberant jubilation. Camusot had left his wife at home, and they were applauding Coralie to the skies! All the rich man's citizen-vanity was summed up and gratified in Coralie; in Coralie's lodging he gave himself the airs of a great lord of a bygone day; now, at this moment, he felt that half of her success was his; the knowledge that he had paid for it confirmed him in this idea. Camusot's conduct was sanctioned by the presence of his father-in-law, a little old fogey with powdered hair and leering eyes, highly respected nevertheless.

Again Lucien felt disgust rising within him. He thought of the year when he loved Mme. de Bargeton with an exalted and disinterested love; and at that thought love, as a poet understands it, spread its white wings about him; countless memories drew a circle of distant blue horizon about the great man of Angoulême, and again he fell to dreaming.

Up went the curtain, and there stood Coralie and Florine upon the stage.

"He is thinking about as much of you as of the Grand Turk, my dear girl," Florine said in an aside while Coralie was finishing her speech.

Lucien could not help laughing. He looked at Coralie. She was one of the most charming and captivating actresses in Paris, rivaling Mme. Perrin and Mlle. Fleuriet, and destined likewise to share their fate. Coralie was a woman of a type that exerts at will a power of fascination over men. With an oval face of deep ivory tint, a mouth red as a pomegranate, and a chin subtly delicate in its contour as the edge of a porcelain cup, Coralie was a Jewess of the sublime type. The jet black eyes behind their curving lashes seemed to scorch her eyelids; you could guess how soft they might grow, or how sparks of the heat of the desert might flash from them in response to a summons from within. The circles of olive shadow about them were bounded by thick arching lines of eyebrow. Magnificent mental power, well-nigh amounting to genius, seemed to dwell in the swarthy forehead beneath the double curve of ebony hair that lay upon it like a crown, and gleamed in the light like a varnished surface; but, like many another actress, Coralie had little wit in spite of her aptness at green-room repartee and scarcely any education in spite of her boudoir experience. Her brain was prompted by her senses, her kindness was the impulsive warm-heartedness of girls of her class. But who could trouble over Coralie's psychology when his eyes were dazzled by those smooth, round arms of hers, the spindle-shaped fingers, the fair, white shoulders, and breast celebrated in the Song of Songs, the flexible curving lines of throat, the graciously moulded outlines beneath the scarlet silk stockings? And this beauty, worthy of an Eastern poet, was brought into relief by the conventional Spanish costume of the stage. Coralie was the delight of the pit; all eyes dwelt on the outlines moulded by the clinging folds of her bodice, and lingered over the Andalusian contour of the hips from which her skirt hung, fluttering wantonly with every movement. To Lucien, watching this creature, who played for him alone, caring no more for Camusot than a street-boy in the gallery cares for an apple-paring, there came a moment when he set desire above love, and enjoyment above desire, and the demon of lust stirred strange thoughts in him.

"I know nothing of the love that wallows in luxury and

11

wine and sensual pleasure," he said within himself. " I have
lived more with ideas than with realities. You must pass
through all experience if you mean to render all experience.
This will be my first great supper, my first orgie in a new and
strange world; why should I not know, for once, the delights
which the great lords of the eighteenth century sought so
eagerly of wantons of the opera?   Must one not first learn of
courtesans and actresses the delights, the perfections, the
transports, the resources, the subtleties of love, if only to
translate them afterward into the regions of a higher love
than this?   And what is all this, after all, but the poetry of
the senses?   Two months ago these women seemed to me to
be goddesses guarded by dragons that no one dared approach ;
I was envying Lousteau just now, but here is another handsomer than Florine; why should I not profit by her fancy,
when the greatest nobles buy a night with such women with
their richest treasures?   When ambassadors set foot in these
depths they fling aside all thought of yesterday or to-morrow.
I should be a fool to be more squeamish than princes, especially as I love no one as yet."

Lucien had quite forgotten Camusot.   To Lousteau he had
expressed the utmost disgust for this most hateful of all parti-
tions, and now he himself had sunk to the same level, and,
carried away by the casuistry of his vehement desire, had
given the reins to his fancy.

" Coralie is raving about you," said Lousteau as he came
in.   " Your countenance, worthy of the greatest Greek sculp-
tors, has worked unutterable havoc behind the scenes.   You
are in luck, my dear boy.   Coralie is eighteen years old, and
in a few days' time she may be making sixty thousand francs
a year by her beauty.   She is an honest girl still.   Since her
mother sold her three years ago for sixty thousand francs, she
has tried to find happiness and found nothing but annoyance.
She took to the stage in a desperate mood ; she has a horror
of her first purchaser, de Marsay ; and when she came out of

the galleys, for the King of dandies soon dropped her, she picked up old Camusot. She does not care much about him, but he is like a father to her, and she endures him and his love. Several times already she has refused the handsomest proposals; she is faithful to Camusot, who lets her live in peace. So you are her first love. The first sight of you went to her heart like a pistol-shot, Florine has gone to her dressing-room to bring the girl to reason. She is crying over your cruelty; she has forgotten her part, the play will go to pieces, then good-day to the engagement at the Gymnase which Camusot had planned for her."

"Pooh! Poor thing!" said Lucien. Every instinct of vanity was tickled by the words; he felt his heart swell high with self-conceit. "More adventures have befallen me this one evening, my dear fellow, than in all the first eighteen years of my life." And Lucien related the history of his love affairs with Mme. de Bargeton, and of the cordial hatred he bore the Baron du Châtelet.

"Stay though! the newspaper wants a *bête noire* (wild boar); we will take him up. The Baron is a buck of the Empire and a Ministerialist; he is the man for us; I have seen him many a time at the opera. I can see your great lady as I sit here; she is often in the Marquise d'Espard's box. The Baron is paying court to your lady-love, a cuttlefish bone that she is. Wait! Finot has just sent a special messenger round to say that they are short of copy at the office. Young Hector Merlin has left them in the lurch because they did not pay for white lines. Finot, in despair, is knocking off an article against the opera. Well now, my dear fellow, you can do this play; listen to it and think it over, and I will go to the manager's office and think out three columns about your man and your disdainful fair one. They will be in no pleasant predicament to-morrow."

"So this is how a newspaper is written?" said Lucien.

"It is always like this," answered Lousteau. "These ten

months that I have been a journalist, they have always run
short of copy at eight o'clock in the evening."

Manuscript sent to the printer is spoken of as "copy,"
doubtless because the writers are supposed to send in a fair
copy of their work ; or possibly the word is ironically derived
from the Latin word *copia*, for copy is invariably scarce.

"We always mean to have a few numbers ready in advance,
a grand idea that will never be realized," continued Lousteau.
"It is ten o'clock, you see, and not a line has been written.
I shall ask Vernou and Nathan for a score of epigrams on
deputies, or on 'Chancellor Cruzoé,' or on the Ministry, or
on friends of ours if it needs must be. A man in this pass
would slaughter his parent, just as a privateer will load his
guns with silver pieces taken out of the booty sooner than
perish. Write a brilliant article, and you will make brilliant
progress in Finot's estimation ; for Finot has a lively sense of
benefits to come, and that sort of gratitude is better than any
kind of pledge, pawntickets always excepted, for they invariably represent something solid."

"What kind of men can journalists be? Are you to sit
down at a table and be witty to order?"

"Just exactly as a lamp begins to burn when you apply a
match—so long as there is any oil in it."

Lousteau's hand was on the lock when du Bruel came in
with the manager.

"Permit me, monsieur, to take a message to Coralie ; allow
me to tell her that you will go home with her after supper, or
my play will be ruined. The wretched girl does not know
what she is doing or saying ; she will cry when she ought to
laugh, and laugh when she ought to cry. She has been hissed
once already. You can still save the piece, and, after all,
pleasure is not a misfortune."

"I am not accustomed to rivals, sir," Lucien answered.

"Pray don't tell her that !" cried the manager. "Coralie
is just the girl to fling Camusot overboard and ruin herself in

good earnest. The proprietor of the ' Golden Cocoon,' worthy man, allows her two thousand francs a month and pays for all her dresses and her *claqueurs* " (paid applauders).

" As your promise pledges me to nothing, save your play," said Lucien, with a sultan's airs.

"But don't look as if you meant to snub that charming creature," pleaded du Bruel.

" Dear me ! am I to write the notice of your play and smile on your heroine as well ? " exclaimed the poet.

The author vanished with a signal to Coralie, who began to act forthwith in a marvelous way. Vignol, who played the part of the alcalde, and revealed for the first time his genius as an actor of old men, came forward amid a storm of applause to make an announcement to the house.

" The piece which we have the honor of playing for you this evening, gentlemen, is the work of Messieurs Raoul and de Cursy."

"Why, Nathan is partly responsible," said Lousteau. " I don't wonder that he looked in."

"*Coralie ! Coralie !* " loudly shouted the enraptured house. " Florine, too ! " roared a voice of thunder from the opposite box, and then other voices took up the cry, " Florine and Coralie ! "

The curtain rose and Vignol reappeared between the two actresses ; Matifat and Camusot flung wreaths on the stage, and Coralie stooped for her flowers and held them out to Lucien.

For him those two hours spent in the theatre seemed to be a dream. The spell that held him had begun to work when he went behind the scenes ; and, in spite of its horrors, the atmosphere of the place, its sensuality and dissolute morals had affected the poet's still untainted nature. A sort of malaria that infects the soul seems to lurk among those dark, filthy passages filled with machinery, and lit with smoky, greasy lamps. The solemnity and reality of life disappear,

the most sacred things are matter for a jest, the most impossible things seem to be true.   Lucien felt as if he had taken
some narcotic, and Coralie had completed the work.   He
plunged into this joyous intoxication.

The lights in the great chandelier were extinguished; there
was no one left in the house except the boxkeepers, busy taking away footstools and shutting doors, the noises echoing
strangely through the empty theatre.   The footlights, blown
out as one candle, sent up a fetid reek of smoke.   The curtain rose again, a lantern was lowered from the ceiling, and
firemen and stage carpenters departed on their rounds.   The
fairy scenes of the stage, the rows of fair faces in the boxes,
the dazzling lights, the magical illusion of new scenery and
costume had all disappeared, and dismal darkness, emptiness,
and cold reigned in their stead.   It was hideous.   Lucien sat
on in bewilderment.

"Well! are you coming, my boy?" Lousteau's voice
called from the stage.   "Jump down."

Lucien sprang over.   He scarcely recognized Florine and
Coralie in their ordinary quilted paletots and cloaks, with
their faces hidden by hats and thick black veils.   Two butter-
flies returned to the chrysalis stage could not be more completely transformed.

"Will you honor me by giving me your arm?" Coralie
asked tremulously.

"With pleasure," said Lucien.   He could feel the beating
of her heart throbbing against his like some snared bird as
she nestled closely to his side, with something of the delight
of a cat that rubs herself against her master with eager silken
caresses.

"So we are supping together!" she said.

The party of four found two cabs waiting for them at the
door in the Rue des Fossés-du-Temple.   Coralie drew Lucien
to one of the two, in which Camusot and his father-in-law,
old Cardot, were seated already.   She offered du Bruel a fifth

place, and the manager drove off with Florine, Matifat, and Lousteau.

"These hackney cabs are abominable things," said Coralie.

"Why don't you have a carriage?" returned du Bruel. ·

"*Why?*" she asked pettishly. "I do not like to tell you before Monsieur Cardot's face; for he trained his son-in-law, no doubt. Would you believe it, little and old as he is, Monsieur Cardot only gives Florentine five hundred francs a month, just about enough to pay for her rent and her grub and her clothes. The old Marquis de Rochegude offered me a brougham two months ago and he has six hundred thousand francs a year, but I am an artist and not a common hussy."

"You shall have a carriage the day after to-morrow, miss," said Camusot benignly; "you never asked me for one."

"As if one *asked* for such a thing as that? What! you love a woman and let her paddle about in the mud at the risk of breaking her legs? Nobody but a knight of the yardstick likes to see a draggled skirt-hem."

As she uttered the sharp words that cut Camusot to the quick, she groped for Lucien's knee, and pressed it between her own and clasped her fingers tightly upon his hand. She was silent. All her power to feel seemed to be concentrated upon the ineffable joy of a moment which brings compensation for the whole wretched past of a life such as these poor creatures lead, and develops within their souls a poetry of which other women, happily ignorant of these violent revulsions, know nothing.

"You played like Mademoiselle Mars herself toward the end," said du Bruel.

"Yes," said Camusot, "something put her out at the beginning; but from the middle of the second act to the very end she was enough to drive you wild with admiration. Half of the success of your play was due to her."

"And half of her success is due to me," said du Bruel.

"This is all much ado about nothing," said Coralie in an

unfamiliar voice. And, seizing an opportunity in the darkness, she carried Lucien's hand to her lips and kissed it and drenched it with tears. Lucien felt thrilled through and through by that touch, for in the humility of the courtesan's love there is a magnificence which might set an example to angels.

"Are you writing the dramatic criticism, monsieur?" said du Bruel, addressing Lucien; "you can write a charming paragraph about our dear Coralie."

"Oh! do us that little service!" pleaded Camusot, down on his knees, metaphorically speaking, before the critic. "You will always find me ready to do you a good turn at any time."

"Do leave him his independence," Coralie exclaimed angrily; "he will write what he pleases. Papa Camusot, buy carriages for me instead of praises."

"You shall have them on very easy terms," Lucien answered politely. "I have never written for newspapers before, so I am not accustomed to their ways, my maiden pen is at your disposal——"

"That is funny," said du Bruel.

"Here we are in the Rue de Bondy," said Cardot. Coralie's sally had quite crushed the little old man.

"If you are giving me the firstfruits of your pen, the first love that has sprung up in my heart shall be yours," whispered Coralie in the brief instant that they remained alone together in the cab; then she went up to Florine's bedroom to change her dress for a toilet previously sent.

Lucien had no idea how lavishly a prosperous merchant will spend money upon an actress or a mistress when he means to enjoy a life of pleasure. Matifat was not nearly so rich a man as his friend Camusot, and he had done his part rather shabbily, yet the sight of the dining-room took Lucien by surprise. The walls were hung with green cloth with a border of gilded nails, the whole room was artistically decorated, lighted by handsome lamps, stands full of flowers stood in every direction. The drawing-room was resplendent with the furniture in fashion in those days—a Thomire chandelier, a carpet of Eastern design, and yellow silken hangings relieved by a brown border. The candlesticks, and irons, and clock were all in good taste; for Matifat had left everything to Grindot, a rising architect, who was building a house for him, and the young man had taken great pains with the rooms when he knew that Florine was to occupy them.

Matifat, a tradesman to the backbone, went about carefully, afraid to touch the new furniture; he seemed to have the totals of the bills always before his eyes, and to look upon the splendors about him as so much jewelry imprudently withdrawn from the case.

"And I shall be obliged to do as much for Florentine!" old Cardot's eyes seemed to say.

Lucien at once began to understand Lousteau's indifference to the state of his garret. Étienne was the real king of these festivals; Étienne enjoyed the use of all these fine things. He was standing just now on the hearth-rug with his back to the fire, as if he were the master of the house, chatting with the manager, who was congratulating du Bruel.

"Copy, copy!" called Finot, coming into the room. "There is nothing in the box; the printers are setting up my article, and they will soon have finished."

"We will manage," said Étienne. "There is a fire burning in Florine's boudoir; there is a table there; and if Monsieur Matifat will find us paper and ink, we will knock off the newspaper while Florine and Coralie are dressing."

Cardot, Camusot, and Matifat disappeared in search of quills, penknives, and everything necessary. Suddenly the door was flung open, and Tullia, one of the prettiest opera-dancers of the day, dashed into the room.

"They agree to take the hundred copies, dear boy!" she cried, addressing Finot; "they won't cost the management anything, for the chorus and the orchestra and the *corps de ballet* are to take them whether they like it or not; but your paper is so clever that nobody will grumble. And you are going to have your boxes. Here is the subscription for the first quarter," she continued, holding out a couple of bank-notes; "so don't cut me up!"

" It is all over with me! " groaned Finot; " I must suppress my abominable diatribe and I haven't another notion in my head."

"What a happy inspiration, divine Laïs!" exclaimed Blondet, who had followed the lady upstairs and brought Nathan, Vernou, and Claud Vignon with him. "Stop to supper, there is a dear, or I will crush thee, butterfly as thou art. There will be no professional jealousies, as you are a dancer; and as to beauty, you have all of you too much sense to show jealousy in public."

" Oh dear! " cried Finot, " Nathan, Blondet, du Bruel, help, friends! I want five columns."

" I can make two of the play," said Lucien.

" I have enough for one," added Lousteau.

" Very well; Nathan, Vernou, and du Bruel will make the jokes at the end; and Blondet, good fellow, surely will vouchsafe a couple of short columns for the first sheet. I will run round to the printer. It is lucky that you brought your carriage, Tullia."

" Yes, but the Duke is waiting below in it and he has a German minister with him."

" Ask the Duke and the minister to come up," said Monsieur Nathan.

" A German? They are the ones to drink, and they listen too; he shall hear some astonishing things to send home to his government," cried Blondet.

" Is there any sufficiently serious personage to go down to speak to him?" asked Finot. " Here, du Bruel, you are an official; bring up the Duc de Rhétoré and the minister, and give your arm to Tullia. Dear me! Tullia, how handsome you are to-night!"

"We shall be thirteen at table!" exclaimed Matifat, paling visibly.

"No, fourteen," said a voice in the doorway, and Florentine appeared. "I have come to look after 'milord Cardot,'" she added, speaking with a burlesque English accent.

"And beside," said Lousteau, "Claud Vignon came with Blondet."

"I brought him here to drink," returned Blondet, taking up an inkstand. "Look here, all of you, you must use all your wit before those fifty-six bottles of wine drive it out. And, of all things, stir up du Bruel; he is a vaudevilliste, he is capable of making bad jokes if you get him to concert pitch."

And Lucien wrote his first newspaper article at the round table in Florine's boudoir, by the light of the pink candles lighted by Matifat; before such a remarkable audience he was eager to show what he could do.

THE PANORAMA-DRAMATIQUE.

First performance of the "Alcalde in a Fix," an imbroglio in three acts. First appearance of Mademoiselle Florine. Mademoiselle Coralie. Vignol.

People are coming and going, walking and talking, everybody is looking for something, nobody finds anything. General hubbub. The Alcalde has lost his daughter and found his cap, but the cap does not fit; it must belong to some thief. Where is the thief? People walk and talk, and come and go more than ever. Finally, the Alcalde finds a man without his daughter, and his daughter without the man, which is satisfactory for the magistrate, but not for the audience. Quiet being restored, the Alcalde tries to examine the man. Behold a venerable Alcalde, sitting in an Alcalde's great armchair, arranging the sleeves of his Alcalde's gown. Only in Spain do Alcaldes cling to their enormous sleeves and wear plaited lawn ruffles about the magisterial throat, a good half of an Alcalde's business on the stage in Paris. This particular Alcalde, wheezing and waddling about like an asthmatic old man, is Vignol, on whom Potier's mantle has fallen ; a young actor who personates old age so admirably that the oldest men in the audience cannot help laughing. With that quavering voice of his, that bald forehead, and those spindle shanks trembling under the weight of a senile frame, he may look forward to a long career of decrepitude. There is something alarming about the young actor's old age ; he is so very old ; you feel nervous lest senility should be infectious. And what an admirable Alcalde he makes ! What a delightful, uneasy smile ! what pompous stupidity ! what wooden dignity ! what judicial hesitation ! How well the man knows that black may be white, or white black ! How eminently well he is fitted to be minister to a constitutional monarch ! The stranger answers every one of his inquiries by a question ; Vignol re-torts in such a fashion that the person under examination elicits all the truth from the Alcalde. This piece of pure comedy, with a breath of Molière throughout, put the house in good humor. The people on the stage all seemed to understand what they were about, but I am quite unable to clear up the mystery, or to say wherein it lay ; for the Alcalde's daughter was there, personified by a living, breathing Andalusian, a Spaniard with a Spaniard's eye, a Spaniard's complexion, a Spaniard's gait and figure, a Spaniard from top to toe, with her poniard in her garter, love in her heart, and a cross on the ribbon about her neck. When the act was over, and somebody asked me how the piece was going, I answered, "She wears scarlet stockings with green clocks to them ; she has a little foot, no larger than *that*, in her patent-leather shoes, and the prettiest pair of ankles in Andalusia !" Oh ! that Alcalde's daughter brings your heart into your mouth ;

she tantalizes you so horribly, that you long to spring upon
the stage and offer her your thatched hovel and your heart, or
thirty thousand livres per annum and your pen. The Andalusian is the loveliest actress in Paris. Coralie, for she must be
called by her real name, can be a countess or a *grisette*, and
in which part she would be more charming one cannot tell.
She can be anything that she chooses ; she is born to achieve
all possibilities ; can more be said of a boulevard actress?

With the second act, a Parisian Spaniard appeared upon
the scene, with her features cut like a cameo and her dangerous eyes. "Where does she come from?" I asked in my
turn, and was told that she came from the green-room, and
that she was Mademoiselle Florine, but, upon my word, I
could not believe a syllable of it, such spirit was there in her
gestures, such frenzy in her love. She is the rival of the
Alcalde's daughter, and married to a grandee cut out to wear
an Almaviva's cloak, with stuff sufficient in it for a hundred
boulevard noblemen. Mlle. Florine wore neither scarlet
stockings with green clocks nor patent-leather shoes, but she
appeared in a mantilla, a veil which she put to admirable uses,
like the great lady that she is! She showed to admiration
that the tigress can be a cat. I began to understand, from
the sparkling talk between the two, that some drama of
jealousy was going on ; and just as everything was put right,
the Alcalde's stupidity embroiled everybody again. Torch-
bearers, rich men, footmen, Figaros, grandees, alcaldes, dames,
and damsels—the whole company on the stage began to eddy
about, and come and go, and look for one another. The plot
thickened, again I left it to thicken ; for Florine the jealous
and the happy Coralie had entangled me once more in the
folds of mantilla and basquina, and their little feet were twinkling in my eyes.

I managed, however, to reach the third act without any
mishap. The commissary of police was not compelled to in-
terfere, and I did nothing to scandalize the house, wherefore

I begin to believe in the influence of that "public and religious morality," about which the chamber of deputies is so
anxious, that any one might think there was no morality left
in France. I even contrived to gather that a man was in love
with two women who failed to return his affection, or else
that two women were in love with a man who loved neither
of them; the man did not love the Alcalde, or the Alcalde
had no love for the man, who was nevertheless a gallant gentleman, and in love with somebody, with himself, perhaps, or
with heaven, if the worst came to the worst, for he becomes a
monk. And if you want to know any more, you can go to
the Panorama-Dramatique. You are hereby given fair warning—you must go once to accustom yourself to those irresistible scarlet stockings with the green clocks, to little feet full
of promises, to eyes with a ray of sunlight shining through
them, to the subtle charm of a Parisienne disguised as an
Andalusian girl, and of an Andalusian masquerading as a
Parisienne. You must go a second time to enjoy the play, to
shed tears over the love-distracted grandee, and die of laughing at the old Alcalde. The play is twice a success. The
author, who writes, it is said, in collaboration with one of the
great poets of the day, was called before the curtain, and appeared with a love-distraught damsel on each arm, and fairly
brought down the excited house. The two dancers seemed
to have more wit in their legs than the author himself; but
when once the fair rivals left the stage, the dialogue seemed
witty at once, a triumphant proof of the excellence of the
piece. The applause and calls for the author caused the
architect some anxiety; but M. de Cursy, the author, being
accustomed to the volcanic eruptions of the reeling Vesuvius
beneath the chandelier, felt no tremor. As for the actresses,
they danced the famous bolero of Seville, which once found
favor in the sight of a council of reverend fathers, and escaped
ecclesiastical censure in spite of its wanton dangerous grace.
The bolero in itself would be enough to attract old age while

there is any lingering heat of youth in the veins, and, out of charity, I warn these persons to keep the lenses of their opera-glasses well polished.

While Lucien was writing a column which was to set a new fashion in journalism and reveal a fresh and original gift, Lousteau indited an article of the kind described as *mœurs**— a sketch of contemporary manners, entitled " The Elderly Beau."

" The buck of the empire," he wrote, " is invariably long, slender, and well preserved. He wears a corset and the cross of the Legion of Honor. His name was originally Potelet, or something very like it; but to stand well with the court, he conferred a *du* upon himself, and *du* Potelet he is until another revolution. A baron of the empire, a man of two ends, as his name (*Potelet*, a post) implies, he is paying his court to the Faubourg Saint-Germain, after a youth gloriously and usefully spent as the agreeable trainbearer of a sister of the man whom decency forbids me to mention by name. Du Potelet has forgotten that he was once in waiting upon her imperial highness; but he still sings the songs composed for the benefactress who took such a tender interest in his career," and so forth, and so forth; it was a tissue of personalities, silly enough for the most part, such as they used to write in those days. Other papers, and notably the " Figaro," have brought the art to a curious perfection since. Lousteau compared the Baron to a heron, and introduced Mme. de Bargeton, to whom he was paying his court, as a cuttlefish bone, a burlesque absurdity which amused readers who knew neither of the per-sonages. The tales of the loves of the heron, who tried in vain to swallow the cuttlefish bone, which broke into three pieces when he dropped it, was irresistibly ludicrous. Every-body remembers the sensation which the pleasantry made in the Faubourg Saint-Germain ; it was the first of a series of

* Lit.: Manners; meaning personal squibs.

similar articles, and was one of the thousand and one causes which provoked the rigorous press legislation of Charles X.

An hour later, Blondet, Lousteau, and Lucien came back to the drawing-room, where the other guests were chatting. The Duke was there and the minister, the four women, the three merchants, the manager, and Finot. A printer's devil, with a paper-cap on his head, was waiting even then for copy.

"The men are just going off, if I have nothing to take them," he said.

"Stay a bit, here are ten francs, and tell them to wait," said Finot.

"If I give them the money, sir, they would take to tipple-ography, and good-night to the newspaper."

"That boy's commonsense is appalling to me," remarked Finot; and the minister was in the middle of a prediction of a brilliant future for the urchin, when the three came in. Blondet read aloud an extremely clever article against the Romantics; Lousteau's paragraph drew laughter, and by the Duc de Rhétoré's advice an indirect eulogium of Mme. d'Espard was slipped in, lest the whole Faubourg Saint-Germain should take offense.

"And now what have *you* written?" asked Finot, turning to Lucien.

And Lucien read, quaking for fear, but the room rang with applause when he finished; the actresses embraced the neophyte; and the two merchants, following suit, half-choked the breath out of him. There were tears in du Bruel's eyes as he grasped his critic's hand, and the manager invited him to dinner.

"There are no children nowadays," said Blondet. "Since Monsieur de Chateaubriand called Victor Hugo a 'sublime child,' I can only tell you quite simply that you have spirit and taste, and write like a gentleman."

"He is on the newspaper," said Finot, as he thanked Étienne and gave him a shrewd glance.

" What jokes have you made?" inquired Lousteau, turning to Blondet and du Bruel.

" Here are du Bruel's," said Nathan.

*** "Now that M. le Vicomte d'A—— is attracting so much attention, they will perhaps let *me* alone," M. le Vicomte Demosthenes was heard to say yesterday.

*** An Ultra, condemning M. Pasquier's speech, said his programme was only a continuation of Decaze's policy. " Yes," said a lady, " but he stands on a Monarchical basis, he has just the kind of leg for a Court suit."

" With such a beginning, I don't ask more of you," said Finot; " it will be all right. Run round with this," he added, turning to the boy; "the paper is not exactly a genuine article, but it is our best number yet," and he turned to the group of writers. Already Lucien's colleagues were privately taking his measure.

" That fellow has brains," said Blondet.

" His article is well written," said Claud Vignon.

" Supper!" cried Matifat.

The Duke gave his arm to Florine, Coralie went across to Lucien, and Tullia went in to supper between Emile Blondet and the German minister.

" I cannot understand why you are making an onslaught on Madame de Bargeton and the Baron du Châtelet; they say that he is prefect-designate of the Charente, and will be a master of requests some day."

" Madame de Bargeton showed Lucien the door as if he had been an impostor," said Lousteau.

" Such a fine young fellow!" exclaimed the minister.

Supper, served with new plate, Sèvres porcelain and white damask, was redolent of opulence. The dishes were from Chevet, the wines from a celebrated merchant on the Quai

12

Saint-Bernard, a personal friend of Matifat's. For the first time Lucien beheld the luxury of Paris displayed; he went from surprise to surprise, but he kept his astonishment to himself, like a man who had spirit and taste and wrote like a gentleman, as Blondet had said.

As they crossed the drawing-room Coralie bent to Florine, "Make Camusot so drunk that he will be compelled to stop here all night," she whispered.

"So you have hooked your journalist, have you?" returned Florine, using the idiom of women of her class.

"No, dear; I love him," said Coralie, with an adorable little shrug of the shoulders.

Those words rang in Lucien's ears, borne to them by the fifth deadly sin. Coralie was perfectly dressed. Every woman possesses some personal charm in perfection, and Coralie's toilet brought her characteristic beauty into prominence. Her dress, moreover, like Florine's, was of some exquisite stuff, unknown as yet to the public, a *mousseline de soie*, with which Camusot had been supplied a few days before the rest of the world; for, as owner of the "Golden Cocoon," he was a kind of Providence in Paris to the Lyons silk-weavers.

Love and the toilet are like color and perfume for a woman, and Coralie in her happiness looked lovelier than ever. A looked-for delight which cannot elude the grasp possesses an immense charm for youth; perhaps in their eyes the secret of the attraction of a house of pleasure lies in the certainty of gratification; perhaps many a long fidelity is attributable to the same cause. Love for love's sake, first love indeed, had blended with one of the strange violent fancies which sometimes possess these poor creatures; and love and admiration of Lucien's great beauty taught Coralie to express the thoughts in her heart.

"I should love you if you were ill and ugly," she whispered as they sat down.

What a saying for a poet! Camusot vanished utterly,

Lucien had forgotten his existence, he saw Coralie, and had eyes for nothing else. How should he draw back—this creature, all sensation, all enjoyment of life, tired of the monotony of existence in a country town, weary of poverty, harassed by enforced continence, impatient of the claustral life of the Rué de Cluny, of toiling without reward? The fascination of the underworld of Paris was upon him; how should he rise and leave this brilliant gathering? Lucien stood with one foot in Coralie's chamber and the other in the quicksands of journalism. After so much vain search and climbing of so many stairs, after standing about and waiting in the Rue de Sentier, he had found journalism a jolly boon companion, joyous over the wine. His wrongs had just been avenged. There were two for whom he had vainly striven to fill the cup of humiliation and pain which he had been made to drink to the dregs, and now to-morrow they should receive a stab in their very hearts. "Here is a real friend!" he thought, as he looked at Lousteau. It never crossed his mind that Lousteau already regarded him as a dangerous rival. He had made a blunder; he had done his very best when a color-less article would have served him admirably well. Blondet's remark to Finot, that it would be better to come to terms with a man of that calibre, had counteracted Lousteau's gnawing jealousy. He reflected that it would be prudent to keep on good terms with Lucien, and, at the same time, to arrange with Finot to exploit this formidable new-comer—he must be kept in poverty. The decision was made in a moment and the bargain made in a few whispered words.

"He has talent."

"He will want the more."

"Ah?"

"Good!"

"A supper among French journalists always fills me with dread," said the German diplomatist, with serene urbanity; he looked as he spoke at Blondet, whom he had met at the

Comtesse de Montcornet's. "It is laid upon you, gentlemen, to fulfill the prophecy of Blücher's."

"What prophecy?" asked Nathan.

"When Blücher and Sacken arrived on the heights of Montmartre in 1814 (pardon me, gentlemen, for recalling a day unfortunate for France), Sacken (a rough brute), re-marked, 'Now we will set Paris alight!' 'Take very good care that you don't,' said Blücher. 'France will die of *that*, nothing else can kill her,' and he waved his hand over the glowing, seething city, that lay like a huge canker in the valley of the Seine. There are no journalists in our country, thank heaven!" continued the minister, after a pause. "I have not yet recovered from the fright that little fellow gave me, a boy of ten, in a paper-cap, with the sense of an old diplomatist. And to-night I feel as if I were supping with lions and panthers, who graciously sheathe their claws in my honor."

"It is clear," said Blondet, "that we are at liberty to in-form Europe that a serpent dropped from your excellency's lips this evening, and that the venomous creature failed to inoculate Mademoiselle Tullia, the prettiest dancer in Paris; and to follow up the story with a commentary on Eve, and the Scriptures, and the first and last transgression. But have no fear, you are our guest."

"It would be funny," said Finot.

"We would begin with a scientific treatise on all the serpents found in the human heart and human body, and so proceed to the diplomatic corps," said Lousteau.

"And we could exhibit one in spirits, in a bottle of bran-died cherries," said Vernou.

"Till you yourself would end by believing in the story," added Vignon, looking at the diplomatist.

"Gentlemen," cried the Duc de Rhétoré, "let sleeping claws lie."

"The influence and power of the press is only dawning,"

said Finot. "Journalism is in its infancy; it will grow. In ten years' time everything will be brought into publicity. The light of thought will be turned on all subjects, and——" .

"The blight of thought will be over it all," corrected Blondet.

"Here is an apophthegm," cried Claud Vignon.

"Thought will make kings," said Lousteau.

"And undo monarchs," said the German.

"And, therefore," said Blondet, "if the press did not exist, it would be necessary to invent it forthwith. But here we have it, and live by it."

"You will die of it," returned the German diplomatist. "Can you not see that if you enlighten the masses and raise them in the political scale, you make it all the harder for the individual to rise above their level? Can you not see that if you sow the seeds of reasoning among the working-classes, you will reap revolt, and be the first to fall victims? What do they smash in Paris when a riot begins?"

"The street-lamps," said Nathan, in reply to the German; "but we are too modest to fear for ourselves, we only run the risk of cracks."

"As a nation you have too much mental activity to allow any government to run its course without interference. But for that, you would make the conquest of Europe a second time, and win with the pen all that you failed to keep with the sword."

"Journalism is an evil," said Claud Vignon. "The evil may have its uses, but the present government is resolved to put it down. There will be a battle over it. Who will give way? That is the question."

"The government will give way," said Blondet. "I keep telling people that with all my might! Intellectual power is *the* great power in France; and the press has more wit than all men of intellect put together, and the hypocrisy of Tartufe beside."

" Blondet ! Blondet ! you are going too far ! " called Finot.
" Subscribers are present."

" You are the proprietor of one of these poison shops ! you have reason to be afraid ; but I can laugh at the whole business, even if I live by it."

"Blondet is right," said Claud Vignon. " Journalism, so far from being in the hands of a priesthood, came to be first a party weapon, and then a commercial speculation, carried on without conscience or scruple, like other commercial speculations. Every newspaper, as Blondet says, is a shop to which people come for opinions of the right shade. If there was a paper for hunchbacks, it would set forth plainly, morning and evening, in its columns, the beauty, the utility, and necessity of deformity. A newspaper is not supposed to enlighten its readers, but to supply them with congenial opinions. Give any newspaper time enough, and it will be base, hypocritical, shameless, and treacherous ; the periodical press will be the death of ideas, systems, and individuals ; nay, it will flourish upon their decay. It will take the credit of all creations of the brain ; the harm that it does is done anonymously. We, for instance—I, Claud Vignon ; you, Blondet ; you, Lousteau ; and you, Finot—we are all Platos, Aristides, and Catos, Plutarch's men, in short ; we are all immaculate ; we may wash our hands of all iniquity. Napoleon's sublime aphorism, suggested by his study of the convention, ' No one individual is responsible for a crime committed collectively,' sums up the whole significance of a phenomenon, moral or immoral, whichever you please. However shamefully a newspaper may behave, the disgrace attaches to no one person."

" The authorities will resort to repressive legislation," interposed du Bruel. "A law is going to be passed, in fact."

" Pooh ! " retorted Nathan. " What is the law in France against the spirit in which it is received, the most subtle of all solvents ? "

" Ideas and opinions can only be counteracted by opinions

and ideas," Vignon continued. "By sheer terror and des-
potism, and by no other means, can you extinguish the genius
of the French nation ; for the language lends itself admirably
to allusion and ambiguity. Epigram breaks out the more for
repressive legislation ; it is like steam in an engine without a
safety-valve. The King, for example, does right ; if a newspaper is against him, the minister gets all the credit of the
measure, and *vice versâ.* A newspaper invents a scandalous
libel—it has been misinformed. If the victim complains, the
paper gets off with an apology for taking so great a freedom.
If the case is taken into court, the editor complains that nobody asked him to rectify the mistake ; but ask for redress,
and he will laugh in your face and treat his offense as a mere
trifle. The paper scoffs if the victim gains the day; and if
heavy damages are awarded, the plaintiff is held up as an
unpatriotic obscurantist and a menace to the liberties of the
country. In the course of an article purporting to explain
that Monsieur So-and-so is as honest a man as you will find in
the kingdom, you are informed that he is no better than a
common thief. The sins of the press ? Pooh ! mere trifles ;
the curtailers of its liberties are monsters ; and give him time
enough, the constant reader is persuaded to believe anything
you please. Everything which does not suit the newspaper
will be unpatriotic, and the press will be infallible. One
religion will be played off against another, and the charter
against the King. The press will hold up the magistracy to
scorn for meting out rigorous justice to the press, and applaud its action when it serves the cause of party hatred.
The most sensational fictions will be invented to increase the
circulation ; journalism will descend to mountebanks' tricks
worthy of Bobêche ; journalism would serve up its father with
the attic salt of its own wit sooner than fail to interest or
amuse the public ; journalism will outdo the actor who put
his son's ashes into the urn to draw real tears from his eyes,
or the mistress who sacrifices everything to her lover."

"Journalism is, in fact, the people in folio form," interrupted Blondet.

"The people with hypocrisy added and generosity lacking," said Vignon. "All real ability will be driven out from the ranks of journalism, as Aristides was driven into exile by the Athenians. We shall see newspapers started in the first instance by men of honor, falling sooner or later into the hands of men of abilities even lower than the average, but endowed with the resistance and flexibility of india-rubber, qualities denied to noble genius; nay, perhaps the future newspaper proprietor will be the tradesman with capital sufficient to buy venal pens. We see such things already indeed, but in ten years' time every little youngster that has left school will take himself for a great man, slash his predecessors from the lofty height of a newspaper column, drag them down by the feet, and take their place.

"Napoleon did wisely when he muzzled the press. I would wager that the opposition papers would batter down a government of their own setting up, just as they are battering the present government, if any demand was refused. The more they have, the more they will want in the way of concessions. The parvenu journalist will be succeeded by the starveling hack. There is no salve for this sore. It is a kind of corruption which grows more and more obtrusive and malignant; the wider it spreads, the more patiently it will be endured, until the day comes when newspapers shall so increase and multiply in the earth that confusion will be the result—a second Babel. We, all of us, such as we are, have reason to know that crowned kings are less ungrateful than kings of our profession; that the most sordid man of business is not so mercenary nor so keen in speculation; that our brains are consumed to furnish their daily supply of poisonous trash. And yet we, all of us, will continue to write, like men who work in quicksilver mines, knowing that they are doomed to die of their trade.

" Look there," he continued, " at that young man sitting beside Coralie—what is his name? Lucien! He has a beautiful face ; he is a poet ; and what is more, he is witty— so much the better for him. Well, he will cross the threshold of one of those dens where a man's intellect is prostituted ; he will put all his best and finest thought into his work ; he will blunt his intellect and sully his soul ; he will be guilty of anonymous meannesses which take the place of stratagem, pillage, and ratting to the enemy in the warfare of *condottieri*. And when, like hundreds more, he has squandered his genius in the service of others who find the capital and do no work, those dealers in poisons will leave him to starve if he is thirsty, and to die of thirst if he is starving."

" Thanks," said Finot.

" But, dear me," continued Claud Vignon, "*I* knew all this, yet here am I in the galleys, and the arrival of another convict gives me pleasure. We are cleverer, Blondet and I, than Messieurs This and That, who speculate in our abilities, yet nevertheless we are always exploited by them. We have a heart somewhere beneath the intellect ; we have *not* the grim qualities of the man who makes others work for him. We are indolent, we like to look on at the game, we are meditative, and we are fastidious ; they will sweat our brains and blame us for improvidence."

" I thought you would be more amusing than this ! " said Florine.

"Florine is right," said Blondet ; " let us leave the cure of public evils to those quacks the statesmen. As Charlet says, ' Quarrel with my own bread and butter? *Never !* ' "

" Do you know what Vignon puts me in mind of ?" said Lousteau. " Of one of those fat women in the Rue du Péli- can telling a school-boy, ' My boy, you are too young to come here.' "

A burst of laughter followed the sally, but it pleased Cora- lie. The merchants meanwhile ate and drank and listened,

" What a nation this is ! You see so much good in it and
so much evil," said the minister, addressing the Duc de Rhétoré. "You are prodigals who cannot ruin yourselves, gentlemen."

And so, by the blessing of chance, Lucien, standing on the
brink of the precipice over which he was destined to fall,
heard warnings on all sides. D'Arthez had set him on the
right road, had shown him the noble method of work and
aroused in him the spirit before which all obstacles disappear.
Lousteau himself (partly from selfish motives) had tried to
warn him away by describing journalism and literature in
their practical aspects. Lucien had refused to believe that
there could be so much hidden corruption ; but now he had
heard the journalists themselves crying woe for their hurt, he
had seen them at their work, had watched them tearing their
foster-mother's heart to read auguries of the future.

That evening he had seen things as they are. He beheld
the very heart's core of corruption of that Paris which Blücher so aptly described ; and, so far from shuddering at the
sight, he was intoxicated with enjoyment of the intellectually
stimulating society in which he found himself.

These extraordinary men, clad in armor damascened by
their vices, these intellects environed by cold and brilliant
analysis, seemed so far greater in his eyes than the grave and
earnest members of the brotherhood. And, beside all this,
he was reveling in his first taste of luxury; he had fallen
under the spell. His capricious instincts awoke; for the first
time in his life he drank exquisite wines, this was his first experience of cookery carried to the pitch of a fine art. A
minister, a duke, and an opera-dancer had joined the party
of journalists, and wondered at their sinister power. Lucien
felt a horrible craving to reign over these kings, and he
thought that he had power to win his kingdom. Finally,
there was this Coralie, made happy by a few words of his. By
the bright light of the wax-candles, through the steam of the

dishes and the fumes of wine, she looked sublimely beautiful to his eyes, so fair had she grown with love. She was the loveliest, the most beautiful actress in Paris. The brotherhood, the heaven of noble thoughts, faded away before a temptation that appealed to every fibre of his nature. How could it have been otherwise? Lucien's author's vanity had just been gratified by the praises of those who know; by the appreciation of his future rivals; the success of his articles and his conquest of Coralie might have turned an older head than his.

During the discussion, moreover, every one at table had made a remarkably good supper, and such wines are not met with every day. Lousteau, sitting beside Camusot, furtively poured cherry-brandy several times into his neighbor's wineglass, and challenged him to drink. And Camusot drank, all unsuspicious, for he thought himself, in his own way, a match for a journalist. The jokes became more personal when dessert appeared and the wine began to circulate. The German minister, a keen-witted man of the world, made a sign to the Duke and Tullia, and the three disappeared with the first symptoms of vociferous nonsense which precede the grotesque scenes of an orgie in its final stage. Coralie and Lucien had been behaving like children all the evening; as soon as the wine was uppermost in Camusot's head they made good their escape down the staircase and sprang into a cab. Camusot subsided under the table; Matifat, looking round for him, thinking that he had gone home with Coralie, left his guests to smoke, laugh, and argue, and followed Florine to her room. Daylight surprised the party, or, more accurately, the first dawn of light discovered one man still able to speak, and Blondet, that intrepid champion, was proposing to the assembled sleepers a health to Aurora the rosy-fingered.

Lucien was unaccustomed to orgies of this kind. His head was very tolerably clear as he came down the staircase, but

the fresh air was too much for him ; he was horribly drunk.
When they reached the handsome house in the Rue de Vendôme, where the actress lived, Coralie and her waiting-woman
were obliged to assist the poet to climb to the second floor.
Lucien was ignominiously sick, and very nearly fainted on
the staircase.

"Quick, Bérénice, some tea ! Make some tea," cried Coralie.

"It is nothing; it is the air," Lucien got out, "and I
have never taken so much before in my life."

" Poor boy ! He is as innocent as a lamb," said Bérénice,
a stalwart Norman peasant-woman as ugly as Coralie was
pretty. Lucien, half-unconscious, was laid at last in bed.
Coralie, with Bérénice's assistance, undressed the poet with
all a mother's tender care.

"It is nothing," he murmured again and again. "It is the
air. Thank you, mamma."

" How charmingly he says 'mamma,'" cried Coralie, putting a kiss on his hair.

" What happiness to love such an angel, mademoiselle !
Where did you pick him up? I did not think a man could
be as beautiful as you are," said Bérénice, when Lucien lay
in bed. He was very drowsy; he knew nothing and saw
nothing; Coralie made him swallow several cups of tea, and
left him to sleep.

" Did the porter see us ? Was there any one else about ? "
she asked.

" No ; I was sitting up for you."

"Does Victoire know anything ? "

" Rather not ! " returned Bérénice.

Ten hours later Lucien awoke to meet Coralie's eyes. She
had watched by him as he slept ; he knew it, poet that he was.
It was almost noon, but she still wore the delicate dress,
abominably stained, which she meant to lay up as a relic.
Lucien understood all the self-sacrifice and delicacy of love,

fain of its reward. He looked into Coralie's eyes. In a moment she had flung off her clothing and slipped like a serpent to Lucien's side.

At five o'clock in the afternoon Lucien was still sleeping, cradled in this voluptuous paradise. He had caught glimpses of Coralie's chamber, an exquisite creation of luxury, a world of rose-color and white. He had admired Florine's apartments, but this surpassed them in its dainty refinement.

Coralie had already risen; for, if she was to play her part as the Andalusian, she must be at the theatre by seven o'clock. Yet she had returned to gaze at the unconscious poet, lulled to sleep in bliss; she could not drink too deeply of this love that rose to rapture, drawing close the bond between the heart and the senses, to steep both in ecstasy. For in that apotheosis of human passion, which of those that were twain on earth that they might know bliss to the full creates one soul to rise to love in heaven, lay Coralie's justification. Who, moreover, would not have found excuse in Lucien's more than human beauty? To the actress kneeling by the bedside, happy in the love within her, it seemed that she had received love's consecration. Bérénice broke in upon Coralie's rapture.

"Here comes Camusot!" cried the maid. "And he knows that you are here."

Lucien sprang up at once. Innate generosity suggested that he was doing Coralie an injury. Bérénice drew aside a curtain, and he fled into a dainty dressing-room, whither Coralie and the maid brought his clothes with magical speed.

Camusot appeared, and only then did Coralie's eyes alight on Lucien's boots, warming in the fender. Bérénice had privately varnished them and put them before the fire to dry; and both mistress and maid alike forgot that tell-tale witness. Bérénice left the room with a scared glance at Coralie. Coralie flung herself into the depths of a settee, and bade Camusot seat himself in the *gondole*, a round-backed chair that stood opposite. But Coralie's adorer, honest soul, dared not look his mistress in the face; he could not take his eyes off the pair of boots.

"Ought I to make a scene and leave Coralie?" he ponderered. "Is it worth while to make a fuss about a trifle? There is a pair of boots wherever you go. These would be more in place in a store window or taking a walk on the boulevard on somebody's feet; here, however, without a pair of feet in them, they tell a pretty plain tale. I am fifty years old, and that is the truth; I ought to be as blind as Cupid himself."

There was no excuse for this mean-spirited monologue. The boots were not the high-lows at present in vogue, which an unobservant man may be allowed to disregard up to a certain point. They were the unmistakable, uncompromising hessians then prescribed by fashion, a pair of extremely elegant betasseled boots, which shone in glistening contrast against tight-fitting trousers invariably of some light color, and reflected their surroundings like a mirror. The boots stared the honest silk-mercer out of countenance, and, it must be added, they pained his heart.

"What is it?" asked Coralie.

"Nothing."

"Ring the bell," said Coralie, smiling to herself at Camusot's want of spirit. "Bérénice," she said, when the Norman handmaid appeared, "just bring me a button-hook, for I must put on these confounded boots again. Don't forget to bring them to my dressing-room to-night."

"What?——*your* boots?"——faltered Camusot, breathing more freely.

"And whose should they be?" she demanded haughtily. "Were you beginning to believe?—great stupid! Oh! and he would believe it, too," she went on, addressing Bérénice. "I have a man's part in What's-his-name's piece, and I have never worn a man's clothes in my life before. The boot-

maker for the theatre brought me these things to try if I could
walk in them, until a pair can be made to measure. He put
them on, but they hurt me so much that I have taken them
off, and after all I must wear them."

"Don't put them on again if they are uncomfortable,"
said Camusot. (The boots had made him feel so very uncomfortable himself.)

"Mademoiselle would do better to have a pair made of
very thin morocco, sir, instead of torturing herself as she did
just now; but the management is so stingy. She was crying,
sir; if I was a man, and loved a woman, I wouldn't let her
shed a tear, I know. You ought to order a pair for her at
once——"

"Yes, yes," said Camusot. "Are you just getting up,
Coralie?"

"Just at this moment; I only came in at six o'clock after
looking for you everywhere. I was obliged to keep the cab
for seven hours. So much for your care of me; you forget
me for a wine-bottle. I ought to take care of myself now
when I am to play every night so long as the 'Alcalde'
draws. I don't want to fall off after that young man's notice
of me."

"That is a handsome boy," said Camusot.

"Do you think so? I don't admire men of that sort; they
are too much like women; and they do not understand how
to love like you stupid old business men. You are so bored
with your own society."

"Is monsieur dining with madame?" inquired Bérénice
of Camusot.

"No, my mouth is clammy."

"You were nicely screwed yesterday. Ah! Papa Camusot,
I don't like men who drink, I tell you at once——"

"You will give that young man a present, I suppose?"
interrupted Camusot.

"Oh! yes. I would rather do that than pay as Florine

does. There, go away with you, good-for-nothing that one loves; or give me a carriage to save time in future," Coralie rejoined.

"You shall go in your own carriage to-morrow to your manager's dinner at the 'Rocher de Cancale.' The new piece will not be given next Sunday."

"Come, I am just going to dine," said Coralie, hurrying Camusot out of the room.

An hour later Bérénice came to release Lucien. Bérénice, Coralie's companion since her childhood, had a keen and subtle brain in her unwieldy frame.

"Stay here," she said. "Coralie is coming back alone; she even talked of getting rid of Camusot if he is in your way; but you are too much of an angel to ruin her, her heart's darling as you are. She wants to clear out of this, she says; to leave this paradise and go and live in your garret. Oh! there are those that are jealous and envious of you, and they have told her that you haven't a brass farthing and live in the Latin Quarter; and I should go, too, you see, to do the housework. But I have just been comforting her, poor child! I have been telling her that you were too clever to do anything so silly. I was right, wasn't I, sir? Oh! you will see that you are her darling, her love, the god to whom she gives her soul; yonder old fool has nothing but the body. If you only knew how nice she is when I hear her say her part over! My Coralie, my little pet, she is! She deserved that God in heaven should send her one of His angels. She was sick of the life. She was so unhappy with her mother that used to beat her, and sold her. Yes, sir, sold her own child! If I had a daughter, I would wait on her hand and foot as I wait on Coralie; she is like my own child to me. These are the first good times she has seen since I have been with her; the first time that she has been really applauded. You have written something, it seems, and they have gotten up a famous

claque for the second performance. Braulard has been going
through the play with her while you were asleep."

"Who? Braulard?" asked Lucien; it seemed to him that
he had heard the name before.

"He is the head of the *claqueurs*, and she was arranging
with him the places where she wished him to look after her.
Florine might try to play her some shabby trick, and take all
for herself, for all she calls herself her friend. There is such
a talk about your article on the boulevards. Isn't it a bed fit
for a prince," she said, smoothing the lace bed-spread.

She lighted the wax-candles, and, to Lucien's bewildered
fancy, the house seemed to be some palace in the "Cabinet
des Fées." Camusot had chosen the richest stuffs from the
"Golden Cocoon" for the hangings and window curtains.
A carpet fit for a king's palace was spread upon the floor.
The carving of the rosewood furniture caught and imprisoned
the light that rippled over its surface. Priceless trifles gleamed
from the white marble mantel. The rug beside the bed
was of swans' skins bordered with sable. A pair of little,
black velvet slippers lined with purple silk told of happiness
awaiting the poet of "The Marguerites." A dainty lamp
hung from the ceiling draped with silk. The room was full
of flowering plants, delicate white heaths and scentless camel-
lias, in stands marvelously wrought. Everything called up
associations of innocence. How was it possible in these rooms
to see the life that Coralie led in its true colors? Bérénice
noticed Lucien's bewildered expression.

"Isn't it nice?" she said coaxingly. "You would be
more comfortable here, wouldn't you, than in a garret? You
won't let her do anything rash?" she continued, setting a
costly stand before him, covered with dishes abstracted from
her mistress' dinner-table, lest the cook should suspect that
her mistress had a lover in the house.

Lucien made a good dinner. Bérénice waited on him, the
dishes were of wrought silver, the painted porcelain plates had

13

cost a louis d'or apiece. The luxury was producing exactly the same effect upon him that the sight of a girl walking the pavement, with bare flaunting throat and neat ankles, produces upon a school-boy.

"How lucky Camusot is!" cried he.

"Lucky?" repeated Bérénice. "He would willingly give all that he is worth to be in your place; he would be glad to barter his gray hair for your golden head."

She gave Lucien the richest wine that Bordeaux keeps for the wealthiest English purchaser, and persuaded Lucien to go to bed to take a preliminary nap; and Lucien, in truth, was quite willing to sleep on the couch that he had been admiring. Bérénice had read his wish, and felt glad for her mistress.

At half-past ten that night Lucien awoke to look into eyes brimming over with love. There stood Coralie in most luxurious night attire. Lucien had been sleeping; Lucien was intoxicated with love, and not with wine. Bérénice left the room with the inquiry, "What time to-morrow morning?"

"At eleven o'clock. We will have breakfast in bed. I am not at home to anybody before two o'clock."

At two o'clock in the afternoon Coralie and her lover were sitting together. The poet, to all appearance, had come to pay a call. Lucien had been bathed and combed and dressed. Coralie had sent to Colliau's for a dozen fine shirts, a dozen cravats, and a dozen pocket-handkerchiefs for him, as well as twelve pairs of gloves in a cedar-wood box. When a carriage stopped at the door they both rushed to the window, and watched Camusot alight from a handsome coupé.

"I would not have believed that one could so hate a man and luxury——"

"I am too poor to allow you to ruin yourself for me," he replied. And thus Lucien passed under the Caudine Forks.

"Poor pet," said Coralie, holding him tightly to her, "do you love me so much? I persuaded this gentleman to call on me this morning," she continued, indicating Lucien to

Camusot, who entered the room. "I thought that we might take a drive in the Champs Élysées to try the carriage."

"Go without me," said Camusot in a melancholy voice; "I shall not dine with you. It is my wife's birthday, I had forgotten that."

"Poor Musot, how badly bored you will be!" she said, putting her arms about his neck.

She was wild with joy at the thought that she and Lucien would handsel this gift together; she would drive with him in the new carriage; and in her happiness she seemed to love Camusot, she lavished caresses upon him.

"If only I could give you a carriage every day!" said the poor fellow.

"Now, sir, it is two o'clock," she said, turning to Lucien, who stood in distress and confusion, but she comforted him with an adorable gesture.

Down the stairs she went, several steps at a time, drawing Lucien after her; the elderly merchant following in their wake like a seal on land, and quite unable to catch them up.

Lucien enjoyed the most intoxicating of pleasures; happiness had increased Coralie's loveliness to the highest possible degree; she appeared before all eyes an exquisite vision in her dainty toilet. All Paris in the Champs Élysées beheld the lovers.

In an avenue of the Bois de Boulogne they met a calèche; Mme. d'Espard and Mme. de Bargeton looked in surprise at Lucien, and met a scornful glance from the poet. He saw glimpses of a great future before him and was about to make his power felt. He could fling them back in a glance some of the revengeful thoughts which had gnawed his heart ever since they planted them there. That moment was one of the sweetest in his life, and perhaps decided his fate. Once again the Furies seized on Lucien at the bidding of pride. He would reappear in the world of Paris; he would take a signal revenge; all the social pettiness hitherto trodden under foot by the worker, the member of the brotherhood, sprang up again afresh in his soul.

Now he understood all that Lousteau's attack had meant. Lousteau had served his passions; while the brotherhood, that collective mentor, had seemed to mortify them in the interests of tiresome virtues and work which began to look useless and hopeless in Lucien's eyes. Work! What is it but death to an eager pleasure-loving nature? And how easy it is for the man of letters to slide into a *far niente* existence of self-indulgence, into the luxurious ways of actresses and women of easy virtues! Lucien felt an overmastering desire to continue the reckless life of the last two days.

The dinner at the " Rocher de Cancale " was exquisite. All Florine's supper guests were there except the minister, the Duke, and the dancer; Camusot, too, was absent; but these gaps were filled by two famous actors and Hector Merlin and his mistress. This charming woman, who chose to be known as Mme. du Val-Noble, was the handsomest and most fashionable of the class of women now euphemistically styled *lorettes*.

Lucien had spent the forty-eight hours since the success of his article in paradise. He was fêted and envied; he gained self-possession; his talk sparkled; he was the brilliant Lucien de Rubempré who shone for a few months in the world of letters and art. Finot, with his infallible instinct for discovering ability, scenting it afar as an ogre might scent human flesh, cajoled Lucien, and did his best to secure a recruit for the squadron under his command. And Coralie watched the manœuvres of this purveyor of brains, saw that Lucien was nibbling at the bait, and tried to put him on his guard.

"Don't make any engagement, dear boy; wait. They want to exploit you; we will talk of it to-night."

" Pshaw ! " said Lucien. " I am sure I am quite as sharp and shrewd as they can be."

Finot and Hector Merlin evidently had not fallen out over

that affair of the white lines and spaces in the columns, for it
was Finot who introduced Lucien to the journalist. Coralie
and Mme. du Val-Noble were overwhelmingly amiable and
polite to each other, and Mme. du Val-Noble asked Lucien
and Coralie to dine with her.

Hector Merlin, short and thin, with lips always tightly
compressed, was the most dangerous journalist present. Un-
bounded ambition and jealousy smoldered within him; he
took pleasure in the pain of others, and fomented strife to
turn it to his own account. His abilities were but slender,
and he had little force of character; but the natural instinct
which draws the upstart toward money and power served him
as well as fixity of purpose. Lucien and Merlin at once took
a dislike to one another, for reasons not far to seek. Merlin,
unfortunately, proclaimed aloud the thoughts that Lucien
kept to himself. By the time the dessert was put on the table,
the most touching friendship appeared to prevail among the
men, each one of whom in his heart thought himself a cleverer
fellow than the rest; and Lucien as the new-comer was made
much of by them all. They chatted frankly and unrestrain-
edly. Hector Merlin, alone did not join in the laughter.
Lucien asked the reason of his reserve.

"You are just entering the world of letters, I can see," he
said; "you are a journalist with all your illusions left. You
believe in friendship. Here we are friends or foes, as it happens; we strike down a friend with the weapon which by
rights should only be turned against an enemy. You will find
out, before very long, that fine sentiments will do nothing for
you. If you are naturally kindly, learn to be ill-natured, to
be consistently spiteful. If you have never heard this golden
rule before, I give it you now in confidence, and it is no
small secret. If you have a mind to be loved, never leave
your mistress until you have made her shed a tear or two;
and if you mean to make your way in literature, let other
people continually feel your teeth; make no exception even

of your friends; wound their susceptibilities and everybody will fawn upon you."

Hector Merlin watched Lucien as he spoke, saw that his words went to the neophyte's heart like a stab, and Hector Merlin was glad. Play followed, Lucien lost all his money, and Coralie brought him away; and he forgot for a while, in the delights of love, the fierce excitement of the gambler, which was to gain so strong a hold upon him.

When he left Coralie in the morning and returned to the Latin Quarter, he took out his purse and found the money he had lost. At first he felt miserable over the discovery, and thought of going back at once to return a gift which humili-ated him; but—he had already come as far as the Rue de la Harpe; he would not return now that he had almost reached the Hôtel de Cluny. He pondered over Coralie's forethought as he went, till he saw in it a proof of the maternal love which is blended with passion in women of her stamp. For Coralie and her like, passion includes every human affection. Lucien went from thought to thought, and argued himself into ac-cepting the gift. "I love her," he said; "we shall live to-gether as husband and wife; I will never forsake her!"

What mortal, short of a Diogenes, could fail to understand Lucien's feelings as he climbed the dirty fetid staircase to his lodging, turned the key that grated in the lock, and entered and looked around at the unswept brick floor, at the cheerless grate, at the ugly poverty and bareness of the room.

A package of manuscript was lying on the table. It was his novel; a note from Daniel d'Arthez lay beside it :

"Our friends are almost satisfied with your work, dear poet," d'Arthez wrote. "You will be able to present it with more confidence now, they say, to friends and enemies. We saw your charming article on the Panorama-Dramatique; you are sure to excite as much jealousy in the profession as re-gret among your friends here.   DANIEL."

"Regrets! What does he mean?" exclaimed Lucien. The polite tone of the note astonished him. Was he to be henceforth a stranger to the brotherhood? He had learned to set a higher value on the good opinion and the friendship of the circle in the Rue des Quatre-Vents since he had tasted of the delicious fruits offered to him by the Eve of the theatrical underworld. For some moments he stood in deep thought; he saw his present in the garret, and foresaw his future in Coralie's rooms. Honorable resolution struggled with temptation and swayed him now this way, now that. He sat down and began to look through his manuscript, to see in what condition his friends had returned it to him. What was his amazement, as he read chapter after chapter, to find his poverty transmuted into riches by the cunning of the pen, and the devotion of the unknown great men, his friends of the brotherhood. Dialogue, closely packed, nervous, pregnant, terse, and full of the spirit of the age, replaced his conversations, which seemed poor and pointless prattle in comparison. His characters, a little uncertain in the drawing, now stood out in vigorous contrast of color and relief; physiological observations, due no doubt to Horace Bianchon, supplied links of interpretation between human character and the curious phenomena of human life—subtle touches which made his men and women live. His wordy passages of description were condensed and vivid. The misshapen, illclad child of his brain had returned to him as a lovely maiden, with white robes and rosy-hued girdle and scarf—an entrancing creation. Night fell and took him by surprise, reading through rising tears, stricken to earth by such greatness of soul, feeling the worth of such a lesson, admiring the alterations, which taught him more of literature and art than all his four years' apprenticeship of study and reading and comparison. A master's correction of a line made upon the study always teaches more than all the theories and criticisms in the world.

"What friends are these! What hearts! How fortunate I am!" he cried, grasping his manuscript tightly and descending the stairs.

With the quick impulsiveness of a poetic and mobile temperament, he rushed off to Daniel's lodging. As he climbed the stairs, and thought of these friends, who refused to leave the path of honor, he felt conscious that he was less worthy of them than before. A voice spoke within him, telling him that if d'Arthez had loved Coralie, he would have had her break with Camusot. And, beside this, he knew that the brotherhood held journalism in utter abhorrence, and that he himself was already, to some small extent, a journalist. All of them, except Meyraux, who had just gone out, were in d'Arthez's room when he entered it, and saw that all their faces were full of sorrow and despair.

"What is it?" he cried.

"We have just heard news of a dreadful catastrophe; the greatest thinker of the age, our most loved friend, who was like a light among us for two years——"

"Louis Lambert!"

"Has fallen a victim to catalepsy. There is no hope for him," said Bianchon.

"He will die, his soul wandering in the skies, his body unconscious on earth," said Michel Chrestien solemnly.

"He will die as he lived," said d'Arthez.

"Love fell like a firebrand in the vast empire of his brain and burned him away," said Léon Giraud.

"Yes," said Joseph Bridau, "he has reached a height that we cannot so much as see."

"*We* are to be pitied, not Louis," said Fulgence Ridal.

"Perhaps he will recover," exclaimed Lucien.

"From what Meyraux has been telling us, recovery seems impossible," answered Bianchon. "Medicine has no power over the change that is working in his brain."

"Yet there are physical means," said d'Arthez.

"Yes," said Bianchon; "we might produce imbecility instead of catalepsy."

"Is there no way of offering another head to the spirit of evil? I would give mine to save him!" cried Michel Chrestien.

"And what would become of European federation?" asked d'Arthez.

"Ah! true," replied Michel Chrestien. "Our duty to humanity comes first; to one man afterward."

"I came here with a heart full of gratitude to you all," said Lucien. "You have changed my alloy into golden coin."

"Gratitude! For what do you take us?" asked Bianchon.

"We had the pleasure," added Fulgence.

"Well; so you are a journalist, are you?" asked Léon Giraud. "The fame of your first appearance has reached even the Latin Quarter."

"I am not a journalist yet," returned Lucien.

"Aha! So much the better," said Michel Chrestien.

"I told you so!" said d'Arthez. "Lucien knows the value of a clean conscience. When you can say to yourself as you lay your head on the pillow at night, 'I have not sat in judgment on another man's work; I have given pain to no one; I have not used the edge of my wit to deal a stab to some harmless soul; I have sacrificed no one's success to a jest; I have not even troubled the happiness of imbecility; I have not added to the burdens of genius; I have scorned the easy triumphs of epigram; in short, I have not acted against my convictions,' is not this a viaticum that gives one daily strength?"

"But one can say all this, surely, and yet work on a newspaper," said Lucien. "If I had absolutely no other way of earning a living, I should certainly come to this."

"Oh! oh! oh!" cried Fulgence, his voice raising a note each time; "we are capitulating, are we?"

"He will turn journalist," Léon Giraud said gravely. "Oh, Lucien, if you would only stay and work with us! We are about to bring out a periodical in which justice and truth shall never be violated; we will spread doctrines that, perhaps, will be of real service to mankind——"

"You will not have a single subscriber," Lucien broke in with Machiavellian wisdom.

"There will be five hundred of them," asserted Michel Chrestien, "but they will be worth five hundred thousand."

"You will need a lot of capital," continued Lucien.

"No, only devotion," said d'Arthez.

"Anybody might take him for a perfumer's assistant," burst out Michel Chrestien, looking at Lucien's head and sniffing comically. "You were seen driving about in a very smart turnout with a pair of thoroughbreds, and a mistress for a prince, Coralie herself."

"Well, and is there any harm in it?"

"You would not say that if you thought that there was no harm in it," said Bianchon.

"I could have wished Lucien a Beatrice," said d'Arthez, "a noble woman, who would have been a help to him in life——"

"But, Daniel," asked Lucien, "love is love wherever you find it, is it not?"

"Ah!" said the republican member, "on that one point I am an aristocrat. I could not bring myself to love a woman who must rub shoulders with all sorts of people in the green-room; whom an actor kisses on the stage; she must lower herself before the public, smile on every one, lift her skirt as she dances, and dress like a man, that all the world may see what none should see save I alone. Or, if I loved such a woman, she should leave the stage, and my love should cleanse her from the stain of it."

"And if she would not leave the stage?"

"I should die of mortification, jealousy, and all sorts of

pain. You cannot pluck love out of your heart as you draw a tooth."

Lucien's face grew dark and thoughtful.

"When they find out that I am tolerating Camusot, how they will despise me," he thought.

"Look here," said the fierce republican with a humorous fierceness, "you can be a great writer, but a little play-actor you shall never be," and he took up his hat and went out.

"He is hard, is Michel Chrestien," commented Lucien.

"Hard and salutary, like the dentist's pincers," said Bianchon. "Michel foresees your future; perhaps in the street, at this moment, he is thinking of you with tears in his eyes."

D'Arthez was kind, and talked comfortingly, and tried to cheer Lucien. The poet spent an hour with his friends, then he went, but his conscience treated him hardly, crying to him, "You will be journalist—a journalist!" as the witch cried to Macbeth that he should be king hereafter!

Out on the street, he looked up at d'Arthez's windows, and saw a faint light shining in them, and his heart sank. A dim foreboding told him that he had bidden his friends good-by for the last time.

As he turned out of the Place de la Sorbonne into the Rue de Cluny, he saw a carriage at the door of his lodging. Coralie had driven all the way from the Boulevard du Temple for the sake of a moment with her lover and a "good-night." Lucien found her sobbing in his garret. She would be as wretchedly poor as her poet, she wept, as she arranged his shirts and gloves and handkerchiefs in the crazy chest of drawers. Her distress was so real and so great that Lucien, but even now chidden for his connection with an actress, saw Coralie as a saint ready to assume the hair-shirt of poverty. The adorable girl's excuse for her visit was an announcement that the firm of Camusot, Coralie, and Lucien meant to invite Matifat, Florine, and Lousteau (the second trio) to supper; had Lucien any invitations to issue to people who might be useful to him? Lucien said that he would take counsel of Lousteau.

A few moments were spent together, and Coralie hurried away. She spared Lucien the knowledge that Camusot was waiting for her below.

Next morning, at eight o'clock, Lucien went to Étienne Lousteau's room, found it empty, and hurried away to Florine. Lousteau and Florine settled into possession of their new quarters like a married couple, received their friend in the pretty bedroom, and all three breakfasted sumptuously together. After talking over various subjects, Lucien stated the object of his call and asked Lousteau's advice.

"Why, I should advise you, my boy, to come with me to see Félicien Vernou," said Lousteau, when they sat at table, and Lucien had mentioned Coralie's projected supper; "ask him to be of the party, and keep well with him, if you can keep well with such a rascal. Félicien Vernou does a *feuilleton* for a political paper; he might perhaps introduce you, and you could blossom out into leaders in it at your ease. It is a Liberal paper, like ours; you will be a Liberal, that is the popular party; and, beside, if you mean to go over to the Ministerialists, you would do better for yourself if they had reason to be afraid of you. Then there is Hector Merlin and his Madame du Val-Noble; you meet great people at their house—dukes and dandies and millionaires; didn't they ask you and Coralie to dine with them?"

"Yes," replied Lucien; "you are going too, and so is Florine." Lucien and Étienne were now on familiar terms after Friday's debauch and the dinner at the "Rocher de Cancale."

"Very well, Merlin is on the paper; we shall come across him pretty often; he is the chap to follow close on Finot's heels. You would do well to pay him attention; ask him and Madame du Val-Noble to supper. He may be useful to you before long; for rancorous people are always in need of others, and he may do you a good turn if he can reckon on your pen."

"Your beginning has made enough sensation to smooth your way," said Florine; "take advantage of it at once, or you will soon be forgotten."

"The bargain, the great business, is concluded," Lousteau continued. "That Finot, without a spark of talent in him, is to be editor of Dauriat's weekly paper, with a salary of six hundred francs per month, and owner of a sixth share, for which he has not paid one penny. And I, my dear fellow, am now editor of our little paper. Everything went off as I expected; Florine managed superbly, she could give points to Talleyrand himself."

"We have a hold on men through their pleasures," said Florine, "while a diplomatist only works on their self-love. A diplomatist sees a man made up for the occasion; we know him in his moments of folly, so our power is greater."

"And when the thing was settled, Matifat made the first and last joke of his whole druggist's career," put in Lousteau. "He said, 'This affair is quite in my line; I am supplying drugs to the public.'"

"I suspect that Florine put him up to it," cried Lucien.

"And by these means, my little dear, your foot is in the stirrup," continued Lousteau.

"You were born with a silver spoon in your mouth," remarked Florine. "What lots of young fellows wait for years, wait till they are sick of waiting, for a chance to get an article into a paper! You will do like Emile Blondet. In six months' time you will be giving yourself high and mighty airs," she added, with a mocking smile, in the language of her class.

"Haven't I been in Paris for three years?" said Lousteau, "and only yesterday Finot began to pay me a fixed monthly salary of three hundred francs, and a hundred francs per sheet for his paper."

"Well; you are saying nothing!" exclaimed Florine, with her eyes turned on Lucien.

"We shall see," said Lucien.

"My dear boy, if you had been my brother, I could not have done more for you," retorted Lousteau, somewhat nettled, "but I won't answer for Finot.   Scores of sharp fellows will besiege Finot for the next two days with offers to work for low pay.   I have promised for you, but you can draw back if you like.   You little know how lucky you are," he added after a pause.   "All those in our set combine to attack an enemy in various papers and lend each other a helping hand all round."

"Let us go, in the first place, to Félicien Vernou," said Lucien.   He was eager to conclude an alliance with such formidable birds of prey.

Lousteau sent for a cab and the pair of friends drove to Vernou's house, on a second floor, up an alley, in the Rue Mandar.   To Lucien's great astonishment, the harsh, fastidious, and severe critic's surroundings were vulgar to the last degree.   A marbled paper, cheap and shabby, with a meaningless pattern repeated at regular intervals, covered the walls, and a series of aqua tints in gilt frames decorated the apartment, where Vernou sat at table with a woman so plain that she could only be the legitimate mistress of the house, and two very small children perched on high chairs with a bar in front to prevent the infants from tumbling out.   Félicien Vernou, in a cotton dressing-gown contrived out of the remains of one of his wife's dresses, was not over well pleased by this invasion.

"Have you breakfasted, Lousteau?" he asked, placing a chair for Lucien.

"We have just left Florine; we have been breakfasting with her."

Lucien could not take his eyes off Madame Vernou.   She looked like a stout, homely cook, with a tolerably fair com-

plexion, but commonplace to the last degree. The lady wore
a bandana tied over her night-cap, the strings of the latter
article of dress being tied so tightly under the chin that her
puffy cheeks stood out on either side. A shapeless, beltless
garment, fastened by a single button at the throat, enveloped
her from head to foot in such a fashion that a comparison to
a milestone at once suggested itself. Her health left no room
for hope; her cheeks were almost purple; her fingers looked
like sausages. In a moment it dawned upon Lucien how it
was that Vernou was always so ill at ease in society; here
was the living explanation of his misanthropy. Sick of his
marriage, unable to bring himself to abandon his wife and
family, he had yet sufficient of the artistic temper to suffer
continually from their presence; Vernou was an actor by
nature bound never to pardon the success of another, condemned to chronic discontent because he was never content
with himself. Lucien began to understand the sour look
which seemed to add to the bleak expression of envy on
Vernou's face; the acerbity of the epigrams with which his
conversation was sown, the journalist's pungent phrases—keen,
polished, and elaborately wrought as a stiletto—were at once
explained.

"Let us go into my study," Vernou said, rising from the
table; "you have come on business, no doubt?"

"Yes and no," replied Étienne Lousteau. "It is a supper,
old chap."

"I have brought a message. from Coralie," said Lucien
(Madame Vernou looked up at once at the name), "to ask
you to supper to-night at her house to meet the same company
as before at Florine's, and a few more besides—Hector Merlin
and Madame du Val-Noble and some others. There will be
play afterward."

"But we are engaged to Madame Mahoudeau this evening,
dear," put in the wife.

"What does that matter?" returned Vernou.

"She will take offense if we don't go; and you are very glad of her when you have a bill to discount."

"This wife of mine, my dear boy, can never be made to understand that a supper engagement for twelve o'clock does not prevent you from going to an evening party that comes to an end at eleven. She is always with me while I work," he added.

"You have so much imagination!" said Lucien, and thereby made a mortal enemy of Vernou.

"Well," continued Lousteau, "you are coming; but that is not all. Monsieur de Rubempré is about to be one of us, so you must push him in your paper. Give him out for a chap that will make a name for himself in literature, so that he can put in at least a couple of articles every month."

"Yes, if he means to be one of us, and will attack our enemies, as we will attack his, I will say a word for him at the opera to-night," replied Vernou.

"Very well—good-by till to-morrow, my boy," said Lousteau, shaking hands with every sign of cordiality. "When is your book coming out?"

"That depends on Dauriat; it is ready," said Vernou *paterfamilias*.

"Are you satisfied?"

"Yes and no——"

"We will get up a success," said Lousteau, and he rose with a bow to his colleague's wife.

The abrupt departure was necessary indeed; for the two infants, engaged in a noisy quarrel, were fighting with their spoons and flinging the pap in each other's faces.

"That, my boy, is a woman who all unconsciously will work great havoc in contemporary literature," said Étienne, when they came away. "Poor Vernou cannot forgive us for his wife. He ought to be relieved of her in the interests of the public; and a deluge of blood-thirsty reviews and stinging sarcasms against successful men of every sort would be averted. What is to become of a man with such a wife and that pair of abominable brats? Have you seen Rigaudin in Picard's 'La Maison en Loterie?' You have? Well, like Rigaudin, Vernou will not fight himself, but he will set others fighting; he would give an eye to put out both eyes in the head of the best friend he has. You will see him using the bodies of the slain for a stepping-stone, rejoicing over every one's misfortunes, attacking princes, dukes, marquises, and nobles, because he himself is a commoner; reviling the work of unmarried men because he forsooth has a wife; and everlastingly preaching morality, the joys of domestic life, and the duties of the citizen. In short, this very moral critic will spare no one, not even infants of tender age. He lives in the Rue Mandar with a wife who might be the 'Mamamouchi' of the 'Bourgeois gentilhomme' and a couple of little Vernous as ugly as sin. He tries to sneer at the Faubourg Saint-Germain, where he will never set foot, and makes his duchesses talk like his wife. That is the sort of man to raise a howl at the Jesuits, insult the court, and credit the court party with the design of restoring feudal rights and the right of primogeniture—just the one to preach a crusade for equality, he that thinks himself the equal of no one. If he were a bachelor, he would go into society; if he were in a fair way to be a royalist poet with a pension and the cross of the Legion of Honor, he would be an optimist, and journalism offers starting-points by the hundred. Journalism is a giant catapult set in motion by pigmy hatreds. Have you any wish to marry after this? Vernou has none of the milk of human kindness in him, it is all turned to gall; and he is emphatically the journalist, a tiger with two hands that tears everything to pieces, as if his pen had the hydrophobia."

"It is a case of gunophobia," said Lucien. "Has he ability?"

"He is witty, he is a writer of articles. He incubates articles; he does that all his life and nothing else. The most

14

dogged industry would fail to graft a book on his prose. Félicien is incapable of conceiving a work on a larger scale, of broad effects, of fitting characters harmoniously in a plot which develops till it reaches a climax. He has ideas, but he has no knowledge of facts; his heroes are utopian creatures, philosophical or liberal notions masquerading. He is at pains to write an original style, but his inflated periods would collapse at a pin-prick from a critic; and therefore he goes in terror of reviews, like every one else who can only keep his head above water with the bladders of newspaper puffs."

" What an article you are making out of him ! "

" That particular kind, my boy, must be spoken and never written."

" You are turning editor," said Lucien.

" Where shall I put you down ? "

"At Coralie's."

"Ah ! we are infatuated," said Lousteau. " What a mistake ! Do as I do with Florine, let Coralie be your housekeeper, and take your fling."

" You would send a saint to perdition," laughed Lucien.

"Well, there is no damning a devil," quickly retorted Lousteau.

The flippant tone, the brilliant talk of this new friend, his views of life, his paradoxes, the axioms of Parisian Machiavellism—all these things impressed Lucien unawares. Theoretically the poet knew that such thoughts were perilous; but he believed them practically useful.

Arrived in the Boulevard du Temple, the friends agreed to meet at the office between four and five o'clock. Hector Merlin would doubtless be there. Lousteau was right. The infatuation of desire was upon Lucien; for the courtesan who loves knows how to grapple her lover to her by every weakness in his nature, fashioning herself with incredible flexibility to his every wish, encouraging the soft, effeminate habits which strengthen her hold. Lucien was thirsting already for enjoyment; he was in love with the easy, luxurious, and expensive life which the actress led.

He found Coralie and Camusot intoxicated with joy. The Gymnase offered Coralie an engagement after Easter on terms for which she had never dared to hope.

"And this great success is owing to you," said Camusot.

"Yes, surely. The 'Alcalde' would have fallen flat but for him," cried Coralie; "if there had been no article, I should have been in for another six years of the boulevard theatres."

She danced up to Lucien and flung her arms around him, putting an indescribable silken softness and sweetness into her enthusiasm. Love had come to Coralie. And Camusot? his eyes fell. Looking down after the wont of mankind in moments of sharp pain, he saw the seam of Lucien's boots, a deep yellow thread used by the best bootmakers of that time, in strong contrast with the glistening leather. The color of that seam had tinged his thoughts during a previous conversation with himself, as he sought to explain the presence of a mysterious pair of hessians in Coralie's fender. He remembered now that he had seen the name of "Gay, Rue de la Michodière," printed in black letters on the soft white kid lining.

"You have a handsome pair of boots, sir," he said.

"Like everything else about him," said Coralie.

"I should be very glad of your bootmaker's address."

"Oh, how like the Rue des Bourdonnais to ask for a tradesman's address," cried Coralie. "Do *you* intend to patronize a young man's bootmaker? A nice young man you would make! Do keep to your own top-boots; they are the kind for a steady-going man with a wife and family and a mistress."

"Indeed, if you would take off one of your boots, sir, I should be very much obliged," persisted Camusot.

"I could not get it on again without a button-hook," said Lucien, flushing up.

"Bérénice will fetch you one ; we can do with some here," jeered Camusot.

"Papa Camusot ! " said Coralie, looking at him with cruel scorn, "have the courage of your pitiful baseness. Come, speak out ! You think that this gentleman's boots are very like mine, do you not ? I forbid you to take off your boots," she added, turning to Lucien. "Yes, Monsieur Camusot. Yes, you saw some boots lying about in the fender here the other day, and that is the identical pair, and this gentleman was hiding in my dressing-room at the time waiting for them ; and he had passed the night here. This was what you were thinking, *hein ?* Think so ; I would rather you did. It is the simple truth. I am deceiving you. And if I am ? I do it to please myself."

She sat down. There was no anger in her face, no embarrassment ; she looked from Camusot to Lucien. The two men avoided each other's eyes.

"I will believe nothing that you do not wish me to believe," said Camusot. " Don't play with me, Coralie ; I was wrong——"

"I am either a shameless baggage that has taken a sudden fancy ; or a poor, unhappy girl who feels what love really is for the first time, the love that all women long for. And whichever way it is, you must leave me or take me as I am," she said, with a queenly gesture that completely crushed the wretched Camusot.

"Is it really true ? " he asked, seeing from their faces that this was no jest, yet begging to be deceived.

"I love mademoiselle," Lucien faltered out.

At that word, Coralie sprang to her poet and held him tightly to her ; then, with her arms still about him, she turned to the silk-mercer, as if to bid him see the beautiful picture made by two young lovers.

"Poor Musot, take all that you gave to me back again ; I do not want to keep anything of yours ; for I love this boy here madly, not for his intellect, but for his beauty. I would rather starve with him than have millions with you."

Camusot sank into a low chair, hid his face in his hands, and said not a word.

"Would you like us to go away?" she asked. There was a note of ferocity in her voice which no words can describe.

Cold chills ran down Lucien's spine; he beheld himself burdened with a woman, an actress, and a household.

"Stay here, Coralie; keep it all," the old tradesman said at last, in a faint, unsteady voice that came from his heart; "I don't want anything back. There is the worth of sixty thousand francs here in the furniture; but I could not bear to think of my Coralie in want. And yet, it will not be long before you come to want. However great this gentleman's talent may be, he can't afford to keep you. We old fellows must expect this sort of thing. Coralie, let me come and see you sometimes; I may be of use to you. And—I confess it; I cannot live without you."

The poor man's gentleness, stripped as he was of his happiness just as happiness had reached its height, touched Lucien deeply. Coralie was quite unsoftened by it.

"Come as often as you wish, poor Musot," she said; "I shall like you all the better when I don't pretend to love you."

Camusot seemed to be resigned to his fate so long as he was not driven out of the earthly paradise, in which his life could not have been all joy; he trusted to the chances of life in Paris and to the temptations that would beset Lucien's path; he would wait a while, and all that had been his should be his again. Sooner or later, thought the wily tradesman, this handsome young fellow would be unfaithful; he would keep a watch on him; and the better to do this and use his opportunity with Coralie, he would be their friend. The persistent passion that could consent to such humiliation terrified Lucien. Camusot's proposal of a dinner at Véry's in the Palais Royal was accepted.

"What joy!" cried Coralie, as soon as Camusot had departed. "You will not go back now to your garret in the Latin Quarter; you will live here. We shall always be together. You can take a room in the Rue Charlot for the sake of appearances and *vogue la galère!*" (come what may).

She began to dance her Spanish dance, with an excited eagerness that revealed the strength of the passion in her heart.

"If I work hard, I may make five hundred francs a month," Lucien said.

"And I shall make as much again at the theatre, without counting extras. Camusot will pay for my dresses as before. He is fond of me! We can live like Crœsus on fifteen hundred francs a month."

"And the horses? and the coachman? and the footman?" inquired Bérénice.

"I will get into debt," said Coralie. And she began to dance with Lucien.

"I must close with Finot after this," Lucien exclaimed.

"There!" said Coralie, "I will dress and take you to your office. I will wait outside in the boulevard for you with the carriage."

Lucien sat down on the sofa and made some very sober reflections as he watched Coralie at her toilet. It would have been wiser to leave Coralie free than to start all at once with such an establishment; but Coralie was there before his eyes, and Coralie was so lovely, so graceful, so bewitching, that the more picturesque aspects of bohemia were in evidence, and he flung down the gauntlet to fortune.

Bérénice was ordered to superintend Lucien's removal and installation; and Coralie, triumphant, radiant, and happy, carried off her love, her poet, and must needs go all over Paris on the way to the Rue Saint-Fiacre. Lucien sprang lightly up the staircase and entered the office with an air of being quite at home. Coloquinte was there with the stamped paper still on his head; and old Giroudeau told him again, hypocritically enough, that no one had yet come in.

"But the editor and contributors *must* meet somewhere or other to arrange about the journal," said Lucien.

"Very likely; but I have nothing to do with the writing of the paper," said the Emperor's captain, resuming his occupation of checking off wrappers with his eternal *broum! broum!*

Was it lucky or unlucky? Finot chanced to come in at that very moment to announce his sham abdication and to bid Giroudeau watch over his interests.

"No shilly-shally with this gentleman; he is on the staff," Finot added for his uncle's benefit, as he grasped Lucien by the hand.

"Oh! he is on the paper," exclaimed Giroudeau, much surprised at this friendliness. "Well, sir, you came on without much difficulty."

"I want to make things snug for you here, lest Étienne should bamboozle you," continued Finot, looking knowingly at Lucien. "This gentleman will be paid three francs per column all around, including theatres."

"You have never taken any one on such terms before," said Giroudeau, opening his eyes.

"And he will take the four boulevard theatres. See that nobody sneaks his boxes and that he gets his share of tickets. I should advise you, nevertheless, to have them sent to your address," he added, turning to Lucien. "And he agrees to write beside ten miscellaneous articles of two columns each, for fifty francs per month, for one year. Does that suit you?"

"Yes," said Lucien. Circumstances had forced his hand.

"Draw up the agreement, uncle, and we will sign it when we come downstairs."

"Who is the gentleman?" inquired Giroudeau, rising and taking off his black silk skull-cap.

"Monsieur Lucien de Rubempré, who wrote the article on 'The Alcalde.'"

"Young man, you have a gold mine *there*," said the old soldier, tapping Lucien on the forehead. "I am not literary myself, but I read that article of yours, and I liked it. That is the kind of thing! There's gaiety for you! 'That will bring us new subscribers,' says I to myself. And so it did. We sold fifty more numbers."

"Is my agreement with Lousteau made out in duplicate and ready to sign?" asked Finot, speaking aside.

"Yes."

"Then antedate this gentleman's agreement by one day, so that Lousteau will be bound by the previous contract."

Finot took his new contributor's arm with a friendliness that charmed Lucien, and drew him out on the landing to say—

"Your position is made for you. I will introduce you to *my* staff myself, and to-night Lousteau will go round with you to the theatres. You can make a hundred and fifty francs per month on this little paper of ours with Lousteau as its editor, so try to keep well with him. The rogue bears a grudge against me as it is, for tying his hands so far as you are concerned; but you have ability, and I don't choose that you shall be subjected to the whims of the editor. You might let me have a couple of sheets every month for my review, and I will pay you two hundred francs. This is between ourselves, don't mention it to anybody else; I should be laid open to the spite of every one whose vanity is mortified by your good fortune. Write four articles, fill your two sheets, sign two with your own name and two with a pseudonym, so that you may not seem to be taking the bread out of anybody else's mouth. You owe your position to Blondet and Vignon; they think that you have a future before you. So keep out of scrapes, and, above all things, be on your guard against your friends. As for us, we shall always get on

well together, you and I. Help me, and I will help you.
You have forty francs' worth of boxes and tickets to sell, and
sixty francs' worth of books to convert into cash. With that
and your work on the paper, you will be making four hundred
and fifty francs every month. If you use your wits, you will
find ways of making another two hundred francs, at least,
among the publishers ; they will pay you for reviews and prospectuses. But you are mine, are you not ? I can count upon
you."

Lucien squeezed Finot's hand in transports of joy which
no words can express.

" Don't let any one see that anything has passed between
us," said Finot in his ear, and he flung open a door of a
room in the roof at the end of a long passage on the fifth floor.

A table covered with a green cloth was drawn up to a
blazing fire, and seated in various chairs and lounges Lucien
discovered Lousteau, Félicien Vernou, Hector Merlin, and
two others unknown to him, all laughing or smoking. A real
inkstand, full of ink this time, stood on the table among a
great litter of papers; while a collection of pens, the worse
for wear, but still serviceable for journalists, told the new
contributor very plainly that the mighty enterprise was carried
on in this apartment.

"Gentlemen," said Finot, "the object of this gathering
is the installation of our friend Lousteau in my place as
editor of the newspaper which I am compelled to relinquish.
But although my opinions will necessarily undergo a transformation when I accept the editorship of a review of which
the politics are known to you, my *convictions* remain the
same, and we shall be friends as before. I am quite at your
service, and you likewise will be ready to do anything for me.
Circumstances change ; principles are fixed. Principles are
the pivot on which the hands of the political barometer
turn."

There was an instant shout of laughter.

"Who, pray, put that into your mouth?" asked Lousteau.

"Blondet!" said Finot.

"Windy, showery, stormy, settled fair," said Merlin; "we will all row in the same boat."

"In short," continued Finot, "not to muddle our wits with metaphors, any one who has an article or two for me will always find Finot.   This gentleman," turning to Lucien, "will be one of you.   I have arranged with him, Lousteau."

Every one congratulated Finot on his advance and new prospects.

"So there you are, mounted on our shoulders," said a contributor whom Lucien did not know.   "You will be the Janus of journal——"

"So long as he isn't the Janot," put in Vernou.

"Are you going to allow us to make attacks on our *bêtes noires?*" (wild boars).

"Any one you like."

"Ah, yes!" said Lousteau; "but the paper must keep on its lines.   Monsieur Châtelet is very wroth; we shall not let him off for a week yet."

"What has happened?" asked Lucien.

"He came here to ask for an explanation," said Vernou. "The imperial buck found old Giroudeau at home; and old Giroudeau told him, with all the coolness in the world, that Philippe Bridau wrote the article.   Philippe asked the Baron to mention the time and the weapons, and there it ended. We are engaged at this moment in offering excuses to the Baron in to-morrow's issue.   Every phrase is a stab for him."

"Keep your teeth in him and he will come round to me," said Finot; "and it will look as if I was obliging him by appeasing you.   He can say a word to the Ministry, and we can get something or other out of him—an assistant schoolmaster's place or a tobacconist's license.   It is a lucky thing for us that we flicked him on the raw.   Does anybody here care to take a serious article on Nathan for my new paper?"

"Give it to Lucien," said Lousteau. "Hector and Vernou will write articles in their papers at the same time."

"Good-day, gentlemen; we shall meet each other face to face at Barbin's," said Finot, laughing.

Lucien received some congratulations on his admission to the mighty army of journalists, and Lousteau explained that they could be sure of him. "Lucien wants you all to sup in a body at the house of the fair Coralie."

"Coralie is going on at the Gymnase," said Lucien.

"Very well, gentlemen; it is understood that we push Coralie, eh? Put a few lines about her new engagement in your papers and say something about her talent. Credit the management of the Gymnase with tact and discernment; will it do to say intelligence?"

"Yes, say intelligence," said Merlin; "Frédéric has something of Scribe's."

"Oh! Well, then, the manager of the Gymnase is the most perspicacious and far-sighted of men of business," said Vernou.

"Look here! don't write your articles on Nathan until we have come to an understanding; you shall hear why," said Étienne Lousteau. "We ought to do something for our new comrade. Lucien here has two books to bring out—a volume of sonnets and a novel. The power of the paragraph should make him a great poet due in three months; and we will make good use of his sonnets ('Marguerites' is the title) to run down odes, ballads, and reveries, and all the romantic poetry."

"It would be a droll thing if the sonnets were no good after all," said Vernou. "What do you yourself think of your sonnets, Lucien?"

"Yes, what do you think of them?" asked one of the two whom Lucien did not know.

"They are all right, gentlemen; I give you my word," said Lousteau.

" Very well, that will do for me," said Vernou; " I will heave your book at the poets of the sacristy; I am tired of them."

" If Dauriat declines to take the ' Marguerites ' this evening, we will attack him by pitching into Nathan."

" But what will Nathan say ? " cried Lucien.

His five colleagues burst out laughing.

" Oh ! he will be delighted," said Vernou.   " You will see how we manage these things."

" So he is one of us ? " said one of the two (to Lucien) unknown journalists.

" Yes, yes, Frédéric ; no tricks.   We are all working for you, Lucien, you see ; you must stand by us when your turn comes.   We are all friends of Nathan's, and we are attacking him.   Now, let us divide Alexander's empire.   Frédéric, will you take the Français and the Odéon ? "

" If these gentlemen are willing," returned the person addressed as Frédéric.   The others nodded assent, but Lucien saw a gleam of jealousy here and there.

" I am keeping the Opera, the Italiens, and the Opera-Comique," put in Vernou.

" And how about me ?   Am I to have no theatres at all ? " asked the second stranger.

" Oh well, Hector can let you have the Variétés, and Lucien can spare you the Porte Saint-Martin.   Let him have the Porte Saint-Martin, Lucien, he is wild about Fanny Beaupré ; and you can take the Cirque-Olympique in exchange.   I shall have Bobino and the Funambules and Madame Saqui.   Now, what have we for to-morrow ? "

" Nothing."

" Nothing ? "

" Nothing."

" Gentlemen, be brilliant for my first number.   The Baron du Châtelet and his cuttlefish-bone will not last for a week, and the writer of ' Le Solitaire ' is worn out."

"And 'Sosthenes-Demosthenes' is stale too," said Vernou; "everybody has taken it up."

"The fact is, we want a new set of ninepins," said Frédéric.

"Suppose that we take the virtuous representatives of the Right?" suggested Lousteau. "We might say that Monsieur de Bonald has sweaty feet."

"Let us begin a series of sketches of Ministerialist orators," suggested Hector Merlin.

"You do that, youngster; you know them; they are your own party," said Lousteau; "you could indulge any little private grudges of your own. Pitch into Beugnot and Syrieys de Mayrinhac and the rest. You might have the sketches ready in advance, and we shall have something to fall back upon."

"How if we invented one or two cases of refusal of burial with aggravating circumstances?" asked Hector.

"Do not follow in the tracks of the big constitutional papers; they have pigeon-holes full of ecclesiastical *canards*," retorted Vernou.

"*Canards?*" repeated Lucien.

"That is our word for a scrap of fiction told for true, put in to enliven the column of morning news when it is flat. We owe the discovery to Benjamin Franklin, the inventor of the lightning conductor and the republic. That journalist completely deceived the encyclopædists by his transatlantic *canards*. Raynal gives two of them for facts in his 'Histoire philosphique des Indes.' "

"I did not know that," said Vernou. "What were the stories?"

"One was a tale about an Englishman and a negress who helped him to escape; he sold the woman for a slave after getting her with child himself to enhance her value. The other was the eloquent defense of a young woman brought before the authorities for bearing a child out of wedlock. Franklin owned to the fraud in Necker's house when he came to Paris, much to the confusion of French philosophism. Behold how the New World twice set a bad example to the Old!"

"In journalism," said Lousteau, "everything that is probable is true. That is an axiom."

"Criminal procedure is based on the same rule," said Vernou.

"Very well, we meet here at nine o'clock," and with that they rose, and the sitting broke up with the most affecting demonstrations of intimacy and good-will.

"What have you done to Finot, Lucien, that he should make a special arrangement with you? You are the only one that he has bound to himself," said Étienne Lousteau, as they came downstairs.

"I? Nothing. It was his own proposal," said Lucien.

"As a matter of fact, if you should make your own terms with him, I should be delighted; we should, both of us, be the better for it."

On the first floor they found Finot. He stepped across to Lousteau and asked him into the so-called private office. Giroudeau immediately put a couple of stamped agreements before Lucien.

"Sign your agreement," he said, "and the new editor will think the whole thing was arranged yesterday."

Lucien, reading the document, overheard fragments of a tolerably warm dispute within as to the line of conduct and profits of the paper. Étienne Lousteau wanted his share of the blackmail levied by Giroudeau; and, in all probability, the matter was compromised, for the pair came out perfectly good friends.

"We will meet at Dauriat's, Lucien, in the Wooden Galleries, at eight o'clock," said Étienne Lousteau.

A young man appeared, meanwhile, in search of employment, wearing the same nervous, shy look with which Lucien himself had come to the office so short a while ago; and in his secret soul Lucien felt amused as he watched Giroudeau playing off the same tactics with which the old campaigner had previously foiled him. Self-interest opened his eyes to the necessity of the manœuvres which raised well-nigh insurmountable barriers between beginners and the upper room where the elect were gathered together.

"Contributors don't get very much as it is," he said, addressing Giroudeau.

"If there were more of you, there would be so much less," retorted the captain. "So there!"

The old campaigner swung his loaded cane, and went down, coughing as usual. Out in the street he was amazed to see a handsome carriage waiting on the boulevard for Lucien.

"*You* are the army nowadays," he said, "and we are the civilians."

"Upon my word," said Lucien, as he drove away with Coralie, "these young writers seem to me to be the best fellows alive. Here am I a journalist, sure of making six hundred francs a month if I work like a horse. But I shall find a publisher for my two books, and I will write others; for my friends will insure a success. And so, Coralie, '*vogue la galère !*' (come what may) as you say."

"You will make your way, dear boy; but you must not be as good-natured as you are good-looking; it would be the ruin of you. Be ill-natured, that is the proper thing."

Coralie and Lucien drove in the Bois de Boulogne, and again they met the Marquise d'Espard, Mme. de Bargeton, and the Baron du Châtelet. Mme. de Bargeton gave Lucien a languishing glance which might be taken as a greeting. Camusot had ordered the best possible dinner; and Coralie, feeling that she was rid of her adorer, was more charming to the poor silk-mercer than she had ever been in the fourteen months during which their connection lasted; he had never seen her so kindly, so enchantingly lovely.

"Come," he thought, "let us keep near her anyhow!"

In consequence, Camusot made secret overtures. He promised Coralie an income of six thousand livres; he would
transfer the stock in the funds into her name (his wife knew
nothing about the investment) if only she would consent to
be his mistress still. He would shut his eyes to her lover.

"And betray such an angel? Why, just look at him,
you old fossil, and look at yourself!" and her eyes turned to
her poet. Camusot had pressed Lucien to drink till the
poet's head was rather cloudy.

There was no help for it; Camusot made up his mind to
wait till sheer want should give him this woman a second
time.

"Then I can only be your friend," he said, as he kissed
her on the forehead.

Lucien went from Coralie and Camusot to the Wooden
Galleries. What a change had been wrought in his mind by
his initiation into journalism! He mixed fearlessly now with
the crowd which surged to and fro in the buildings; he even
swaggered a little because he had a mistress; and he walked
into Dauriat's shop in an off-hand manner because he was a
journalist.

He found himself among distinguished men; gave a hand
to Blondet and Nathan and Finot, and to all the coterie with
whom he had been fraternizing for a week. He was a personage, he thought, and he flattered himself that he surpassed
his comrades. That little flick of the wine did him admirable
service; he was witty; he showed that he could "howl with
the wolves."

And yet the tacit approval, the praises spoken and un-
spoken on which he had counted, were not forthcoming. He
noticed the first stirrings of jealousy among a group, less
curious, perhaps, than anxious to know the place which this
new-comer might take, and the exact portion of the sum-total
of profits which he would probably secure and swallow.
Lucien only saw smiles on two faces—Finot, who regarded

him as a mine to be exploited, and Lousteau, who considered that he had proprietary rights in the poet, looked glad to see him. Lousteau had begun already to assume the airs of an editor; he tapped sharply on the window-panes of Dauriat's private office.

"One moment, my friend," cried a voice within as the publisher's face appeared above the green curtains of the window.

The moment lasted an hour, and finally Lucien and Étienne were admitted into the sanctum.

"Well, have you thought over our friend's proposal?" asked Étienne Lousteau, now an editor.

"To be sure," said Dauriat, lolling like a sultan in his chair. "I have read the volume. And I submitted it to a man of taste, a good judge; for I don't pretend to understand these things myself. I myself, my friend, buy reputations ready-made, as the Englishman bought his love affairs. You are as great as a poet as you are handsome as a man, my boy," pronounced Dauriat. "Upon my word and honor (I don't tell you that as a publisher, mind), your sonnets are magnificent; no sign of effort about them, as is natural when a man writes with inspiration and *verve*. You know your craft, in fact, one of the good points of the new school. Your volume of 'Marguerites' is a fine book, but there is no business in it, and it is not worth my while to meddle with anything but a very big affair. In conscience, I won't take your sonnets. It would be impossible to push them; there is not enough in the thing to pay the expenses of a big success. Beside, you will not keep to poetry; this book of yours will be your first and last attempt of the kind. You are young; you bring me the everlasting volume of early verse which every man of letters writes when he leaves school; he thinks a lot of it at the time, and laughs at it later on. Lousteau, your friend, has a poem put away somewhere among his old socks, I'll warrant. Haven't you a poem that you thought a good deal

15

of once, Lousteau?'' inquired Dauriat, with a knowing glance at the other.

'' How should I be writing prose otherwise, eh?'' asked Lousteau.

'' There, you see! He has never said a word to me about it, for our friend understands business and the trade,'' continued Dauriat. '' For me the question is not whether you are a great poet, I know that,'' he added, stroking down Lucien's pride; '' you have a great deal, a very great deal of merit; if I were only just starting in business, I should make the mistake of publishing your book. But, in the first place, my sleeping partners and those at the back of me are cutting off my supplies; I dropped twenty thousand francs over poetry last year, and that is enough for them; they will not hear of any more just now, and they are my masters. Nevertheless, that is not the question. I admit that you may be a great poet, but will you be a prolific writer? Will you hatch sonnets regularly? Will you run into ten volumes? Is there business in it? Of course not. You will be a delightful prose writer; you have too much sense to spoil your style with tagging rhymes together. You have a chance to make thirty thousand francs per annum by writing for the papers, and you will not exchange that chance for three thousand francs made with difficulty by your hemistitches and strophes and tomfoolery——''

'' You know that he is on the paper, Dauriat?'' put in Lousteau.

'' Yes,'' Dauriat answered. '' Yes, I saw his article, and in his own interest I decline the 'Marguerites.' Yes, sir, in six months' time I shall have paid you more money for the articles that I shall ask you to write than for your poetry that will not sell.''

'' And fame?'' said Lucien.

Dauriat and Lousteau laughed.

'' Oh, dear!'' said Lousteau, '' there be illusions left.''

" Fame means ten years of sticking to work, and a hundred thousand francs lost or made in the publishing trade. If you find anybody mad enough to print your poetry for you, you will feel some respect for me in another twelvemonth, when you have had time to see the outcome of the transaction."

" Have you the manuscript here?" Lucien asked the bookseller coldly.

" Here it is, my friend," said Dauriat. The publisher's manner toward Lucien had sweetened singularly.

Lucien took up the roll without looking at the string, so sure he felt that Dauriat had read his " Marguerites." He went out with Lousteau, seemingly neither disconcerted nor dissatisfied. Dauriat went with them into the shop, talking of his newspaper and Lousteau's daily, while Lucien played with the manuscript of the " Marguerites."

" Do you suppose that Dauriat has read your sonnets or sent them to any one else?" Étienne Lousteau snatched an opportunity to whisper.

" Yes," said Lucien.

" Look at the string." Lucien looked down at the blot of ink, and saw that the mark on the string still coincided ; he turned white with rage.

" Which of the sonnets was it that you particularly liked?" he asked, turning to the publisher.

" They are all of them remarkable, my friend ; but the sonnet on the Marguerite is delightful, the closing thought is fine, and exquisitely expressed. I felt sure from that sonnet that your prose work would command a success, and I spoke to Finot about you at once. Write articles for us and we will pay you well for them. Fame is a very fine thing, you see, but don't forget the practical and solid, and take every chance that turns up. When you have made money, you can write poetry."

The poet dashed out of the store to avoid an explosion. He was furious. Lousteau followed.

" Well, my boy, pray keep cool.   Take men as they are—
for means to an end.   Do you wish for revenge ? "

"At any price," muttered the poet.

" Here is a copy of Nathan's book.   Dauriat has just given
it to me.   The second edition is coming out to-morrow ; read
the book again, and knock off an article demolishing it.
Félicien Vernou cannot endure Nathan, for he thinks that
Nathan's success will injure his own forthcoming book.   It is
a craze with these little minds to fancy that there is not room
for two successes under the sun ; so he will see that your article
finds a place in the big paper for which he writes."

" But what is there to be said against the book ? it is good
work," cried Lucien.

" Oh, I say ! you must learn your trade," said Lousteau,
laughing.   " Given that the book is a masterpiece, under the
stroke of your pen it must turn to dull trash, dangerous and
unwholesome stuff."

" But how ? "

" You turn all the good points into bad ones."

" I am incapable of such a juggler's feat."

" My dear boy, a journalist is a juggler ; a man must make
up his mind to the drawbacks of the calling.   Look here ! I
am not a bad fellow ; this is the way *I* should set to work myself.   Attention ! You might begin by praising the book,
and amuse yourself a while by saying what you really think.
' Good,' says the reader, ' this critic is not jealous ; he will
be impartial, no doubt,' and from that point your public will
think that your criticism is a piece of conscientious work.
Then, when you have won your reader's confidence, you will
regret that you must blame the tendency and influence of such
work upon French literature.   ' Does not France,' you will
say, ' sway the whole intellectual world ? French writers
have kept Europe in the path of analysis and philosophical
criticism from age to age by their powerful style and the
original turn given by them to ideas.'   Here, for the benefit

of the Philistine, insert a panegyric on Voltaire, Rousseau, Diderot, Montesquieu, and Buffon. Hold forth upon the inexorable French language. Show how it spreads a varnish, as it were, over thought. Let fall a few aphorisms, such as:— 'A great writer in France is invariably a great man ; he writes in a language which compels him to think ; it is otherwise in other countries'—and so on, and so on. Then, to prove your case, draw a comparison between Rabener, the German satirical moralist, and La Bruyère. Nothing gives a critic such an air as an apparent familiarity with foreign literature. Kant is Cousin's pedestal.

" Once on that ground you bring out a word which sums up the French men of genius of the eighteenth century for the benefit of simpletons—you call that literature the ' literature of ideas.' Armed with this expression, you fling all the mighty dead at the heads of the illustrious living. You explain that in the present day a new form of literature has sprung up; that dialogue (the easiest form of writing) is overdone, and description dispenses with any need for thinking on the part of the author or reader. You bring up the fiction of Voltaire, Diderot, Sterne, and Le Sage, so trenchant, so compact of the stuff of life ; and turn from them to the modern novel, composed of scenery and word-pictures and metaphor and the dramatic situations, of which Scott is full. Invention may be displayed in such work, but there is no room for anything else. ' The romance after the manner of Scott is a mere passing fashion in literature,' you will say, and fulminate against the fatal way in which ideas are diluted and beaten thin ; cry out against a style within the reach of any intellect, for any one can commence author at small expense in a way of literature, which you can nickname the ' literature of imagery.'

" Then you fall upon Nathan with your argument, and establish it beyond cavil that he is a mere imitator with an appearance of genius. The concise, grand style of the eighteenth

century is lacking; you show that the author substitutes events
for sentiments. Action and stir is not life; he gives you
pictures, but no ideas.

"Come out with such phrases, and people will take them
up. In spite of the merits of the work, it seems to you to be
a dangerous, nay, a fatal precedent. It throws open the gates
of the temple of Fame to the crowd; and in the distance you
descry a legion of petty authors hastening to imitate this
novel and easy style of writing.

"Here you launch out into resounding lamentations over
the decadence and decline of taste, and slip in eulogies of
Messieurs Étienne Jouy, Tissot, Gosse, Duval, Jay, Benjamin
Constant, Aignan, Baour-Lormian, Villemain, and the whole
Liberal-Bonapartist chorus who patronize Vernou's paper.
Next you draw a picture of that glorious phalanx of writers
repelling the invasion of the romantics; these are the up-
holders of ideas and style as against metaphor and balder-
dash; the modern representatives of the school of Voltaire
as opposed to the English and German schools, even as the
seventeen heroic deputies of the Left fought the battle for the
nation against the Ultras of the Right.

"And then, under cover of names respected by the immense majority of Frenchmen (who will always be against the
government), you can crush Nathan; for although his work
is far above the average, it confirms the bourgeois taste for
literature without ideas. And after that, you understand, it
is no longer a question of Nathan and his book, but of France
and the glory of France. It is the duty of all honest and
courageous pens to make strenuous opposition to these foreign
importations. And with that you flatter your readers. Shrewd
French mother-wit is not easily caught napping. If publishers, by ways which you do not choose to specify, have
stolen a success, the reading public very soon judges for itself,
and corrects the mistakes made by some five hundred fools,
who always rush to the fore.

"Say that the publisher who sold a first edition of the book is audacious indeed to issue a second, and express regret that so clever a man does not know the taste of the country better. There is the gist of it. Just a sprinkle of the salt of wit and a dash of vinegar to bring out the flavor, and Dauriat will be done to a turn. But mind that you end with seeming to pity Nathan for a mistake, and speak of him as of a man from whom contemporary literature may look for great things if he renounces these ways."

Lucien was amazed at this talk from Lousteau. As the journalist spoke, the scales fell from his eyes; he beheld new truths of which he had never before caught so much as a glimpse.

"But all this that you are saying is quite true and just," cried he.

"If it were not, how could you make it tell against Nathan's book?" asked Lousteau. "That is the first manner of demolishing a book, my boy; it is the pickaxe style of criticism. But there are plenty of other ways. Your education will complete itself in time. When you are absolutely obliged to speak of a man whom you do not like, for proprietors and editors are sometimes under compulsion, you bring out a neutral special article. You put the title of the book at the head of it, and begin with general remarks, on the Greeks and the Romans if you like, and wind up with—'and this brings us to Mr. So-and-so's book, which will form the subject of a second article.' The second article never appears, and in this way you snuff out the book between two promises. But in this case you are writing down, not Nathan, but Dauriat; he needs the pickaxe style. If the book is really good, the pickaxe does no harm; but it goes to the core of it if it is bad. In the first case, no one but the publisher is any the worse; in the second, you do the public a service. Both methods, moreover, are equally serviceable in political criticism."

Étienne Lousteau's cruel lesson opened up possibilities for Lucien's imagination. He understood this craft to admiration.

"Let us go to the office," said Lousteau; "we shall find our friends there, and we will agree among ourselves to charge at Nathan; they will laugh, you will see."

Arrived in the Rue Saint-Fiacre, they went up to the room in the roof where the paper was made up, and Lucien was surprised, and gratified no less, to see the alacrity with which his comrades proceeded to demolish Nathan's book. Hector Merlin took up a piece of paper and wrote a few lines for his own newspaper:

"A second edition of M. Nathan's book is announced. We had intended to keep silence with regard to that work, but its apparent success obliges us to publish an article, not so much upon the book itself as upon certain tendencies of the new school of literature."

At the head of the "Facetiæ" in the morning's paper, Lousteau inserted the following note:

"M. Dauriat is bringing out a second edition of Monsieur Nathan's book. Evidently he does not know the legal maxim, *Non bis in idem.* All honor to rash courage."

Lousteau's words had been like a torch for burning; Lucien's hot desire to be revenged on Dauriat took the place of conscience and inspiration. For three days he never left Coralie's room; he sat at work by the fire, waited upon by Bérénice; petted, in moments of weariness, by the silent and attentive Coralie; till, at the end of that time, he had made a fair copy of about three columns of criticism, and an astonishingly good piece of work.

It was nine o'clock in the evening when he ran round to the office, found his associates, and read over his work to an attentive audience. Félicien said not a syllable. He took up the manuscript, and made off with it pellmell down the staircase.

" What has come to him? " cried Lucien.

" He has taken your article straight to the printer," said Hector Merlin. " 'Tis a masterpiece ; not a line to add, nor a word to take out."

" There was no need to do more than show you the way," said Lousteau.

" I should like to see Nathan's face when he reads this to-morrow," said another contributor, beaming with gentle satisfaction.

" It is as well to have you for a friend," remarked Hector Merlin.

" Then it will do? " Lucien asked quickly.

" Blondet and Vignon will feel bad," said Lousteau.

" Here is a short article which I have knocked together for you," began Lucien ; " if it takes, I could write you a series."

"Read it over," said Lousteau, and Lucien read the first of the delightful short papers which made the fortune of the little newspaper ; a series of sketches of Paris life, a portrait, a type, an ordinary event, or some of the oddities of the great city. This specimen—" The Man in the Street "—was written in a way that was fresh and original ; the thoughts were struck out by the shock of the words, the sounding ring of the adverbs and adjectives caught the reader's ear. The paper was as different from the serious and profound article on Nathan as the "Lettres persanes " from the " Esprit des lois."

"You are a born journalist," said Lousteau. " It shall go in to-morrow. Do as much of this sort of thing as you like."

" Ah, by-the-by," said Merlin, " Dauriat is furious about those two bombshells hurled into his magazine. I have just come from him. He was hurling imprecations, and in such a rage with Finot, who told him that he had sold his paper to you. As for me, I took him aside and just said a word in his

ear.   'The "Marguerites" will cost you dear,' I told him.
'A man of talent comes to you, you turn the cold shoulder
on him and send him into the arms of the newspapers.' "

"Dauriat will be dumfounded by the article on Nathan,"
said Lousteau.   "Do you see now what journalism is, Lucien?
Your revenge is beginning to tell.   The Baron Châtelet came
here this morning for your address.   There was a cutting
article upon him in this morning's issue; he is a weakling,
that buck of the empire, and he has lost his head.   Have
you seen the paper?   It is a funny article.   Look, 'Funeral
of the Heron and the Cuttlefish-bone's Lament.'   Madame
de Bargeton is called the Cuttlefish-bone now, and no mistake, and Châtelet is known everywhere as Baron Heron."

Lucien took up the paper, and could not help laughing at
Vernou's extremely clever skit.

"They will capitulate soon," said Hector Merlin.

Lucien merrily assisted at the manufacture of epigrams and
jokes at the end of the paper; and the associates smoked and
chatted over the day's adventures, over the foibles of some
among their number, or some new bit of personal gossip.
From their witty, malicious, bantering talk, Lucien gained a
knowledge of the inner life of literature and of the manners
and customs of the craft.

"While they are setting up the paper, I will go round with
you and introduce you to the managers of your theatres, and
take you behind the scenes," said Lousteau.   "And then we
will go to the Panorama-Dramatique and have a frolic in their
dressing-rooms."

Arm-in-arm they went from theatre to theatre.   Lucien was
introduced to this one and that and enthroned as a dramatic
critic.   Managers complimented him, actresses flung him side-
glances; for every one of them knew that this was the critic
who, by a single article, had gained an engagement at the
Gymnase, with twelve thousand francs a year, for Coralie, and
another for Florine at the Panorama-Dramatique with eight

thousand francs. Lucien was a man of importance. The little ovations raised Lucien in his own eyes, and taught him to know his power. At eleven o'clock the pair arrived at the Panorama-Dramatique; Lucien with a careless air that worked wonders. Nathan was there. Nathan held out a hand, which Lucien squeezed.

"Ah! my masters, so you have a mind to floor me, have you?" said Nathan, looking from one to the other.

"Just you wait until to-morrow, my dear fellow, and you shall see how Lucien has taken you in hand. Upon my word, you will be pleased. A piece of serious criticism like that is sure to do a book good."

Lucien reddened with confusion.

"Is it severe?" inquired Nathan.

"It is serious," said Lousteau.

"Then there is no harm done," Nathan rejoined. "Hector Merlin, in the green-room of the Vaudeville, was saying that I had been cut up."

"Let him talk and wait," cried Lucien, and took refuge in Coralie's dressing-room. Coralie, in her alluring costume, had just come off the stage.

Next morning, as Lucien and Coralie sat at breakfast, a carriage drove along the Rue du Vendôme. The street was quiet enough, so that they could hear the light sound made by an elegant cabriolet; and there was that in the pace of the horse, and the manner of pulling up at the door, which tells unmistakably of a thoroughbred. Lucien went to the window, and there, in fact, beheld a splendid English horse, and no less a person than Dauriat flinging the reins to his man as he stepped down.

"'Tis the publisher, Coralie," said Lucien.

"Let him wait, Bérénice," Coralie said at once.

Lucien smiled at her presence of mind and kissed her with a great rush of tenderness. This mere girl had made his interests hers in a wonderful way; she was quick-witted where he was concerned. The apparition of the insolent publisher, the sudden and complete collapse of that prince of charlatans, was due to circumstances almost entirely forgotten, so utterly has the booktrade changed during the last fifteen years.

From 1816 to 1827, when the newspaper reading-rooms were only just beginning to lend new books, the fiscal law pressed more heavily than ever upon periodical publications and necessity created the invention of advertisements. Paragraphs and articles in the newspapers were the only means of advertisement known in those days; and French newspapers, before the year 1822, were so small that the largest sheet of those times was not so large as the smallest daily paper of ours. Dauriat and Ladvocat, the first publishers to make a stand against the tyranny of journalists, were also the first to use the placards which caught the attention of Paris by strange type, striking colors, vignettes, and (at a later time) by lithograph illustrations, till a placard became a fairy-tale for the eyes, and not unfrequently a snare for the purse of the amateur. So much originality indeed was expended on placards in Paris, that one of that peculiar kind of maniacs, known as a collector, possesses a complete series.

At first the placard was confined to the store windows and stalls upon the boulevards in Paris; afterward it spread all over France, till it was supplanted to some extent by a return to advertisements in the newspapers. But the placard, nevertheless, which continues to strike the eye, after the advertisement and the book which it advertised are both forgotten, will always be among us; it took a new lease of life when walls were plastered with posters.

Newspaper advertising, the offspring of heavy stamp duties, a high rate of postage, and the heavy deposit of caution-money required by the government as security for good behavior, is within the reach of all who care to pay for it, and has turned the fourth page of every journal into a harvest-field alike for the speculator and the Internal Revenue Department. The press restrictions were invented in the time of M. de Villèle, who had a chance, if he had but known it, of destroying the power of journalism by allowing newspapers to multiply till no one took any notice of them; but he missed his opportunity, and a sort of privilege was created, as it were, by the almost insuperable difficulties put in the way of starting a new venture. So, in 1821, the periodical press might be said to have power of life and death over the creations of the brain and the publishing trade. A few lines among the items of news cost a fearful amount. Intrigues were multiplied in newspaper offices; and of a night when the columns were divided up, and this or that article was put in or left out to suit the space, the printing-room became a sort of battlefield; so much so, that the largest publishing firms had writers in their pay to insert short articles in which many ideas are put in little space. Obscure journalists of this stamp were only paid after the insertion of the items, and not unfrequently spent the night in the printing-office to make sure that their contributions were not omitted; sometimes putting in a long article, obtained heaven knows how, sometimes a few lines of a puff.

The manners and customs of journalism and of the publishing houses have since changed so much that many people nowadays will not believe what immense efforts were made by writers and publishers of books to secure a newspaper puff; the martyrs of glory, and all those who are condemned to the penal servitude of a life-long success, were reduced to such shifts, and stooped to the depths of bribery and corruption as seem fabulous to-day. Every kind of persuasion was brought to bear on journalists—dinners, flattery, and presents. The following story will throw more light on the close connection between the critic and the publisher than any quantity of flat assertions:

There was once upon a time an editor of an important paper, a clever writer with the prospect of becoming a statesman; he was young in those days and fond of pleasure, and he became the favorite of a well-known publishing house. One Sunday the wealthy head of the firm was entertaining several of the foremost journalists of the time in the country, and the mistress of the house, then a young and pretty woman, went to walk in her park with the illustrious visitor. The head clerk of the firm, a cool, steady, methodical German with nothing but business in his head, was discussing a project with one of the journalists, and as they chatted they walked on into the woods beyond the park. In among the thickets the German thought he caught a glimpse of his hostess, put up his eyeglass, made a sign to his young companion to be silent, and turned back, stepping softly. "What did you see?" asked the journalist. "Nothing particular," said the clerk. "Our affair of the long article is settled. To-morrow we shall have at least three columns in the 'Débats.'"

Another anecdote will again show the influence of a single article :

A book of M. de Chateaubriand's on the last of the Stuarts was for some time a "nightingale" on the bookseller's shelves. A single article in the "Journal des Débats" sold the work in a week. In those days, when there were no lending libraries, a publisher would sell an edition of ten thousand copies of a book by a Liberal if it was well reviewed by the opposition papers; but then the Belgian pirated editions were not as yet.

The preparatory attacks made by Lucien's friends, followed up by his article on Nathan, proved efficacious; they stopped the sale of his book. Nathan escaped with the mortification; he had been paid; he had nothing to lose; but Dauriat was likely to lose thirty thousand francs. The trade in new books may, in fact, be summed up much on this wise: A ream of blank paper costs fifteen francs, a ream of printed paper is worth anything between a hundred sous and a hundred crowns, according to its success; a favorable or unfavorable review at a critical time often decides the question; and Dauriat, having five hundred reams of printed paper on hand, hurried to make terms with Lucien. The sultan was now the slave.

After waiting for some time, fidgeting and making as much noise as he could while parleying with Bérénice, he at last obtained speech of Lucien; and, arrogant publisher though he was, he came in with the radiant air of a courtier in the royal presence, mingled, however, with a certain self-sufficiency and easy good-humor.

"Don't disturb yourselves, my little dears! How nice they look, just like a pair of turtle-doves. Who would think now, mademoiselle, that he, with that girl's face of his, could be a tiger with claws of steel, ready to tear a reputation to rags, just as he tears your wrappers, I'll be bound, when you are not quick enough to unfasten them," and he laughed before he had finished his jest.

"My dear boy——" he began, sitting down beside Lucien. "Mademoiselle, I am Dauriat," he said, interrupting himself. He judged it expedient to fire his name at her like a pistol-shot, for he considered that Coralie was less cordial than she should have been.

"Have you breakfasted, monsieur; will you keep us company?" asked Coralie.

"Why, yes; it is easier to talk at table," said Dauriat. "Beside, by accepting your invitation I shall have a right to expect you to dine with my friend Lucien here, for we must be close friends now, hand and glove!"

"Bérénice! Bring oysters, lemons, fresh butter, and champagne," said Coralie.

"You are too clever not to know what has brought me here," said Dauriat, fixing his eyes on Lucien.

"You have come to buy my sonnets."

"Precisely. First of all, let us lay down our arms on both

sides." As he spoke he took out a neat pocket-book, drew from it three bills for a thousand francs each, and laid them before Lucien with a suppliant's air. "Is monsieur content?" he asked.

"Yes," said the poet. A sense of beatitude, for which no words exist, flooded his soul at the sight of that unhoped wealth. He controlled himself, but he longed to sing aloud, to jump for joy; he was ready to believe in Aladdin's lamp and in enchantment; he believed in his own genius, in short.

"Then the 'Marguerites' are mine," continued Dauriat; "but you will undertake not to attack my publications, won't you?"

"The 'Marguerites' are yours, but I cannot pledge my pen; it is at the service of my friends, as theirs are mine."

"But you are one of my authors now. All my authors are my friends. So you won't spoil my business without warning me beforehand, so that I am prepared, will you?"

"I agree to that."

"To your fame!" and Dauriat raised his glass.

"I see that you have read the 'Marguerites,'" said Lucien. Dauriat was not disconcerted.

"My boy, a publisher cannot pay a greater compliment than by buying your 'Marguerites' unread. In six months' time you will be a great poet. You will be written up; people are afraid of you; I shall have no difficulty in selling your book. I am the same man of business that I was four days ago. It is not I who have changed; it is *you*. Last week your sonnets were so many cabbage-leaves for me; to-day your position has ranked them beside Delavigne."

"Ah, well," said Lucien, "if you have not read my sonnets you have read my article." With the sultan's pleasure of possessing a fair mistress, and the certainty of success, he had grown satirical and adorably impertinent of late.

"Yes, my friend; do you think I should have come here in such a hurry but for that? That terrible article of yours is very well written, worse luck. Oh ! you have a very great gift, my boy. Take my advice and make the most of your vogue," he added, with good humor, which masked the extreme insolence of the speech. "But have you yourself a copy of the paper? Have you seen your article in print?"

"Not yet," said Lucien, "though this is the first long piece of prose which I have published ; but Hector will have sent a copy to my address in the Rue Charlot."

"Here—read !" cried Dauriat, copying Talma's gesture in "Manlius."

Lucien took the paper, but Coralie snatched it from him.

"The firstfruits of your pen belong to me, as you well know," she laughed.

Dauriat was unwontedly courtier-like and complimentary. He was afraid of Lucien, and, therefore, he asked him to a great dinner which he was giving to a party of journalists toward the end of the week, and Coralie was included in the invitation. He took the "Marguerites" away with him when he went, asking *his* poet to look in when he pleased in the Wooden Galleries, and the agreement should be ready for his signature. Dauriat never forgot the royal airs with which he endeavored to overawe superficial observers and to impress them with the notion that he was a Mæcenas rather than a publisher ; at this moment he left the three thousand francs, waving away in lordly fashion the receipt which Lucien offered, kissed Coralie's hand, and took his departure.

"Well, dear love, would you have seen many of these bits of paper if you had stopped in your hole in the Rue de Cluny, prowling about among the musty old books in the Bibliothèque (Library) de Sainte-Geneviève?" asked Coralie, for she knew the whole story of Lucien's life by this time. "Those little friends of yours in the Rue des Quatre-Vents are great ninnies, it seems to me."

His brothers of the *cénacle !* * And Lucien could hear

* Lit.: The chamber in which the Last Supper was given.

16

the verdict and join heartily in the laughter excited by the remark.

He had seen himself in print; he had just experienced the ineffable joy of the author, that first pleasurable thrill of gratified vanity which comes but once. The full import and bearing of his article became apparent to him as he read and re-read it. The garb of print is to manuscript as the stage is to women; it brings beauties and defects to light, killing and giving life; the fine thoughts and the faults alike stare you in the face.

Lucien, in his excitement and rapture, gave not another thought to Nathan. Nathan was a stepping-stone for him— that was all; and he (Lucien) was happy exceedingly—he thought himself rich. The money brought by Dauriat was a very Potosi for the lad who used to go about unnoticed through the streets of Angoulême and down the steep path into L'Houmeau to Postel's garret, where his whole family had lived upon an income of twelve hundred francs. The pleasures of his life in Paris must inevitably dim the memories of those days; but so keen were they, that, as yet, he seemed to be back again in the Place du Mûrier. He thought of Eve, his beautiful, noble sister, of David his friend, and of his poor mother, and he sent Bérénice out to change one of the notes. While she went he wrote a few lines to his family, and on the maid's return he sent her to the coach-office with a packet of five hundred francs addressed to his mother. He could not trust himself; he wanted to send the money at once; later he might not be able to do it. Both Lucien and Coralie looked upon this restitution as a meritorious action. Coralie put her arms about her lover and kissed him, and thought him a model son and brother; she could not make enough of him, for generosity is a trait of character which delights these kindly creatures, who always carry their hearts in their hands.

"We have a dinner now every day for a week," she said;

"we will make a little carnival; you have worked quite hard enough."

Coralie, fain to delight in the beauty of a man whom all other women should envy her, took Lucien back to Staub. He was not dressed finely enough for her. Thence the lovers went to drive in the Bois de Boulogne, and came back to dine at Mme. du Val-Noble's. Rastignac, Bixiou, des Lupeaulx, Finot, Blondet, Vignon, the Baron de Nucingen, Beaudenord, Philippe Bridau, Conti, the great musician, all the artists and speculators, all the men who seek for violent sensations as a relief from immense labors, gave Lucien a welcome among them. And Lucien had gained confidence; he gave himself out in talk as though he had not to live by his wit, and was pronounced to be a "clever fellow" in the slang of the coterie of semi-comrades.

"Oh! we must wait and see what he has in him," said Theodore Gaillard, a poet patronized by the court, who thought of starting a royalist paper, to be entitled the "Réveil," at a later day.

After dinner, Merlin and Lucien, Coralie and Mme. du Val-Noble, went to the opera, where Merlin had a box. The whole party adjourned thither, and Lucien triumphant reappeared upon the scene of his first serious check.

He walked in the lobby, arm-in-arm with Merlin and Blondet, looking the dandies, who had once made merry at his expense, between the eyes. Châtelet was under his feet. He clashed glances with de Marsay, Vandenesse, and Manerville, the bucks of that day. And indeed Lucien, beautiful and elegantly arrayed, had caused a discussion in the Marquise d'Espard's box; Rastignac had paid a long visit, and the Marquise and Mme. de Bargeton put up their opera-glasses at Coralie. Did the sight of Lucien send a pang of regret through Mme. de Bargeton's heart? This thought was uppermost in the poet's mind. The longing for revenge aroused in him by the sight of the Corinne of Angoulême was as fierce as on that day when the lady and her cousin had cut him in the Champs-Élysées.

"Did you bring an amulet with you from the provinces?" It was Blondet who made this inquiry some few days later, when he called at eleven o'clock in the morning and found that Lucien was not yet risen. "His good looks are making ravages from cellar to garret, high and low," continued Blondet, kissing Coralie on the forehead. "I have come to enlist you, dear fellow," he continued, grasping Lucien by the hand. "Yesterday, at the Italiens, the Comtesse de Montcornet asked me to bring you to her house. You will not give a refusal to a charming woman? You meet people of the first fashion there."

"If Lucien is nice, he will not go to see your Countess," put in Coralie. "What call is there for him to show his face in fine society? He would only be bored there."

"Have you a vested interest in him? Are you jealous of fine ladies?"

"Yes," cried Coralie. "They are worse than we are."

"How do you know that, my pet?" asked Blondet.

"From their husbands," retorted she. "You are forgetting that I once had six months of de Marsay."

"Do you suppose, child, that *I* am particularly anxious to take such a handsome fellow as your poet to Madame de Montcornet's house? If you object, let us consider that nothing has been said. But I don't fancy that the women are so much in the question as a poor devil that Lucien pilloried in his newspaper; he is begging for mercy and peace. The Baron du Châtelet is imbecile enough to take the thing seriously. The Marquise d'Espard, Mme. de Bargeton, and Mme. de Montcornet's set have taken up the heron's cause; and I have undertaken to reconcile Petrarch and his Laura—Mme. de Bargeton and Lucien."

"Aha!" cried Lucien, the glow of the intoxication of

revenge throbbing full-pulsed through every vein. "Aha ! so my foot is on their necks ! You make me adore my pen, worship my friends, bow down to the fate-dispensing power of the press. I have not written a single sentence as yet upon the heron and the cuttlefish-bone. I will go with you, my boy," he cried, catching Blondet by the waist ; " yes, I will go ; but, first, the couple shall feel the weight of *this*, for so light as it is." He flourished the pen which had written the article upon Nathan.

" To-morrow," he cried, "I will hurl a couple of columns at their heads. Then, we will see. Don't be frightened, Coralie, it is not love but revenge; revenge ! And I will have it to the full ! "

" What a man it is ! " said Blondet. "If you but knew, Lucien, how rare such explosions are in this jaded Paris, you might appreciate yourself. You will be a precious scamp " (the actual expression was a trifle stronger) ; " you are in a fair way to be a power in the land."

" He will get on," said Coralie.

" Well, he has come a good way already in six weeks."

" And if he should climb so high that he can reach a sceptre by treading over a corpse, he shall have Coralie's body for a stepping-stone," said the girl.

"You are a pair of lovers of the Golden Age," said Blondet. "I congratulate you on your big article," he added, turning to Lucien. " There were a lot of new things in it. You are pastmaster ! "

Lousteau called with Hector Merlin and Vernou. Lucien was immensely flattered by this attention. Félicien Vernou brought a hundred francs for Lucien's article ; it was felt that such a contributor must be well paid to attach him to the paper.

Coralie, looking round at the chapter of journalists, ordered in a breakfast from the " Cadran Bleau," the nearest restaurant, and asked her visitors to adjourn to her handsomely furnished dining-room when Bérénice announced that the meal was ready.   In the middle of the repast, when the champagne had gone to all heads, the motive of the visit came out.

"You do not mean to make an enemy of Nathan, do you?" asked Lousteau.   "Nathan is a journalist, and he has friends; he might play you an ugly trick with your first book.   You have your 'Archer of Charles IX.' to sell, have you not? We went around to Nathan this morning; he is in a terrible way.   But you will set about another article and puff praise in his face."

"What!   After my article against his book, would you have me say——" began Lucien.

The whole party cut him short with a shout of laughter.

"Did you ask him to supper here the day after to-morrow?" asked Blondet.

"Your article was not signed," added Lousteau.   "Félicien, not being quite such a new hand as you are, was careful to put an initial C at the bottom.   You can do that now with all your articles in his paper, which is pure unadulterated Left. We are all of us in the opposition.   Félicien was tactful enough not to compromise your future opinions.   Hector's shop is Right Centre; you might sign your work on it with an L.   If you cut a man up, you do it anonymously; if you praise him, it is just as well to put your name to your article."

"It is not the signatures that trouble me," returned Lucien, "but I cannot see anything to be said in favor of the book."

"Then did you really think as you wrote?" asked Hector.

"Yes."

"Oh!   I thought you were cleverer than that, youngster," said Blondet.   "No.   Upon my word, as I looked at that forehead of yours I credited you with the omnipotence of the great mind—the power of seeing both sides of everything. In literature, my boy, every idea is reversible, and no man can take upon himself to decide which is the right or wrong side.   Everything is bilateral in the domain of thought.

Ideas are binary. Jānus is a fable signifying criticism and the symbol of genius. The Almighty alone is triform. What raises Molière and Corneille above the rest of us but the faculty of saying one thing with an Alceste or an Octave, and another with a Philinte or a Cinna? Rousseau wrote a letter against dueling in the 'Nouvelle Héloïse,' and another in favor of it. Which of the two represented his own opinion? will you venture to take it upon yourself to decide? Which of us could give judgment for Clarissa or Lovelace, Hector or Achilles? Who was Homer's hero? What did Richardson himself think? It is the function of criticism to look at a man's work in all its aspects. We draw up our case, in short."

"Do you really stick to your written opinions?" asked Vernou, with a satirical expression. "Why, we are retailers of phrases; that is how we make a livelihood. When you try to do a good piece of work—to write a book, in short—you can put your thoughts, yourself into it, and cling to it, and fight for it; but as for newspaper articles, read to-day and forgotten to-morrow, they are worth nothing in my eyes but the money that is paid for them. If you attach any importance to such drivel, you might as well make the sign of the cross and invoke heaven when you sit down to write a tradesman's circular."

Every one apparently was astonished at Lucien's scruples. The last rags of the boyish conscience were torn away, and he was invested with the *toga virilis* of journalism.

"Do you know what Nathan said by way of comforting himself after your criticism?" asked Lousteau.

"How should I know?"

"Nathan exclaimed, 'Paragraphs pass away; but a great work lives!' He will be here to supper in two days, and he will be sure to fall flat at your feet, and kiss your claws, and swear that you are a great man."

"That would be a funny thing," was Lucien's comment.

"Funny!" repeated Blondet. " He can't help himself."

" I am quite willing, my friends," said Lucien, on whom the wine had begun to take effect. " But what am I to say?"

" Oh, well, refute yourself in three good columns in Merlin's paper. We have been enjoying the sight of Nathan's wrath; we have just been telling him that he owes us no little gratitude for getting up a hot controversy that will sell his second edition in a week. In his eyes at this present moment you are a spy, a scoundrel, a caitiff wretch; the day after tomorrow you will be a genius, an uncommonly clever fellow, one of Plutarch's men. Nathan will hug you and call you his best friend. Dauriat has been to see you; you have your three thousand francs; you have worked the trick! Now you want Nathan's respect and esteem. Nobody ought to be let in except the publisher. We must not immolate any one but an enemy. We should not talk like this if it were a question of some outsider, some inconvenient person who had made a name for himself without us and was not wanted; but Nathan is one of us. Blondet got some one to attack him in the ' Mercure ' for the pleasure of replying in the ' Débats.' For which reason the first edition went off at once."

" My friends, upon my word and honor, I cannot write two words in praise of that book——"

" You will have another hundred francs," interrupted Merlin. " Nathan will have brought you in ten louis d'or, to say nothing of an article that you might put in Finot's paper; you would get a hundred francs for writing that, and another hundred francs from Dauriat—total, twenty louis."

" But what am I to say?"

" Here is your way out of the difficulty," said Blondet, after some thought. " Say that the envy that fastens on all good work, like wasps on ripe fruit, has attempted to set its fangs in this production. The captious critic, trying his best to find fault, has been obliged to invent theories for that purpose and has drawn a distinction between two kinds of literature—

'the literature of ideas and the literature of imagery,' as he calls them. On the heads of that, youngster, say that to give expression to ideas through imagery is the highest form of art. Try to show that all poetry is summed up in that, and lament that there is so little poetry in French; quote foreign criticisms on the unimaginative precision of our style, and then extol M. de Canalis and Nathan for the services they have done France by infusing a less prosaic spirit into the language. Knock your previous argument to pieces by calling attention to the fact that we have made progress since the eighteenth century. (Discover the 'progress,' a beautiful word to mystify the bourgeois public.) Say that the new methods in literature concentrate all styles, comedy and tragedy, description, character-drawing and dialogue, in a series of pictures set in the brilliant frame of a plot which holds the reader's interest. The novel which demands sentiment, style, and imagery is the greatest creation of modern days; it is the successor of stage comedy grown obsolete with its restrictions. Facts and ideas are all within the province of fiction. The intellect of an incisive moralist, like La Bruyère, the power of treating character as Molière could treat it, the grand machinery of a Shakespeare, together with the portrayal of the most subtle shades of passion (the one treasury left untouched by our predecessors)—for all this the modern novel affords free scope. How far superior in all this to the cut-and-dried logic-chopping, the cold analysis to the eighteenth century! 'The novel,' say sententiously, 'is the epic grown amusing.' Instance 'Corinne,' bring Madame de Staël up to support your argument. The eighteenth century called all things in question; it is the task of the nineteenth to conclude and speak the last word; and the last word of the nineteenth century has been for realities—realities which live, however, and move. Passion, in short, an element unknown in Voltaire's philosophy, has been brought into play. Here a diatribe against Voltaire, and, as for Rousseau, his characters are polemics and systems masquerading.   Julie and Claire are entelechies—informing spirit awaiting flesh and bones.

" You might slip off on a side-issue at this, and say that we owe a new and original literature to the peace and the restoration of the Bourbons, for you are writing for a Right Centre paper.

" Scoff at founders of systems.   And cry with a glow of fine enthusiasm, ' Here are errors and misleading statements in abundance in our contemporary's work, and to what end ? To depreciate a fine work, to deceive the public, and to arrive at this conclusion—"A book that sells, does not sell." ' *Proh pudor !* (Mind you put *Proh pudor !* 'tis a harmless expletive that stimulates the reader's interest.)   Foresee the approaching decadence of criticism, in fact.   Moral—' There is but one kind of literature, the literature which aims to please.   Nathan has started upon a new way ; he understands his epoch and fulfills the requirements of his age—the demand for drama, the natural demand of a century in which the political stage has become a permanent puppet show.   Have we not seen four dramas in a score of years—the Revolution, the Directory, the Empire, and the Restoration ? '   With that, wallow in dithyramb and eulogy, and the second edition shall vanish like smoke.   This is the way to do it.   Next Saturday put a review in our magazine, and sign it ' de Rubempré,' out in full.

" In that final article say that ' fine work always brings about abundant controversy.   This week such and such a paper contained such and such an article on Nathan's book, and such another paper made a vigorous reply.'   Then you criticise the critics ' C ' and ' L ; ' pay me a passing compliment on the first article in the ' Débats,' and end by averring that Nathan's work is the great book of the epoch ; which is all as if you had said nothing at all ; they say the same of everything that comes out.

" And so," continued Blondet, " you will have made four

hundred francs in a week, to say nothing of the pleasure of now and again saying what you really think. A discerning public will maintain that either C or L or Rubempré is in the right of it, or mayhap all the three. Mythology, beyond doubt one of the grandest inventions of the human brain, places truth at the bottom of a well; and what are we to do without buckets? You will have supplied the public with three for one. There you are, my boy. Go ahead!"

Lucien's head was swimming with bewilderment. Blondet kissed him on both cheeks.

"I am going to my shop," said he. And every man likewise departed to his shop. For these "*hommes forts*" (dexterous men), a newspaper office was nothing but a shop.

They were to meet again in the evening in the Wooden Galleries, and Lucien would sign his treaty of peace with Dauriat. Florine and Lousteau, Lucien and Coralie, Blondet and Finot were to dine in the Palais-Royal; du Bruel was giving the manager of the Panorama-Dramatique a dinner.

"They are right," exclaimed Lucien, when he was alone with Coralie. "Men are made to be tools in the hands of stronger spirits. Four hundred francs for three articles! Doguereau would scarcely give me as much for a book which cost me two years of work."

"Write criticism," said Coralie, "have a good time! Look at me, I am an Andalusian girl to-night, to-morrow I may be a gypsy, and a man the night after. Do as I do, give them grimaces for their money and let us live happily."

Lucien, smitten with love of paradox, set himself to mount and ride that unruly hybrid product of pegasus and Balaam's ass; started out at a gallop over the fields of thought while he took a turn in the Bois, and discovered new possibilities in Blondet's outline.

He dined as happy people dine, and signed away all his rights in the "Marguerites." It never occurred to him that any trouble might arise from that transaction in the future.

He took a turn of work at the office, wrote off a couple of columns, and came back to the Rue de Vendôme. Next morning he found that the germs of yesterday's ideas had sprung up and developed in his brain, as ideas develop while the intellect is yet unjaded and the sap is rising ; and thoroughly did he enjoy the projection of this new article. He threw himself into it with enthusiasm. At the summons of the spirit of contradiction, new charms met beneath his pen. He was witty and satirical ; he rose to yet newer views of sentiment, of ideas and imagery in literature. With subtle ingenuity, he went back to his own first impressions of Nathan's work, when he read it in the newsroom of the Cour du Commerce ; and the ruthless, bloodthirsty critic, the lively mocker, became a poet in the final phrases which rose and fell with majestic rhythm like the swaying censer before the altar.

"One hundred francs, Coralie ! " cried he, holding up eight sheets of paper covered with writing while she dressed.

The mood was upon him ; he went on to indite, stroke by stroke, the promised terrible article on Châtelet and Mme. de Bargeton. That morning he experienced one of the keenest personal pleasures of journalism ; he knew what it was to forge the epigram, to whet and polish the cold blade to be sheathed in a victim's heart, to make of the hilt a cunning piece of workmanship for the reader to admire. For the public admires the handle, the delicate work of the brain, while the cruelty is not apparent ; how should the public know that the steel of the epigram, tempered in the fire of revenge, has been plunged deftly, to rankle in the very quick of a victim's vanity, and is reeking from wounds innumerable which it has inflicted ? It is a hideous joy, that grim, solitary pleasure, relished without witnesses ; it is like a duel with an absent enemy, slain at a distance by a quill ; a journalist might really possess the magical power of talismans in Eastern tales. Epigram is distilled rancor, the quintessence of a hate derived from all the worst passions of man, even as

love concentrates all that is best in human nature. The man does not exist who cannot be witty to avenge himself; and, by the same rule, there is not one to whom love does not bring delight. Cheap and easy as this kind of wit may be in France, it is always relished. Lucien's article was destined to raise the previous reputation of the paper for venomous spite and evil-speaking. His article probed two hearts to the depths; it dealt a grievous wound to Mme. de Bargeton, his Laura of old days, as well, also, as to his rival, the Baron du Châtelet.

"Well, let us go for a drive in the Bois," said Coralie, "the horses are fidgeting. There is no need to kill yourself."

"We will take the article on Nathan to Hector. Journalism is really very much like Achilles' lance, it salves the wounds that it makes," said Lucien, correcting a phrase here and there.

The lovers started forth in splendor to show themselves to the Paris which had but lately given Lucien the cold shoulder, and now was beginning to talk about him. To have Paris talking of you! and this after you have learned how large the great city is, how hard it is to be anybody there—it was this thought that turned Lucien's head with exultation.

"Let us go by way of your tailor's, dear boy, and tell him to be quick with your clothes, or try them on if they are ready. If you are going to your fine ladies' houses, you shall eclipse that monster of a de Marsay and young Rastignac, and any Ajuda-Pinto or Maxime de Trailles or Vandenesse of them all. Remember that your mistress is Coralie! But you will not play me any tricks, eh?"

Two days afterward, on the eve of the supper-party at Coralie's house, there was a new play at the Ambigu, and it fell to Lucien to write the dramatic criticism. Lucien and Coralie walked together after dinner from the Rue de Vendôme to the Panorama-Dramatique, going along the Café Turc side of the Boulevard du Temple, a lounge much fre-

quented at that time.   People wondered at his luck and praised
Coralie's beauty.   Chance remarks reached his ears; some
said that Coralie was the finest woman in Paris, others that
Lucien was a match for her.   The romantic youth felt that
he was in his atmosphere.   This was the life for him.   The
brotherhood was so far away that it was almost out of sight.
Only two months ago how he had looked up to those lofty
great natures; now he asked himself if they were not just a
trifle ridiculous with their notions and their puritanism.   Coralie's careless words had lodged in Lucien's mind, and begun
already to bear fruit.   He took Coralie to her dressing-room,
and strolled about like a sultan behind the scenes; the actresses gave him burning glances and flattering speeches.

"I must go to the Ambigu and attend to business," said he.

At the Ambigu the house was full; there was not a seat left
for him.   Indignant complaints behind the scenes brought no
redress; the box-office keeper, who did not know him as yet,
said that they had sent orders for two boxes to his paper, and
sent him about his business.

"I shall speak of the play as I find it," said Lucien, nettled
at this.

"What a dunce you are!" said the leading lady, addressing the box-office keeper, "that is Coralie's adorer."

The box-office keeper turned round immediately at this.
"I will speak to the manager at once, sir," he said.

In all these small details Lucien saw the immense power
wielded by the press.   His vanity was gratified.   The manager appeared to say that the Duc de Rhétoré and Tullia the
opera-dancer were in the stage-box, and they had consented
to allow Lucien to join them.

"You have driven two people to distraction," remarked
the young Duke, mentioning the names of the Baron du
Châtelet and Mme. de Bargeton.

"Distraction?   What will it be to-morrow?" said Lucien.
"So far, my friends have been mere skirmishers, but I have

given them red-hot shot to-night. To-morrow you will know why we are making game of 'Potelet.' The article is called 'Potelet from 1811 to 1821.' Châtelet will be a by-word, a name for the type of courtier who deny their benefactor and rally to the Bourbons. When I have done with him, I am going to Madame de Montcornet's."

Lucien's talk was sparkling. He was eager that this great personage should see how gross a mistake Mesdames d'Espard and de Bargeton had made when they slighted Lucien de Rubempré. But he showed the tip of his ear when he asserted his right to bear the name of Rubempré, the Duc de Rhétoré having purposely addressed him as Chardon.

"You should go over to the Royalists," said the Duke. "You have proved yourself a man of ability; now show your good sense. The one way of obtaining a patent of nobility and the right to bear the title of your mother's family is by asking for it in return for services to be rendered to the court. The Liberals will never make a count of you. The restoration will get the better of the press, you see, in the long run, and the press is the only formidable power. They have borne with it too long as it is; the press is sure to be muzzled. Take advantage of the last moments of liberty to make yourself formidable, and you will have everything — intellect, nobility, and good looks; nothing will be out of your reach. So if you are a Liberal, let it be simply for the moment, so that you can make a better bargain for your Royalism."

With that the Duke intreated Lucien to accept an invitation to dinner, which the German minister (of Florine's supper-party) was about to send. Lucien fell under the charm of the noble peer's arguments; the salons from which he had been exiled for ever, as he thought, but a few months ago, would shortly open their doors for him! He was delighted. He marveled at the power of the press; Intellect and the Press, these then were the real powers in society. Another thought shaped itself in his mind—Was Étienne Lousteau sorry that he had opened the gate of the temple to a new-comer? Even now he (Lucien) felt on his own account that it was strongly advisable to put difficulties in the way of eager and ambitious recruits from the provinces. If a poet should come to him as he had flung himself into Étienne's arms, he dared not think of the reception that he would give him.

The youthful Duke meanwhile saw that Lucien was deep in thought and made a pretty good guess at the matter of his meditations. He himself had opened out wide horizons of public life before an ambitious poet, with a vacillating will, it is true, but not without aspirations; and the journalists had already shown the neophyte, from a pinnacle of the temple, all the kingdoms of the world of letters and its riches.

Lucien himself had no suspicion of a little plot that was being woven, nor did he imagine that M. de Rhétoré had a hand in it. M. de Rhétoré had spoken of Lucien's clever-ness, and Mme. d'Espard's set had taken alarm. Mme. de Bargeton had commissioned the Duke to sound Lucien, and with that object in view the noble youth had come to the Ambigu-Comique.

Do not believe in stories of elaborate treachery. Neither the great world nor the world of journalists laid any deep schemes; definite plans are not made by either; their Machi-avellism lives from hand to mouth, so to speak, and consists, for the most part, in being always on the spot, always on the alert to turn everything to account, always on the watch for the moment when a man's ruling passion shall deliver him into the hands of his enemies. The young Duke had seen through Lucien at Florine's supper-party; he had just touched his vain susceptibilities; and now he was trying his first efforts in diplomacy upon the living subject.

Lucien hurried to the Rue Saint-Fiacre after the play to write his article. It was a piece of savage and bitter criticism, written in pure wantonness; he was amusing himself by trying his power. The melodrama, as a matter of fact, was a better piece than the "Alcalde;" but Lucien wished to see whether he could damn a good play and send everybody to see a bad one, as his associates had said.

He unfolded the sheet at breakfast next morning, telling Coralie as he did so that he had cut up the Ambigu-Comique; and not a little astonished was he to find below his paper on Mme. de Bargeton and Châtelet a notice of the Ambigu, so mellowed and softened in the course of the night that, although the witty analysis was still preserved, the judgment was favorable. The article was more likely to fill the house than to empty it. No words can describe his wrath. He determined to have a word or two with Lousteau. He had begun already to think himself an indispensable man, and he vowed that he would not submit to be tyrannized over and treated like a fool. To establish his power beyond cavil, he wrote the article for Dauriat's review, summing up and weighing all the various opinions concerning Nathan's book; and while he was in the humor, he hit off another of his short sketches for Lousteau's newspaper. Inexperienced journalists, in the first effervescence of youth, make a labor of love of ephemeral work and lavish their best thought unthriftily thereon.

The manager of the Panorama-Dramatique gave a first performance of a vaudeville that night, so that Florine and Coralie might be free for the evening. There were to be cards before supper. Lousteau came for the short notice of the vaudeville; it had been written beforehand after the general rehearsal, for Étienne wished to have the paper off his mind. Lucien read over one of the charming sketches of Parisian whimsicalities which made the fortune of the paper, and Lousteau kissed him on both eyelids and called him the providence of journalism.

"Then why do you amuse yourself by turning my article inside out?" asked Lucien. He had written his brilliant sketch simply and solely to give emphasis to his grievance.

"*I?*" exclaimed Lousteau.

17

"Well, who else can have altered my article?" said Lucien.

"You do not know all the ins and outs yet, dear fellow. The Ambigu pays for thirty copies, and only takes nine for the manager and box-office keeper and their mistresses, and for the three lessees of the theatre. Every one of the boulevard theatres pays eight hundred francs in this way to the paper ; and there is quite as much again in boxes and orders for Finot, to say nothing of the contributions of the company. And if the minor theatres do this, you may imagine what the big ones do ! Now you understand ? We are bound to show a good deal of indulgence."

"I understand this, that I am not at liberty to write as I think——"

"Eh ! what does that matter, so long as you turn an honest penny?" cried Lousteau. "Beside, my boy, what grudge had you against the theatre? You must have had some reason for it, or you would not have cut up the play as you did. If you slash for the sake of slashing the paper will get into trouble, and when there is good reason for hitting hard it will not tell. Did the manager leave you out in the cold?"

"He had not kept a place for me."

"Good," said Lousteau. "I shall let him see your article, and tell him that I softened it down ; you will find it serve you better than if it had appeared in print. Go and ask him for tickets to-morrow and he will sign forty blank orders every month. I know a man who can get rid of them for you ; I will introduce you to him, and he will buy them all up at half-price. There is a trade done in theatre tickets, just as Barbet trades in reviewers' copies. This is another Barbet, the leader of the *claque* (hired applauders). He lives near-by ; come and see him, there is time enough."

"But, my dear fellow, it is a scandalous thing that Finot should levy blackmail in matters intellectual. Sooner or later——"

"Really !" cried Lousteau, "where do you come from?

For what do you take Finot? Beneath his pretense of good-
nature, his ignorance and stupidity, and those Turcaret's airs
of his, there *is* all the cunning of his father the hatter. Did
you notice an old soldier of the empire in the den at the office?
That is Finot's uncle. The uncle is not only one of the right
sort, he has the luck to be taken for a fool; and he takes
all that kind of business upon his shoulders. An ambitious
man in Paris is well off indeed if he has a willing scapegoat
at hand. In public life, as in journalism, there are hosts of
emergencies in which the chiefs cannot afford to appear. If
Finot should enter on a political career, his uncle would be
his secretary, and receive all the contributions levied in his
department on big affairs. Anybody would take Giroudeau
for a fool at first sight, but he has just enough shrewdness to
be an inscrutable old file. He is on picket duty; he sees
that we are not pestered with hubbub, beginners wanting a
job, or advertisements. No other paper has his equal, I
think."

"He plays his part well," said Lucien; "I saw him at
work."

Étienne and Lucien reached a handsome house in the Rue
du Faubourg-du-Temple.

"Is Monsieur Braulard in?" Étienne asked of the porter.

"*Monsieur?*" said Lucien. "Then is the leader of the
claque 'Monsieur?'"

"My dear boy, Braulard has twenty thousand francs of income. All the dramatic authors of the boulevards are in his
clutches, and have a standing account with him as if he were
a banker. Orders and complimentary tickets are sold here.
Braulard knows where to get rid of such merchandise. Now
for a turn at statistics, a useful science enough in its way. At
the rate of fifty complimentary tickets every evening for each
theatre, you have two hundred and fifty tickets daily. Suppose, taking one with another, that they are worth a couple of
francs apiece, Braulard pays a hundred and twenty-five francs

daily for them, and takes his chance of making cent. per cent.
In this way author's tickets alone bring him in about four
thousand francs every month, or forty-eight thousand francs
per annum.   Allow twenty thousand francs for loss, for he
cannot always place all his tickets——''

" Why not ? ''

" Oh ! the people who pay at the door go in with the
holders of complimentary tickets for unreserved seats, and the
theatres reserve the right of admitting those who pay.   There
are fine warm evenings to be reckoned with beside, and poor
plays.   Braulard makes, perhaps, thirty thousand francs every
year in this way, and he has his *claqueurs* beside, another industry.   Florine and Coralie pay tribute to him; if they did
not there would be no applause when they come on or go
off.''

Lousteau gave this explanation in a low voice as they went
up the stair.

" Paris is a queer place," said Lucien ; it seemed to him
that he saw self-interest squatting in every corner of that great
city.

A smart maidservant opened the door.   At the sight of
Étienne Lousteau, the dealer in orders and tickets rose from a
study chair before a large cylinder desk, and Lucien beheld
the leader of the *claque*, Braulard himself, dressed in a gray
molleton jacket, footed trousers, and red slippers ; for all the
world like a doctor or an attorney.   He was a typical self-made
man, Lucien thought—a vulgar-looking face with a pair of
exceedingly cunning gray eyes, hands made for hired applause,
a complexion over which hard living had passed like rain over
a roof, grizzled hair, and a somewhat husky voice.

" You have come from Mademoiselle Florine, no doubt,
sir, and this gentleman for Mademoiselle Coralie," said
Braulard ; " I know you very well by sight.   Don't you trouble
yourself, sir," he continued, addressing Lucien ; " I am buying the Gymnase connection, I will look after your lady, and

I will give her notice of any tricks that they may try to play
on her."

"That is not an offer to be refused, my dear Braulard,
but we have come about the press orders for the boulevard
theatres—I as editor and this gentleman as dramatic critic."

"Oh! ah, yes! Finot has sold his paper. I heard about
it. He is getting on, is Finot. I have asked him to dine
with me at the end of the week; if you will do me the honor
and pleasure of coming, you may bring your ladies, and there
will be a grand jollification. Adèle Dupuis is coming, and
Ducange, and Frédéric du Petit-Méré, and Mademoiselle
Millot, my mistress. We shall have good fun and better
liquor."

"Ducange must be in difficulties. He has lost his lawsuit."

"I have lent him ten thousand francs; if 'Calas' succeeds,
it will repay the loan, so I have been organizing a success.
Ducange is a clever man; he has brains——"

Lucien fancied that he must be dreaming when he heard a
claqueur appraising a writer's value.

"Coralie has improved," continued Braulard, with the air
of a competent critic. "If she is a good girl, I will take her
part, for they have got up a cabal against her at the Gymnase.
This is how I mean to do it: I will have a few well-dressed
men in the balconies to smile and make little murmurs, and
the applause will follow. That is a dodge which makes a
position for an actress. I have a liking for Coralie, and you
ought to be satisfied, for she has feeling. Aha! I can hiss
any one on the stage if I like."

"But let us settle this business about the tickets," put in
Lousteau.

"Very well, I will come to this gentleman's lodging for
them at the beginning of the month. He is a friend of
yours, and I will treat him as I do you. You have five
theatres; you will get thirty tickets—that will be something
like seventy-five francs a month. Perhaps you will be want-

ing an advance?" added Braulard, lifting a cash-box full of coin out of his desk.

"No, no," said Lousteau; "we will keep that shift against a rainy day."

"I will work with Coralie, sir, and we will come to an understanding," said Braulard, addressing Lucien, who was looking about him, not without profound astonishment. There was a bookcase in Braulard's study, there were framed engravings and good furniture; and, as they passed through the drawing-room, he noticed that the fittings were neither too luxurious nor yet mean. The dining-room seemed to be the best-ordered room, he remarked on this jokingly.

"But Braulard is an epicure," said Lousteau; "his dinners are famous in dramatic literature, and they are what you might expect from his cash-box."

"I have good wine," Braulard replied modestly. "Ah! here are my lamplighters," he added, as a sound of hoarse voices and strange footsteps came up from the staircase.

Lucien on his way down saw a march past of *claqueurs* and retailers of tickets. It was an ill-smelling squad, attired in caps, seedy trousers, and threadbare overcoats; a flock of gallows-birds with bluish and greenish tints in their faces, neglected beards, and a strange mixture of savagery and subservience in their eyes. A horrible population lives and swarms upon the Paris boulevards; selling watch-guards and brass jewelry in the streets by day, applauding under the chandeliers of the theatre at night, and ready to lend themselves to any dirty business in the great city.

"Behold the Romans!" laughed Lousteau; "behold fame incarnate for actresses and dramatic authors. It is no prettier than our own when you come to look at it closely."

"It is difficult to keep illusions on any subject in Paris," answered Lucien as they turned in at his door. "There is a tax upon everything—everything has its price, and anything can be made to order—even success."

Thirty guests were assembled that evening in Coralie's rooms; her dining-room would not hold more. Lucien had asked Dauriat and the manager of the Panoroma-Dramatique, Matifat and Florine, Camusot, Lousteau, Finot, Nathan, Hector Merlin and Mme. du Val-Noble, Félicien Vernou, Blondet, Vignon, Philippe Bridau, Mariette, Giroudeau, Cardot and Florentine, and Bixiou. He had also asked all his friends of the Rue des Quatre-Vents. Tullia the dancer, who was not unkind, said gossip, to du Bruel, had come without her duke. The proprietors of the newspapers, for whom most of the journalists wrote, were also of the party.

At eight o'clock, when the lights of the candles in the chandeliers shone over the furniture, the hangings, and the flowers, the rooms wore the festal air that gives to Parisian luxury the appearance of a dream; and Lucien felt indefinable stirrings of hope and gratified vanity and pleasure at the thought that he was the master of the house. But how and by whom the magic wand had been waved he no longer sought to remember. Florine and Coralie, dressed with the fanciful extravagance and magnificent artistic effect of the stage, smiled on the poet like two fairies at the gates of the Palace of Dreams. And Lucien was almost in a dream.

His life had been changed so suddenly during the last few months; he had gone so swiftly from the depths of penury to the last extreme of luxury, that at moments he felt as uncomfortable as a dreaming man who knows that he is asleep. And yet he looked around at the fair reality about him with a confidence to which envious minds might have given the name of fatuity.

Lucien himself had changed. He had grown paler during these days of continual enjoyment; languor had lent a humid look to his eyes; in short, to use Madame d'Espard's expression, he looked like a man who is loved. He was the handsomer for it. Consciousness of his powers and his strength was visible in his face, enlightened as it was by love and experience. Looking out over the world of letters and of men, it seemed to him that he might go to and fro as lord of it all. Sober reflection never entered his romantic head unless it was driven in by the pressure of adversity, and just now the present held not a care for him. The breath of praise swelled the sails of his skiff; all the instruments of success lay there to his hand; he had an establishment, a mistress whom all Paris envied him, a carriage, and untold wealth in his inkstand. Heart and soul and brain were alike transformed within him; why should he care to be overnice about the means, when the great results were visible there before his eyes.

As such a style of living will seem, and with good reason, to be anything but secure to economists who have any experience of Paris, it will not be superfluous to give a glance to the foundation, uncertain as it was, upon which the prosperity of the pair was based.

Camusot had given Coralie's tradesmen instructions to grant her credit for three months at least, and this had been done without her knowledge. During those three months, therefore, horses and servants, like everything else, waited as if by enchantment at the bidding of two children, eager for enjoyment, and enjoying to their hearts' content.

Coralie had taken Lucien's hand and given him a glimpse of the transformation scene in the dining-room, of the splendidly appointed table, of chandeliers, each fitted with forty wax-lights, of the royally luxurious dessert, and a menu of Chevet's. Lucien kissed her on the forehead and held her closely to his heart.

"I shall succeed, child," he said, "and then I will repay you for such love and devotion."

"Pshaw!" said Coralie. "Are you satisfied?"

"I should be very hard to please if I was not."

"Very well, then, that smile of yours pays for everything," she said, and with a serpentine movement she raised her head and laid her lips against his.

When they went back to the others, Florine, Lousteau, Matifat, and Camusot were setting out the card-tables. Lucien's friends began to arrive, for already these folk began to call themselves "Lucien's friends;" and they sat over the cards from nine o'clock till midnight. Lucien was unacquainted with a single game, but Lousteau lost a thousand francs, and Lucien could not refuse to lend him the money when he asked for it.

Michel, Fulgence, and Joseph appeared about ten o'clock; and Lucien, chatting with them in a corner, saw that they looked sober and serious enough, not to say ill at ease. D'Arthez could not come, he was finishing his book; Léon Giraud was busy with the first number of his review; so the brotherhood had sent the three artists among their number, thinking that they would feel less out of their element in an uproarious supper-party than the rest.

"Well, my dear fellows," said Lucien, assuming a slightly patronizing tone, "the 'comical fellow' may become a great public character yet, you see."

"I wish I may be mistaken; I don't ask better," said Michel.

"Are you living with Coralie until you can do better?" asked Fulgence.

"Yes," said Lucien, trying to look unconscious. "Coralie had an elderly adorer, a merchant, and she showed him the door, poor fellow. I am better off than your brother Philippe," he added, addressing Joseph Bridau; "he does not know how to manage Mariette."

"You are a man like another now; in short, you will make your way," said Fulgence.

"A man that will always be the same for you, under all circumstances," returned Lucien.

Michel and Fulgence exchanged incredulous, scornful smiles at this. Lucien saw the absurdity of his remark.

"Coralie is wonderfully beautiful," exclaimed Joseph Bridau. "What a magnificent portrait she would make!"

"Beautiful and good," said Lucien; "she is an angel, upon my word. And you shall paint her portrait; she shall sit to you if you like for your Venetian lady brought by the old woman to the senator."

"All women who love are angelic," said Michel Chrestien.

Just at that moment Raoul Nathan flew upon Lucien, and grasped both his hands and shook them in a sudden access of violent friendship.

"Oh, my good friend, you are something more than a great man, you have a heart," he cried, "a much rarer thing than genius in these days. You are a devoted friend. I am yours, in short, through thick and thin; I shall never forget all that you have done for me this week."

Lucien's joy had reached the highest point; to be thus caressed by a man of whom every one was talking! He looked at his three friends of the brotherhood with something like a superior air. Nathan's appearance upon the scene was the result of an overture from Merlin, who sent him a proof of the favorable review to appear in to-morrow's issue.

"I only consented to write the attack on condition that I should be allowed to reply to it myself," Lucien said in Nathan's ear. "I am one of you." This incident was opportune; it justified the remark which amused Fulgence. Lucien was radiant.

"When d'Arthez's book comes out," he said, turning to the three, "I am in a position to be useful to him. That thought in itself would induce me to remain a journalist."

"Can you do as you like?" Michel asked quickly.

"So far as one can when one is indispensable," said Lucien modestly.

It was almost midnight when they sat down to supper, and

the fun grew fast and furious. Talk was less restrained in Lucien's house than at Matifat's, for no one suspected that the representatives of the brotherhood and the newspaper writers held divergent opinions. Young intellects, depraved by arguing for either side, now came into conflict with each other, and fearful axioms of the journalistic jurisprudence, then in its infancy, hurtled to and fro. Claud Vignon, upholding the dignity of criticism, inveighed against the tendency of the smaller newspapers, saying that the writers of personalities lowered themselves in the end. Lousteau, Merlin, and Finot took up the cudgels for the system known by the name of *blague;* puffery, gossip, and humbug, they said, was the test of talent, and set the hall-mark, as it were, upon it. " Any man who can stand that test has real power," said Lousteau.

" Beside," cried Merlin, "when a great man receives ovations, there ought to be a chorus of insults to balance, as in a Roman triumph."

" Oho ! " put in Lucien ; " then every one held up to ridicule in print will fancy that he has made a success."

"Any one would think that the question interested you," exclaimed Finot.

"And how about our sonnets," said Michel Chrestien ; " is that the way they will win us the fame of a second Petrarch ? "

" Laura already counts for something in his fame," said Dauriat, a pun [Laure (*l'or*) gold] received with acclamations.

"*Faciamus experimentum in anima vili,*" retorted Lucien with a smile.

"And woe unto him whom reviewers shall spare, flinging him crowns at his first appearance, for he shall be shelved like the saints in their shrines and no man shall pay him the slightest attention," said Vernou.

" People will say, ' Look elsewhere, simpleton ; you have had your due already,' as Champcenetz said to the Marquis de Genlis, who was looking too fondly at his wife," added Blondet.

" Success is the ruin of a man in France," said Finot. " We are so jealous of one another that we try to forget, and to make others forget, the triumphs of yesterday."

" Contradiction is the life of literature, in fact," said Claud Vignon.

" In art as in nature, there are two principles everywhere at strife," said Fulgence ; " victory for either means death."

" So it is with politics," added Michel Chrestien.

" We have a case in point," said Lousteau. " Dauriat will sell a couple of thousand copies of Nathan's book in the coming week. And why? Because the book that was cleverly attacked will be ably defended."

Merlin took up the proof of to-morrow's paper. " How can such an article fail to sell an edition ? " he asked.

" Read the article," said Dauriat. " I am a publisher wherever I am, even at supper."

Merlin read Lucien's triumphant refutation aloud and the whole party applauded.

" How could that article have been written unless the attack had preceded it ? " asked Lousteau.

Dauriat drew the proof of the third article from his pocket and read it over, Finot listening closely; for it was to appear in the second number of his own review, and as editor he exaggerated his enthusiasm.

" Gentlemen," said he, " so and not otherwise would Bossuet have written if he had lived in our day."

" I am sure of it," said Merlin. " Bossuet would have been a journalist to-day."

" To Bossuet the Second ! " cried Claud Vignon, raising his glass with an ironical bow.

" To my Christopher Columbus ! " returned Lucien, drinking a health to Dauriat.

" Bravo ! " cried Nathan.

" Is it a nickname?" Merlin inquired, looking maliciously from Finot to Lucien.

"If you go on at this pace, you will be quite beyond us," said Dauriat; "these gentlemen" (indicating Camusot and Matifat) "cannot follow you as it is. A joke is like a bit of thread ; if it is spun too fine, it breaks, as the great Bonaparte said."

"Gentlemen," said Lousteau, "we have been eye-witnesses of a strange, portentous, unheard-of, and truly surprising phenomenon. Admire the rapidity with which our friend here has been transformed from a provincial into a journalist of Paris ! "

" He is a born journalist," said Dauriat.

"Children ! " called Finot, rising to his feet, "all of us here present have encouraged and protected our amphitryon in his entrance upon a career in which he has already surpassed our hopes. In two months he has shown us what he can do in a series of excellent articles known to us all. I propose to baptize him in form as a journalist."

"A crown of roses ! to signalize a double conquest," cried Bixiou, glancing at Coralie.

Coralie made a sign to Bérénice. That portly handmaid went to Coralie's dressing-room and brought back a box of tumbled artificial flowers. The more incapable members of the party were grotesquely tricked out in these blossoms, and a crown of roses was soon woven. Finot, as high-priest, sprinkled a few drops of champagne on Lucien's golden curls, pronouncing with delicious gravity the words—" In the name of the Government Stamp, the Caution-money, and the Fine, I baptize thee, Journalist. May thy articles sit lightly on thee ! "

" And may they be paid for, including white lines ! " cried Merlin.

Just at that moment Lucien caught sight of three melancholy faces. Michel Chrestien, Joseph Bridau, and Fulgence

Ridal took up their hats and went out amid a storm of invective.

" Queer customers ! " said Merlin.

" Fulgence used to be a good fellow," added Lousteau, " before they perverted his morals."

" Who are ' they?' " asked Claud Vignon.

" Some very serious young men," said Blondet, "·who meet at a philosophico-religious symposium in the Rue des Quatre-Vents, and worry themselves about the meaning of human life——"

"Oh ! oh ! "

" They are trying to find out whether it goes round in a circle or makes some progress," continued Blondet. " They were very hard put to it between the straight line and the curve ; the triangle, warranted by scripture, seemed to them to be nonsense, when, lo ! there arose among them some prophet or other who declared for the spiral."

" Men might meet to invent more dangerous nonsense than that ! " exclaimed Lucien, making a faint attempt to champion the brotherhood.

"You take theories of that sort for idle words," said Félicien Vernou ; " but a time comes when the arguments take the form of gunshot and the guillotine."

" They have not come to that yet," said Bixiou ; "they have only come as far as the designs of Providence in the invention of champagne, the humanitarian significance of breeches, and the blind deity who keeps the world going. They pick up fallen great men like Vico, Saint-Simon, and Fourier. I am much afraid that they will turn poor Joseph Bridau's head among them."

" Bianchon, my old school-fellow, gives me the cold shoulder now," said Étienne Lousteau ; " it is all their doing and——"

" Do they give lectures on orthopedy and intellectual gymnastics? " asked Merlin.

"Very likely," answered Finot, "if Bianchon has any hand in their theories."

" Pshaw !" said Lousteau ; "he will be a great physician anyhow."

" Isn't d'Arthez their visible head?" asked Nathan ; "a little youngster that is going to swallow all of us up."

" He is a genius ! " cried Lucien.

"Genius, is he ! Well, give me a glass of sherry ! " said Claud Vignon, smiling.

Every one thereupon began to explain his character for the benefit of his neighbor ; and when a clever man feels a pressing need of explaining himself, and of unlocking his heart, it is pretty clear that wine has gotten the upper hand. An hour later, all the men in the company were the best friends in the world, addressing each other as great men and bold spirits who held the future in their hands. Lucien, in his quality of host, was sufficiently clear-headed to apprehend the meaning of the sophistries which impressed him and completed his demoralization.

"The Liberal party," announced Finot, " is compelled to stir up discussion somehow. There is no fault to find with the action of the government, and you may imagine what a fix the opposition is in. Which of you now cares to write a pamphlet in favor of the system of primogeniture, and raise a cry against the secret designs of the court? The pamphlet will be paid for handsomely."

" I will write it," said Hector Merlin. " It is my own point of view."

" Your party will complain that you are compromising them," said Finot. " Félicien, you must undertake it ; Dauriat will bring it out and we will keep the secret."

" How much shall I get ? "

" Six hundred francs. Sign it ' Le Comte C., three stars,' " Finot replied.

" It's a bargain," said Félicien Vernou.

"So you are introducing the *canard* to the political world," remarked Lousteau.

"It is simply the Chabot affair carried into the region of abstract ideas," said Finot. "Fasten intentions on the government, and then let loose public opinion."

"How a government can leave the control of ideas to such a pack of scamps as we are is matter for perpetual and profound astonishment to me," said Claud Vignon.

"If the ministry blunders so far as to come down into the arena, we can give them a drubbing. If they are nettled by it, the thing will rankle in people's minds, and the government will lose its hold on the masses. The newspaper risks nothing, and the authorities have everything to lose."

"France will be a cipher until newspapers are abolished by law," said Claud Vignon. "You are making progress hourly," he added, addressing Finot. "You are a modern order of Jesuits, lacking the creed, the fixed idea, the discipline, and the union."

They went back to the card-tables; and before long the light of the candles grew feeble in the dawn.

"Lucien, your friends from the Rue des Quatre-Vents looked as dismal as criminals going to be hanged," said Coralie.

"They were the judges, not the criminals," replied her poet.

"Judges are more amusing than *that*," said Mademoiselle Coralie.

For a month Lucien's whole time was taken up with supper parties, dinner engagements, breakfasts, and evening parties; he was swept away by an irresistible current into the vortex of dissipation and easy work. He no longer thought of the future. The power of calculation amid the complications of life is the sign of a strong will which poets, weaklings, and men who live a purely intellectual life can never counterfeit.

Lucien was living from hand to mouth, spending his money as fast as he made it, like many another journalist; nor did he give so much as a thought to those periodically recurrent days of reckoning which checker the life of the bohemian in Paris so sadly.

In dress and figure he was a rival for the great dandies of the day. Coralie, like all zealots, loved to adorn her idol. She ruined herself to give her beloved poet the accoutrements which had so stirred his envy in the garden of the Tuileries. Lucien had wonderful canes and a charming eyeglass; he had diamond studs, and scarf-rings, and signet-rings, beside an assortment of waistcoats marvelous to behold, and in sufficient number to match every color in a variety of costumes. His transition to the estate of dandy swiftly followed. When he went to the German minister's dinner, all the young men regarded him with suppressed envy; yet de Marsay, Vandenesse, Ajuda-Pinto, Maxime de Trailles, Rastignac, Beaudenord, Manerville, and the Duc de Maufrigneuse gave place to none in the kingdom of fashion. Men of fashion are as jealous among themselves as women, and in the same way. Lucien was placed between Mme. de Montcornet and Mme. d'Espard, in whose honor the dinner was given; both ladies overwhelmed him with flatteries.

"Why did you turn your back on society when you would have been so well received?" asked the Marquise. "Every one was prepared to make much of you. And I have a quarrel with you too. You owed me a call—I am still waiting to receive it. I saw you at the opera the other day, and you would not deign to come to see me nor to take any notice of me."

"Your cousin, madame, so unmistakably dismissed me——"

"Oh! you do not know women," the Marquise d'Espard broke in upon him. "You have wounded the most angelic heart, the noblest nature that I know. You do not know all that Louise was trying to do for you, nor how tactfully she
18

laid her plans for you. Oh ! and she would have succeeded,"
the Marquise continued, replying to Lucien's mute incredulity.
" Her husband is now dead; died, as he was bound to die,
of an indigestion; could you doubt that she would be free
sooner or later ? And can you suppose that she would like
to be Madame Chardon ? It was worth while to take some
trouble to gain the title of Comtesse de Rubempré. Love,
you see, is a great vanity, which requires the lesser vanities to
be in harmony with itself—especially in marriage. I might
love you to madness—which is to say, sufficiently to marry
you—and yet I should find it very unpleasant to be called
Madame Chardon. You can see that. And now that you
understand the difficulties of Paris life, you will know how
many roundabout ways you must take to reach your end ;
very well, then, you must admit that Louise was aspiring to
an all but impossible piece of court favor ; she was quite unknown, she is not rich, and therefore she could not afford to
neglect any means of success.

"You are clever," the Marquise d'Espard continued ; " but
we women, when we love, are cleverer than the cleverest man.
My cousin tried to make that absurd Châtelet useful——
Oh !" she broke off, " I owe not a little amusement to you ;
your articles on Châtelet made me laugh heartily."

Lucien knew not what to think of all this. Of the treachery
and bad faith of journalism he had had some experience ; but,
in spite of his perspicacity, he scarcely expected to find bad
faith or treachery in society. There were some sharp lessons
in store for him.

" But, madame," he objected, for her words aroused a lively
curiosity, " is not the heron under your protection ? "

" One is obliged to be civil to one's worst enemies in society," protested she ; " one may be bored, but one must look
as if the talk was amusing, and not seldom one seems to sacrifice friends the better to serve them. Are you still a novice ?
You mean to write, and yet you know nothing of current

deceit? My cousin apparently sacrificed you to the heron, but how could she dispense with his influence for you? Our friend stands well with the present ministry; and we have made him see that your attacks will do him service—up to a certain point, for we want you to make it up again some of these days. Châtelet has received compensations for his troubles; for, as des Lupeaulx said, 'While the newspapers are making Châtelet ridiculous, they will leave the ministry in peace.'"

There was a pause; the Marquise left Lucien to his own reflections.

"Monsieur Blondet led me to hope that I should have the pleasure of seeing you in my house," said the Comtesse de Montcornet. "You will meet a few artists and men of letters, and some one else who has the keenest desire to become acquainted with you—Mademoiselle des Touches, the owner of talents rare among our sex. You will go to her house, no doubt. Mademoiselle des Touches (or Camille Maupin, if you prefer it) is prodigiously rich, and presides over one of the most remarkable salons in Paris. She has heard that you are as handsome as you are clever, and is dying to meet you."

Lucien could only pour out incoherent thanks and glance enviously at Emile Blondet. There was as great a difference between a great lady like Mme. de Montcornet and Coralie as between Coralie and a girl out of the streets. The Countess was young and witty and beautiful, with the very white fairness of women of the North. Her mother was the Princess Scherbellof, and the minister before dinner had paid her the most respectful attention.

By this time the Marquise had made an end of trifling disdainfully with the wing of a chicken.

"My poor Louise felt so much affection for you," she said. "She took me into her confidence; I knew her dreams of a great career for you. She would have borne a great deal, but what scorn you showed her when you sent back her letters! Cruelty we can forgive; those who hurt us must still have some faith in us; but indifference! Indifference is like polar snows. It extinguishes all life. So, you must see that you have lost a precious affection through your own fault. Why break with her? Even if she had scorned you, you had your way to make, had you not?—your name to win back? Louise thought of all that.''

"Then why was she silent?''

"*Eh! mon Dieu!*'' cried the Marquise, ''it was I myself who advised her not to take you into her confidence. Between ourselves, you know, you seemed so little used to the ways of the world that I took alarm. I was afraid that your inexperience and rash ardor might wreck our carefully made schemes. Can you recollect yourself as you were then? You must admit that if you could see your double to-day, you would say the same yourself. You are not like the same man. That was our one mistake. But would one man in a thousand combine such intellectual gifts with such a wonderful aptitude for taking the tone of society? I did not think that you would be such an astonishing exception. You were transformed so quickly, you acquired the manner of Paris so easily, that I did not recognize you in the Bois de Boulogne a month ago.''

Lucien heard the great lady with inexpressible pleasure; the flatteries were spoken with such a petulant, childlike, confiding air, and she seemed to take such a deep interest in him, that he thought of his first evening at the Panorama-Dramatique, and began to fancy that some such miracle was about to take place a second time. Everything had smiled upon him since that happy evening; his youth, he thought, was the talisman that worked this change. He would prove this great lady; she should not take him at unawares.

"Then, what were these schemes which have turned to chimeras, madame?'' asked he.

"Louise meant to obtain a royal patent permitting you to bear the name and title of Rubempré. She wished to put Chardon out of sight. Your opinions have put that out of the question now, but *then* it would not have been so hard to manage, and a title would mean a fortune for you.

"You will look on these things as trifles and visionary ideas," she continued; "but we know something of life, and we know, too, all the solid advantages of a count's title when it is borne by a fashionable and extremely charming young man. Announce 'Monsieur Chardon' and 'Monsieur le Comte de Rubempré' before heiresses or English girls with a million to their fortune and note the difference of the effect. The Count might be in debt, but he would find open hearts ; his good looks, brought into relief by his title, would be like a diamond in a rich setting ; Monsieur Chardon would not be so much as noticed. *We* have not invented these notions ; they are everywhere in the world, even among the bourgeois. You are turning your back on fortune at this minute. Do you see that good-looking young man, he is the Vicomte Félix de Vandenesse, one of the King's private secretaries. The King is fond enough of young men of talent, and Vandenesse came from the provinces with baggage nearly as light as yours. You are a thousand times cleverer than he ; but do you belong to a great family, have you a name? You know des Lupeaulx ; his name is very much like yours, for he was born a Chardin ; well, he would not sell his little farm of Lupeaulx for a million, he will be Comte des Lupeaulx some day, and perhaps his grandson may be a duke. You have made a false start ; and if you continue in that way it will be all over with you. See how much wiser Monsieur Emile Blondet has been ! He is engaged on a government newspaper ; he is well looked on by those in authority ; he can afford to mix with Liberals, for he holds sound opinions ; and sooner or later he will succeed. But then he understood how to choose his opinions and his protectors.

"Your charming neighbor" (Mme. d'Espard glanced at Mme. de Montcornet) "was a Troisville; there are two peers of France in the family and two deputies. She made a wealthy marriage with her name; she sees a great deal of society at her house; she has influence, she will move the political world for young Monsieur Blondet. Where will a Coralie take you? In a few years' time you will be hopelessly in debt and weary of pleasure. You have chosen badly in love and you are arranging your life ill. The woman whom you delight to wound was at the opera the other night, and this was how she spoke of you. She deplored the way in which you were throwing away your talent and the prime of youth; she was thinking of you, and not of herself, all the while."

"Ah! if only you were telling me truth, madame!" cried Lucien.

"What object should I have in telling lies?" returned the Marquise, with a glance of cold disdain which annihilated him. He was so dashed by it that the conversation dropped, for the Marquise was offended and said no more.

Lucien was nettled by her silence, but he felt that it was due to his own clumsiness and promised himself that he would repair his error. He turned to Mme. de Montcornet and talked to her of Blondet, extolling that young writer for her benefit. The Countess was gracious to him, and asked him (at a sign from Mme. d'Espard) to spend an evening at her house. It was to be a small and quiet gathering to which only friends were invited—Mme. de Bargeton would be there in spite of her mourning; Lucien would be pleased, she was sure, to meet Mme. de Bargeton.

"Madame la Marquise says that all the wrong is on my side," said Lucien; "so surely it rests with her cousin, does it not, to decide whether she will meet me?"

"Put an end to those ridiculous attacks, which only couple her name with the name of a man for whom she does not care at all, and you will soon sign a treaty of peace. You thought that she had used you ill, I am told, but I myself have seen her in sadness because you had forsaken her. Is it true that she left the provinces on your account?"

Lucien smiled; he did not venture to make any other reply.

"Oh! how could you doubt the woman who made such sacrifices for you? Beautiful and intellectual as she is, she deserves beside to be loved for her own sake; and Madame de Bargeton cared less for you than for your talents. Believe me, women value intellect more than good looks," added the Countess, stealing a glance at Emile Blondet.

In the minister's hôtel Lucien could see the differences between the great world and that other world beyond the pale in which he had lately been living. There was no sort of resemblance between the two kinds of splendor, no single point in common. The loftiness and disposition of the rooms in one of the handsomest houses in the Faubourg Saint-Germain, the ancient gilding, the breadth of decorative style, the subdued richness of the accessories, all this was strange and new to him; but Lucien had learned very quickly to take luxury for granted, and he showed no surprise. His behavior was as far removed from assurance or fatuity on the one hand as from complacency and servility on the other. His manner was good; he found favor in the eyes of all who were not prepared to be hostile, like the younger men, who resented his sudden intrusion into the great world and felt jealous of his good looks and his success.

When they arose from table, he offered his arm to Madame d'Espard, and was not refused. Rastignac, watching him, saw that the Marquise was gracious to Lucien, and came in the character of a fellow-countryman to remind the poet that they had met once before at Madame du Val-Noble's. The young patrician seemed anxious to find an ally in the great man from his own province, asked Lucien to breakfast with him some morning, and offered to introduce him to some young men of fashion. Lucien was nothing loth.

" The dear Blondet is coming," said Rastignac.

The two were standing near the Marquis de Ronquerolles, the Duc de Rhétoré, de Marsay, and General Montriveau. The minister came across to join the group.

" Well," said he, addressing Lucien with the bluff German heartiness that concealed his dangerous subtlety; " well, so you have made your peace with Madame d'Espard; she is delighted with you, and we all know," he added, looking around the group, " how difficult it is to please her."

" Yes, but she adores intellect," said Rastignac, " and my illustrious fellow-countryman has wit enough to sell."

" He will soon find out that he is not doing well for himself," Blondet put in briskly. " He will come over; he will soon be one of us."

Those who stood about Lucien rang the changes on this theme.; the older and responsible men laid down the law with one or two profound remarks; the younger ones made merry at the expense of the Liberals.

" He simply tossed up head or tails for Right or Left, I am sure," remarked Blondet, " but now he will choose for himself."

Lucien burst out laughing; he thought of his talk with Lousteau that evening in the Luxembourg Gardens.

" He has taken on a bear-leader," continued Blondet, " one Étienne Lousteau, a newspaper hack who sees a five-franc piece in a column. Lousteau's politics consist in a belief that Napoleon will return, and (and this seems to me to be still more simple) in a confidence in the gratitude and patriotism of their worships the gentlemen of the Left. As a Rubempré, Lucien's sympathies should lean toward the aristocracy; as a journalist, he ought to be for authority, or he will never be either Rubempré or a secretary-general."

The minister now asked Lucien to take a hand at whist;

but, to the great astonishment of those present, he declared
that he did not know the game.

"Come early to me on the day of that breakfast affair,"
Rastignac whispered, "and I will teach you to play. You are
a discredit to the royal city of Angoulême; and, to repeat
Monsieur de Talleyrand's saying, you are laying up an unhappy old age for yourself."

Des Lupeaulx was announced. He remembered Lucien,
whom he had met at Mme. du Van-Noble's, and bowed with
a semblance of friendliness which the poet could not doubt.
Des Lupeaulx was in favor, he was a master of requests, and
did the ministry secret services; he was, moreover, cunning
and ambitious, slipping himself in everywhere; he was everybody's friend, for he never knew whom he might need. He
saw plainly that this was a young journalist whose social
success would probably equal his success in literature; saw,
too, that the poet was ambitious, and overwhelmed him with
protestations and expressions of friendship and interest, till
Lucien felt as if they were old friends already, and took his
promises and speeches for more than their worth. Des
Lupeaulx made a point of knowing a man thoroughly well if
he wanted to get rid of him or feared him as a rival. So, to
all appearance, Lucien was well received. He knew that
much of his success was owing to the Duc de Rhétoré, the
Minister, Mme. d'Espard, and Mme. de Montcornet, and went
to spend a few moments with the two ladies before taking
leave, and talked his very best for them.

"What a coxcomb!" said des Lupeaulx, turning to the
Marquise when he had gone.

"He will be rotten before he is ripe," de Marsay added,
smiling. "You must have private reasons of your own,
madame, for turning his head in this way."

When Lucien stepped into the carriage in the courtyard, he
found Coralie waiting for him. She had come to fetch him.

The little attention touched him; he told her the history of his evening; and, to his no small astonishment, the new notions which even now were running in his head met with Coralie's approval. She strongly advised him to enlist under the ministerial banner.

"You have nothing to expect from the Liberals but hard knocks," she said. "They plot and conspire; they murdered the Duc de Berri. Will they upset the government? Never! You will never come to anything through them, while you will be the Comte de Rubempré if you throw in your lot with the other side. You might render services to the state, and be a peer of France, and marry an heiress. Be an Ultra. It is the proper thing beside," she added, this being the last word with her on all subjects. "I dined with the Val-Noble; she told me that Théodore Gaillard is really going to start his little royalist 'Revue,' so as to reply to your witticisms and the jokes in 'The Miroir.' To hear them talk, Monsieur Villèle's party will be in office before the year is out. Try to turn the change to account before they come to power; and say nothing to Étienne and your friends, for they are quite equal to playing you some ill turn."

A week later Lucien went to Mme. de Montcornet's house, and saw the woman whom he had so loved, whom later he had stabbed to the heart with a jest. He felt the most violent agitation at the sight of her, for Louise also had undergone a transformation. She was the Louise that she would always have been but for her detention in the provinces—she was a great lady. There was a grace and refinement in her mourning dress which told that she was a happy widow; Lucien fancied that this coquetry was aimed in some degree at him, and he was right; but, like an ogre, he had tasted flesh, and all that evening he vacillated between Coralie's warm, voluptuous beauty and the dried-up, haughty, cruel Louise. He could not make up his mind to sacrifice the actress to the great lady; and Mme. de Bargeton—all the old feeling reviving in her at the sight of Lucien, Lucien's beauty, Lucien's cleverness—was waiting and expecting that sacrifice all evening; and after all her insinuating speeches and her fascinations, she had her trouble for her pains. She left the room with a fixed determination to be revenged.

"Well, dear Lucien," she had said, and in her kindness there was both generosity and Parisian grace; "well, dear Lucien, so you, that were to have been my pride, took me for your first victim; and I forgave you, my dear, for I felt that in such a revenge there was a trace of love still left."

With that speech, and the queenly way in which it was uttered, Mme. de Bargeton recovered her position. Lucien, convinced that he was a thousand times in the right, felt that he had been put in the wrong. Not one word of the causes of the rupture! not one syllable of the terrible farewell letter! A woman of the world has a wonderful genius for diminishing her faults by laughing at them; she can obliterate them all with a smile or a question of feigned surprise, and she knows this. She remembers nothing, she can explain everything; she is amazed, asks questions, comments, amplifies, and quarrels with you, till in the end her sins disappear like stains on the application of a little soap and water; black as ink you knew them to be; and lo! in a moment, you behold immaculate, white innocence, and lucky are you if you do not find that you yourself have sinned in some way beyond redemption.

In a moment old illusions regained their power over Lucien and Louise; they talked like friends, as before; but when the lady, with a hesitating sigh, put the question, "Are you happy?" Lucien was not ready with a prompt, decided answer; he was intoxicated with gratified vanity; Coralie, who (let us admit it) had made life easy for him, had turned his head. A melancholy "No" would have made his fortune, but he must needs begin to explain his position with regard to Coralie. He said that he was loved for his own sake; he said a good many foolish things that a man will say when he is smitten with a tender passion, and thought the while that he was doing a clever thing.

Mme. de Bargeton bit her lips.   There was no more to be said.   Mme. d'Espard brought Mme. de Montcornet to her cousin, and Lucien became the hero of the evening, so to speak.   He was flattered, petted, and made much of by the three women ; he was entangled with art which no words can describe.   His social success in this fine and brilliant circle was at least as great as his triumphs in journalism.   Beautiful Mlle. des Touches, so well known as "Camille Maupin," asked him to one of her Wednesday dinners ; his beauty, now so justly famous, seemed to have made an impression upon her.   Lucien exerted himself to show that his wit equaled his good looks, and Mlle. des Touches expressed her admiration with a playful outspokenness and a pretty fervor of friendship which deceives those who do not know life in Paris to its depths, nor suspect how continual enjoyment whets the appetite for novelty.

"If she should like me as much as I like her, we might abridge the romance," said Lucien, addressing de Marsay and Rastignac.

"You both of you write romances too well to care to live them," returned Rastignac.   "Can men and women who write ever fall in love with each other ?   A time is sure to come when they begin to make little cutting remarks."

"It would not be a bad dream for you," laughed de Marsay.   "The charming young lady is thirty years old, it is true, but she has an income of eighty thousand livres.   She is adorably capricious, and her style of beauty wears well. Coralie is a silly little fool, my dear boy, well enough for a start, for a young spark must have a mistress ; but unless you make some great conquest in the great world, an actress will do you harm in the long run.   Now, my boy, go and cut out Conti.   Here he is, just about to sing with Camille Maupin. Poetry has taken precedence of music ever since time began."

But when Lucien heard Mlle. des Touches' voice blending with Conti's, his hopes fled.

"Conti sings too well," he told des Lupeaulx; and he went back to Mme. de Bargeton, who carried him off to Mme. d'Espard in another room.

"Well, will you not interest yourself in him?" asked Mme. de Bargeton.

The Marquise spoke with an air half-kindly, half-insolent. "Let Monsieur Chardon first put himself in such a position that he will not compromise those who take an interest in him," she said. "If he wishes to drop his patronymic and to bear his mother's name, he should at any rate be on the right side, should he not?"

"In less than two months I will arrange everything," said Lucien.

"Very well," returned Mme. d'Espard. "I will speak to my father and uncle; they are in waiting, they will speak to the chancellor for you."

The diplomatist and the two women had very soon discovered Lucien's weak side. The poet's head was turned by the glory of the aristocracy; every man who entered the rooms bore a sounding name mounted in a glittering title and he himself was plain Chardon. Unspeakable mortification filled him at the sound of it. Wherever he had been during the last few days that pang had been constantly present with him. He felt, moreover, a sensation quite as unpleasant when he went back to his desk after an evening spent in the great world, in which he made a tolerable figure, thanks to Coralie's carriage and Coralie's servants. It was, in fact, a constant mortification.

He learned to ride, in order to escort Mme. d'Espard, Mlle. des Touches, and the Comtesse de Montcornet when they drove in the Bois, a privilege which he had envied other young men so greatly when he first came to Paris. Finot was delighted to give his right-hand man an order for the opera, so

Lucien wasted many an evening there, and thenceforward he was one among the exquisites of the day, most of whom he outshone.

The poet asked Rastignac and his new associates to a breakfast, and made the blunder of giving it in Coralie's rooms in the Rue de Vendôme ; he was too young, too much of a poet, too self-confident, to discern certain shades and distinctions in conduct ; and how should an actress, a good-hearted but uneducated girl, teach him life ? His guests were anything but charitably disposed toward him ; it was clearly proven to their minds that Lucien the critic and the actress were in collusion for their mutual interests, and all of the young men were jealous of an arrangement which all of them stigmatized. The most pitiless of those who laughed that evening at Lucien's expense was Rastignac himself. Rastignac had made and held his position by very similar means ; but so careful had he been of appearances that he could afford to treat scandal as slander.

Lucien proved an apt pupil at whist. Play became a passion with him ; and, so far from disapproving, Coralie encouraged his extravagance with the peculiar shortsightedness of an all-absorbing love, which sees nothing beyond the moment and is ready to sacrifice anything, even the future, to the present enjoyment. Coralie looked on cards as a safeguard against rivals. A great love has much in common with childhood—a child's heedless, careless, spendthrift ways, a child's laughter and tears.

In those days there lived and flourished a set of young men, some of them rich, some poor, and all of them idle, called " free-livers " (*viveurs*); and, indeed, they lived with incredible insolence—unabashed and unproductive consumers and yet more intrepid drinkers. These spendthrifts mingled the roughest practical jokes with a life not so much reckless as suicidal; they drew back from no impossibility, and gloried in pranks which, nevertheless, were confined within certain limits; and as they showed the most original wit in their escapades, it was impossible not to pardon them.

No sign of the times more plainly discovered the helotism to which the restoration had condemned the young manhood of the epoch. The younger men, being at a loss to know what to do with themselves, were compelled to find other outlets for their superabundant energy beside journalism, or conspiracy, or art, or letters. They squandered their strength in the wildest excesses, such sap and luxuriant power were there in young France. The hard workers among these gilded youths wanted power and pleasure; the artists wished for money; the idle sought to stimulate their appetites or wished for excitement; one and all of them wanted a place, and one and all were shut out from politics and public life. Nearly all the "free-livers" were men of unusual mental powers; some held out against the enervating life, others were ruined by it. The most celebrated and the cleverest among them was Eugène Rastignac, who entered, with de Marsay's help, upon a political career, in which he has since distinguished himself. The practical jokes in which the set indulged became so famous that not a few vaudevilles have been founded upon them.

Blondet introduced Lucien to this society of prodigals, of which he became a brilliant ornament, ranking next to Bixiou, one of the most mischievous and untiring scoffing wits of his time. All through that winter Lucien's life was one long fit of intoxication, with intervals of easy work. He continued his series of sketches of contemporary life, and very occasionally made great efforts to write a few pages of serious criticism, on which he brought his utmost power of thought to bear. But study was the exception, not the rule, and only undertaken at the bidding of necessity; dinners and breakfasts, parties of pleasure and play, took up most of his time and Coralie absorbed all that was left. He would not think of the morrow. He saw beside that his so-called friends were leading the same life, earning money easily by writing publishers' prospectuses and articles paid for by speculators; all of them lived beyond their incomes, none of them thought seriously of the future.

Lucien had been admitted into the ranks of journalism and of literature on terms of equality; he foresaw immense difficulties in the way if he should try to rise above the rest. Every one was willing to look upon him as an equal; no one would have him for a superior. Unconsciously he gave up the idea of winning fame in literature, for it seemed easier to gain success in politics.

"Intrigue raises less opposition than talent," du Châtelet had said one day (for Lucien and the Baron had made up their quarrel); "a plot below the surface rouses no one's attention. Intrigue, moreover, is superior to talent, for it makes something out of nothing; while, for the most part, the immense resources of talent only injure a man."

So Lucien never lost sight of his principal idea; and though to-morrow, following close upon the heels of to-day in the midst of an orgie, never found the promised work accomplished, Lucien was assiduous in society. He paid court to Mme. de Bargeton, the Marquise d'Espard, and the Comtesse de Montcornet; he never missed a single party given by Mlle. des Touches, appearing in society after a dinner given by authors or publishers and leaving the salons for a supper given in consequence of a bet. The demands of conversation and . the excitement of play absorbed all the ideas and energy left by excess. The poet had lost the lucidity of judgment and coolness of head which must be preserved if a man is to see all that is going on around him, and never to lose the exquisite tact which the *parvenu* needs at every moment. How should he know how many a time Mme. de Bargeton left him with wounded susceptibilities, how often she forgave him or added one more condemnation to the rest?

Châtelet saw that his rival had still a chance left, so he became Lucien's friend. He encouraged the poet in dissipation that wasted his energies. Rastignac, jealous of his fellow-countryman, and thinking, beside, that Châtelet would be a surer and more useful ally than Lucien, had taken up the Baron's cause. So, some few days after the meeting of the Petrarch and Laura of Angoulême, Rastignac brought about a reconciliation between the poet and the elderly beau at a sumptuous supper given at the "Rocher de Cancale." Lucien never returned home till morning, and rose in the middle of the day; Coralie was always at his side, he could not forego a single pleasure. Sometimes he saw his real position, and made good resolutions, but they came to nothing in his idle, easy life; and the mainspring of will grew slack, and only responded to the heaviest pressure of necessity.

Coralie had been glad that Lucien should amuse himself; she had encouraged him in this reckless expenditure, because she thought that the cravings which she fostered would bind her lover to her; he could not lead his present life without her. But tender-hearted and loving as she was, she found courage to advise Lucien not to forget his work, and once or twice was obliged to remind him that he had earned very little during the month. Their debts were growing frightfully fast. The fifteen hundred francs which remained from the purchase-money of the "Marguerites" had been swallowed up at once, together with Lucien's first five hundred livres. In three months he had only made a thousand francs, yet he felt as though he had been working tremendously hard. But by this time Lucien had adopted the "free-liver's" pleasant theory of debts.

Debts are becoming to a young man, but after the age of five-and-twenty they are inexcusable. It should be observed that there are certain natures in which a really poetic temper is united with a weakened will; and these while absorbed in feeling, that they may transmute personal experience, sensation, or impression into some permanent form, are essentially deficient in the moral sense which should accompany all ob-

19

servation. Poets prefer rather to receive their own impressions than to enter into the souls of others to study the mechanism of their feelings and thoughts. So Lucien neither asked his associates what became of those who disappeared from among them, nor looked into the futures of his so-called friends. Some of them were heirs to property, others had definite expectations; yet others either possessed names that were known in the world, or a most robust belief in their destiny and a fixed resolution to circumvent the law. Lucien, too, believed in his future on the strength of various profound axiomatic sayings of Blondet's: "Everything comes out all right at last. If a man has nothing, his affairs cannot be embarrassed. We have nothing to lose but the fortune that we seek. Swim with the stream; it will take you somewhere. A clever man with a footing in society can make a fortune whenever he pleases."

That winter, filled as it was with so many pleasures and dissipations, was a necessary interval employed in finding capital for the new royalist paper; Théodore Gaillard and Hector Merlin only brought out the first number of the "Réveil" in March, 1822. The affair had been settled at Mme. du Val-Noble's house. Mme. du Val-Noble exercised a certain influence over the great personages, royalist writers, and bankers who met in her splendid rooms—"fit for a tale out of the 'Arabian Nights,'" as the elegant and clever courtesan herself used to say—to transact business which could not well be arranged elsewhere. The editorship had been promised to Hector Merlin. Lucien, Merlin's intimate, was pretty certain to be his right-hand man, and a *feuilleton* in a ministerial paper had been promised to him beside. All through the dissipations of that winter Lucien had been secretly making ready for this change of front. Child as he was, he fancied that he was a deep politician because he concealed the preparation for the approaching transformation scene, while he was counting upon ministerial largesses to extricate himself from embarrassment and to lighten Coralie's secret cares. Coralie said nothing of her distress; she smiled now, as always; but Bérénice was bolder, she kept Lucien informed of their difficulties; and the budding great man, moved, after the fashion of poets, by the tale of disasters, would vow that he would begin to work in earnest, and then forget his resolution, and drown his fleeting. cares in excess. One day Coralie saw the poetic brow overcast, scolded Bérénice, and told her lover that everything would be settled.

Mme. d'Espard and Mme. de Bargeton were waiting for Lucien's profession of his new creed, so they said, before applying through Châtelet for the patent which should permit Lucien to bear the so-much desired name. Lucien had proposed to dedicate the "Marguerites" to Mme. d'Espard, and the Marquise seemed to be not a little flattered by a compliment which authors have been somewhat chary of paying since they became a power in the land; but when Lucien went to Dauriat and asked after his book, that worthy publisher met him with excellent reasons for the delay in its appearance. Dauriat had this and that in hand, which took up all his time; a new volume by Canalis was coming out and he did not want the two books to clash; M. de Lamartine's second series of "Meditations" was in the press, and two important collections of poetry ought not to appear together.

By this time, however, Lucien's needs were so pressing that he had recourse to Finot, and received an advance on his work. When, at a supper-party that evening, the poet-journalist explained his position to his friends in the fast set, they drowned his scruples in champagne, iced with pleasantries. Debts! There was never yet a man of any power without debts! Debts represented satisfied cravings, clamorous vices. A man only succeeds under the pressure of the iron hand of necessity. Debts forsooth!

"Why, the one pledge of which a great man can be sure is given him by his friend the pawnbroker," cried Blondet.

"If you want everything, you must owe for everything," called Bixiou.

"No," corrected des Lupeaulx, "if you owe for everything, you have had everything."

The party contrived to convince the novice that his debts were a golden spur to urge on the horses of the chariot of his fortunes. There is always the stock example of Julius Cæsar with his debt of forty millions, and Friedrich II. on an allowance of one ducat a month, and a host of other great men whose failings are held up for the corruption of youth, while not a word is said of their wide-reaching ideas, their courage equal to all odds.

Creditors seized Coralie's horses, carriage, and furniture at last, for an amount of four thousand francs. Lucien went to Lousteau and asked his friend to meet his bill for the thousand francs lent to pay gaming debts; but Lousteau showed him certain pieces of stamped paper which proved that Florine was in much the same case. Lousteau was grateful, however, and offered to take the necessary steps for the sale of Lucien's "Archer of Charles IX."

"How came Florine to be in this plight?" asked Lucien.

"The Matifat took alarm," said Lousteau. "We have lost him; but, if Florine chooses, she can make him pay dear for his treachery. I will tell you all about it."

Three days after this bootless errand, Lucien and Coralie were breakfasting in melancholy spirits beside the fire in their pretty bedroom. Bérénice had cooked a dish of eggs for them over the grate; for the cook had gone, and the coachman and servants had taken leave. They could not sell the furniture, for it had been attached; there was not a single object of any value in the house; a goodly collection of pawntickets, forming a very instructive octavo volume, represented all the gold, silver, and jewelry. Bérénice had kept back a couple of spoons and forks, that was all.

Lousteau's newspaper was of service now to Coralie and

Lucien, little as they suspected it; for the tailor, dressmaker, and milliner were afraid to meddle with a journalist who was quite capable of writing down their establishments.

Étienne Lousteau broke in upon their breakfast with a shout of "Hurrah! Long live 'The Archer of Charles IX.!' And I have converted a hundred francs' worth of books into cash, children. We will go halves."

He handed fifty francs to Coralie, and sent Bérénice out in quest of a more substantial breakfast.

"Hector Merlin and I went to a booksellers' trade dinner yesterday, and prepared the way for your romance with cunning insinuations. Dauriat is in treaty, but Dauriat is haggling over it; he won't give more than four thousand francs for two thousand copies, and you want six thousand francs. We made you out twice as great as Sir Walter Scott! Oh! you have such novels as never were in the inwards of you. It is not a mere book for sale, it is a big business; you are not simply the writer of one more or less ingenious novel, you are going to write a whole series. That word 'series' did it! So, mind you, don't forget that you have a great historical series on hand—'La Grande Mademoiselle, or The France of Louis Quatorze;' 'Cotillon I., or The Early Days of Louis Quinze;' 'The Queen and the Cardinal, or Paris and the Fronde;' 'The Son of the Concini, or Richelieu's Intrigue.' These novels will be announced on the wrapper of the book. We call this manœuvre 'giving a success a toss in the coverlet,' for the titles are all to appear on the cover, till you will be better known for the books that you have not written than for the work you have done. And 'In the Press' is a way of gaining credit in advance for work that you will do. Come now, let us have a little fun! Here comes the champagne. You can understand, Lucien, that our men opened eyes as big as saucers. By-the-by, I see that you have saucers still left."

"They are attached," explained Coralie.

"I understand, and I resume: Show a publisher one manuscript volume and he will believe in all the rest. A publisher asks to see your manuscript and gives you to understand that he is going to read it. Why disturb his harmless vanity. They never read a manuscript; they would not publish so many if they did. Well, Hector and I allowed it to leak out that you might consider an offer of five thousand francs for three thousand copies, in two editions. Let me have your 'Archer;' the day after to-morrow we are to breakfast with the publishers, and we will get the upper hand of them."

"Who are they?" asked Lucien.

"Two partners named Fendant and Cavalier; they are two good fellows, pretty straightforward in business. One of them used to be with Vidal and Porchon, the other is the cleverest hand on the Quai des Augustins. They only started in business last year, and have lost a little on translations of English novels; so now my gentlemen have a mind to exploit the native product. There is a rumor current that these dealers in spoiled white paper are trading on other people's capital; but I don't think it matters very much to you who finds the money so long as you are paid."

Two days later the pair went to a breakfast in the Rue Serpente, in Lucien's old quarter of Paris. Lousteau still kept his room in the Rue de la Harpe; and it was in the same state as before, but this time Lucien felt no surprise; he had been initiated into the life of journalism; he knew all its ups and downs. Since that evening of his introduction to the Wooden Galleries, he had been paid for many an article, and gambled away the money along with the desire to write. He had filled columns, not once but many times, in the ingenious ways described by Lousteau on that memorable evening as they went to the Palais Royal. He was dependent upon Barbet and Braulard; he trafficked in books and theatre-tickets; he shrank no longer from any attack, from writing any panegyric; and at this moment he was in some sort rejoicing to make all that he could out of Lousteau before turning his back on the Liberals. His intimate knowledge of the party would stand him in good stead in future. And Lousteau, on his side, was privately receiving five hundred francs of the purchase-money, under the name of commission, from Fendant and Cavalier for introducing the future Sir Walter Scott to two enterprising tradesmen in search of a French author of "Waverley."

The firm of Fendant and Cavalier had started in business without any capital whatsoever. A great many publishing houses were established at that time in the same way, and are likely to be established so long as papermakers and printers will give credit for the time required to play some seven or eight of the games of chance called "new publications." At that time, as at present, the author's copyright was paid for in bills at six, nine, and twelve months—a method of payment determined by the custom of the trade, for booksellers settle accounts between themselves by bills at even longer dates. Papermakers and printers are paid in the same way, so that in practice the publisher-bookseller has a dozen or a score of works on sale for a twelvemonth before he pays for them. Even if only two or three of these hit the public taste, the profitable speculations pay for the bad and the publisher pays his way by grafting, as it were, one book upon another. But if all of them turn out badly, or if, for his misfortune, the publisher-bookseller happens to bring out some really good literature which stays on hand until the right public discovers and appreciates it ; or, if it costs too much to discount the paper that he receives, then, resignedly, he files his schedule and becomes a bankrupt with an untroubled mind. He was prepared all along for something of the kind. So, all the chances being in favor of the publishers, they staked other people's money, not their own, upon the gambling-table of business speculation.

This was the case with Fendant and Cavalier. Cavalier

brought his experience, Fendant his industry; the capital was a joint-stock affair, and very accurately described by that word, for it consisted in a few thousand francs scraped together with difficulty by the mistresses of the pair. Out of this fund they allowed each other a fairly handsome salary and scrupulously spent it all in dinners to journalists and authors, or at the theatre, where their business was transacted, as they said. This questionably honest couple were both supposed to be clever men of business, but Fendant was more slippery than Cavalier. Cavalier, true to his name, traveled about; Fendant looked after business in Paris. A partnership between two publishers is always more or less of a duel, and so it was with Fendant and Cavalier.

They had brought out plenty of romances already, such as the "Tour du Nord," "Le Marchand de Benares," "La Fontaine du Sépulcre," and "Tékéli," translations of the works of Galt, an English novelist who never attained much popularity in France. The success of translations of Scott had called the attention of the trade to English novels. The race of publishers, all agog for a second Norman Conquest, were seeking industriously for a second Scott, just as at a rather later day every one must needs look for asphalt in stony soil or bitumen in marshes, and speculate in projected railways. The stupidity of the Paris commercial world is conspicuous in these attempts to do the same thing twice, for success lies in contraries; and in Paris, of all places in the world, success spoils success. So beneath the title of "Strelitz, or Russia a Hundred Years Ago," Fendant and Cavalier rashly added in big letters the words, "In the style of Scott."

Fendant and Cavalier were in great need of a success. A single good book might float their sunken bales, they thought; and there was the alluring prospect beside of articles in the newspapers, the great way of promoting sales in those days. A book is very seldom bought and sold for its just value, and purchases are determined by considerations quite other than the merits of the work. So Fendant and Cavalier thought of Lucien as a journalist and of his book as a salable article, which would help them to tide over their monthly settlement.

The partners occupied the ground floor of one of the great old-fashioned houses in the Rue Serpente ; their private office had been contrived at the further end of a suite of large drawing-rooms, now converted into warehouses for books. Lucien and Étienne found the publishers in their office, the agreement drawn up, and the bills ready. Lucien wondered at such prompt action.

Fendant was short and thin and by no means reassuring of aspect. With his low, narrow forehead, sunken nose, and hard mouth, he looked like a Kalmuck Tartar ; a pair of small, wide-awake, black eyes, the crabbed irregular outline of his countenance, a voice like a cracked bell—the man's whole appearance, in fact, combined to give the impression that this was a consummate rascal. A honeyed tongue compensated for these disadvantages and he gained his ends by talk. Cavalier, a stout, thick-set young fellow, looked more like the driver of a mail-coach than a publisher ; he had hair of a sandy color, a fiery-red countenance, and the heavy build and untiring tongue of a commercial traveler.

" There is no need to discuss this affair," said Fendant, addressing Lucien and Lousteau. " I have read the work, it is very literary, and so exactly the kind of thing we want, that I have sent it off as it is to the printer. The agreement is drawn on the lines laid down, and, beside, we always make the same stipulations in all cases. The bills fall due in six, nine, and twelve months respectively ; you will meet with no difficulty in discounting them, and we will refund you the discount. We have reserved the right of giving a new title to the book. We don't care for 'The Archer of Charles IX. ;' it does not tickle the reader's curiosity sufficiently ; there were several kings of that name, you see, and there were so many archers in the Middle Ages. If you had only called it

'The Soldier of Napoleon,' now! But 'The Archer of Charles IX. !' why, Cavalier would have to give a course of history lessons before he could place a copy anywhere in the provinces.''

"If you but knew the class of people that we have to do with!'' exclaimed Cavalier.

"''Saint Bartholomew' would suit better,'' continued Fendant.

"''Catherine de Medici, or France under Charles IX.,' would sound more like one of Scott's novels,'' added Cavalier.

"We will settle it when the work is printed,'' said Fendant.

"Do as you please, so long as I approve your title,'' said Lucien.

The agreement was read over, signed in duplicate, and each of the contracting parties took their copy. Lucien put the bills in his pocket with unequaled satisfaction, and the four repaired to Fendant's abode, where they breakfasted on beefsteaks and oysters, kindeys in champagne, and Brie cheese; but if the fare was something of the homeliest, the wines were exquisite; Cavalier had an acquaintance a traveler in the wine trade. Just as they sat down to table the printer appeared, to Lucien's surprise, with the first two proof-sheets.

"We want to get on with it,'' Fendant said; "we are counting on your book; we want a success confoundedly badly.''

The breakfast, begun at noon, lasted till five o'clock.

"Where shall we get cash for these things?'' asked Lucien as they came away, somewhat heated and flushed with the wine.

"We might try Barbet,'' suggested Étienne, and they turned down to the Quai des Augustins.

"Coralie is astonished to the highest degree over Florine's loss. Florine only told her about it yesterday; she seemed to lay the blame of it on you, and was so vexed that she was ready to throw you over."

"That's true," said Lousteau. Wine had gotten the better of prudence, and he unbosomed himself to Lucien, ending up with : "My friend—for you are my friend, Lucien ; you lent me a thousand francs, and you have only once asked me for the money—shun play ! If I had never touched a card, I should be a happy man. I owe money all around. At this moment I have the bailiffs at my heels ; indeed, when I go to the Palais Royal I have dangerous capes to double."

In the language of the fast set, doubling a cape meant dodging a creditor or keeping out of his way. Lucien had not heard the expression before, but he was familiar with the practice by this time.

"Are your debts so heavy ? "

"A mere trifle," said Lousteau. "A thousand crowns would pull me through. I have resolved to turn steady and give up play, and I have done a little 'chantage' to pay my debts."

"What is 'chantage?'" asked Lucien.

"It is an English invention recently imported. A 'chanteur' is a man who can manage to put a paragraph in the papers—never an editor nor a responsible man, for they are not supposed to know anything about it, and there is always a Giroudeau or a Philippe Bridau to be found. A bravo of this stamp finds up somebody who has his own reasons for not wanting to be talked about. Plenty of people have a few peccadilloes, or some more or less original sin, upon their consciences ; there are plenty of fortunes made in ways that would not bear looking into ; sometimes a man has kept the letter of the law and sometimes he has not ; and, in either case, there is a tidbit of tattle for the inquirer, as, for instance, that tale of Fouché's police surrounding the spies of the prefect of police, who, not being in the secret of the fabrication of forged English banknotes, were just about to pounce on the clandestine printers employed by the minister; or there is the story of Prince Galathionne's diamonds, the Maubreuil affair, or the Pombreton will case. The 'chanteur' gets possession of some compromising letter, asks for an interview; and if the man that made the money does not buy silence, the 'chanteur' draws a picture of the press ready to take the matter up and unravel his private affairs. The rich man is frightened, he comes down with the money, and the trick succeeds.

"You are committed to some risky venture, which might easily be written down in a series of articles; a 'chanteur' waits upon you and offers to withdraw the articles —for a consideration. 'Chanteurs' are sent to men in office, who will bargain that their acts and not their private characters are to be attacked, or they are heedless of their characters and anxious only to shield the woman they love. One of your acquaintances, that charming master of requests, des Lupeaulx, is a kind of agent for affairs of this sort. The rascal has màde a position for himself in the most marvelous way in the very centre of power; he is the middleman of the press and the ambassador of the ministers; he works upon a man's self-love; he bribes newspapers to pass over a loan in silence, or to make no comment on a contract which was never put up for public tender, and the jackals of Liberal bankers get a share out of it. That was a bit of 'chantage' that you did with Dauriat; he gave you a thousand crowns to let Nathan alone. In the eighteenth century, when journalism was still in its infancy, this kind of blackmail was levied by pamphleteers in the pay of favorites and great lords. The original inventor was Pietro Aretino, a great Italian. Kings went in fear of him, as stage-players go in fear of a newspaper to-day."

"What did you do to the Matifat to make the thousand crowns?"

"I attacked Florine in half a dozen papers. Florine complained to Matifat. Matifat went to Braulard to find out what the attacks meant. I did my 'chantage' for Finot's benefit, and Finot put Braulard on the wrong scent; Braulard told the man of drugs that *you* were demolishing Florine in Coralie's interest. Then Giroudeau went round to Matifat and told him (in confidence) that the whole business could be accommodated if he (Matifat) would consent to sell his sixth share of Finot's review for ten thousand francs. Finot was to give me a thousand crowns if the dodge succeeded. Well, Matifat was only too glad to get back ten thousand francs out of the thirty thousand invested in a risky speculation, as he thought, for Florine had been telling him for several days past that Finot's review was doing badly; and, instead of paying a dividend, something was said of calling up more capital. So Matifat was just about to close with the offer, when the manager of the Panorama-Dramatique comes to him with some accommodation bills that he wanted to negotiate before filing his schedule. To induce Matifat to take them of him, he let out a word of Finot's trick. Matifat, being a shrewd man of business, took the hint, held tight to his sixth, and is laughing in his sleeve at us. Finot and I are howling with despair. We have been so misguided as to attack a man who has no affection for his mistress, a heartless, soulless wretch. Unluckily, too, for us, Matifat's business is not amenable to the jurisdiction of the press, and he cannot be made to smart for it through his interests. A druggist is not like a hatter or a milliner, or a theatre or a work of art; he is above criticism; you can't run down his opium and dyewoods, nor cocoa-beans, paint, and pepper. Florine is at her wits' end; the Panorama closes to-morrow, and what will become of her she does not know."

"Coralie's engagement at the Gymnase begins in a few days," said Lucien; "she might do something for Florine."

"Not she!" said Lousteau. "Coralie is not clever, but she is not quite simple enough to help herself to a rival. We are in a mess with a vengeance. And Finot is in such a hurry to buy back his sixth——"

" Why ? "

" It is a capital bit of business, my dear fellow. There is a chance of selling the paper for three hundred thousand francs ; Finot would have one-third, and his partners beside are going to pay him a commision, which he will share with des Lupeaulx. So I propose to do another turn of ' chantage.' "

" ' Chantage ' seems to mean your money or your life ? "

" It is better than that," said Lousteau ; " it is your money or your character. A short time ago the proprietor of a minor newspaper was refused credit. The day before yester-day it was announced in his columns that a gold repeater set with diamonds belonging to a certain notability had found its way in a curious fashion into the hands of a private sol-dier in the Guards ; the story promised to the readers might have come from the 'Arabian Nights.' The notability lost no time in asking that editor to dine with him ; the editor was dis-tinctly a gainer by the transaction, and contemporary history has lost an anecdote. Whenever the press makes vehement onslaughts upon some one in power, you may be sure that there is some refusal to do a service behind it. Blackmailing with regard to private life is the terror of the richest English-man and a great source of wealth to the press in England, which is infinitely more corrupt than ours. We are children in comparison ! In England they will pay five or six thousand francs for a compromising letter to sell again."

" Then how can you lay hold of Matifat ? " asked Lucien.

" My dear boy, that low tradesman wrote the queerest letters to Florine ; the spelling, style, and matter of them is ludicrous to the last degree. We can strike him in the very midst of his Lares and Penates, where he feels himself safest, without so much as mentioning his name ; and he cannot complain, for he lives in fear and terror of his wife. Imagine his wrath when he sees the first number of a little serial entitled the

'Amours of a Druggist,' and is given fair warning that his love-letters have fallen into the hands of certain journalists. He talks about the 'little god Cupid,' he tells Florine that she enables him to cross the desert of life (which looks as if he took her for a camel), and spells 'never' with two v's. There is enough in that immensely funny correspondence to bring an influx of subscribers for a fortnight. He will shake in his shoes lest an anonymous letter should supply his wife with a key to the riddle. The question is whether Florine will consent to appear to persecute Matifat. She has some principles, which is to say, some hopes, still left. Perhaps she means to keep the letters and to make something for herself out of them. She is cunning, as befits my pupil. But as soon as she finds out that a bailiff is no laughing matter, or Finot gives her a suitable present or hopes of an engagement, she will give me the letters and I shall sell them to Finot. Finot will put the correspondence in his uncle's hands, and Giroudeau will bring Matifat to terms."

These confidences sobered Lucien. His first thought was that he had some extremely dangerous friends; his second, that it would be impolitic to break with them; for if Mme. d'Espard, Mme. de Bargeton, and Châtelet should fail to keep their word with him, he might need their terrible power yet. By this time Étienne and Lucien had reached Barbet's miserable bookshop on the quai. Étienne addressed Barbet—

"We have five thousand francs' worth of bills at six, nine, and twelve months, given by Fendant and Cavalier. Are you willing to discount them for us?"

"I will give you three thousand francs for them," said Barbet with imperturbable coolness.

"Three thousand francs!" echoed Lucien.

"Nobody else will give you as much," rejoined the bookseller. "The firm will go bankrupt before three months are out; but I happen to know that they have some good books that are hanging on hand; they cannot afford to wait, so I shall buy their stock for cash and pay them with their own bills, and get the books at a reduction of two thousand francs. That's how it is.''

'' Do you mind losing a couple of thousand francs, Lucien ?'' asked Lousteau.

'' Yes ! '' Lucien answered vehemently. He was dismayed by this first rebuff.

'' You are making a mistake,'' said Étienne.

'' You won't find any one that will take their paper,'' said Barbet. '' Your book is their last stake, sir. The printer will not trust them ; they are obliged to leave the copies in pawn with him. If they make a hit now, it will only stave off bankruptcy for another six months, sooner or later they will have to go. They are cleverer at tippling than at book-selling. In my own case, their bills mean business ; and that being so, I can afford to give more than a professional dis-counter who simply looks at the signatures. It is a bill-discounter's business to know whether three names on a bill are each good for thirty per cent. in case of bankruptcy. And here at the outset you only offer two signatures, and neither of them worth ten per cent.''

The two journalists exchanged glances in surprise. Here was a little scrub of a bookseller putting the essence of the art and mystery of bill-discounting in these few words.

'' That will do, Barbet,'' said Lousteau. '' Can you tell us of a bill-broker that will look at us ? ''

'' There is Daddy Chaboisseau, on the Quai Saint-Michel, you know. He tided Fendant over his last monthly settle-ment. If you won't listen to my offer, you might go and see what he says to you ; but you would only come back to me, and then I shall offer you two thousand francs instead of three.''

Étienne and Lucien betook themselves to the Quai Saint-Michel and found Chaboisseau in a little house with a passage entry. Chaboisseau, a bill-discounter, whose dealings were principally with the booktrade, lived in a third-floor lodging furnished in the most eccentric manner. A brevet-rank banker and a millionaire to boot, he had a taste for the classical style. The cornice was in the classical style; the bedstead, in the purest classical taste, dated from the time of the empire, when such things were in fashion; the purple hangings fell over the wall like the classic draperies in the background of one of David's pictures. Chairs and tables, lamps and sconces, and every least detail had evidently been sought with patient care in furniture warehouses. There was the elegance of antiquity about the classic revival as well as its fragile and somewhat arid grace. The man himself, like his manner of life, was in grotesque contrast with the airy mythological look of his rooms; and it may be remarked that the most eccentric characters are found among men who give their whole energies to money-making.

Men of this stamp are, in a certain sense, intellectual libertines. Everything is within their reach, consequently their fancy is jaded, and they will make immense efforts to shake off their indifference. The student of human nature can always discover some hobby, some accessible weakness and sensitive spot in their hearts. Chaboisseau might have intrenched himself in antiquity as in an impregnable and fortified camp.

"The man will be an antique to match, no doubt," said Étienne, smiling.

Chaboisseau, a little old person with powdered hair, wore a greenish coat and snuff-brown waistcoat; he was tricked out beside in black small-clothes, ribbed stockings, and shoes that creaked as he came forward to take the bills. After a short scrutiny, he returned them to Lucien with a serious countenance.

"Messieurs Fendant and Cavalier are delightful young fellows; they have plenty of intelligence; but I have no money," he said blandly.

20

"My friend here would be willing to meet you in the matter of discount——" Étienne began.

"I would not take the bills on any consideration," returned the little broker. The words slid down upon Lousteau's suggestion like the blade of the guillotine on a man's neck.

The two friends withdrew; but as Chaboisseau went prudently out with them across the antechamber, Lucien noticed a pilè of second-hand books. Chaboisseau had been in the trade, and this was a recent purchase. Shining conspicuous among them, he noticed a copy of a work by the architect Ducerceau, which gives exceedingly accurate plans of various royal palaces and châteaux in France.

"Could you let me have that book?" he asked.

"Yes," said Chaboisseau, transformed into a bookseller.

"How much?"

"Fifty francs."

"It is dear, but I want it. And I can only pay you with one of the bills which you refuse to take."

"You have a bill there for five hundred francs at six months; I will take that one of you," said Chaboisseau.

Apparently at the last statement of accounts, there had been a balance of five hundred francs in favor of Fendant and Cavalier.

They went back to the classical apartment. Chaboisseau made out a little memorandum, interest so much and commission so much, total deduction thirty francs, then he subtracted fifty francs for Ducerceau's book; finally, from a cashbox full of coin, he took four hundred and twenty francs.

"Look here, though, Monsieur Chaboisseau, the bills are either all of them good or all bad alike; why don't you take the rest?"

"This is not discounting; I am paying myself for a sale," said the old man.

Étienne and Lucien were still laughing at Chaboisseau,

without understanding him, when they reached Dauriat's shop, and Étienue asked Gabusson to give them the name of a bill-broker. Gabusson thus appealed to gave them a letter of introduction to a broker in the Boulevard Poissonnière, telling them at the same time that this was the " oddest and queerest party" (to use his own expression) that he, Gabusson, had come across. The friends took a cab by the hour, and went to the address.

" If Samanon won't take your bills," Gabusson had said, " nobody else will look at them."

A second-hand bookseller on the first floor, a second-hand clothes-dealer on the second floor, and a seller of indecent prints on the third, Samanon carried on a fourth business— he was a money-lender into the bargain. No character in Hoffmann's romances, no sinister-brooding miser of Scott's, can compare with this freak of human and Parisian nature (always admitting that Samanon was human). In spite of himself, Lucien shuddered at the sight of the dried-up little old creature, whose bones seemed to be cutting a leather skin, spotted with all sorts of little green and yellow patches, like a portrait by Titian or Veronese when you look at it closely. One of Samanon's eyes was fixed and glassy, the other lively and bright ; he seemed to keep that dead eye for the bill-discounting part of his profession, and the other for the trade in the pornographic curiosities upstairs. A few stray white hairs, escaping from under a small, sleek, rusty black wig, stood erect above a sallow forehead with a suggestion of menace about it ; a hollow trench in either cheek defined the outline of the jaws ; while a set of projecting teeth, still white, seemed to stretch the skin of the lips with the effect of an equine yawn. The contrast between the ill-assorted eyes and grinning mouth gave Samanon a passably ferocious air ; and the very bristles on the man's chin looked stiff and sharp as pins.

Nor was there the slightest sign about him of any desire to redeem a sinister appearance by attention to the toilet ; his threadbare jacket was all but dropping to pieces; a cravat, which had once been black, was frayed by contact with a stubble chin, and left on exhibition a throat as wrinkled as a turkey-gobbler's.

This was the individual whom Étienne and Lucien discovered in his filthy counting-house, busily affixing tickets to the backs of a parcel of books from a recent sale. In a glance, the friends exchanged the innumerable questions raised by the existence of such a creature; then they presented Gabusson's introduction and Fendant and Cavalier's bills. Samanon was still reading the note when a third-comer entered, the wearer of a short jacket, which seemed in the dimly lighted shop to be cut out of a piece of zinc roofing, so solid was it by reason of alloy with all kinds of foreign matter. Oddly attired as he was, the man was an artist of no small intellectual power, and ten years later he was destined to assist in the inauguration of the great, but ill-founded, Saint-Simonian system.*

"I want my coat, my black trousers, and satin waistcoat," said this person, pressing a numbered ticket on Samanon's attention. Samanon touched the brass button of a bell-pull, and a woman came down from some upper region, a Normande apparently, to judge by her rich, fresh complexion.

"Let the gentleman have his clothes," said Samanon, holding out a hand to the new-comer. "It's a pleasure to do business with you, sir; but that youngster whom one of your friends introduced to me took me in most abominably."

"Took *him* in!" chuckled the new-comer, pointing out Samanon to the two journalists with an extremely comical gesture. The great man dropped thirty sous into the money-lender's yellow, wrinkled hand; like the Neapolitan's *lazzaroni* (beggars), he was taking his best clothes out of pawn

* A kind of communism.

for a state occasion. The coins dropped jingling into the till.

"What queer business are you up to?" asked Lousteau of the artist, an opium-eater who dwelt among visions of enchanted palaces till he either could not or would not create.

" *He* lends you a good deal more than an ordinary pawn-broker on anything you pledge; and, beside, he is so awfully charitable, he allows you to take your clothes out when you must have something to wear. I am going to dine with the Kellers and my mistress to-night," he continued; "and to me it is easier to find thirty sous than two hundred francs, so I keep my wardrobe here. It has brought the charitable usurer a hundred francs in the last six months. Samanon has devoured my library already, volume by volume" (*livre à livre*).

"And sou by sou," Lousteau said with a laugh.

"I will let you have fifteen hundred francs," said Samanon, looking up.

Lucien started, as if the bill-broker had thrust a red-hot skewer through his heart. Samanon was subjecting the bills and their dates to a close scrutiny.

"And even then," he added, "I must see Fendant first. He ought to deposit some books with me. You aren't worth much" (turning to Lucien); "you are living with Coralie, and your furniture has been attached."

Lousteau, watching Lucien, saw him take up his bills, and dash out into the street. "He is the devil himself!" exclaimed the poet. For several seconds he stood outside gazing at the shop-front. The whole place was so pitiful that a passer-by could not see it without smiling at the sight, and wondering what kind of business a man could do among those mean, dirty shelves of ticketed books.

A few moments later, the great man, in incognito, came out, very well dressed, smiled at the friends, and turned to go with them in the direction of the Passage des Panoramas, where he meant to complete his toilet by the polishing of his shoes.

"If you see Samanon in a bookseller's shop, or calling on a paper-merchant or a printer, you may know that it is all over with that man," said the artist. "Samanon is the undertaker come to take the measurements for a coffin."

"You won't discount your bills now, Lucien," said Étienne.

"If Samanon will not take them, nobody else will; he is the *ultima ratio*," said the stranger. "He is one of Gigonnet's lambs, a spy for Palma, Werbrust, Gobseck, and the rest of those crocodiles who swim in the Paris money-market. Every man with a fortune to make, or unmake, is sure to come across one of them sooner or later."

"If you cannot discount your bills at fifty per cent.," remarked Lousteau, "you must exchange them for hard cash."

"How?"

"Give them to Coralie; Camusot will cash them for her. You are disgusted," added Lousteau, as Lucien cut him short with a start. "What nonsense! How can you allow such a silly scruple to turn the scale, when your future is in the balance?"

"I shall take this money to Coralie in any case," began Lucien.

"Here is more folly!" cried Lousteau. "You will not keep your creditors quiet with four hundred francs when you must have four thousand. Let us keep a little and get drunk on it, if we lose the rest at *rouge et noir*."

"That is sound advice," said the great man.

Those words, spoken not four paces from Frascati's, were magnetic in their effect. The friends dismissed their cab and went up to the gaming-table.

At the outset they won three thousand francs, then they lost and fell to five hundred; again they won three thousand seven hundred francs, and again they lost all but a five-franc piece. After another turn of luck they staked two thousand francs on an even number to double the stake at a stroke ; an even number had not turned up for five times in succession, and this was the sixth time. They punted the whole sum, and an odd number turned up once more.

After two hours of all-absorbing, frenzied excitement, the two dashed down the staircase with the hundred francs kept back for the dinner. Upon the steps, between the two pillars which support the little sheet-iron verandah to which so many eyes have been upturned in longing or despair, Lousteau stopped and looked into Lucien's flushed, inflamed, and excited face.

" Let us just try fifty francs," he said.

And up the stairs again they went. An hour later they owned a thousand crowns. Black had turned up for the fifth consecutive time ; they trusted that their previous luck would not repeat itself, and put the whole sum on the red—black turned up for the sixth time. They had lost. It was now six o'clock.

" Let us just try twenty-five francs," said Lucien.

The new venture was soon made—and lost. The twenty-five francs went in five stakes. Then Lucien, in a frenzy, flung down his last twenty-five francs on the number of his age, and won. No words can describe how his hands trembled as he raked in the coins which the bank paid him one by one. He handed ten louis to Lousteau.

" Fly ! " he cried ; " take it to Véry's."

Lousteau took the hint and went to order dinner. Lucien, left alone, laid his thirty louis on the red and won. Emboldened by the inner voice which a gambler always hears, he staked the whole again on the red, and again he won. He felt as if there was a furnace within him. Without heeding the voice, he laid a hundred and twenty louis on the black and lost. Then to the torturing excitement of suspense succeeded the delicious feeling of relief known to the gambler who has nothing left to lose, and must perforce leave the palace of fire in which his dreams melt and vanish.

He found Lousteau at Vèry's, and flung himself upon the cookery (to make use of La Fontaine's expression), and drowned his cares in wine. By nine o'clock his ideas were so confused that he could not imagine why the portress in the Rue 'de Vendôme persisted in sending him to the Rue de la Lune.

"Mademoiselle Coralie has gone," said the woman. "She has taken lodgings elsewhere. She left her address with me on this scrap of paper."

Lucien was too far gone to be surprised at anything. He went back to the cab which had brought him, and was driven to the Rue de la Lune, making puns to himself on the name of the street as he went.

The news of the failure of the Panorama-Dramatique had come like a thunder-clap. Coralie, taking alarm, made haste to sell her furniture (with the consent of her creditors) to little, old Cardot, who installed Florentine in the rooms at once. The tradition of the house remained unbroken. Coralie paid her creditors and satisfied the landlord, proceeding with her "washing-day," as she called it, while Bérénice bought the absolutely indispensable necessaries to furnish a fourth-floor lodging in the Rue de la Lune, a few doors from the Gymnase. Here Coralie was waiting for Lucien's return. She had brought her love unsullied out of the shipwreck and twelve hundred francs.

Lucien, more than half-intoxicated, poured out his woes to Coralie and Bérénice.

"You did quite right, my angel," said Coralie, with her arms about his neck. "Bérénice can easily negotiate your bills with Braulard."

The next morning Lucien awoke to an enchanted world of happiness made about him by Coralie. She was more loving and tender in these days than she had ever been ; perhaps she thought that the wealth of love in her heart should make him amends for the poverty of their lodging. She looked bewitchingly charming, with the loose hair straying from under the crushed, white silk handkerchief about her head; there was soft laughter in her eyes; her words were as bright as the first rays of sunrise that shone in through the windows, pouring a flood of gold upon such charming poverty.

Not that the room was squalid. The walls were covered with a sea-green paper, bordered with red; there was one mirror over the chimney-piece and a second above the chest of drawers. The bare boards were covered with a cheap carpet, which Bérénice had bought in spite of Coralie's orders, and paid for out of her own little store. A wardrobe, with a glass door and a chest, held the lovers' clothing, the mahogany chairs were covered with blue cotton stuff, and Bérénice had managed to save a clock and a couple of china vases from the catastrophe, as well as four spoons and forks and half-a-dozen little spoons. The bedroom was entered from the dining-room, which might have belonged to a clerk with an income of twelve hundred francs. The kitchen was next the landing, and Bérénice slept above in an attic. The rent was not more than a hundred crowns.

The dismal house boasted a sham carriage entrance, the porter's box being contrived behind one of the useless leaves of the gate and lighted by a peephole through which that personage watched the comings and goings of seventeen families, for this hive was a "good-paying property," in auctioneer's phrase.

Lucien, looking round the room, discovered a desk, an easy-chair, paper, pens, and ink. The sight of Bérénice in high spirits (she was building hopes on Coralie's *début* at the Gymnase), and of Coralie herself conning her part with a knot of blue ribbon tied about it, drove all cares and anxieties from the sobered poet's mind.

"So long as nobody in society hears of this sudden come-

down, we shall pull through," he said. "After all, we have
four thousand five hundred francs before us. I will turn my
new position in royalist journalism to account. To-morrow
we shall start the 'Réveil;' I am an old hand now, and I
will make something out."

And Coralie, seeing nothing but love in the words, kissed
the lips that uttered them. By this time Bérénice had set the
table near the fire and served a modest breakfast of scrambled
eggs, a couple of cutlets, coffee, and cream. Just then there
came a knock at the door, and Lucien, to his astonishment,
beheld three of the loyal friends of old days—d'Arthez, Léon
Giraud, and Michel Chrestien. He was deeply touched, and
asked them to share the breakfast.

" No; we have come on more serious business than con-
dolence," said d'Arthez; "we know the whole story, we
have just come from the Rue de Vendôme. You know my
opinions, Lucien. Under any other circumstances I should
be glad to hear that you had adopted my political convictions;
but situated as you are with regard to the Liberal press, it is
impossible for you to go over to the Ultras. Your life will be
sullied, your character blighted for ever. We have come to
entreat you in the name of our friendship, weakened though
it may be, not to soil yourself in this way. You have been
prominent in attacking the Romantics, the Right, and the
Government; you cannot now declare for the Government,
the Right, and the Romantics."

" My reasons for the change are based on lofty grounds;
the end will justify the means," said Lucien.

" Perhaps you do not fully comprehend our position on the
side of the government," said Léon Giraud. " The government, the court, the Bourbons, the absolutist party, or, to sum
up in a general expression, the whole system opposed to the
constitutional system, may be divided upon the question of
the best means of extinguishing the revolution, is unanimous
as to the advisibility of extinguishing the newspapers. The

'Réveil, the 'Foudre,' and the 'Drapeau Blanc' have all been founded for the express purpose of replying to the slander, gibes, and railing of the Liberal press. I cannot approve them, for it is precisely this failure to recognize the grandeur of our priesthood that has led us to bring out a serious and self-respecting paper; which perhaps," he added parenthetically, "may exercise a worthy influence before very long, and win respect, and carry weight; but this royalist artillery is destined for a first attempt at reprisals, the Liberals are to be paid back in their own coin—shaft for shaft, wound for wound.

"What can come of it, Lucien? The majority of newspaper readers incline for the Left; and in the press, as in warfare, the victory is with the big battalions. You will be blackguards, liars, enemies of the people; the other side will be defenders of their country, martyrs, men to be held in honor, though they may be even more hypocritical and slippery than their opponents. In these ways the pernicious influence of the press will be increased, while the most odious form of journalism will receive sanction. Insult and personalities will have become a recognized privilege of the press; newspapers have taken this tone in the subscribers' interests; and when both sides have recourse to the same weapons, the standard is set and the general tone of journalism taken for granted. When the evil is developed to its fullest extent, restrictive laws will be followed by prohibitions; there will be a return of the censorship of the press imposed after the assassination of the Duc de Berri, and repealed since the opening of the Chambers. And do you know what the nation will conclude from the debate? The people will believe the insinuations of the Liberal press; they will think that the Bourbons mean to attack the rights of property acquired by the revolution, and some fine day they will rise and shake off the Bourbons. You are not only soiling your life, Lucien, you are going over to the losing side. You are too young, too lately a journalist, too little initiated into the secret springs of motive and the tricks of the craft, you have aroused too much jealousy, not to fall a victim to the general hue and cry that will be raised against you in the Liberal newspapers. You will be drawn into the fray by party spirit now still at fever-heat; though the fever, which spent itself in violence in 1815 and 1816, now appears in debates in the Chamber and polemics in the papers."

"I am not quite a featherhead, my friends," said Lucien, "though you may choose to see a poet in me. Whatever may happen, I shall gain one solid advantage which no Liberal victory can give me. By the time your victory is won, I shall have gained my end."

"We will cut off—your hair," said Michel Chrestien, with a laugh.

"I shall have children by that time," said Lucien; "and if you cut off my head it will not matter."

The three could make nothing of Lucien. Intercourse with the great world had developed in him the pride of caste, the vanities of the aristocrat. The poet thought, and not without reason, that there was a fortune in his good looks and intellect, accompanied by the name and title of Rubempré. Mme. d'Espard and Mme. de Bargeton held him fast by this clue, as a child holds a cockroach by a string. Lucien's flight was circumscribed. The words, "He is one of us, he is sound," accidentally overheard but three days ago in Mlle. des Touches' salon, had turned his head. The Duc de Lenoncourt, the Duc de Navarreins, the Duc de Grandlieu, Rastignac, Blondet, the lovely Duchesse de Maufrigneuse, the Comte d'Escrignon, and des Lupeaulx, all the most influential people at court, in fact, had congratulated him on his conversion, and completed his intoxication.

"Then there is no more to be said," d'Arthez rejoined. "You, of all men, will find it hard to keep clean hands and self-respect. I know you, Lucien; you will feel it acutely when you are despised by the very men to whom you offer yourself."

"OH! NEVER MIND THOSE NINNIES," CRIED CORALIE.

The three took leave, and not one of them gave him a friendly handshake. Lucien was thoughtful and sad for a few minutes.

"Oh! never mind those ninnies," cried Coralie, springing upon his knee and putting her beautiful arms about his neck. "They take life seriously, and life is a joke. Beside, you are going to be Count Lucien de Rubempré. I will wheedle the Chancellors if there is no other way. I know how to come round that rake of a des Lupeaulx, who will sign your patent. Did I not tell you, Lucien, that at the last you should have Coralie's dead body for a stepping-stone?"

Next day Lucien allowed his name to appear in the list of contributors to the "Réveil." His name was announced in the prospectus with a flourish of trumpets, and the ministry took care that a hundred thousand copies should be scattered abroad far and wide. There was a dinner at Robert's, two doors away from Frascati's, to celebrate the inauguration, and the whole band of royalist writers for the press were present. Martainville was there, and Auger and Destains, and a host of others, still living, who "did monarchy and religion," to use the familiar expression coined for them. Nathan had also enlisted under the banner, for he was thinking of starting a theatre, and not unreasonably held that it was better to have the licensing authorities for him than against him.

"We will pay the Liberals out?" cried Hector Merlin energetically.

"Gentlemen," said Nathan, "if we are for war, let us have war in earnest; we must not carry it on with pop-guns. Let us fall upon all Classicals and Liberals without distinction of age or sex, and put them all to the sword with ridicule. There must be no quarter."

"We must act honorably; there must be no bribing with copies of books or presents; no taking money of publishers. We must inaugurate a restoration of journalism."

"Good!" said Martainville. *"Justum et tanacem pro-*

positi virum!   Let us be implacable and virulent.   I will give out La Fayette for the prince of harlequins that he is!'' he went on.

'' And I will undertake the heroes of the ' Constitutionnel,' '' added Lucien ; '' Sergeant Mercier, Monsieur Jouy's Complete Works, and ' the illustrious orators of the Left.' ''

A war of extermination was unanimously resolved upon, and by one o'clock in the morning all shades of opinion were merged and drowned, together with every glimmer of sense, in a flaming bowl of punch.

'' We have had a fine monarchical and religious jollification,'' remarked an illustrious reveler in the doorway as he went.

That comment appeared in the next day's issue of the '' Miroir'' through the good offices of a publisher among the guests, and became historic.   Lucien was supposed to be the traitor who blabbed.   His defection gave the signal for a terrific hubbub in the Liberal camp ; Lucien was the butt of the opposition newspapers, and ridiculed unmercifully.   The whole history of his sonnets was given to the public.   Dauriat was said to prefer a first loss of a thousand crowns to the risk of publishing the verses ; Lucien was called '' the Poet *sans* Sonnets ;'' and one morning, in that very paper in which he had so brilliant a beginning, he read the following lines, significant enough for him, but barely intelligible to other readers :

*** If M. Dauriat' persistently withholds the Sonnets of the future Petrarch from publication, we will act like generous foes.   We will open our own columns to his poems, which must be piquant indeed, to judge by the following specimen obligingly communicated by a friend of the author.

And close upon that ominous preface followed a sonnet entitled '' The Thistle '' (*le Chardon*):

A chance-come seedling, springing up one day
  Among the flowers in a garden fair,
  Made boast that splendid colors bright and rare
Its claims to lofty lineage should display.

So for a while they suffered it to stay;
  But with such insolence it flourished there,
  That, out of patience with its braggart's air,
They bade it prove its claims without delay.

It bloomed forthwith; but ne'er was blundering clown
Upon the boards more promptly hooted down;
  The sister flowers began to jeer and laugh,

The owner flung it out. At close of day
A solitary jackass came to bray—
  A common Thistle's fitting epitaph.

Lucien read the words through scalding tears.

Vernou touched elsewhere on Lucien's gambling propensities, and spoke of the forthcoming "Archer of Charles IX." as "anti-national" in its tendency, the writer siding with Catholic cut-throats against their Calvinist victims.

Another week found the quarrel embittered. Lucien had counted upon his friend Étienne; Étienne owed him a thousand francs, and there had been beside a private understanding between them; but Étienne Lousteau during the interval became his sworn foe, and this was the manner of it:

For the past three months Nathan had been smitten with Florine's charms, and much at a loss how to rid himself of Lousteau his rival, who was in fact dependent upon the actress. And now came Nathan's opportunity, when Florine was frantic with distress over the failure of the Panorama-Dramatique, which left her without an engagement, he went as Lucien's colleague to beg Coralie to ask for a part for Florine in a play of his which was about to be produced at the Gymnase. Then Nathan went to Florine and made capital with her out of the service done by the promise of a conditional engagement. Ambition had turned Florine's head; she did not hesitate. She had had time to gauge Lousteau pretty thoroughly. Lousteau's courses were weakening his will, and here was Nathan with his ambitions in politics and literature, and energies strong as his cravings. Florine proposed to reappear on the stage with renewed *éclat*, so she handed over Matifat's correspondence to Nathan. Nathan drove a bargain for them with Matifat, and took the sixth share of Finot's review in exchange for the compromising billets. After this, Florine was installed in sumptuously furnished apartments in the Rue Hauteville, where she took Nathan for her protector in the face of the theatrical and journalistic world.

Lousteau was terribly overcome. He wept (toward the close of a dinner given by his friends to console him in his affliction). In the course of that banquet it was decided that Nathan had not acted unfairly; several writers present— Finot and Vernou, for instance—knew of Florine's fervid admiration for dramatic literature; but they all agreed that Lucien had behaved very ill when he arranged that business at the Gymnase; he had indeed broken the most sacred laws of friendship. Party-spirit and zeal to serve his new friends had led the royalist poet on to sin beyond forgiveness.

"Nathan was carried away by passion," pronounced Bixiou, "while this 'distinguished provincial,' as Blondet calls him, is simply scheming for his own selfish ends."

And so it came to pass that deep plots were laid by all parties alike to rid themselves of this little upstart intruder of a poet who wanted to eat everybody up. Vernou bore Lucien a personal grudge and undertook to keep a tight hand on him; and Finot declared that Lucien had betrayed the secret of the combination against Matifat, and thereby swindled him (Finot) out of fifty thousand francs. Nathan, acting on Florine's advice, gained Finot's support by selling him the sixth share for fifteen thousand francs, and Lousteau consequently lost his commission. His thousand crowns had vanished away; he could not forgive Lucien for this treacherous blow (as he supposed it) dealt to his interests. The wounds of vanity refuse to heal if oxide of silver gets into them.

No words, no amount of description, can depict the wrath of an author in a paroxysm of mortified vanity, nor the energy which he discovers when stung by the poisoned darts of sarcasm; but, on the other hand, the man that is roused to fighting-fury by a personal attack usually subsides very promptly. The more phlegmatic race, who take these things quietly, lay their account with the oblivion which speedily overtakes the spiteful article. These are the truly courageous men of letters; and if the weaklings seem at first to be the strong men, they cannot hold out for any length of time.

During that first fortnight, while the fury was upon him, Lucien poured a perfect hailstorm of articles into the royalist papers, in which he shared the responsibilities of criticism with Hector Merlin. He was always in the breach, pounding away with all his might in the "Réveil," backed up by Martainville, the only one among his associates who stood by him without an after-thought. Martainville was not in the secret of certain understandings made and ratified amid after-dinner jokes, or at Dauriat's in the Wooden Galleries, or behind the scenes at the Vaudeville, when journalists of either side met on neutral ground.

When Lucien went to the green-room of the Vaudeville, he met with no welcome; the men of his own party held out a hand to shake, the others cut him; and all the while Hector Merlin and Théodore Gaillard fraternized unblushingly with Finot, Lousteau, and Vernou, and the rest of the journalists who were known for "good fellows."

The green-room of the Vaudeville in those days was a hotbed of gossip, as well as a neutral ground where men of every shade of opinion could meet; so much so that the president

21

of a court of law, after reproving a learned brother in a certain council chamber for "sweeping the green-room with his gown," met the subject of his strictures, gown to gown, in the green-room of the Vaudeville.   Lousteau, in time, shook hands again with Nathan; Finot came thither almost every evening; and Lucien, whenever he could spare the time, went to the Vaudeville to watch the enemies, who showed no sign of relenting toward the unfortunate boy. They all appeared determined to down him.

   In the time of the restoration party hatred was far more bitter than in our day.   Intensity of feeling is diminished in our high-pressure age.   The critic cuts a book to pieces and shakes hands with the author afterward, and the victim must keep on good terms with his slaughterer, or run the gantlet of innumerable jokes at his expense.   If he refuses, he is unsociable, eaten up with self-love, he is sulky and rancorous, he bears malice, he is a bad fellow.   To-day let an author receive a treacherous stab in the back, let him avoid the snares set for him with base hypocrisy, and endure the most unhandsome treatment, he must still exchange greetings with his assassin, who, for that matter, claims the esteem and friendship of his victim.   Everything can be excused and justified in an age which has transformed vice into virtue and virtue into vice.   Good-fellowship has come to be the most sacred of our liberties ; the representatives of the most opposite opinions courteously blunt the edge of their words and fence with buttoned foils.   But in those almost forgotten days the same theatre could scarcely hold certain Royalist and Liberal journalists ; the most malignant provocation was offered, glances were like pistol-shots, the least spark produced an explosion of quarrel.   Who has not heard his neighbor's half-smothered oath on the entrance of some man in the forefront of the battle on the opposing side ?   There were but the two parties—Royalists and Liberals, Classics and Romantics.   You found the same hatred masquerading in either form, and no longer wondered at the scaffolds of the convention.

Lucien had been a Liberal and a hot Voltairean; now he was a rabid Royalist and a Romantic. Martainville, the only one among his colleagues who really liked him and stood by him loyally, was more hated by the Liberals than any man on the Royalist side, and this fact drew down all the hate of the Liberals on Lucien's head. Martainville's stanch friendship injured Lucien. Political parties show scanty gratitude to outpost sentinels, and leave leaders of forlorn hopes to their fate; 'tis a rule of warfare, which holds equally good in matters political, to keep with the main body of the army if you mean to succeed. The spite of the small Liberal papers fastened at once on the opportunity of coupling the two names, and flung them into each other's arms. Their friendship, real or imaginary, brought down upon them both a series of articles written by pens dipped in gall. Félicien Vernou was furious with jealousy of Lucien's social success; and believed, like all his old associates, in the poet's approaching elevation.

The fiction of Lucien's treason was embellished with every kind of aggravating circumstance; he was called Judas the Less, Martainville being Judas the Great, for Martainville was supposed (rightly or wrongly) to have given up the Bridge of Pecq to the foreign invaders. Lucien said jestingly to des Lupeaulx that he himself, surely, had given up the Asses' Bridge.

Lucien's luxurious life, hollow though it was, and founded on expectations, had estranged his friends. They could not forgive him for the carriage which he had put down—for them he was still rolling about in it—nor yet for the splendors of the Rue de Vendôme which he had left. All of them felt instinctively that nothing was beyond the reach of this young and handsome poet, with intellect enough and to spare; they themselves had trained him in corruption; and, therefore, they left no stone unturned to ruin him.

Some few days before Coralie's first appearance at the Gymnase, Lucien and Hector Merlin went arm-in-arm to the Vaudeville. Merlin was scolding his friend for giving a helping hand to Nathan in Florine's affair.

"You then and there made two mortal enemies of Lousteau and Nathan," he said. "I gave you good advice, and you took no notice of it. You gave praise, you did them a good turn—you will be well punished for your kindness. Florine and Coralie will never live in peace on the same stage ; both will wish to be first. You can only defend Coralie in our papers ; and Nathan not only has a pull as a dramatic author, he can control the dramatic criticism in the Liberal newspapers. He has been a journalist a little longer than you!"

The words responded to Lucien's inward misgivings. Neither Nathan nor Gaillard was treating him with the frankness which he had a right to expect, but so new a convert could hardly complain. Gaillard utterly confounded Lucien by saying roundly that new-comers must give proofs of their sincerity for some time before their party could trust them. There was more jealousy than he had imagined in the inner circles of royalist and ministerial journalism. The jealousy of curs fighting for a bone is apt to appear in the human species when there is a loaf to divide ; there is the same growling and showing of teeth, the same characteristics come out.

In every possible way these writers of articles tried to injure each other with those in power ; they brought reciprocal accusations of lukewarm zeal ; they invented the most treacherous ways of getting rid of a rival. There had been none of this internecine warfare among the Liberals ; they were too far from power, too hopelessly out of favor ; and Lucien, amid the inextricable tangle of ambitions, had neither the courage to draw sword and cut the knot nor the patience to unravel it. He could not be the Beaumarchais, the Aretino, the Fréron of his epoch ; he was not made of such stuff ; he thought of nothing but his own desire, the patent of nobility; for he saw clearly that for him such a restoration meant a wealthy marriage, and, the title once secured, chance and his good looks would do the rest. This was all his plan; and Étienne Lousteau, who had confided so much to him, knew his secret, knew how to deal a death-blow to the poet of Angoulême. That very night, as Lucien and Merlin went to the Vaudeville, Étienne had laid a terrible trap into which an inexperienced boy could not but fall.

"Here is our handsome Lucien," said Finot, drawing des Lupeaulx in the direction of the poet, and shaking hands with feline amiability. "I cannot think of another example of such rapid success," continued Finot, looking from des Lupeaulx to Lucien. "There are two sorts of success in Paris: there is a fortune in solid cash, which any one can amass, and there is the intangible fortune of connections, position, or a footing in certain circles inaccessible for certain persons, however rich they may be. Now my friend here——"

"Our friend," interposed des Lupeaulx, smiling blandly.

"Our friend," repeated Finot, patting Lucien's hand, "has made a brilliant success from this point of view. Truth to tell, Lucien has more in him, more gift, more wit than the rest of us that envy him, and he is enchantingly handsome beside; his old friends cannot forgive him for his success—they call it luck."

"Luck of that sort never comes to fools or incapables," said des Lupeaulx. "Can you call Bonaparte's fortune luck, eh? There were a score of applicants for the command of the army of Italy, just as there are a hundred young men at this moment who would like to have an entrance to Mademoiselle des Touches' house; people are coupling her name with yours already in society, my dear boy," said des Lupeaulx, clapping Lucien on the shoulder. "Ah! you are in high favor. Madame d'Espard, Madame de Bargeton, and Madame de Montcornet are wild about you. You are going

to Madame Firmiani's party to-night, are you not, and to the
Duchesse de Grandlieu's rout to-morrow?"

"Yes," said Lucien.

"Allow me to introduce a young banker to you, a Monsieur
du Tillet ; you ought to be acquainted, he has contrived to
make a great fortune in a short time."

Lucien and du Tillet bowed, and entered into conversation,
and the banker asked Lucien to dinner. Finot and des Lu-
pleaux, a well-matched pair, knew each other well enough to
keep upon good terms ; they turned away to continue their
chat on one of the sofas in the green-room, and left Lucien
with du Tillet, Merlin, and Nathan.

"By the way, my friend," said Finot, "tell me how things
stand. Is there really somebody behind Lucien ? For he is
the *bête noir* (wild boar) of my staff; and before allowing
them to plot against him, I thought I should like to know
whether, in your opinion, it would be better to baffle them
and keep well with him."

The master of requests and Finot looked at each other very
closely for a moment or two.

"My dear fellow," said des Lupeaulx, "how can you imagine that the Marquise d'Espard, or Châtelet, or Madame de
Bargeton—who has procured the Baron's nomination to the
prefecture and the title of Count, so as to return in triumph
to Angoulême—how can you suppose that any of them will
forgive Lucien for his attacks on them ? They dropped him
down in the royalist ranks to crush him out of existence.
At this moment they are looking around for any excuse for
not fulfilling the promises they made to that boy. Help them
to some ; you will do the greatest possible service to the two
women, and some day or other they will remember it. I am
in their secrets ; I was surprised to find how much they hated
the little fellow. This Lucien might have rid himself of his
bitterest enemy (Madame de Bargeton) by desisting from his
attacks on terms which a woman loves to grant—do you take

me? He is young and handsome, he should have drowned her hate in torrents of love, he would be Comte de Rubempré by this time ; the cuttlefish-bone would have obtained some sinecure for him, some post in the royal household. Lucien would have made a very pretty reader to Louis XVIII.; he might have been librarian somewhere or other, master of requests for a joke, master of the revels, what you please. The young fool has missed his chance. Perhaps that is his unpardonable sin. Instead of imposing his conditions, he has accepted them. When Lucien was caught with the bait of the patent of nobility, the Baron Châtelet made a great step. Coralie has been the ruin of that boy. If he had not had the actress for his mistress, he would have turned again to the cuttlefish-bone ; and he would have had her, too."

" Then we can knock him over ? "

" How ? " des Lupeaulx asked carelessly. He saw a way of gaining credit with the Marquise d'Espard for this service.

" He is under contract to write for Lousteau's paper and we can the better hold him to his agreement because he has not a sou. If we tickle up the keeper of the seals with a facetious article, and prove that Lucien wrote it, he will consider that Lucien is unworthy of the King's favor. We have a plot on hand beside. Coralie will be ruined, and our distinguished provincial will lose his head when his mistress is hissed off the stage and left without an engagement. When once the patent is suspended, we will laugh at the victim's aristocratic pretensions, and allude to his mother the nurse and his father the apothecary. Lucien's courage is only skin-deep, he will collapse ; we will send him back to his provinces. Nathan made Florine sell me Matifat's sixth share of the review, I was able to buy ; Dauriat and I are the only proprietors now ; we might come to an understanding, you and I, and the review might be taken over for the benefit of the court. I stipulated for the restitution of my sixth before I undertook to protect Nathan and Florine ;

they let me have it, and I must help them; but I wished to know first how Lucien stood——"

"You deserve your name," said des Lupeaulx. "I like a man of your sort——"

"Very well. Then can you arrange a definite engagement for Florine?" asked Finot.

"Yes, but rid us of Lucien, for Rastignac and de Marsay never wish to hear of him again."

"Sleep in peace," returned Finot. "Nathan and Merlin will always have articles ready for Gaillard, who will promise to take them; Lucien will never get a line into the paper. We will cut off his supplies. There is only Martainville's paper left him in which to defend himself and Coralie; what can a single paper do against so many?"

"I will let you know the weak points of the Ministry; but get Lucien to write that article and hand over the manuscript," said des Lupeaulx, who refrained carefully from informing Finot that Lucien's promised patent was nothing but a joke.

When des Lupeaulx had gone, Finot went to Lucien, and taking the good-natured tone which deceives so many victims, he explained that he could not possibly afford to lose his contributor and at the same time he shrank from taking proceedings which might ruin him with his friends of the other side. Finot himself liked a man who was strong enough to change his opinions. They were pretty sure to come across one another, he and Lucien, and might be mutually helpful in a thousand little ways. Lucien, beside, needed a sure man in the Liberal party to attack the Ultras and men in office who might refuse to help him.

"Suppose they play you false, what will you do?" Finot ended. "Suppose that some minister fancies that he has you fast by the halter of your apostasy, and turns the cold shoulder on you? You will be glad to set on a few dogs to snap at his legs, will you not? Very well. But you have made a deadly enemy of Lousteau; he is thirsting for your blood. You and Félicien are not on speaking terms. I only remain to you. It is a rule of the craft to keep a good understanding with every man of real ability. In the world which you are about to enter you can do me services in return for mine with the press. But business first. Let me have purely literary articles; they will not compromise you, and we shall have executed our agreement."

Lucien saw nothing but good-fellowship and a shrewd eye to business in Finot's offer; Finot and des Lupeaulx had flattered him, and he was in a good humor. He actually thanked Finot!

Ambitious men, like all those who can only make their way by the help of others and of circumstances, are bound to lay their plans very carefully and to adhere very closely to the course of conduct on which they determine; it is a cruel moment in the lives of such aspirants when some unknown power brings the fabric of their fortunes to some severe test and everything gives way at once; threads are snapped or entangled, and misfortune appears on every side. Let a man lose his head in the confusion, it is all over with him; but if he can resist this first revolt of circumstance, if he can stand erect until the tempest passes over, or make a supreme effort and reach the serene sphere about the storm—then he is really strong. To every man, unless he is born rich, there comes, sooner or later, "his fatal week," as it must be called. For Napoleon, for instance, that week was the retreat from Moscow. It had begun now for Lucien.

Social and literary success had come to him too easily; he had had such luck that he was bound to know reverses and to see men and circumstances turn against him.

The first blow was the heaviest and the most keenly felt, for it touched Lucien where he thought himself invulnerable —in his heart and his love. Coralie might not be clever, but hers was a noble nature, and she possessed the great actress' faculty of suddenly standing aloof from self. This strange phenomenon is subject, until it degenerates into a habit with long practice, to the caprices of character, and not seldom to an admirable delicacy of feeling in actresses who are still young. Coralie, to all appearance bold and wanton, as her part required, was in reality girlish and timid, and love had wrought in her a revulsion of her woman's heart against the comedian's mask. Art, the supreme art of feigning passion and feeling, had not yet triumphed over nature in her; she shrank before a great audience from the utterance that belongs to love alone; and Coralie suffered beside from another true woman's weakness—she needed success, born stage queen though she was. She could not confront an audience with which she was out of sympathy; she was nervous when she appeared on the stage, a cold reception paralyzed her. Each new part gave her the terrible sensations of a first appearance. Applause produced a sort of intoxication which gave her encouragement without flattering her vanity; at a murmur of dissatisfaction or before a silent house, she flagged; but a great audience following attentively, admiringly, willing to be pleased, electrified Coralie. She felt at once in communication with the nobler qualities of all those listeners; she felt that she possessed the power of stirring their souls and carrying them with her. But if this action and reaction of the audience upon the actress reveals the nervous organization of genius, it shows no less clearly the poor child's sensitiveness and delicacy. Lucien had discovered the treasures of her nature; had learned in the past months that this woman who loved him was still so much of a girl. And Coralie was unskilled in the wiles of an actress—she could not fight her own battles nor protect herself against the machinations of jealousy behind the scenes. Florine was jealous of her, and Florine was as dangerous and depraved as Coralie was simple and generous. Rôles must come to find Coralie; she was too proud to implore authors or to submit to dishonoring conditions; she would not give herself to the first journalist who persecuted her with his advances and threatened her with his pen. Genius is rare enough in the extraordinary art of the stage; but genius is only one condition of success among many, and is positively hurtful unless it is accompanied by a genius for intrigue, in which Coralie was utterly lacking.

Lucien knew how much his friend would suffer on her first appearance at the Gymnase, and was anxious at all costs to obtain a success for her; but all the money remaining from the sale of the furniture and all Lucien's earnings had been sunk in costumes, in the furniture of a dressing-room, and the expenses of a first appearance.

A few days later, Lucien made up his mind to a humiliating step for love's sake. He took Fendant and Cavalier's bills and went to the "Golden Cocoon" in the Rue des Bourdonnais. He would ask Camusot to discount them. The poet had not fallen so low that he could make this attempt coolly. There had been many a sharp struggle first, and the way to that decision had been paved with many dreadful thoughts. Nevertheless, he arrived at last in the dark, cheerless little private office that looked out upon a yard, and found Camusot seated gravely there; this was not Coralie's infatuated adorer, not the easy-natured, indolent, incredulous libertine whom he had known hitherto as Camusot, but a heavy father of a family, a merchant grown old in shrewd expedients of business and respectable virtues, wearing a magistrate's mask of judicial prudery; this Camusot was the cool, business-like head of the firm surrounded by clerks, green cardboard boxes, pigeonholes, invoices, and samples, and fortified by the presence of a wife and a plainly-dressed daughter. Lucien trembled from head to foot as he timidly approached; for the worthy merchant, like the moneylenders, turned cool, indifferent eyes upon him, as though he was an entire stranger.

"Here are two or three bills, monsieur," he said, standing

beside the merchant, who did not rise from his desk. "If you will take them of me, you will oblige me extremely."

"You have taken something of *me*, monsieur," said Camusot; "I do not forget it."

On this, Lucien explained Coralie's predicament. He spoke in a low voice, bending to murmur his explanation, so that Camusot could hear the heavy throbbing of the humiliated poet's heart. It was no part of Camusot's plans that Coralie should suffer a check. He listened, smiling to himself over the signatures on the bills (for, as a judge at the Tribunal of Commerce, he knew how the booksellers stood), but in the end he gave Lucien four thousand five hundred francs for them, stipulating that he should add the formula, "For value received in silks."

Lucien went straight to Braulard, and made arrangements for a good reception. Braulard promised to come to the dress-rehearsal, to determine on the points where his "Romans" should work their fleshy clappers to bring down the house in applause. Lucien gave the rest of the money to Coralie (he did not tell her how he had come by it), and allayed her anxieties and the fears of Bérénice, who was sorely troubled over their daily expenses.

Martainville came several times to hear Coralie rehearse, and he knew more of the stage than most men of his time; several royalist writers had promised favorable articles; Lucien had not a suspicion of the impending disaster.

A fatal event occurred on the evening before Coralie's *début*. D'Arthez's book had appeared; and the editor of Merlin's paper, considering Lucien to be the best qualified man on the staff, gave him the book to review. He owned his unlucky reputation to those articles on Nathan's work. There were several men in the office at the time, for all the staff had been summoned; Martainville was explaining that the party warfare with the Liberals must be waged on certain lines. Nathan, Merlin, all the contributors in fact, were talking of Léon Giraud's paper, and remarking that its influence was the more pernicious because the language was guarded, cool, moderate. People were beginning to speak of the circle in the Rue des Quatre-Vents as a second convention. It had been decided that the royalist papers were to wage a systematic war of extermination against these dangerous opponents, who, indeed, at a later day, were destined to sow the doctrines that drove the Bourbons into exile; but that was only after the most brilliant of royalist writers had joined them for the sake of a mean revenge.

D'Arthez's absolutist opinions were not known; it was taken for granted that he shared the views of his clique, he fell under the same anathema, and he was to be the first victim. His book was to be honored with "a slashing article," to use the consecrated formula. Lucien refused to write the article. Great was the commotion among the leading royalist writers thus met in conclave. Lucien was told plainly that a renegade could not do as he pleased; if it did not suit his views to take the side of the monarchy and religion, he could go back to the other camp. Merlin and Martainville took him aside and begged him, as his friends, to remember that he would simply hand Coralie over to the tender mercies of the Liberal papers, for she would find no champions on the royalist and ministerial side. Her acting was certain to provoke a hot battle, and the kind of discussion which every actress longs to arouse.

"You don't understand it in the least," said Martainville; "if she plays for three months amid a cross-fire of criticism, she will make thirty thousand francs when she goes on tour in the provinces at the end of the season; and here you are about to sacrifice Coralie and your own future, and to quarrel with your own bread and butter, all for a scruple that will always stand in your way, and ought to be gotten rid of at once."

Lucien was forced to choose between d'Arthez and Coralie.

His mistress would be ruined unless he dealt his friend a death-blow in the " Réveil " and the great newspaper. Poor poet ! He went home with death in his soul; and by the fireside he sat and read that finest production of modern literature. Tears fell fast over it as the pages turned. For a long while he hesitated, but at last he took up the pen and wrote a sarcastic article of the kind that he understood so well, taking the book as children might take some bright bird to strip it of its plumage and torture it. His sardonic jests were sure to tell. Again he turned to the book, and as he read it over a second time, his better self awoke. In the dead of night he hurried across Paris and stood outside d'Arthez's house. He looked up at the windows and saw the faint pure gleam of light in the panes, as he had so often seen it, with a feeling of admiration for the noble steadfastness of that truly great nature. For some moments he stood irresolute on the curbstone; he had not courage to go further; but his good angel urged him on. He tapped at the door and opened, and found d'Arthez sitting reading in a fireless room.

" What has happened ? " asked d'Arthez, for news of some dreadful kind was visible in Lucien's ghastly face.

" Your book is sublime, d'Arthez," said Lucien, with tears in his eyes, " and they have ordered me to write an attack upon it."

" Poor boy ! the bread that they give you is hard indeed ! " said d'Arthez.

" I only ask for one favor, keep my visit a secret and leave me to my hell, to the occupations of the damned. Perhaps it is impossible to attain to success until the heart is seared and callous in every most sensitive spot."

" The same as ever ! " cried d'Arthez.

" Do you think me a base poltroon ? No, d'Arthez ; no, I am a boy half-crazed with love," and he told his story.

" Let us look at the article," said d'Arthez, touched by all that Lucien said of Coralie.

Lucien held out the manuscript; d'Arthez read, and could not help smiling.

"Oh, what a fatal waste of intellect!" he began. But at the sight of Lucien overcome with grief in the opposite armchair he checked himself.

"Will you leave it with me to correct? I will let you have it again to-morrow," he went on. "Flippancy depreciates a work; serious and conscientious criticism is sometimes praise in itself. I know the way to make your article more honorable both for yourself and for me. Beside, I know my faults well enough."

"When you climb a hot, shadowless hillside, you sometimes find fruit to quench your torturing thirst; and I have found it here and now," said Lucien, as he sprang sobbing to d'Arthez's arms and kissed his friend on the forehead. "It seems to me that I am leaving my conscience in your keeping; some day I will come to you and ask for it again."

"I look upon a periodical repentance as great hypocrisy," d'Arthez said solemnly; "repentance becomes a sort of indemnity for wrongdoing. Repentance is virginity of soul, which we must keep for God; a man who repents twice is a horrible sycophant. I am afraid that you regard repentance as absolution."

Lucien went slowly back to the Rue de la Lune, stricken dumb by those words.

Next morning d'Arthez sent back his article, recast throughout, and Lucien sent it in to the review; but from that day melancholy preyed upon him and he could not always disguise his mood. That evening, when the theatre was full, he experienced for the first time the paroxysm of nervous terror caused by a *début;* terror aggravated in his case by all the strength of his love. Vanity of every kind was involved. He looked over the rows of faces as a criminal eyes the judges and the jury on whom his life depends. A murmur would have set him quivering; any slight incident upon the stage,

Coralie's exits and entrances, the slightest modulation of the tones of her voice, would perturb him beyond all reason.

The play in which Coralie made her first appearance at the Gymnase was a piece of the kind which sometimes falls flat at first, and afterward has immense success. It fell flat that night. Coralie was not applauded when she came on, and the chilly reception reacted upon her. The only applause came from Camusot's box, and various persons posted in the balcony and galleries silenced Camusot with repeated cries of "Hush!" The galleries even silenced the *claqueurs* when they led off with exaggerated salvoes. Martainville applauded bravely; Nathan, Merlin, and the treacherous Florine followed his example; but it was clear that the piece was a failure. A crowd gathered in Coralie's dressing-room and consoled her, till she had no courage left. She went home in despair, less for her own sake than for Lucien's.

"Braulard has betrayed us," Lucien said.

Coralie was heart-stricken. The next day found her in a high fever, utterly unfit to play, face to face with the thought that she had been cut short in her career. Lucien hid the papers from her and looked them over in the dining-room. The reviewers one and all attributed the failure of the piece to Coralie; she had overestimated her strength; she might be the delight of a boulevard audience, but she was out of her element at the Gymnase; she had been inspired by a laudable ambition, but she has not taken her powers into account; she had chosen a part to which she was quite unequal. Lucien read on through a pile of penny-a-lining, put together on the same system as his attack upon Nathan. Milo of Crotona, when he found his hands fast in the oak which he himself had cleft, was not more furious than Lucien. He grew haggard with rage. His friends gave Coralie the most treacherous advice, in the language of kindly counsel and friendly interest. She should play (according to these authorities) all kinds of rôles, which the treacherous writers of these unblushing *feuilletons* knew to be utterly unsuited to her genius. And these were the royalist papers, led off by Nathan. As for the Liberal press, all the weapons which Lucien had used were now turned against him.

Coralie heard a sob, followed by another and another. She sprang out of bed to find Lucien and saw the papers. Nothing would satisfy her but she must read them all; and when she had read them she went back to bed and lay there in silence.

Florine was in the plot ; she had foreseen the outcome; she had studied Coralie's part, and was ready to take her place. The management, unwilling to give up the piece, was ready to take Florine in Coralie's stead. When the manager came, he found poor Coralie sobbing and exhausted on her bed ; but when he began to say, in Lucien's presence, that Florine knew the part, and that the play must be given that evening, Coralie sprang up at once.

" I will play ! " she cried, and sank fainting on the floor.

So Florine took the part and made her reputation in it ; for the piece succeeded, the newspapers all sang her praises, and from that time forth Florine was the great actress whom we all know. Florine's success exasperated Lucien to the highest degree.

"A wretched girl, whom you helped to earn her bread ! If the Gymnase prefers to do so, let the management pay you to cancel your engagement. I shall be the Comte de Rubempré ; I will make my fortune and you shall be my wife."

" What nonsense ! " said Coralie, looking at him with wan eyes.

" Nonsense ! " repeated he. " Very well, wait a few days, and you shall live in a fine house, you shall have a carriage and I will write a part for you."

He took two thousand francs and hurried to Frascati's. For seven hours the unhappy victim of the Furies watched his varying luck, and outwardly seemed cool and self-contained.

22

He experienced both extremes of fortune during that day and part of the night that followed; at one time he possessed as much as thirty thousand francs, and he came out at last without a sou. In the Rue de la Lune he found Finot waiting for him with a request for one of his short articles. Lucien so far forgot himself that he complained.

"Oh, it is not all rosy," returned Finot. "You made your right-about-face in such a way that you were bound to lose the support of the Liberal press, and the Liberals are far stronger in print than all the Ministerialist and Royalist papers put together. A man should never leave one camp for another until he has made a comfortable berth for himself, by way of consolation for the losses that he must expect; and in any case a prudent politician will see his friends first, and give them his reasons for going over, and take their opinions. You can still act together, they sympathize with you, and you agree to give mutual help. Nathan and Merlin did that before they went over. Hawks don't pike out hawks' eyes. You were as innocent as a lamb; you will be forced to show your teeth to your new party to make anything out of them. You have been necessarily sacrificed to Nathan. I cannot conceal from you that your article on d'Arthez has roused a terrific hubbub. Marat is a saint compared with you. You will be attacked and your book will be a failure. How far have things gone with your romance?"

"These are the last proof-sheets."

"All the anonymous articles against that young d'Arthez in the Ministerialist and Ultra papers are set down to you. The 'Réveil' is poking fun at the set in the Rue des Quatre-Vents, and the hits are the more telling because they are funny. There is a whole serious political coterie at the back of Léon Giraud's paper; they will come into power, too, sooner or later."

"I have not written a line in the 'Réveil' this week past."

"Very well. Keep my short articles in mind. Write fifty of them straight off, and I will pay you for them in a lump; but they must be of the same color as the paper." And Finot, with seeming carelessness, gave Lucien an edifying anecdote of the keeper of the seals, a piece of current gossip, he said, for the subject of one of the papers.

Eager to retrieve his losses at play, Lucien shook off his dejection, summoned up his energy and youthful force, and wrote thirty articles of two columns each. These finished, he went to Dauriat's, partly because he felt sure of meeting Finot there, and he wished to give the articles to Finot in person; partly because he wished for an explanation of the non-appearance of the "Marguerites." He found the bookseller's shop full of his enemies. All the talk immediately ceased as he entered. Put under the ban of journalism, his courage rose, and once more he said to himself, as he had said in the alley at the Luxembourg, "I will triumph."

Dauriat was neither amiable nor inclined to patronize; he was sarcastic in tone and determined not to abate an inch of his rights. The "Marguerites" should appear when it suited his purpose; he should wait until Lucien was in a position to secure the success of the book; it was his, he had bought it outright. When Lucien asserted that Dauriat was bound to publish the "Marguerites" by the very nature of the contract, and the relative positions of the parties to the agreement, Dauriat flatly contradicted him, said that no publisher could be compelled by law to publish at a loss, and that he himself was the best judge of the expediency of producing the book. There was, beside, a remedy open to Lucien, as any court of law would admit—the poet was quite welcome to take his verses to a royalist publisher upon the repayment of the thousand crowns.

Lucien went away. Dauriat's moderate tone had exasperated him even more than his previous arrogance at their first interview. So the "Marguerites" would not appear until

Lucien had found a host of formidable supporters, or grown formidable himself. He walked home slowly, so oppressed and out of heart that he felt ready for suicide. Coralie lay in bed, looking white and ill.

" She must have a part or she will die," said Bérénice, as Lucien dressed for a great evening party at Mlle. des Touches' house in the Rue du Mont Blanc. Des Lupeaulx and Vignon and Blondet were to be there, as well as Mme. d'Espard and Mme. de Bargeton.

The party was given in honor of Conti, the great composer, owner likewise of one of the most famous voices off the stage, Cinti, Pasta, Garcia, Levasseur, and two or three celebrated amateurs in society not excepted. Lucien saw the Marquise, . her cousin, and Mme. de Montcornet sitting together, and made one of the party. The unhappy young fellow to all appearance was light-hearted, happy, and content ; he jested, he was the Lucien de Rubempré of his days of splendor, he would not seem to need help from any one. He dwelt on his services to the Royalist party, and cited the hue and cry raised after him by the Liberal press as a proof of his zeal.

" And you will be well rewarded, my friend," said Mme. de Bargeton, with a gracious smile. " Go to the Chancellor the day after to-morrow with ' the heron ' and des Lupeaulx, and you will find your patent signed by his majesty. The keeper of the seals will take it to-morrow to the Tuileries, but there is to be a meeting of the council, and he will not come back till late. Still, if I hear the result to-morrow evening, I will let you know. Where are you living ? "

" I will come to you," said Lucien, ashamed to confess that he was living in the Rue de la Lune.

" The Duc de Lenoncourt and the Duc de Navarreins have made mention of you to the King," added the Marquise ; " they praised your absolute and entire devotion, and said that some distinction ought to avenge your treatment on the Liberal press. The name and title of Rubempré, to which you have a claim through your mother, would become illustrious through you, they said. The King gave his lordship instructions that evening to prepare a patent authorizing the Sieur Lucien Chardon to bear the arms and title of the Comtes de Rubempré, as grandson of the last Count by the mother's side. ' Let us favor the songsters ' (*chardonnerets*) ' of Pindus,' said his majesty, after reading your sonnet on the Lily, which my cousin luckily remembered to give the Duke. ' Especially when the King can work miracles, and change the song-bird into an eagle,' de Navarreins replied.''

Lucien's expansion of feeling would have softened the heart of any woman less deeply wounded than Louise d'Espard de Nègrepelisse ; but her thirst for vengeance was only increased by Lucien's graciousness. Des Lupeaulx was right ; Lucien was wanting in tact. It never crossed his mind that this history of the patent was one of the mystifications at which Madame d'Espard was an adept. Emboldened with success and the flattering distinction shown to him by Mademoiselle des Touches, he stayed till two o'clock in the morning for a word in private with his hostess. Lucien had learned in royalist newspaper offices that Mademoiselle des Touches was the author of a play in which "La Petite Fay,'' the marvel of the moment, was about to appear. As the rooms emptied, he drew Mademoiselle des Touches to a sofa in the boudoir, and told the story of Coralie's misfortune and his own so touchingly that Mademoiselle des Touches promised to give the heroine's part to his friend.

That promise put new life into Coralie. But the next day, as they breakfasted together, Lucien opened Lousteau's newspaper and found that unlucky anecdote of the keeper of the seals and his wife. The story was full of the blackest malice lurking in the most caustic wit. Louis XVIII. was brought into the story in a masterly fashion and held up to ridicule in such a way that prosecution was impossible. Here is the substance of a fiction for which the Liberal party attempted to win credence, though they only succeeded in adding one more to the tale of their ingenious calumnies.

The King's passion for pink-scented notes and a correspondence full of madrigals and sparkling wit was declared to be the last phase of the tender passion; love had reached the doctrinaire stage; or had passed, in other words, from the concrete to the abstract. The illustrious lady, so cruelly ridiculed under the name of Octavie by Béranger, had conceived (so it was said) the gravest fears. The correspondence was languishing. The more Octavie displayed her wit, the cooler grew the royal lover. At last Octavie discovered the cause of her decline; her power was threatened by the novelty and piquancy of a correspondence between the august scribe and the wife of his keeper of the seals. That excellent woman was believed to be incapable of writing a note; she was simply and solely godmother to the efforts of audacious ambition. Who could be hidden behind her petticoats? Octavie decided, after making observations of her own, that the King was corresponding with his minister.

She laid her plans. With the help of a faithful friend, she arranged that a stormy debate should detain the minister at the Chamber; then she contrived to secure a *tête-à-tête*, and to convince outraged majesty of the fraud. Louis XVIII. flew into a royal and truly Bourbon passion, but the tempest broke on Octavie's head. He would not believe her. Octavie offered immediate proof, begging the King to write a note which must be answered at once. The unlucky wife of the keeper of the seals sent to the Chamber for her husband; but precautions had been taken, and at that moment the minister was on his legs addressing the Chamber. The lady racked her brains and replied to the note with such intellect as she could improvise.

"Your Chancellor will supply the rest," cried Octavie, laughing at the King's chagrin.

There was not a word of truth in the story; but it struck

home to three persons—the keeper of the seals, his wife, and the King. It was said that des Lupeaulx had invented the tale, but Finot always kept his counsel. The article was caustic and clever, the Liberal papers and the Orleanists were delighted with it, and Lucien himself laughed, and thought of it merely as a very amusing *canard*.

He called next day for des Lupeaulx aud the Baron du Châtelet. The Baron had just been to thank his lordship. The Sieur Châtelet, newly appointed councilor extraordinary, was now Comte du Châtelet, with a promise of the prefecture of the Charente so soon as the present prefect should have completed the term of office necessary to receive the maximum retiring pension. The Comte *du* Châtelet (for the *du* had been inserted in the patent) drove with Lucien to the Chancellor's, and treated his companion as an equal. But for Lucien's articles, he said, his patent would not have been granted so soon; Liberal persecution had been a stepping-stone to advancement. Des Lupeaulx was waiting for them in the secretary-general's office. That functionary started with surprise when Lucien appeared and looked at des Lupeaulx.

"What!" he exclaimed, to Lucien's utter bewilderment. "Do you dare to come here, sir? Your patent was made out, but his lordship has torn it up. Here it is!" (the secretary-general caught up the first torn sheet that came to hand). "The minister wished to discover the author of yesterday's atrocious article, and here is the manuscript," added the speaker, holding out the sheets of Lucien's article. "You call yourself a royalist, sir, and you are on the staff of that detestable paper which turns the minister's hair gray, harasses the Centre, and is dragging the country headlong to ruin? You breakfast on the 'Corsaire,' the 'Miroir,' the 'Constitutionnel,' and the 'Courier;' you dine on the 'Quotidienne' and the 'Réveil,' and then sup with Martainville, the worst enemy of the government? Martainville urges the government on to absolutist measures; he is more likely to bring on another revolution than if he had gone over to the extreme Left. You are a very clever journalist, but you will never make a politician. The minister denounced you to the King, and the King was so angry that he scolded Monsieur le Duc de Navarreins, his first gentleman of the bedchamber. Your enemies will be all the more formidable because they have hitherto been your friends. Conduct that one expects from an enemy is atrocious in a friend."

" Why really, my dear fellow, are you a child ? " said des Lupeaulx. " You have compromised me. Madame d'Espard, Madame de Bargeton, and Madame de Montcornet, who were responsible for you, must be furious. The Duke is sure to have handed on his annoyance to the Marquise, and the Marquise will have scolded her cousin. Keep away from them and wait."

" Here comes his lordship—go !" said the secretary-general.

Lucien went out into the Place Vendôme ; he was stunned by this bludgeon blow. He walked home along the boulevards trying to think over his position. He saw himself a plaything in the hands of envy, treachery, and greed. What was he in this world of contending ambitions? A child sacrificing everything to the pursuit of pleasure and the gratification of vanity; a poet whose thoughts never went beyond the moment, a moth flitting from one bright gleaming object to another. He had no definite aim ; he was the slave of circumstance— meaning well, doing ill. Conscience tortured him remorselessly. And, to crown it all, he was penniless and exhausted with work and emotion. His articles could not compare with Merlin's or Nathan's work.

He walked on at random, absorbed in these thoughts. As he passed some of the reading-rooms which were already lending books as well as newspapers, a placard caught his eyes. It was an advertisement of a book with a grotesque title, but beneath the announcement he saw his name in brilliant letters

—"By Lucien Chardon de Rubempré." So his book had come out, and he had heard nothing of it! All the newspapers were silent. He stood motionless before the placard, his arms hanging at his sides. He did not notice a little knot of acquaintances—Rastignac and de Marsay and some other fashionable young men; nor did he see that Michel Chrestien and Léon Giraud were coming toward him.

"Are you Monsieur Chardon?" It was Michel who spoke, and there was that in the sound of his voice that set Lucien's heartstrings vibrating.

"Do you not know me?" he asked, turning very pale.

Michel spat in his face.

"Take that as your wages for your article against d'Arthez. If everybody would do as I do on his own or his friend's behalf, the press would be as it ought to be—a self-respecting and respected priesthood."

Lucien staggered back and caught hold of Rastignac.

"Gentlemen," he said, addressing Rastignac and de Marsay, in an excited manner, "you will not refuse to act as my seconds. But, first, I wish to make matters even and apology impossible."

He struck Michel a sudden, unexpected blow in the face. The rest rushed in between the republican and royalist, to prevent a street brawl. Rastignac dragged Lucien off to the Rue Taitbout, only a few steps away from the Boulevard de Gand, where this scene took place. It was the hour of dinner, or a crowd would have assembled at once. De Marsay came to find Lucien, and the pair insisted that he should dine with them at the Café Anglais, where they drank and made merry.

"Are you a good swordsman?" inquired de Marsay.

"I have never had a foil in my hands."

"A good shot?"

"Never fired a pistol in my life."

"Then you have luck on your side. You are a formidable

antagonist to stand up to; you may kill your man," said de Marsay.

Fortunately, Lucien found Coralie in bed and asleep.

She had played without rehearsal in a one-act play, and taken her revenge.   She had met with genuine applause. Her enemies had not been prepared for this step on her part, and her success had determined the manager to give her the heroine's part in Camille Maupin's play.   He had discovered the cause of her apparent failure, and was indignant with Florine and Nathan.   Coralie should have the protection of the management.

At five o'clock that morning, Rastignac came for Lucien.

"The name of your street, my dear fellow, is particularly appropriate for your lodgings; you are up in the sky," he said, by way of greeting.   "Let us be first upon the ground on the road to Clignancourt; it is good form, and we ought to set them an example."

"Here is the programme," said de Marsay, as the cab rattled through the Faubourg Saint-Denis: "You stand up at twenty-five paces, coming nearer, till you are only fifteen apart.   You have, each of you, five paces to take and three shots to fire—no more.   Whatever happens, that must be the end of it.   We load for your antagonist, and his seconds load for you.   The weapons were chosen by the four seconds at a gunmaker's.   We helped you to a chance, I will promise you; horse-pistols are to be the weapons."

For Lucien, life had become a bad dream.   He did not care whether he lived or died.   The courage of suicide helped him in some sort to carry things off with a dash of bravado before the spectators.   He stood in his place; he would not take a step, a piece of recklessness which the others took for deliberate calculation.   They thought the poet an uncommonly cool hand.   Michel Chrestien came as far as his limit; both fired twice and at the same time, for either party was considered to be equally insulted.   Michel's first bullet grazed

Lucien's chin; Lucien's passed ten feet above Chrestien's head. The second shot hit Lucien's coat collar, but the buckram lining fortunately saved its wearer. The third bullet struck him in the chest, and he dropped.

" Is he dead ? " asked Michel Chrestien.

" No," said the surgeon, " he will pull through."

" So much the worse," answered Michel.

" Yes, so much the worse," said Lucien, as his tears fell fast.

By noon the unhappy boy lay in bed in his own room. With untold pains they had managed to remove him, but it had taken five hours to bring him to the Rue de la Lune. His condition was not dangerous, but precautions were necessary lest fever should set in and bring about troublesome complications. Coralie choked down her grief and anguish. She sat up with him at night through the anxious weeks of his illness, studying her parts by his bedside. Lucien was in danger for two long months; and often at the theatre Coralie acted her frivolous rôle with one thought in her heart, " Perhaps he is dying at this moment."

Lucien owed his life to the skill and devotion of a friend whom he had grievously hurt. Bianchon had come to tend him after hearing the story of the attack from d'Arthez, who told it in confidence and excused the unhappy poet. Bianchon suspected that d'Arthez was generously trying to screen the renegade; but on questioning Lucien during a lucid interval in the dangerous nervous fever, he learned that his patient was only responsible for the one serious article in Hector Merlin's paper.

Before the first month was out, the firm of Fendant and Cavalier filed their schedule. Bianchon told Coralie that Lucien must on no account hear the news. The famous "Archer of Charles IX.," brought out with an absurd title, had been a complete failure. Fendant, being anxious to realize a little ready money before going into bankruptcy, had sold the whole edition (without Cavalier's knowledge) to dealers in printed paper. These, in their turn, had disposed of it at a cheap rate to hawkers, and Lucien's book at that moment was adorning the bookstalls along the quays. The booksellers on the Quai des Augustins, who had previously taken a quantity of copies, now discovered that after this sudden reduction of the price they were likely to lose heavily on their purchases; the four duodecimo volumes, for which they had paid four francs fifty centimes, were being given away for fifty sous. Great was the outcry in the trade; but the newspapers preserved a profound silence. Barbet had not foreseen this "clearance;" he had a belief in Lucien's abilities; for once he had broken his rule and taken two hundred copies. The prospect of a loss drove him frantic; the things he said of Lucien were fearful to hear. Then Barbet took a heroic resolution. He stocked his copies in a corner of his store, with the obstinacy of greed, and left his competitors to sell their wares at a loss. Two years afterward, when d'Arthez's fine preface, the merits of the book, and one or two articles by Léon Giraud had raised the value of the book, Barbet sold his copies, one by one, at ten francs each.

Lucien knew nothing of all this, but Bérénice and Coralie could not refuse to allow Hector Merlin to see his dying comrade, and Hector Merlin made him drink, drop by drop, the whole of the bitter draught brewed by the failure of Fendant and Cavalier, made bankrupts by his first ill-fated book. Martainville, the one friend who stood by Lucien through thick and thin, had written a magnificent article on his work; but so great was the general exasperation against the editor of "L'Aristarque," "L'Oriflamme," and "Le Drapeau Blanc," that his championship only injured Lucien. In vain did the athlete return the Liberal insults tenfold, not a newspaper took up the challenge in spite of all his attacks.

Coralie, Bérénice, and Bianchon might shut the door on Lucien's so-called friends, who raised a great outcry, but it was impossible to keep out creditors and writs. After the failure of Fendant and Cavalier, their bills were taken into the bankruptcy according to that provision of the Code of Commerce most inimical to the claims of third parties, who in this way lose the benefit of delay.

Lucien discovered that Camusot was proceeding against him with great energy. When Coralie heard the name, and for the first time learned the dreadful and humiliating step which her poet had taken for her sake, the angelic creature loved him ten times more than before and would not approach Camusot. The bailiff bringing the warrant of arrest shrank from the idea of dragging his prisoner out of bed, and went back to Camusot before applying to the president of the Tribunal of Commerce for an order to remove the debtor to a private hospital. Camusot hurried at once to the Rue de la Lune, and Coralie went down to him.

When she came up again she held the warrants, in which Lucien was described as a tradesman, in her hand. How had she obtained those papers from Camusot? What promise had she given? Coralie kept a sad, gloomy silence, but when she returned she looked as if all the life had gone out of her. She played in Camille Maupin's play, and contributed not a little to the success of that illustrious literary hermaphrodite; but the creation of this character was the last flicker of a bright, dying lamp. On the twentieth night, when Lucien had so far recovered that he had regained his appetite, and could walk abroad, and talked of getting down to work again, Coralie broke down ; a secret trouble was weighing upon her. Bérénice always believed that she had promised to go back to Camusot to save Lucien.

Another mortification followed. Coralie was obliged to see her part given to Florine. Nathan had threatened the Gymnase with war if the management refused to give the vacant place to Coralie's rival. Coralie had persisted till she could play no longer, knowing that Florine was waiting to step into her place. She had overtasked her strength. The Gymnase had advanced sums during Lucien's illness, she had no money to draw; Lucien, eager to work though he was, was not yet strong enough to write, and he helped, beside, to nurse Coralie and to relieve Bérénice. From poverty they had come to utter distress; but in Bianchon they found a skillful and devoted doctor, who obtained credit for them of the druggist. The landlord of the house and the trades-people knew by this time how matters stood. The furniture was attached. The tailor and dressmaker no longer stood in awe of the journalist and proceeded to extremes; and at last no one, with the exception of the pork-butcher and the drug-gist, gave the two unlucky children credit. For a week or more all three of them—Lucien, Bérénice, and the invalid— were obliged to live on the various ingenious preparations sold by the pork-butcher; the inflammatory diet was little suited to the sick girl and Coralie grew worse. Sheer want compelled Lucien to ask Lousteau for a return of the loan of a thousand francs lost at play by the friend who had deserted him in his hour of need. Perhaps, amid all his troubles, this step cost him most cruel suffering.

Lousteau was not to be found in the Rue de la Harpe. Hunted down like a hare, he was lodging now with this friend, now with that. Lucien found him at last at Flicoteaux's; he was sitting at the very table at which Lucien had found him that evening when, for his misfortune, he forsook d'Arthez for journalism. Lousteau offered him dinner and Lucien ac-cepted the offer.

As they came out of Flicoteaux's with Claud Vignon (who happened to be dining there that day) and the great man in obscurity, who kept his wardrobe at Samanon's, the four among them could not produce enough specie to pay for a cup of coffee at the Café Voltaire. They lounged about the Luxembourg in the hope of meeting with a publisher; and, as it fell out, they met with one of the most famous printers of the day. Lousteau borrowed forty francs of him, and divided the money into four equal parts.

Misery had brought down Lucien's pride and extinguished sentiment; he shed tears as he told the story of his troubles, but each one of his comrades had a tale as cruel as his own; and when the three versions had been given, it seemed to the poet that he was the least unfortunate among the four. All of them craved a respite from remembrance and thoughts which made trouble doubly hard to bear.

Lousteau hurried to the Palais Royal to gamble with his remaining nine francs. The great man unknown to fame, though he had a divine mistress, must needs hie him to a low haunt of vice to wallow in perilous pleasure. Vignon betook himself to the " Rocher de Cancale " to drown memory and thought in a couple of bottles of Bordeaux; Lucien parted company with him on the threshold, declining to share that supper. When he shook hands with the one journalist who had not been hostile to him, it was with a cruel pang in his heart.

"What shall I do?" he asked aloud.

"One must do as one can," the great critic said. "Your book is good, but it excited jealousy and your struggle will be hard and long. Genius is a cruel disease. Every writer carries a canker in his heart, a devouring monster, like the tapeworm in the stomach, which destroys all feeling as it arises in him. Which is the stronger? The man or the disease? One had need be a great man, truly, to keep the balance between genius and character. The talent grows, the heart withers. Unless a man is a giant, unless he has the thews of a Hercules, he must be content either to lose his gift or to live without a heart. You are slender and fragile, you will give way," he added, as he turned into the restaurant.

Lucien returned home, thinking over that terrible verdict. He beheld the life of literature by the light of the profound truths uttered by Vignon.

"Money! money!" a seeming voice cried in his ears; ever "Money! money!"

Then he drew three bills of a thousand francs each, due respectively in one, two, and three months, imitating the handwriting of his brother-in-law, David Séchard, with admirable skill. He indorsed the bills, and took them next morning to Métivier, the paper-dealer in the Rue Serpente, who made no difficulty about taking them. Lucien wrote a few lines to give his brother-in-law notice of this assault upon his cash-box, promising, as usual in such cases, to be ready to meet the bills as they fell due.

When all debts, his own and Coralie's, were paid, he put the three hundred francs which remained into Bérénice's hands, bidding her to refuse him money if he asked her for it. He was afraid of a return of the gambler's frenzy. Lucien worked away gloomily in a sort of cold, speechless fury, putting forth all his powers into witty articles, written by the light of the lamp at Coralie's bedside. Whenever he looked up in search of ideas, his eyes fell on that beloved face, white as porcelain, fair with the beauty that belongs to the dying, and he saw a smile on her pale lips, and her eyes, grown bright with a more consuming pain than physical suffering, always turned on his face.

Lucien sent in his work, but he could not leave the house to worry editors, and his articles did not appear. When he at last made up his mind to go to the office, he met with a cool reception from Théodore Gaillard, who had advanced him money, and turned his literary diamonds to good account afterward.

"Take care, my dear fellow, you are falling off," he said. "You must not let yourself down, your work wants inspiration!"

"That little Lucien has written himself out with his romance and his first articles," cried Félicien Vernou, Merlin, and the whole chorus of his enemies, whenever his name came up at Dauriat's or the Vaudeville. "The work he is sending us is pitiable."

"To have written one's self out" (in the slang of journalism) is a verdict very hard to live down. It passed everywhere from mouth to mouth, ruining Lucien, all unsuspicious as he was. And, indeed, his burdens were too heavy for his strength. In the midst of a heavy strain of work, he was sued for the bills which he had drawn in David Séchard's name. He had recourse to Camusot's experience, and Coralie's sometime adorer was generous enough to assist the man she loved. The intolerable situation lasted for two whole months; the days being diversified by stamped papers in abundance, which Lucien (acting on Camusot's advice) handed over to Desroches, a friend of Bixiou, Bloudet, and des Lupeaulx.

Early in August, Bianchon told them that Coralie's condition was hopeless—she had only a few days to live. Those days were spent in tears by Bérénice and Lucien ; they could not hide their grief from the dying girl, and she was broken-hearted for Lucien's sake.

Some strange change was working in Coralie. She would have Lucien bring a priest ; she must be reconciled to the church and die in peace. Coralie died as a Christian ; her repentance was sincere. Her agony and death took all energy and heart out of Lucien. He sank into a low chair at the foot of the bed, and never took his eyes off her till death brought the end of her suffering. It was five o'clock in the morning. Some singing-bird, lighting upon a flower-pot on the window-sill, twittered a few notes. Bérénice, kneeling by the bedside, was covering a hand fast growing cold with kisses and tears. On the chimney-piece there lay eleven sous.

Lucien went out. Despair bade him beg for money to lay Coralie in her grave. He had wild thoughts of flinging himself at the Marquise d'Espard's feet, of entreating the Comte du Châtelet, Mme. de Bargeton, Mlle. des Touches, nay, that

23

terrible dandy of a de Marsay. All his pride had gone with his strength. He would have enlisted as a common soldier at that moment for money. He walked on with the slouching, feverish gait known to all the unhappy, reached Camille Maupin's house, entered, careless of his disordered dress, and sent in a message. He entreated Mlle. des Touches to see him for a moment.

"Mademoiselle only went to bed at three o'clock this morning," said the servant, "and no one would dare to disturb her until she rings."

"When does she ring?"

"Never before ten o'clock."

Then Lucien wrote one of those harrowing appeals in which the well-dressed beggar flings all pride and self-respect to the winds. One evening, not so very long ago, when Lousteau had told him of the abject begging-letters which Finot received, Lucien had thought it impossible that any creature should sink so low; and now, carried away by his pen, he had gone further, it may be, than other unlucky wretches upon the same road. He did not suspect, in his fever and imbecility, that he had just written a masterpiece of pathos. On his way home along the boulevards he met Barbet.

"Barbet!" he begged, holding out his hand. "Five hundred francs!"

"No. Two hundred," returned the other.

"Ah! then you have a heart."

"Yes; but I am a man of business as well. I have lost a lot of money through you," he concluded, after giving the history of the failure of Fendant and Cavalier, "will you put me in the way of making some?"

Lucien quivered.

"You are a poet. You ought to understand all kinds of poetry," continued the little publisher. "I want a few rollicking songs at this moment to put along with some more by different authors, or they will be down upon me over the copyright. I want to have a good collection to sell on the streets at ten sous. If you care to let me have ten good drinking-songs by to-morrow morning, or something spicy, you know the sort of thing, eh? I will pay you two hundred francs.''

When Lucien returned home, he found Coralie stretched out straight and stiff on a pallet-bed; Bérénice, with many tears, had wrapped her in a coarse linen sheet and put lighted candles at the four corners of the bed. Coralie's face had taken that strange, delicate beauty of death which so vividly impresses the living with the idea of absolute calm; she looked like some white girl in a decline; it seemed as if those pale, crimson lips must open and murmur the name which had blended with the name of God in the last words that she uttered before she died.

Lucien told Bérénice to order a funeral which should not cost more than two hundred francs, including the service at the shabby little church of the Bonne-Nouvelle. As soon as she had gone out, he sat down to a table, and, beside the dead body of his love, he composed, the ten rollicking songs to fit popular airs. The effort cost him untold anguish, but at last the brain began to work at the bidding of necessity, as if suffering were not; and already Lucien had learned to put Claud Vignon's terrible maxims in practice and to raise a barrier between heart and brain. What a night the poor boy spent over those drinking-songs, writing by the light of the tall wax-candles while the priest recited the prayers for the dead!

Morning broke before the last song was finished. Lucien tried it over to a street-song of the day, to the consternation of Bérénice and the priest, who thought that he was mad:

> '' Lads, 'tis tedious waste of time
> To mingle song and reason;
> Folly calls for laughing rhyme
> Sense is out of season.

Let Apollo be forgot
  When Bacchus fills the drinking cup;
And any catch is good I wot,
  If good fellows take it up.
      Let philosophers protest.
        Let us laugh,
          And quaff,
        And a fig for the rest!

" As Hippocrates has said,
    Every jolly fellow,
  When a century has sped,
    Still is fit and mellow.
No more following of a lass
  With the palsy in your legs?—
While your hand can hold a glass,
  You can drain it to the dregs,
      With an undiminished zest.
        Let us laugh,
          And quaff,
        And a fig for the rest.

" Whence we come we know full well.
    Whither are we going?
  Ne'er a one of us can tell,
    'Tis a thing past knowing.
Faith what does it signify,
    Take the good that heaven sends;
It is certain that we die,
    Certain that we live, my friends.
      Life is nothing but a jest.
        Let us laugh,
          And quaff,
        And a fig for the rest!"

He was shouting the reckless refrain when d'Arthez and
Bianchon arrived, to find him in a paroxysm of despair and
exhaustion, utterly unable to make a fair copy of his verses.
A torrent of tears followed; and when, amid his sobs, he had

told his pitiful story, he saw the tears standing in his friends' eyes.

"This wipes out many sins," said d'Arthez.

"Happy are they who suffer for their sins in this world," the priest said solemnly.

At the sight of the fair, dead face smiling at eternity, while Coralie's lover wrote tavern-catches to buy a grave for her, and Barbet paid for the coffin—of the four candles lighted about the dead body of her who had thrilled a great audience as she stood behind the footlights in her Spanish basquina and scarlet, green-clocked stockings; while beyond, in the doorway, stood the priest who had reconciled the dying actress with God, now about to return to the church to say a mass for the soul of her who had "loved much"—all the grandeur and the sordid aspects of the scene, all that sorrow crushed under by necessity, froze the blood of the great writer and the great doctor. They sat down; neither of them could utter a word.

Just at that moment a servant in livery announced Mlle. des Touches. That beautiful and noble woman understood everything at once. She stepped quickly across the room to Lucien, and slipped two thousand-franc notes into his hand as she grasped it.

"It is too late," he said, looking up at her with dull, hopeless eyes.

The three stayed with Lucien, trying to soothe his despair with comforting words; but every spring seemed to be broken. At noon all the brotherhood, with the exception of Michel Chrestien (who, however, had learned the truth as to Lucien's treachery), was assembled in the poor little church of the Bonne-Nouvelle; Mlle. des Touches was present, and Bérénice and Coralie's dresser from the theatre, with a couple of supernumeraries, and the disconsolate Camusot. All the men accompanied the actress to her last resting-place in Père Lachaise. Camusot, shedding hot tears, had solemnly promised Lucien to buy the grave in perpetuity, and to put a headstone above it with the words:

CORALIE

AGED NINETEEN YEARS

August, 1822.

Lucien stayed there, on the sloping ground that looks out over Paris, until the sun had set.

"Who will love me now?" he thought. "My truest friends despise me. Whatever I might have done, she who lies here would have thought me wholly noble and good. I have no one left to me now but my sister and mother and David. And what do they think of me at home?"

Poor distinguished provincial! He went back to the Rue de la Lune; but the sight of the rooms was so acutely painful that he could not stay in them, and he took a cheap lodging elsewhere in the same street. Mlle. des Touches' two thousand francs and the sale of the furniture paid the debts.

Bérénice had two hundred francs left, on which they lived for two months. Lucien was prostrate; he could neither write nor think; he gave way to morbid grief. Bérénice took pity upon him.

"Suppose that you were to go back to your own country, how are you to get there?" she asked one day, by way of reply to an exclamation of Lucien's.

"On foot."

"But even so, you must live and sleep on the way. Even if you walk twelve leagues a day, you will want twenty francs at least."

"I will get them together," he said.

He took his clothes and his best linen, keeping nothing but strict necessaries, and went to Samanon, who offered fifty francs for his entire wardrobe. In vain he begged the money-lender to let him have enough to pay his fare by the coach; Samanon was inexorable. In a paroxysm of fury, Lucien rushed to Frascati's, staked the proceeds of the sale, and lost every farthing. Back once more in the wretched room in the Rue de la Lune, he asked Bérénice for Coralie's shawl. The good girl looked at him and knew in a moment what he meant to do. He had confessed to his loss at the gaming-table; and now he was going to hang himself.

"Are you mad, sir? Go out for a walk, and come back again at midnight. I will get the money for you; but keep to the boulevards, do not go toward the quais."

Lucien paced up and down the boulevards. He was stupid with grief. He watched the passers-by and the stream of traffic, and felt that he was alone and a very small atom in this seething whirlpool of Paris, churned by the strife of innumerable interests. His thoughts went back to the banks of his Charente; a craving for happiness and home awoke in him; and with the craving came one of the febrile bursts of energy which half-feminine natures like his mistake for strength. He would not give up until he had poured out his heart to David Séchard, and taken counsel of the three good angels still left to him on earth.

As he lounged along, he caught sight of Bérénice—Bérénice in her Sunday clothes, speaking to a stranger at the corner of the Rue de la Lune and the filthy Boulevard Bonne-Nouvelle, where she had taken her stand.

"What are you doing?" asked Lucien, dismayed by a sudden suspicion.

"Here are your twenty francs," said the girl, slipping four five-franc pieces into the poet's hand. "They may cost dear yet; but you can go," and she had fled before Lucien could see the way she went; for, in justice to him, it must be said that the money burned his hand, he wanted to return it, but he was forced to keep it, as the final brand set upon him by life in Paris.   PARIS, 1839.

Z. MARCAS.

Translated by CLARA BELL.

*To His Highness Count William of Wurtemberg, as
a token of the author's respectful gratitude.*

DE BALZAC.

I NEVER saw anybody, not even among the most remarkable men of the day, whose appearance was so striking as this
man's; the study of his countenance at first gave me a feeling
of great melancholy, and at last produced an almost painful
impression.

There was a certain harmony between the man and his
name. The Z. preceding Marcas, which was seen on the
addresses of his letters, and which he never omitted from his
signature, as the last letter of the alphabet, suggested some
mysterious fatality.

MARCAS! say this two-syllabled name again and again; do
you not feel as if it had some sinister meaning? Does it not
seem to you that its owner must be doomed to martyrdom?
Though foreign, savage, the name has a right to be handed
down to posterity; it is well constructed, easily pronounced,
and has the brevity that beseems a famous name. Is it not
pleasant as well as odd? But does it not sound unfinished?

I will not take it upon myself to assert that names have no
influence on the destiny of men. There is a certain secret
and inexplicable concord or a visible discord between the
events of a man's life and his name which is truly surprising;
often some remote but very real correlation is revealed. Our
globe is round; everything is linked to everything else.
Some day perhaps we shall revert to the occult sciences.

(360)

Do you not discern in that letter Z an adverse influence? Does it not prefigure the wayward and fantastic progress of a storm-tossed life? What wind blew on that letter, which, whatever language we find it in, begins scarcely fifty words? Marcas' name was Zephirin; Saint Zephirin is highly venerated in Brittany, and Marcas was a Breton.

Study the name once more: Z. Marcas! The man's whole life lies in this fantastic juxtaposition of seven letters; seven! the most significant of all the cabalistic numbers. And he died at five-and-thirty, so his life extended over seven lustres.

Marcas! Does it not hint of some precious object that is broken by a fall, with or without a crash?

I had finished studying the law in Paris in 1836. I lived at that time in the Rue Corneille, in a house where none but students came to lodge, one of those large houses where there is a winding staircase quite at the back, lighted below from the street, higher up by borrowed lights, and at the top by a skylight. There were forty furnished rooms—furnished as students' rooms are! What does youth demand more than was here supplied? A bed, a few chairs, a chest of drawers, a looking-glass and a table. As soon as the sky is blue the student opens his window.

But in this street there are no fair neighbors to flirt with. In front is the Odéon, long since closed, presenting a wall that is beginning to go black, its tiny gallery windows and its vast expanse of slate roof. I was not rich enough to have a good room; I was not even rich enough to have a room to myself. Juste and I shared a double-bedded room on the fifth floor.

On our side of the landing there were but two rooms—ours and a smaller one occupied by Z. Marcas, our neighbor. For six months Juste and I remained in perfect ignorance of the fact. The old woman who managed the house had indeed told us that the room was inhabited, but she had added that we should not be disturbed, that the occupant was exceedingly quiet. In fact, for those six months, we never met our fellow-lodger, and we never heard a sound in his room, in spite of the thinness of the partition that divided us—one of those walls of lath and plaster which are common in Paris houses.

Our room, a little over seven feet high, was hung with a vile cheap paper sprigged with blue. The floor was painted, and knew nothing of the polish given by the rubber's brush. By our beds there was only a scrap of thin carpet. The chimney opened immediately to the roof, and smoked so abominably that we were obliged to provide a stove at our own expense. Our beds were mere painted wooden cribs like those in schools; on the chimney-shelf there were but two brass candlesticks, with or without tallow candles in them, and our two pipes with some tobacco in a pouch or strewn abroad, also the little piles of cigar-ash left there by our visitors or ourselves.

A pair of calico curtains hung from the brass window-rods, and on each side of the window was a small bookcase in cherry-wood, such as every one knows who has stared into the shop windows of the Quartier Latin, and in which we kept the few books necessary for our studies.

The ink in the inkstand was always in the state of lava congealed in the crater of a volcano. May not any inkstand nowadays become a Vesuvius? The pens, all twisted, served to clean the stems of our pipes; and, in opposition to all the laws of credit, paper was even scarcer than coin.

How can young men be expected to stay at home in such furnished lodgings? The students studied in the cafés, the theatre, the Luxembourg gardens, in *grisettes'* rooms, even in the law schools—anywhere rather than in their horrible rooms —horrible for purposes of study, delightful as soon as they are used for gossiping and smoking in. Put a cloth on the table, and the impromptu dinner sent in from the best eating-house in the neighborhood—places for four—two of them in petticoats—show a lithograph of this "Interior" to the veriest bigot, and she will be bound to smile.

We thought only of amusing ourselves. The reason for our dissipation lay in the most serious facts of the politics of the time. Juste and I could not see any room for us in the two professions our parents wished us to take up. There are a hundred doctors, a hundred lawyers, for one that is wanted. The crowd is choking these two paths which are supposed to lead to fortune, but which are merely two arenas; men kill each other there, fighting, not indeed with swords or firearms, but with intrigue and calumny, with tremendous toil, campaigns in the sphere of the intellect as murderous as those in Italy were to the soldiers of the republic. In these days, when everything is an intellectual competition, a man must be able to sit forty-eight hours on end in his chair before a table, as a general could remain for two days on horseback and in his saddle.

The throng of aspirants has necessitated a division of the faculty of medicine into categories. There is the physician who writes and the physician who practices, the political physician and the physician militant—four different ways of being a physician, four classes already filled up. As to the fifth class, that of physicians who sell remedies, there is such a competition that they fight each other with disgusting advertisements on the walls of Paris.

In all the law courts there are almost as many lawyers as there are cases. The pleader is thrown back on journalism, on politics, on literature. In fact, the state, besieged for the smallest appointments under the law, has ended by requiring that the applicants should have some little fortune. The pear-shaped head of the grocer's son is selected in preference to the square skull of a man of talent who has not a sou. Work as he will, with all his energy, a young man, starting from zero, may at the end of ten years find himself below the point he set out from. In these days, talent must have the good-luck which secures success to the most incapable ; nay more, if it scorns the base compromises which insure advancement to crawling mediocrity, it will never get on.

If we thoroughly knew our time, we also knew ourselves, and we preferred the indolence of dreamers to aimless stir, easy-going pleasure to the useless toil which would have exhausted our courage and worn out the edge of our intelligence. We had analyzed social life while smoking, laughing, and loafing. But, though elaborated by such means as these, our reflections were none the less judicious and profound.

While we were fully conscious of the slavery to which youth is condemned, we were amazed at the brutal indifference of the authorities to everything connected with intellect, thought, and poetry. How often have Juste and I exchanged glances when reading the papers as we studied political events, or the debates in the Chamber, and discussed the proceedings of a court whose willful ignorance could find no parallel but in the platitude of the courtiers, the mediocrity of the men forming the hedge round the newly restored throne, all alike devoid of talent or breadth of view, of distinction or learning, of influence or dignity !

Could there be a higher tribute to the court of Charles X. than the present court, if court it may be called ? What a hatred of the country may be seen in the naturalization of vulgar foreigners, devoid of talent, who are enthroned in the Chamber of Peers ! What a perversion of justice ! What an insult to the distinguished youth, the ambitions native to the soil of France ! We looked upon these things as upon a spectacle, and groaned over them, without taking upon ourselves to act.

Juste, whom no one ever sought, and who never sought any one, was, at five-and-twenty, a great politician, a man with a wonderful aptitude for apprehending the correlation between remote history and the facts of the present and of the future. In 1831, he told me exactly what would and did happen—

the murders, the conspiracies, the ascendency of the Jews, the difficulty of doing anything in France, the scarcity of talent in the higher circles, and the abundance of intellect in the lowest ranks, where the finest courage is smothered under cigar ashes.

What was to become of him? His parents wished him to be a doctor. But if he were a doctor, must he not wait twenty years for a practice? You know what he did? No? Well, he is a doctor; but he left France, he is in Asia. At this moment he is perhaps sinking under fatigue in a desert, or dying of the lashes of a barbarous horde—or perhaps he is some Indian prince's prime minister.

Action is my vocation. Leaving a civil college at the age of twenty, the only way for me to enter the army was by enlisting as a common soldier; so weary of the dismal out-look that lay before a lawyer, I acquired the knowledge needed for a sailor. I imitate Juste, and keep out of France, where men waste, in the struggle to make way, the energy needed for the noblest works. Follow my example, friends; I am going where a man steers his destiny as he pleases; is his own navigator.

These great resolutions were formed in the little room in the lodging-house in the Rue Corneille, in spite of our haunt-ing the Bal Musard, flirting with girls of the town, and lead-ing a careless and apparently reckless life. Our plans and arguments long floated in the air.

Marcas, our neighbor, was in some degree the guide who led us to the margin of the precipice or the torrent, who made us sound it, and showed us beforehand what our fate would be if we let ourselves fall into it. It was he who put us on our guard against the time-bargains a man makes with poverty under the sanction of hope, by accepting precarious situations whence he fights the battle, carried along by the devious tide of Paris—that great harlot who takes you up or leaves you stranded, smiles or turns her back on you with equal readiness,

wears out the strongest will in vexatious waiting, and makes
misfortune wait on chance.

At our first meeting, Marcas, as it were, dazzled us. On
our return from the schools, a little before the dinner-hour,
we were accustomed to go up to our room and remain there a
while, either waiting for the other, to learn whether there
were any change in our plans for the evening. One day, at
four o'clock, Juste met Marcas on the stairs, and I saw him
in the street. It was in the month of November, and Marcas
had no cloak; he wore shoes with heavy soles, corduroy trousers, and a blue double-breasted coat buttoned to the throat,
which gave a military air to his broad chest, all the more so
because he wore a black stock. The costume was not in itself
extraordinary, but it agreed well with the man's mien and
countenance.

My first impression on seeing him was neither surprise, nor
distress, nor interest, nor pity, but curiosity mingled with all
these feelings. He walked slowly, with a step that betrayed
deep melancholy, his head forward with a stoop, but not bent
like that of a conscience-stricken man. That head, large and
powerful, which might contain the treasures necessary for a
man of the highest ambition, looked as if it were loaded with
thought; it was weighted with grief of mind, but there was
no touch of remorse in his expression. As to his face, it may
be summed up in a word. A common superstition has it
that every human countenance resembles some animal. The
animal for Marcas was the lion. His hair was like a
mane, his nose was short and flat, broad and dented at the
tip like a lion's; his brow, like a lion's, was strongly marked
with a deep median furrow, dividing two powerful bosses.
His high, hairy cheek-bones, all the more prominent because
his cheeks were so thin, his enormous mouth and hollow jaws,
were accentuated by lines of haughty significance, and marked
by a complexion full of tawny shadows. This almost terrible

countenance seemed illuminated by two lamps—two eyes, black indeed, but infinitely sweet, calm and deep, full of thought. If I may say so, those eyes had a humiliated expression.

Marcas was afraid of looking directly at others, not for himself, but for those on whom his fascinating gaze might rest; he had a power, and he shunned using it; he would spare those he met, and he feared notice. This was not from modesty, but from resignation—not Christian resignation, which implies charity, but resignation founded on reason, which had demonstrated the immediate inutility of his gifts, the impossibility of entering and living in the sphere for which he was fitted. Those eyes could at times flash lightnings. From those lips a voice of thunder must surely proceed; it was a mouth like Mirabeau's.

"I have seen such a grand fellow in the street," said I to Juste on coming in.

"It must be our neighbor," replied Juste, who described, in fact, the man I had just met. "A man who lives like a wood-louse would be sure to look like that," he added.

"What dejection and what dignity!"

"One is the consequence of the other."

"What ruined hopes! What schemes and failures!"

"Seven leagues of ruins! Obelisks—palaces—towers!— The ruins of Palmyra in the desert!" said Juste, laughing.

So we called him the Ruins of Palmyra.

As we went out to dine at the wretched eating-house in the Rue de la Harpe to which we subscribed, we asked the name of Number 37, and then heard the weird name Z. Marcas. Like boys, as we were, we repeated it more than a hundred times with all sorts of comments, absurd or melancholy, and the name lent itself to the jest. Juste would fire off the Z like a rocket rising, *z-z-z-zed;* and after pronouncing the first syllable of the name with great importance, depicted a fall by the dull brevity of the second.

" Now, how and where does the man live ? "

From this query, to the innocent espionage of curiosity there was no pause but that required for carrying out our plan. Instead of loitering about the streets, we both came in, each armed with a novel. We read with our ears open. And in the perfect silence of our attic rooms, we heard the even, dull sound of a sleeping man breathing.

" He is asleep," said I to Juste, noticing this fact.

" At seven o'clock ! " replied the doctor.

This was the name by which I called Juste, and he called me the keeper of the seals.

" A man must be wretched indeed to sleep as much as our neighbor ! " cried I, jumping on to the chest of drawers with a knife in my hand, to which a corkscrew was attached.

I made a round hole at the top of the partition, about as big as a five-sou piece. I had forgotten that there would be no light in the room, and, putting my eyes to the hole, I saw only darkness. At about one in the morning, when we had finished our books and were about to undress, we heard a noise in our neighbor's room. He got up, struck a match, and lighted his dip. I got on to the drawers again, and I then saw Marcas seated at his table and copying law-papers.

His room was about half the size of ours ; the bed stood in a recess by the door, for the passage ended there, and its breadth was added to his garret ; but the ground on which the house was built was evidently irregular, for the party-wall formed an obtuse angle, and the room was not square. There was no fireplace, only a small earthenware stove, white blotched with green, of which the pipe went up through the roof. The window, in the skew side of the room, had shabby, red curtains. The furniture consisted of an armchair, a table, a chair, and a wretched bed-table. A cupboard in the wall held his clothes. The wall-paper was horrible ; evidently only a servant had ever lodged there before Marcas.

" What is to be seen ? " asked the doctor as I got down.

"Look for yourself," said I.

At nine next morning Marcas was in bed. He had break-fasted off a saveloy; we saw on a plate, with some crumbs of bread, the remains of that too familiar delicacy. He was asleep; he did not wake until eleven. He then set to work again on the copy he had begun the night before, which was lying on the table.

On going downstairs we asked the price of that room, and were told fifteen francs a month.

In the course of a few days we were fully informed as to the mode of life of Z. Marcas. He did copying, at so much a sheet no doubt, for a law-writer who lived in the courtyard of the Sainte-Chapelle. He worked half the night; after sleeping from six until ten, he began again and wrote until three. Then he went out to take the copy home before dinner, which he ate at Mizerai's in the Rue Michel-le-Comte, at a cost of nine sous, and came in to bed at six o'clock. It became known to us that Marcas did not utter fifteen sentences in a month; he never talked to anybody, nor said a word to himself in his dreadful garret.

"The Ruins of Palmyra are terribly silent!" said Juste.

This taciturnity in a man whose appearance was so imposing was strangely significant. Sometimes when we met him, we exchanged glances full of meaning on both sides, but they never led to any advances. Insensibly this man became the object of our secret admiration, though we knew no reason for it. Did it lie in his secretly simple habits, his monastic regularity, his hermit-like frugality, his idiotically mechanical labor, allowing his mind to remain neuter or to work on its own lines, seeming to us to hint at an expectation of some stroke of good-luck or at some foregone conclusion as to his life?

After wandering for a long time among the Ruins of Palmyra, we forgot them—we were young! Then came the carnival, the Paris carnival, which, henceforth, will eclipse

24

the old carnival of Venice, unless some ill-advised prefect of police is antagonistic.

Gambling ought to be allowed during the carnival; but the stupid moralists who have had gambling suppressed are inept financiers, and this indispensable evil will be re-established among us when it is proved that France leaves millions at the German tables.

This splendid carnival brought us to utter penury, as it does every student. We got rid of every object of luxury; we sold our second coats, our second boots, our second waist-coats—everything of which we had a duplicate, except our friend. We ate bread and cold sausages; we looked where we walked; we had set to work in earnest. We owed two months' rent, and were sure of having a bill from the porter for sixty or eighty items each, and amounting to forty or fifty francs. We made no noise, and did not laugh as we crossed the little hall at the bottom of the stairs; we commonly took it at a flying leap from the lowest step into the street. On the day when we first found ourselves bereft of tobacco for our pipes, it struck us that for some days we had been eating bread without any kind of butter.

Great was our distress.

"No tobacco!" said the doctor.

"No cloak!" said the keeper of the seals.

"Ah, you young rascals, you would dress as the postillon de Longjumeau, you would appear as Débardeurs, sup in the morning, and breakfast at night at Véry's—sometimes even at the Rocher de Cancale. Dry bread for you, my boys! Why," said I, in a big bass voice, "you deserve to sleep under the bed, you are not worthy to lie in it——"

"Yes, yes; but, keeper of the seals, there is no more tobacco!" said Juste.

"It is high time to write home, to our aunts, our mothers, and our sisters, to tell them that we have no underlinen left, that the wear and tear of Paris would ruin garments of wire. Then we will solve an elegant chemical problem by transmuting linen into silver."

"But we must live till we get the answer."

"Well, I will go and bring out a loan among such of our friends as may still have some capital to invest."

"And how much will you find?"

"Say ten francs!" replied I with pride.

It was midnight. Marcas had heard everything. He knocked at our door.

"Messieurs," said he, "here is some tobacco; you can repay me on the first opportunity."

We were struck, not by the offer, which we accepted, but by the rich, deep, full voice in which it was made; a tone only comparable to the lowest string of Paganini's violin. Marcas vanished without waiting for our thanks.

Juste and I looked at each other without a word. To be rescued by a man evidently poorer than ourselves! Juste sat down to write to every member of his family, and I went off to effect a loan. I brought in twenty francs lent me by a fellow-provincial. In that evil but happy day gambling was still tolerated, and in its lodes, as hard as the rocky ore of Brazil, young men, by risking a small sum, had a chance of winning a few gold-pieces. My friend, too, had some Turkish tobacco brought home from Constantinople by a sailor, and he gave me quite as much as we had taken from Z. Marcas. I conveyed the splendid cargo into port, and we went in triumph to repay our neighbor with a tawny wig of Turkish tobacco for his dark caporal.

"You were determined not to be my debtors," said he. "You are giving me gold for copper. You are boys—good boys——"

The sentences, spoken in varying tones, were variously emphasized. The words were nothing, but the expression! That made us friends of ten years' standing at once.

Marcas, on hearing us coming, had covered up his papers;
we understood that it would be taking a liberty to allude
to his means of subsistence, and felt ashamed of having
watched him.   His cupboard stood open; in it there were
were two shirts, a white necktie, and a razor.   The razor
made me shudder.   A looking-glass, worth five francs perhaps, hung near the window.

The man's few and simple movements had a sort of
savage grandeur.   The doctor and I looked at each other,
wondering what we could say in reply.   Juste, seeing that I
was speechless, asked Marcas jestingly—

" You cultivate literature, monsieur ? "

" Far from it ! " replied Marcas.   " I should not be so
wealthy."

" I fancied," said I, " that poetry alone, in these days, was
amply sufficient to provide a man with lodgings as bad as
ours."

My remark made Marcas smile, and the smile gave a charm
to his yellow face.

" Ambition is not a less severe taskmaster to those who
fail," said he.   " You, who are beginning life, walk in the
beaten paths.   Never dream of rising superior, you will be
ruined ! "

" You advise us to stay just as we are ? " said the doctor,
smiling.

There is something so infectious and childlike in the pleasantries of youth that Marcas smiled again in reply.

" What incidents can have given you this detestable philosophy ? " asked I.

" I forgot once more that chance is the result of an immense equation of which we know not all the factors.   When
we start from zero to work up to the unit, the chances are
incalculable.   To ambitious men Paris is an immense roulette
table, and every young man fancies he can hit on a successful
progression of numbers."

He offered us the tobacco I had brought that we might smoke with him ; the doctor went to fetch our pipes ; Marcas filled his, and then he came to sit in our room, bringing the tobacco with him, since there were but two chairs in his. Juste, as brisk as a squirrel, ran out and returned with a boy carrying three bottles of Bordeaux, some Brie cheese, and a loaf.

"Hah!" said I to myself, "fifteen francs," and I was right to a sou.

Juste gravely laid five francs on the chimney-shelf and seated himself.

There are immeasurable differences between the gregarious man and the man who lives closest to nature. Toussaint Louverture, after he was caught, died without speaking a word. Napoleon, transplanted to a rock, talked like a magpie—he wanted to account for himself. Z. Marcas erred in the same way, but for our benefit only. Silence in all its majesty is to be found only in the savage. There never is a criminal who, though he might let his secrets fall with his head into the basket of sawdust, does not feel the purely social impulse to tell them to somebody.

Nay, I am wrong. We have seen one Iroquois of the Faubourg Saint-Marceau who raised the Parisian to the level of the natural savage—a republican, a conspirator, a Frenchman, an old man, who outdid all we have heard of negro determination, and all that Cooper tells us of the tenacity and coolness of the redskins under defeat. Morey, the Guatimozin of the "Mountain," preserved an attitude unparalleled in the annals of European justice.

This is what Marcas told us during the small hours, sandwiching his discourse with slices of bread spread with cheese and washed down with wine. All the tobacco was burned out. Now and then the hackney coaches clattering across the Place de l'Odéon, or the omnibuses toiling past, sent up their dull rumbling, as if to remind us that Paris was still close to us.

His family lived at Vitré; his father and mother had fifteen hundred francs a year in the funds. He had received an education gratis in a seminary, but had refused to enter the priesthood. He felt in himself the fires of immense ambition, and had come to Paris on foot at the age of twenty, the possessor of two hundred francs. He had studied the law, working in an attorney's office, where he had risen to be senior clerk. He had taken his doctor's degree in law, had mastered the old and modern codes, and could hold his own with the most famous pleaders. He had studied the law of nations, and was familiar with European treaties and international practice. He had studied men and things in five capitals— London, Berlin, Vienna, St. Petersburg, and Constantinople.

No man was better informed than he as to the rules of the Chamber. For five years he had been reporter of the debates for a daily paper. He spoke extempore and admirably, and could go on for a long time in that deep, appealing voice which had struck us to the soul. Indeed, he proved by the narrative of his life that he was a great orator, a concise orator, serious and yet full of piercing eloquence; he resembled Berryer in his fervor and in the impetus which commands the sympathy of the masses, and was like Thiers in refinement and skill; but he would have been less diffuse, less in difficulties for a conclusion. He had intended to rise rapidly to power without burdening himself first with the doctrines necessary to begin with, for a man in opposition, but an incubus later to the statesman.

Marcas had learned everything that a real statesman should know; indeed, his amazement was considerable when he had occasion to discern the utter ignorance of men who have risen to the administration of public affairs in France. Though in him it was vocation that had led to study, nature had been generous and bestowed all that cannot be acquired—keen per-

ceptions, self-command, a nimble wit, rapid judgment, deci-
siveness, and, what is the genius of these men, fertility in
resource.

By the time when Marcas thought himself duly equipped,
France was torn by intestinal divisions arising from the tri-
umph of the house of Orleans over the elder branch of the
Bourbons.

The field of political warfare is evidently changed. Civil
war henceforth cannot last for long, and will not be fought
out in the provinces. In France such struggles will be of
brief duration and at the seat of government; and the battle
will be the close of the moral contest which will have been
brought to an issue by superior minds. This state of things
will continue so long as France has her present singular form
of government, which has no analogy with that of any
other country; for there is no more resemblance between the
English and the French constitutions than between the two
lands.

Thus Marcas' place was in the political press. Being poor
and unable to secure his election, he hoped to make a sudden
appearance. He resolved on making the greatest possible
sacrifice for a man of superior intellect, to work as subordinate
to some rich and ambitious deputy. Like a second Bonaparte,
he sought his Barras; the new Colbert hoped to find a Mazarin.
He did immense services, and he did them then and there; he
assumed no importance, he made no boast, he did not complain of ingratitude. He did them in the hope that his patron
would put him in a position to be elected deputy; Marcas
wished for nothing but a loan that might enable him to purchase a house in Paris, the qualification required by law.
Richard III. asked for nothing but his horse.

In three years Marcas had made his man—one of the fifty
supposed great statesmen who are the battledores with which
two cunning players toss the ministerial portfolios, exactly as
the man behind the puppet-show hits Punch against the con-

stable in his street theatre, and counts on always getting paid. This man existed only by Marcas, but he had just brains enough to appreciate the value of his "ghost," and to know that Marcas, if he ever came to the front, would remain there, would be indispensable, while he himself would be translated to the polar zone of the Luxembourg. So he determined to put insurmountable objects in the way of his mentor's advancement, and hid his purpose under the semblance of the utmost sincerity. Like all mean men, he could dissimulate to perfection, and he soon made progress in the ways of ingratitude, for he felt that he must kill Marcas, not to be killed by him. These two men, apparently so united, hated each other as soon as one had once deceived the other.

The politician was made one of a ministry; Marcas remained in the opposition to hinder his man from being attacked; nay, by skillful tactics he won him the applause of the opposition. To excuse himself for not rewarding his subaltern, the chief pointed out the impossibility of finding a place suddenly for a man on the other side without a great deal of manœuvring. Marcas had hoped confidently for a place to enable him to marry, and thus acquire the qualification he so ardently desired. He was two-and-thirty, and the Chamber ere long must be dissolved. Having detected his man in this flagrant act of bad faith, he overthrew him, or at any rate contributed largely to his overthrow, and covered him with mud.

A fallen minister, if he is to rise again to power, must show that he is to be feared ; this man, intoxicated by royal glibness, had fancied that his position would be permanent ; he acknowledged his delinquencies ; beside confessing them, he did Marcas a small money service, for Marcas had gotten into debt. He subsidized the newspaper on which Marcas worked, and made him the manager of it.

Though he despised the man, Marcas, who, practically, was being subsidized too, consented to take the part of the fallen minister. Without unmasking at once all the batteries of his

superior intellect, Marcas came a little further than before; he
showed half his shrewdness. The ministry lasted only a hundred and eighty days; it was swallowed up. Marcas had
put himself into communication with certain deputies, had
moulded them like dough, leaving each impressed with a
high opinion of his talent; his puppet again became a member of the ministry, and then the paper was ministerial. The
ministry united the paper with another, solely to squeeze out
Marcas, who in this fusion had to make way for a rich and
insolent rival, whose name was well known, and who already
had his foot in the stirrup.

Marcas relapsed into utter destitution; his haughty patron
well knew the depths into which he had cast him.

Where was he to go? The ministerial papers, privily warned,
would have nothing to say to him. The opposition papers
did not care to admit him to their offices. Marcas could side
neither with the Republicans nor with the Legitimists, two
parties whose triumph would mean the overthrow of everything that now is.

"Ambitious men like a fast hold on things," said he with
a smile.

He lived by writing a few articles on commercial affairs,
and contributed to one of those encyclopedias brought out by
speculation and not by learning. Finally a paper was founded
which was destined to live but two years, but which secured
his services. From that moment he renewed his connection
with the minister's enemies; he joined the party who were
working for the fall of the government; and as soon as his
pickaxe had free play, it fell.

This paper had now for six months ceased to exist; he had
failed to find employment of any kind; he was spoken of as
a dangerous man, calumny attacked him; he had unmasked
a huge financial and mercantile job by a few articles and a
pamphlet. He was known to be the mouthpiece of a banker
who was said to have paid him largely, and from whom he

was supposed to expect some patronage in return for his championship. Marcas, disgusted by men and things, worn out
by five years of fighting, regarded as a free-lance rather than
as a great leader, crushed by the necessity for earning his
daily bread, which hindered him from gaining ground, in
despair at the influence exerted by money over mind, and
given over to dire poverty, buried himself in a garret, to
make thirty sous a day, the sum strictly answering to his
needs. Meditation had leveled a desert all around him.
He read the papers to be informed of what was going on.
Pozzo di Borgo had once lived like this for some time.

Marcas, no doubt, was planning a serious attack, accustom-
ing himself to dissimulation, and punishing himself for his
blunders by pythagorean muteness. But he did not tell us
the reasons for his conduct.

It is impossible to give you an idea of the scenes of the
highest comedy that lay behind this algebraic statement of his
career; his useless patience dogging the footsteps of fortune,
which presently took wings, his long tramps over the thorny
brakes of Paris, his breathless chases as a petitioner, his attempts to win over fools; the schemes laid only to fail
through the influence of some frivolous woman; the meetings
with men of business who expected their capital to bring
them places and a peerage, as well as large interest. Then
the hopes rising in a towering wave only to break in foam on
the shoal; the wonders wrought in reconciling adverse interests which, after working together for a week, fell asunder;
the annoyance, a thousand times repeated, of seeing a dunce
decorated with the Legion of Honor, and preferred, though
as ignorant as a shop-boy, to a man of talent. Then, what
Marcas called the stratagems of stupidity—you strike a man,
and he seems convinced, he nods his head—everything is
settled; next day, this india-rubber ball, flattened for a moment, has recovered itself in the course of the night; it is as
full of wind as ever; you must begin all over again; and you

go on till you understand that you are not not dealing with a man, but with a lump of gum that loses shape in the sunshine.

These thousand annoyances, this vast waste of human energy on barren spots, the difficulty of achieving any good, the incredible facility of doing mischief; two strong games played out, twice won and then twice lost; the hatred of a statesman—a blockhead with a painted face and a wig, but in whom the world believed—all these things, great and small, had not crushed, but for the moment had dashed, Marcas. In the days when money had come into his hands, his fingers had not clutched it; he had allowed himself the exquisite pleasure of sending it all to his family—to his sisters, his brothers, his old father. Like Napoleon in his fall, he asked for no more than thirty sous a day, and any man of energy can earn thirty sous for a day's work in Paris.

When Marcas had finished the story of his life, intermingled with reflections, maxims, and observations, revealing him as a great politician, a few questions and answers on both sides as to the progress of affairs in France and in Europe were enough to prove to us that he was a real statesman ; for a man may be quickly and easily judged when he can be brought on to the ground of immediate difficulties : there is a certain shibboleth for men of superior talents, and we are of the tribe of modern Levites without belonging as yet to the temple. As I have said, our frivolity covered certain purposes which Juste has carried out, and which I am about to execute.

When we had done talking, we all three went out, cold as it was, to walk in the Luxembourg gardens till the dinner-hour. In the course of that walk our conversation, grave throughout, turned on the painful aspects of the political situation. Each of us contributed his remarks, his comment, or his jest, a pleasantry or a proverb. This was no longer exclusively a discussion of life on the colossal scale just described by Marcas, the soldier of political warfare. Nor was it the distressful monologue of the wrecked navigator, stranded

in a garret in the Hôtel Corneille; it was a dialogue in which
two well-informed young men, having gauged the times they
lived in, were endeavoring, under the guidance of a man of
talent, to gain some light on their own future prospects.

"Why," asked Juste, "did you not wait patiently for an
opportunity, and imitate the only man who has been able to
keep the lead since the revolution of July by holding his head
above water?"

"Have I not said that we never know where the roots of
chance lie? Carrel was in identically the same position as
the orator you speak of. That gloomy young man, of a bitter
spirit, had a whole government in his head; the man of whom
you speak had no idea beyond mounting on the crupper of
every event. Of the two, Carrel was the better man. Well,
one became a minister, Carrel remained a journalist; the in-
complete but craftier man is living; Carrel is dead.

"I may point out that your man has for fifteen years
been making his way, and is but making it still. He may
yet be caught and crushed between two cars full of intrigues
on the high-road to power. He has no house; he has not the
favor of the palace like Metternich; nor, like Villèle, the
protection of a compact majority.

"I do not believe that the present state of things will last
ten years longer. Hence, supposing I should have such poor
good-luck, I am already too late to avoid being swept away
by the commotion I foresee. I should need to be established
in a superior position."

"What commotion?" asked Juste.

"AUGUST, 1830," said Marcas in solemn tones, holding out
his hand toward Paris; "AUGUST, the offspring of Youth
which bound the sheaves, and of Intellect which had ripened
the harvest, forgot to provide for Youth and Intellect.

"Youth will explode like the boiler of a steam-engine.
Youth has no outlet in France; it is gathering an avalanche
of underrated capabilities, of legitimate and restless ambi-

tions; young men are not marrying now; families cannot tell what to do with their children. What will the thunder-clap be that will shake down these masses? I know not, but they will crash down into the midst of things and overthrow everything. These are laws of hydrostatics which act on the human race; the Roman Empire had failed to understand them, and the barbaric hordes came down.

"The barbaric hordes now are the intelligent class. The laws of overpressure are at this moment acting slowly and silently in our midst. The government is the great criminal; it does not appreciate the two powers to which it owes every-thing; it has allowed its hands to be tied by the absurdities of the Contract; it is bound, ready to be the victim.

"Louis XIV., Napoleon, England, all were or are eager for intelligent youth. In France the young are condemned by the new legislation, by the blundering principles of elective rights, by the unsoundness of the ministerial constitution.

"Look at the elective Chamber; you will find no deputies of thirty; the youth of Richelieu and of Mazarin, of Turenne and of Colbert, of Pitt and of Saint-Just, of Napoleon and of Prince Metternich, would find no admission there; Burke, Sheridan, or Fox could not win seats. Even if political ma-jority had been fixed at one-and-twenty, and eligibility had been relieved of every disabling qualification, the departments would have returned the very same members, men devoid of political talent, unable to speak without murdering French grammar, and among whom, in ten years, scarcely one states-man has been found.

"The causes of an impending event may be seen, but the event itself cannot be foretold. At this moment the youth of France is being driven into republicanism, because it be-lieves that the republic would bring it emancipation. It will always remember the young representatives of the people and the young army leaders! The imprudence of the government is only comparable to its avarice."

That day left its echoes in our lives. Marcas confirmed us in our resolution to leave France, where young men of talent and energy are crushed under the weight of successful commonplace, envious, and insatiable middle age.

We dined together in the Rue de la Harpe. We thenceforth felt for Marcas the most respectful affection; he gave us the most practical aid in the sphere of the mind. That man knew everything; he had studied everything. For us he cast his eye over the whole civilized world, seeking the country where openings would be at once the most abundant and the most favorable to the success of our plans. He indicated what should be the goal of our studies; he bid us make haste, explaining to us that time was precious, that emigration would presently begin, and that its effect would be to deprive France of the cream of its powers and of its youthful talent; that their intelligence, necessarily sharpened, would select the best places, and that the great thing was to be first in the field.

Thenceforward, we often sat late at work under the lamp. Our generous instructor wrote some notes for our guidance— two pages for Juste and three for me—full of invaluable advice —the sort of information which experience alone can supply, such landmarks as only genius can place. In those papers, smelling of tobacco and covered with writing so vile as to be almost hieroglyphic, there are suggestions for a fortune, and forecasts of unerring acumen. There are hints as to certain parts of America and Asia which have been fully justified, both before and since Juste and I could set out.

Marcas, like us, was in the most abject poverty. He earned, indeed, his daily bread, but he had neither linen, clothes, nor shoes. He did not make himself out any better than he was; his dreams had been of luxury as well as of power. He did not admit that this was the real Marcas; he abandoned his person, indeed, to the caprices of life. What he lived by was the breath of ambition; he dreamed of revenge while blaming himself for yielding to so shallow a feeling. The true states-

man ought, above all things, to be superior to vulgar passions;
like the man of science, he should have no passion but for his
science. It was in these days of dire necessity that Marcas
seemed to us so great—nay, so terrible; there was something
awful in the gaze which saw another world than that which
strikes the eyes of ordinary men. To us he was a subject of
comtemplation and astonishment; for the young—which of
us has not known it?—the young have a keen craving to
admire; they love to attach themselves, and are naturally
inclined to submit to the men they feel to be superior, as they
are to devote themselves to a great cause.

Our surprise was chiefly aroused by his indifference in
matters of sentiment; woman had no place in his life. When
we spoke of this matter, a perennial theme of conversation
among Frenchmen, he simply remarked—

"Gowns cost too much."

He saw the look that passed between Juste and me, and
went on—

"Yes, far too much. The woman you buy—and she is the
least expensive—takes a great deal of money. The woman
who gives herself takes all your time! Woman extinguishes
every energy, every ambition. Napoleon reduced her to what
she should be. From that point of view, he really was great.
He did not indulge such ruinous fancies as Louis XIV. and
Louis XV.; at the same time, he could love in secret."

We discovered that, like Pitt, who made England his wife,
Marcas bore France in his heart; he idolized his country; he
had not a thought that was not for his native land. His fury
at feeling that he had in his hands the remedy for the evils
which so deeply saddened him, and could not apply it, ate
into his soul, and this rage was increased by the inferiority of
France at that time, as compared with Russia and England.
France a third-rate power! This cry came up again and
again in his conversation. The intestinal disorders of his
country had entered into his soul. All the contests between

the Court and the Chamber, showing, as they did, incessant change and constant vacillation, which must injure the prosperity of the country, he scoffed at as backstairs squabbles.

"This is peace at the cost of the future," he said.

One evening Juste and I were at work, sitting in perfect silence. Marcas had just risen to toil at his copying, for he had refused our assistance in spite of our most earnest entreaties. We had offered to take it in turns to copy a batch of manuscript, so that he should do but a third of his distasteful task; he had been quite angry, and we had ceased to insist.

We heard the sound of gentlemanly shoes in the passage, and raised our heads, looking at each other. There was a tap at Marcas' door—he never took the key out of the lock—and we heard our hero answer—

"Come in." Then—"What! you here, monsieur!"

"I myself," replied the retired minister.

It was the Diocletian of this unknown martyr.

For some time he and our neighbor conversed in an undertone. Suddenly Marcas, whose voice had been heard but rarely, as is natural in a dialogue in which the applicant begins by setting forth the situation, broke out loudly in reply to some offer we had not overheard.

"You would laugh at me for a fool," he cried, "if I took you at your word. Jesuits are a thing of the past, but Jesuitism is eternal. Your Machiavellism and your generosity are equally hollow and untrustworthy. You can make your own calculations, but who can calculate on you? Your court is made up of owls who fear the light, of old men who quake in the presence of the young, or who simply disregard them. The government is formed on the same pattern as the court. You have hunted up the remains of the empire, as the restoration enlisted the voltigeurs of Louis XIV.

"Hitherto the evasions of cowardice have been taken for

the manœuvring of ability; but dangers will come, and the younger generation will rise as they did in 1790. They did grand things then. Just now you change ministries as a sick man turns in his bed; these oscillations betray the weakness of the government. You work on an underhand system of policy which will be turned against you, for France will be tired of your shuffling. France will not tell you that she is tired of you; a man never knows whence his ruin comes; it is the historian's task to find out; but you will undoubtedly perish as the reward of not having asked the youth of France to lend you its strength and energy; for having hated really capable men; for not having lovingly chosen them from this noble generation; for having in all cases preferred mediocrity.

"You have come to ask my support, but you are an atom in that decrepit heap which is made hideous by self-interest, which trembles and squirms, and, because it is so mean, tries to make France mean too. My strong nature, my ideas, would work like poison in you; twice you have tricked me, twice have I overthrown you. If we unite a third time, it must be a very serious matter. I should kill myself if I allowed myself to be duped; for I should be to blame, not you."

Then we heard the humblest entreaties, the most fervent adjurations, not to deprive the country of such superior talents. The man spoke of patriotism, and Marcas uttered a significant "*Ouh! ouh!*" He laughed at his would-be patron. Then the statesman was more explicit; he bowed to the superiority of his ere-while counselor; he pledged himself to enable Marcas to remain in office, to be elected deputy; then he offered him a high appointment, promising him that he, the speaker, would thenceforth be the subordinate of a man whose subaltern he was only worthy to be. He was in the newly formed ministry, and he would not return to power unless Marcas had a post in proportion to his merit; he had

25

already made it a condition, Marcas had been regarded as indispensable.

Marcas refused.

" I have never before been in a position to keep my promises ; here is an opportunity of proving myself faithful to my word, and you fail me ! "

To this Marcas made no reply. The shoes were again audible in the passage on the way to the stairs.

" Marcas, Marcas ! " we both cried, rushing into his room. " Why refuse ? He really meant it. His offers are very handsome ; at any rate, go to see the ministers."

In a twinkling, we had given Marcas a hundred reasons. The minister's voice was sincere ; without seeing him, we had felt sure that he was honest.

" I have no clothes," replied Marcas.

" Rely on us," said Juste, with a glance at me.

Marcas had the courage to trust us ; a light flashed in his eye, he pushed his fingers through his hair, lifting it from his forehead with a gesture that showed some confidence in his luck ; and when he had thus unveiled his face, so to speak, we saw in him a man absolutely unknown to us—Marcas sublime, Marcas in his power ! His mind in its element—the bird restored to the free air, the fish to the water, the horse galloping across the plain.

It was transient. His brow clouded again ; he had, it would seem, a vision of his fate. Halting doubt had followed close on the heels of white-winged hope.

We left him to himself.

" Now then," said I to the doctor, " we have given our word ; how are we to keep it ? "

" We will sleep upon it," said Juste, " and to-morrow morning we will talk it over."

Next morning we went for a walk in the Luxembourg.

We had had time to think over the incident of the past night, and were both equally surprised at the lack of address shown by Marcas in the minor difficulties of life—he, a man who never saw any difficulties in the solution of the hardest problems of abstract or practical politics. But these elevated characters can all be tripped up on a grain of sand, and will, like the grandest enterprise, miss fire for want of a thousand francs. It is the old story of Napoleon, who, for lack of a pair of boots, did not set out for India.

"Well, what have you hit upon?" asked Juste.

"I have thought of a way to get him a complete outfit."

"Where?"

"From Humann."

"How?"

"Humann, my boy, never goes to his customers—his customers go to him; so that he does not know whether I am rich or poor. He only knows that I dress well and look decent in the clothes he makes for me. I shall tell him that an uncle of mine has dropped in from the country, and that his indifference in matters of dress is quite a discredit to me in the upper circles where I am trying to find a wife. It will not be Humann if he sends in his bill before three months."

The doctor thought this a capital idea for a vaudeville, but poor enough in real life, and doubted my success. But, I give you my word of honor, Humann dressed Marcas, and, being an artist, turned him out as a political personage ought to be dressed.

Juste lent Marcas two hundred francs in gold, the product of two watches bought on credit and pawned at the Mont-de-Piété.* For my part, I had said nothing of six shirts and all necessary linen, which cost me no more than the pleasure of asking for them from a forewoman in a shop whom I had treated to Musard's during the carnival.

Marcas accepted everything, thanking us no more than he ought. He only inquired as to the means by which we had

* State supervised pawnbrokers.

gotten possession of such riches, and we made him laugh for the
last time.   We looked on our Marcas as shipowners, when
they have exhausted their credit and every resource at their
command to fit out a vessel, must look on it as it puts to sea.

Here Charles was silent ; he seemed crushed by his memories.

" Well," cried the audience, " and what happened ? "

" I will tell you in few words—for this is not romance—it
is history."

We saw no more of Marcas.   The administration lasted
for three months ; it fell at the end of the session.   Then Marcas came back to us, worked to death.   He had sounded the
crater of power ; he came away from it with the beginnings
of brain fever.   The disease made rapid progress ; we nursed
him.   Juste at once called in the chief physician of the hospital where he was working as house-surgeon.   I was then
living alone in our room, and I was the most attentive attend-
ant ; but care and science alike were in vain.   By the month
of January, 1838, Marcas himself felt that he had but a few
days to live.

The man whose soul and brain he had been for six months
never even sent to inquire after him.   Marcas expressed the
greatest contempt for the government ; he seemed to doubt
what the fate of France might be, and it was this doubt that
had made him ill.   He had, he thought, detected treason in
the heart of power, not tangible, seizable treason, the result
of facts, but the treason of a system, the subordination of
national interests to selfish ends.   His belief in the degrada-
tion of the country was enough to aggravate his complaint.

I myself was witness to the proposals made to him by one
of the leaders of the antagonistic party which he had fought
against.   His hatred of the men he had tried to serve was so
virulent that he would gladly have joined the coalition that
was about to be formed among certain ambitious spirits who,
at least, had one idea in common—that of shaking off the

yoke of the court. But Marcas could only reply to the envoy in the words of the Hôtel de Ville—

"It is too late!"

Marcas did not leave money enough to pay for his funeral. Juste and I had great difficulty in saving him from the ignominy of a pauper's bier, and we alone followed the coffin of Z. Marcas, which was dropped into the common grave of the cemetery of Mont-Parnasse.

We looked sadly at each other as we listened to this tale, the last we heard from the lips of Charles Rabourdin the day before he embarked at le Havre on a brig that was to convey him to the islands of Malay. We all knew more than one Marcas, more than one victim of his devotion to a party, repaid by betrayal or neglect.

LES JARDIES, *May*, 1840.